Also by Sharon Sala

LAST RITES

SHARON SALA

sourcebooks
casablanca

Published by Sourcebooks Casablanca, an imprint of Sourcebooks
P.O. Box 4410, Naperville, Illinois 60567-4410
(630) 961-3900
sourcebooks.com

Printed and bound in the United States of America.
OPM 10 9 8 7 6 5 4 3 2 1

Chapter 1

Shirley Wallace woke up on the kitchen floor with her son Sean hovering over her. He had a phone in one hand calling for an ambulance, while holding a kitchen towel pressed against the top of her head with the other.

The taste of blood was in her mouth.

Her body was one solid pain, and it hurt to breathe.

She could hear the frantic tone in his voice, but she couldn't focus enough to respond.

"Yes, yes, she's breathing and starting to regain consciousness, but she's bloody as hell, and I don't know where all the blood is coming from. Yes, I know who attacked her. Her husband, Clyde. No, I don't know where he is. Just hurry."

The 911 dispatcher's voice was calm and quiet, even as he was dispatching emergency vehicles to the address.

"Sean, stay on the line with me until help arrives," he said.

"Call my brother," Sean said. "His name is Aaron Wallace. He's an officer with the Conway Police Department."

That was the last thing Shirley heard before darkness claimed her.

The next time she woke up, she was in ER.

"Shirley! Can you hear me? My name is Dr. Malone, and you're in ER."

"Where's my son?" she mumbled.

"He's just outside this room. You're safe. He's safe, and we're going to make you better."

———

Sean was frantically pacing outside the exam bay when he heard the sound of someone running up behind him. He turned to look, then breathed a sigh of relief. Aaron was here!

"How is she?" Aaron asked as he slid a hand across his brother's shoulder.

Sean shuddered. "I don't know. Jesus, Aaron. He's never hurt her like this before. I came in from running errands and found her like that. Her face is bloody and swollen. She's bleeding from both ears and from a huge cut in her scalp, and she has broken ribs, for sure. Scared the hell out of me. Have they found Clyde?"

Aaron lowered his voice. "He's in jail. They're processing him now. Mom got off lucky. Clyde walked into a Quick Loan and shot two people dead. He's high as a kite and talking out of his head."

Sean froze, unable to believe what he was hearing. "What?"

Aaron gripped his brother's shoulders. "Our father just murdered two people in cold blood. Shit has hit the fan. Have you called Wiley? Does B.J. know?"

Sean's eyes welled. "Oh my God. No...not yet."

Aaron nodded. "I'll do it. And I'll call the school for B.J. Did he ride his Harley this morning?"

Sean nodded.

"Okay. You just stay here with Mom. I'm going outside to make some calls."

It was the beginning of the end of life as they'd known it.

Within a week of leaving the hospital, Shirley Pope Wallace had filed for divorce. By the time Clyde Wallace's trial came to court, his family's names and faces were as well-known as his, and they were being judged and found guilty of nothing but bearing his last name.

The Conway, Arkansas, police department decided it would be in the public's best interest if the son of a killer was not on their force, and despite an exemplary record, they let Aaron go. Clyde was in prison for life, and so, it would seem, was his family.

Aaron's wife, Kelly, couldn't handle the pressure and filed for divorce two months before their first anniversary. Again, it was nothing Aaron did. She just didn't want to be associated with the crime.

Sean lost clients through the IT firm he'd worked

for, and was scrambling to make ends meet, and Wiley was reduced to a DoorDash delivery driver, instead of the law enforcement job he'd been hoping for since graduating from the police academy.

B.J. finished his senior year of high school, but skipped the ceremony, unable to face the shame.

Shirley was let go from her job as a receptionist in a dental office and removed from being a volunteer story-teller at a local library. She finally found a job as a dishwasher in a small Mexican restaurant, and was grateful for it.

Then one day, about a year after Clyde's imprison-ment, Shirley got a phone call that changed their world.

═══════════

It was the first week of February and Shirley's day off. She was doing laundry when her phone rang. She recognized the area code, and without looking at the number, just assumed it was her mother, Helen, calling from Kentucky.

"Hello."

"Hi, Shirley. This is your Aunt Annie."

Shirley was a little surprised, but pleased to hear from Annie. She was one of her deceased father's sis-ters, and she adored her.

"Hi, Auntie! It's good to hear your voice."

"Well, sugar, I'm not calling with good news," Annie said. "I'm so sorry to have to tell you, but your mother passed away in her sleep last night."

Shock rolled through Shirley in waves.

"No! Oh my God, no! I just spoke to her day before yesterday. She was in good spirits and said she was feeling fine." She started crying. "Mom was my touchstone to sanity."

"I know. I'm so sorry, Shirley," Annie said.

Shirley was sobbing now, struggling to catch her breath. "Why didn't Mom let me know she was failing?"

"She wasn't. Not in the way you mean. Helen never looked at life like that. She just got old, and she was ready to go," Annie said.

Shirley moaned. "But I could have been there to help."

Annie hesitated before answering. "Honestly, I think Helen knew you already had more on your plate than you could say grace over. This was how she wanted it, and you have to honor that."

"I feel like someone just cut the rope to my anchor," Shirley said, then wiped her eyes and blew her nose. "So, what do I need to know? What do I need to do? I can't be there before tomorrow at the earliest."

"No, no. No need to hurry here at all," Annie said. "Helen always said she didn't want to waste money on some big funeral, and she didn't want people looking at her in a coffin. She wrote it all down years ago and showed me where her papers were kept. She will be cremated, and her ashes will be saved for you. She always said when you come home to claim your heritage, she wants you to sprinkle them where the mountain laurel grows. She said you'd know the place."

Shirley hadn't thought past the shock of the loss until she heard the words, *come home to claim your heritage*.

Her brother and only sibling had died in a car accident some years back, and knowing she was the sole heir to the land and the home in which she'd been raised, felt like one last hug from her mother.

"Yes. Yes, I know right where she means," Shirley said. "Thank you for calling, Aunt Annie. I am so sad right now, but the thought of going home to Pope Mountain feels like a godsend."

"I know," Annie said. "We all know what's been happening to you and your boys, and we're so sorry for your suffering. Come home, darlin'. We love you. You'll be safe here. This is where you'll heal."

"Yes, yes…I will. It will take a while, but I'll let you know. Thank you for calling. I love you, too."

After the call ended, Shirley sent a group text to her sons, calling a family meeting for that evening, and after the year they'd just lived through, the text sent them all into a panic.

Getting that message from his mom stopped Aaron cold. He didn't even go back to his apartment after he got off work at the service station, and drove straight to her home, worried all over again as to what else might be happening.

His younger brothers had all moved home after the fallout to help pay the bills and look after Shirley, but the moment they got her messages, a feeling of dread came over them.

That evening they began arriving within moments of each other, leaving B.J., the youngest, to be the last to get home from his job at a fast-food drive-in. He parked his Harley in a skid, then came running into the house, wide-eyed and pale.

"Mom! What's wrong?"

"Sit down with your brothers," she said, then drew a slow, shaky breath.

"Your grandma has died. Aunt Annie said they found her in her bed. She died in her sleep."

"Oh, Mama!" they said in unison, and jumped up and ran to her, hugging her and commiserating with her, which brought on another round of weeping.

"I'm so sorry," Aaron said. "We were all going back for Easter right after Kelly and I got married, and then Dad broke your nose, and we made excuses. We were going to go a year ago last Christmas, and that shit with Dad happened and we didn't. Now this."

Shirley wiped her eyes. "Your grandma knew what was happening. She always knew. We talked weekly, sometimes more. She didn't blame us for the situation. Aunt Annie said there won't be a funeral. Mom didn't want one. But when we do go there, she wants us to spread her ashes on the mountain."

"So, we're going now? After she's gone?" Wiley asked.

Shirley swallowed past her tears.

"As the only living child, I have inherited the home and land where I grew up. I own it now. We haven't been welcome in this town for a long time. I want to go home to stay, and I'm asking if any of you want to come with me. We'll be living in a home that's paid for, surrounded by family and people who love us, and there is always work to be had in Jubilee."

Sean sighed. "But Mama, what will they think of us? I mean...we'll still be Clyde Wallace's sons."

Shirley's chin came up. Her eyes were still teary, but her voice was sure and strong.

"They'll think I have raised four fine sons," Shirley said. "And none of us have to bear Clyde Wallace's name or sins if we don't want to. You're not just your father's child! You're mine, too, which makes you Popes. You carry the DNA of generations of honorable men within you, and you might as well carry the name as well."

Aaron stood, his fists clenched. "I choose to change."

Sean nodded where he sat. "I choose to change."

Wiley was grim-lipped. "Hell yes, and thank you!" he said.

B.J., the youngest, had tears in his eyes. He'd known nothing but his father's abuse and rage, and now the shame of being his son.

"I choose you, Mama. I always have," B.J. said.

Shirley nodded. "Then we'll do it! Since there are so many of us doing it at once, I'll contact a lawyer to get us through the process."

Within the month, it was done. They'd cut the last link they would ever have with Clyde Wallace by rejecting his name.

After that, leaving Conway was easy.

———

March—Pope Mountain

Shirley Pope's heart was pounding as she and her sons drove their little convoy through the bustling tourist attraction of Jubilee, located in the valley below Pope Mountain. She was coming back to her roots and almost at the end of their journey.

Shirley and B.J. were in the lead.

Aaron was in his SUV behind his mother.

Sean was behind Aaron, driving his car, and Wiley in his car behind Sean, and just ahead of the moving van bringing up the rear.

B.J.'s Harley was in the moving van, and he'd been riding shotgun with his mother all the way.

It had been far too long since Shirley had made this trip. Her eyes were full of tears, but they weren't tears of joy. She was crying because there was no one left to welcome them home.

Even though six weeks had passed since they'd received the news, Shirley was still in shock that it had happened. Her mother had seemed invincible, even immortal, and had been Shirley's steadfast backup through her abusive marriage with Clyde Wallace. Helen had always been the gentle voice and the deep wisdom Shirley needed in times of strife.

As they were driving out of Conway, Shirley made a call to Annie, letting her know they were on the way. But it had taken a long day of traveling before they met their moving van in Frankfort this morning to lead the way home.

This was the last leg of a long trip. They didn't know what lay ahead, but anything would be better than what they'd left behind.

Shirley's sons only knew what she'd told them about her side of the family. Thanks to their dad, their visits to Kentucky had been few and far between. But they knew their ancestors had lived in this place since the early 1800s. And they knew this mountain they were now driving up on bore their family name. Here, in this place, they hoped to regain their sense of self. To be proud of who they were again. And one day, know that their mother was no longer crying herself to sleep.

From the moment they'd started up the tree-covered mountain, B.J. quit talking and became wide-eyed and quiet—too quiet. After the four-lane highways and the busy streets of their city, the two-lane blacktop on which they were traveling seemed little more than a trail cut through a wilderness. Shirley was worried he was not happy about her decision.

"So, B.J., what do you think?" she asked, then heard him sigh.

"I think it feels safe here."

She smiled. "Good. Hold that feeling," and kept on driving. A few miles later, she began slowing down and flipped on her turn signal. "There's where we turn."

One by one, the vehicles behind her did the same as she left the blacktop and began following the gravel road up into the trees.

The house was a hundred yards back, all but buried in

the woods, but as soon as she passed the twin pines, she saw the house, and then gasped at the sight of a half dozen cars in the yard and a whole row of people lining the front porch.

"Mama, who are those people?" B.J. asked as she parked off to the side.

Shirley shivered, seeing herself in their faces. The high cheekbones. The dark hair. The women's curves. The men's broad shoulders.

"Some of our family. Look at them. That's why you're all so tall. That's where your dark hair comes from. Look at them, and you'll see yourself."

"Oh wow," B.J. whispered.

One by one, her sons parked, but when they got out, they headed straight for Shirley, as did the people coming off the porch. After that, they were surrounded, fielding hugs and handshakes.

Then one man who stood a head above the rest spoke up from the crowd.

"Shirley, I'm Cameron Pope, your aunt Georgia's oldest son. This is my wife, Rusty. Welcome home."

Shirley was crying. "You were just a boy last time I saw you. These are my sons, Aaron, Sean, Wiley, and Brendan Pope, but we call him B.J."

Cameron smiled. "Another Brendan, huh? Named after the man who started us all. Good to have some more Pope men on this mountain. I've been the only man left with that name since my father's passing."

And just like that, Shirley's sons took their first steps into the family.

Annie Cauley, Shirley's aunt, slipped up behind Shirley and whispered in her ear.

"We cleaned the house. You have food in your refrigerator. The appliances have been serviced. John will show the boys around outside. You come in now and sit where it's cool while you tell the movers where you want to put your things. After your call, and mentioning your sons were bringing their own things, we took down the old beds in the spare rooms and stored them all in the attic. Your mom's living room furniture was past hope. She'd written in her last wishes to have it donated, so there's plenty of room now for your stuff. And don't worry. All the family heirlooms are still where she had them. The cupboard. The pie safe. The sideboard. And your great-grandpa's old secretary desk. We'll have you set up and comfy before nightfall."

Walking into the old home place without her mother to greet her was bittersweet, but Shirley took the home as the blessing it was, and by the time night fell, the moving van was long gone. All her sons had their own beds up in their own rooms, and she had her things around her again. Clothes were unpacked and put away, and they'd just sat down to supper at the kitchen table.

There were no sirens or dogs barking outside. No cars honking. No streetlights. Just the glow from the security light between the house and the barn, and their cars, lined up in front of the house like a used car lot.

Shirley looked at the faces of her sons, at the food before them and the familiarity of the room in which they were sitting, and then she sighed.

"Well, we're here. And right now, I am at peace. Once again, my mother has saved my sanity and your futures."

"Amen," Aaron said.

"I'm thankful," Sean said.

"I'm thankful," Wiley added.

"Me, too," B.J. said, and then pointed at the platter of cold fried chicken. "Somebody please pass the chicken. I'm starving."

Their laughter was sudden, but it felt good to have something to laugh about.

———

The next few days were about settling in. Shirley walked the woods with her sons, showing them the woods and the creek where she and her brother had played in when they were little, and the pond where fish never quit biting. And then one bright morning, she took them to the place where the mountain laurel grew, and scattered her mother's ashes.

"Love you, Mother. I'll miss you forever. Rest in the peace you have given to us," Shirley said, and wiped tears as her sons gathered around her. On the walk back, she showed them the creek that ran through their property. "This creek water is cold year-round. It comes from a long way up, out of a spring in the rocks at the top of the mountain. It runs all the way down through Jubilee, to a river miles and miles away."

"Did you play here when you were little?" B.J. asked.

Shirley smiled. "When my brother and I weren't doing chores or going to school, we lived in these woods, waded in these waters. Pope Mountain was our playground."

Aaron saw the far-off look in his mother's eyes as she gazed down into the swift running water, and knew she was remembering better days.

As they began to settle in, they talked about getting chickens for a chicken house long since empty, and after a week of sleeping in and lazy days, her sons began looking for jobs. Finding out that their relatives ran a lot of the businesses in Jubilee was a boon they hadn't seen coming.

After getting Wi-Fi and Internet to the house, Sean set up his own IT office in their home, and his online website, then he began growing a new clientele.

Wiley was ecstatic when he got hired as a daytime security guard at one of the music venues and came home beaming, carrying in uniforms, his badge, and the weapon he'd been issued.

Shirley celebrated with him, but the irony was not lost upon her of having an ex-husband serving a life sentence, and two sons who'd chosen careers in law enforcement.

B.J. got a job driving a delivery van for his Aunt Annie at her bakery in Jubilee, but for the time being, Aaron was staying home to help his mother settle in. He missed being on the force and wasn't sure where to go from here.

And then one morning not long after their arrival, Cameron called to ask if it was okay if he dropped by that evening after all of the family was home, that there was some family business they needed to know about.

Instead, Shirley invited him and Rusty to eat supper with them, and they accepted.

———

"I haven't cooked for anyone but family in so long I've forgotten what it's like to have company," Shirley said as she took a big beef roast with vegetables out of the oven and set it on the counter to rest.

Aaron grinned. "You're a good cook, Mama, and you know it. Do you want me to put the leaf in the table?"

Shirley beamed from the compliment as she nodded. "Yes, to the table leaf. With seven at the table, we'll need it."

He went to get the leaf from the hall closet, while Shirley began cleaning fresh vegetables for a tossed salad. She had three apple pies cooling on the sideboard, a basket of dinner rolls beside it, and fresh green beans warming on the stove that she cooked and seasoned with bits of ham. All she needed was for Wiley and B.J. to get home from work, and the company to arrive.

Moments later, she heard a car driving up.

"That's Wiley," Aaron said, and then they heard the rumble of B.J.'s Harley as he pulled up to the house. "And that's B.J."

"Good. Then all we have to do is wait for Cameron and Rusty."

"What does he want to talk to us about?" Aaron asked.

"I don't know, but we'll find out soon enough," Shirley said, then winced when the front door slammed.

"Sorry!" B.J. yelled. "The wind caught it. I'm going to shower! Won't be long!"

Shirley grinned. B.J. had been slamming doors all his life. Today it was the fault of the wind. Tomorrow it would be something else. Truth was, B.J. was always in too big of a hurry to catch it.

Seconds later, Wiley came in the back door. "Thought I'd park out back and leave room for company out front. I'm gonna change."

Now Shirley could relax. All her boys were accounted for.

—————

"Cameron, I need help," Rusty said, and turned her back to him so he could zip up her sundress.

Cameron turned away from the dresser to come to his wife's aid. She was holding her long curly hair up off her neck so it wouldn't get caught in the zipper, and he couldn't resist a kiss below all those red curls.

"I'd just as soon be taking this off you as putting it on," he said.

Rusty laughed. "Hold that thought and you can do that later," she said. "We don't want to be late."

Cameron grabbed the zipper tab and pulled it all the way up, then kissed the back of her neck one last time.

"Done and done," he said as she turned around to face him. "Damn, but you are a beautiful woman, Rusty Pope."

"Flattery will get you everywhere," she said, and kissed him square on the lips before tearing herself away. "All I need are my shoes and I'm ready."

The big white German shepherd who'd been lying in the doorway watching them dress, stood up and whined.

"Ghost is sad," Rusty said.

"He'll be fine. I'm not taking a dog the size of a small polar bear out to dinner."

Rusty frowned. She couldn't bear it when Ghost whined. "Then he gets the big chew bone, right?"

Cameron rolled his eyes. "Yes, he gets the big chew bone. He won't miss us after that. Trust me."

"Ghost. Treat!" Cameron said, and Ghost shot off down the hall at a gallop.

Rusty laughed.

"See?" Cameron said.

As soon as they gave Ghost the bone, he chomped it and carried it to his bed in the living room.

Cameron and Rusty set the security alarm, then locked up and drove away.

It took less than fifteen minutes to get up the mountain to where Shirley and her sons were living now. Just enough time for Rusty to watch the sun moving down behind the tallest treetops. It would be dark in an hour. She loved night on the mountain, almost as much as she loved the man sitting beside her.

They pulled up into the yard and parked at the end of a line of cars.

"Good thing Shirley doesn't have but four sons.

She'd be running out of parking space with any more," Cameron said.

They were on their way up the steps when the front door opened.

Aaron was standing in the doorway. "Welcome to this house," he said, then stepped aside for them to enter.

"Something sure smells good," Rusty said as they entered.

"Mama's a good cook," Aaron said. "We used to say that's why we grew so tall, but after moving here, I'm thinking it was DNA, not roast and mashed potatoes."

"You've got that right," Cameron said as Aaron ushered them into the kitchen. Sean and Wiley were already there and carrying the food to the table.

Shirley met them with a hug.

"Welcome! Ooh, Rusty, I love that blue sundress. It's the perfect foil for your gorgeous hair."

Rusty smiled. "Thank you. Mom and Dad used to blame my hair color on the postman and then laugh hysterically, because no one in our family had red hair. I had to get older to get the joke."

"That hair is a country all its own," Cameron said. "It's what I saw first across a crowded hotel lobby, and then I saw her, and I was done."

"What a storybook meeting," Shirley said.

B.J. walked into the kitchen on that last comment.

"Sorry I kept everyone waiting," he said, then shook hands with Cameron and gave Rusty an appreciative glance, thinking to himself how pretty she was.

Shirley waved a hand toward the table. "Please be seated." Then she nodded at Aaron to sit at the head of the table and saw the pleased expression on his face. As soon as everyone was in their place, Shirley gave the blessing, then as the passing of food began around the table, Shirley shifted her attention to Cameron and Rusty.

"You two are the first guests in our new home, and we are so grateful for your company."

"It's our pleasure," Cameron said.

Chatter filled the room as they filled their plates, and the boys poked fun at the size of B.J.'s helpings.

"Still growing into those long legs," Cameron said.

Shirley laughed and, as she did, realized how long it had been since she'd felt this kind of delight.

As the meal progressed, conversation turned to jobs and work. Cameron heard about Sean's IT business in their home and B.J. making deliveries for Aunt Annie's bakery. He already knew through the family grapevine that Wiley had gone to work at the music venue for country music star Reagan Bullard.

"So, Wiley. What do you think of Reagan Bullard? Have you met him yet?"

"Yes, I met him my first day on the job. He seems nice enough. I also heard he bought the campgrounds outside of Jubilee and is turning it into a whole new venue. Waterslides. A big swimming pool, pony rides, and a concession stand to go with the little cabins and the campgrounds and fireworks every Saturday night."

Cameron glanced at Rusty. That place held a

not-so-nice history for them, but they'd been aware of the changes after the previous owner's arrest.

"I heard a bit about that myself," Cameron said. "A new owner will work wonders for the place." Then he glanced at B.J. "So how do you like working at the bakery?"

B.J. grinned. "I like it. Aunt Annie is awesome, and the free cookies I get are just fine, too."

They laughed, even Aaron, who had been silent during the job discussion. But Rusty had noticed his reticence and was curious about the silence.

"So, Aaron, what kind of job are you looking for?" she asked as Shirley began serving slices of apple pie for their dessert.

He met her gaze, but it took everything within him to not duck his head in shame.

"Before Clyde Wallace's crime spree, I was a police officer for the City of Conway. After Clyde's trial and sentencing, they let me go. I always wanted to be in law enforcement. I had seven years on the force before Clyde's killing spree. After all the bad press and publicity, I guess being the son of a killer tainted the badge and screwed up public relations."

Rusty didn't blink. "Well, that sucks, but we have a lot in common. I was an undercover agent for the FBI for almost ten years. It's what brought me to Jubilee, and where Cameron and I reunited after meeting years earlier."

Aaron blinked. "No joke? A Fed?"

"I liked it, but undercover work is dangerous, and

I had too many close calls. I happily gave it up just to have a family again."

Cameron had been silent through the conversation, but in a lull, he had to ask.

"Have you applied for a job here with the Jubilee PD?"

Aaron shook his head.

"Why not?" Cameron asked.

"We came here to get away from being Clyde Wallace's sons. I don't want to resurrect that again with a simple background check."

Cameron frowned. "Your last name is Pope. That name goes a long way around here. Sonny Warren is the police chief. I grew up with him. He's a good man and a fair man. If you want that career, then fight for it."

"If I thought it wouldn't make trouble for us all over again here, I'd do it in a heartbeat," Aaron said.

"Every family has a cross of some kind to bear. Your reputation should have nothing to do with who you're related to. Trust him. Trust us," Cameron said.

Aaron nodded but stayed silent.

Rusty took a bite of the pie, then rolled her eyes.

"Lord, Shirley. This pie is delicious!"

Shirley beamed. "Thanks. B.J. helped me make them. He's a good hand in the kitchen."

B.J. nodded. "I like to cook. But I like to eat better."

They laughed, and the moment passed, but after the meal was over and the table cleared, Cameron knew it was time to explain why he'd come.

"I know you're all wondering why I needed to talk

to you, so I'll get right to the point. And I need to stress this, above all else…what I say to you tonight stays in the family…in this room. Everybody on the mountain knows it, but we don't talk about it, because it has to stay a secret."

It was the word *secret* that got their attention, and in that moment, Shirley suddenly realized what this was about.

"What's the secret?" Aaron asked.

"The entire town of Jubilee is a very successful tourist attraction, owned by a company called PCG, Incorporated. All of the businesses in town lease the property locations and pay monthly rent to the corporation. The land is never for sale, nor is the mountain on which we live. It's how we are protected from investors and outsiders wanting to clear it for their own gain. That's how it's been since my grandfather's time. And this is how it will always be. But nobody except the families involved know that PCG stands for *Pope, Cauley, and Glass.*"

Shirley was smiling. "I've been gone from here so long I'd completely forgotten about all this."

Aaron leaned forward. "What? What are you saying?"

Cameron glanced at Rusty, and then spoke.

"That we here on the mountain own Jubilee, and all of the members of those families on the mountain are stockholders. We all receive quarterly dividends from the company. Anyone up here automatically becomes eligible for dividends once they reach their eighteenth birthday. Each family is represented by a family member of their choosing to sit on the board. I am, at the present time, the CEO of PCG, Inc. I was the elected member of the Pope family, and the other members of the board selected me as the CEO."

"What kind of money are we talking about?" Sean asked.

"We're in the third generation of PCG's existence. It is a multimillion-dollar company. The dividends are generous and issued quarterly, and the investments from the money grow the coffers, as well. By moving here and coming into Helen's heritage, you will receive your first checks by the end of the month. There are less than two hundred and fifty people still living on Pope Mountain. The money arrives by direct deposit into your personal bank accounts, or into savings accounts per each family's wishes. In the next three days or so, I'll be needing your bank information so I can get it all to the lawyer in Frankfort who oversees the legal end of the corporation, and you will have assigned bank accounts in a bank in Frankfort. That keeps the people down below from finding out we're their landlords. This is never up for discussion. Nobody outside the families ever knows unless they marry into it."

Wiley was stunned.

Sean was grinning.

Aaron was in shock.

"Cool," B.J. said, and served himself another piece of pie.

Shirley's eyes welled. "Just one more gift from Mama," she whispered. "All I had to do was come home to claim it. I didn't remember, but she did."

Cameron nodded. "And just so you know, if any of you ever have problems or want advice, everyone on this mountain is here for you. It's never a burden. It's our way. Now, since I've eaten your wonderful food and said what I came to say, I think Rusty and I better get home. Ghost doesn't like to be left alone for too long."

"Who's Ghost?" B.J. asked.

"Our dog," Cameron said.

Rusty smiled. "He's Cameron's dog, but he loves me, too, now."

"Next time, bring him with you," B.J. said. "I love dogs."

"He's yeti size," Cameron said. "And a bull in a china shop."

Rusty grabbed her phone from her purse and pulled up a photo of her and Ghost, standing out in the yard.

"See," she said.

The shock on their faces was real.

"Holy shit. His head is above your waist," B.J. said.

"Is he a hunting dog?" Aaron asked.

Cameron shook his head. "Not really, but he's damn good at tracking and sniffing out bombs. I found him as a pup when I was still active duty in Iraq. When I came home, he came with me."

"They're quite the team," Rusty said. "I won Ghost's

heart with treats and pets, but he and Cameron are a pack."

"That's amazing," Sean said, eyeing Cameron and Rusty with new respect. A war veteran and an ex-FBI agent with a bomb-sniffing dog.

"I'll see you to the door," Shirley said as they got up from the table, then walked them out onto the porch.

The night birds were calling. A hound bayed from a hollow somewhere above them. The sky was cloudless and full of stars.

"Supper is on us next time," Cameron said.

"Thank you for everything. I'll reinforce the no-talking bit with the boys before I go to bed. Safe travels going home," Shirley said, then stood on the porch and watched until they drove out of sight. She started to go back inside, then hesitated and glanced up at the stars. "Night, Mom. Thank you for still watching over us. Love you. Miss you."

The screen door banged behind her as she went inside. She winced, thinking maybe the banging door wasn't B.J.'s fault after all. Maybe the spring was too tight. But that was something to look at in the bright light of day.

Chapter 2

AARON COULDN'T SLEEP FOR THINKING ABOUT WHAT Cameron said about the job. He didn't like feeling indecisive. He'd lost his wife to circumstances beyond his control. He'd lost his job the same way. He missed belonging to someone, but he'd chosen a woman without substance. He'd never do that again.

And he didn't like the thought of giving up his career out of fear. By the time he was drifting off to sleep, he'd made up his mind to at least apply. The worst that could happen was being turned down.

Shirley was making breakfast when Aaron walked in. He had showered and shaved, and was wearing dark slacks and a light blue knit shirt that accentuated a very fit, muscular body. Family DNA was strong in all her boys. They had the height, the broad shoulders and long legs, even the high cheekbones and handsome faces. Looking back, she wondered if that was one of the reasons Clyde was so mean to her and the boys. Because he saw none of himself in any of them.

"You look nice," she said.

Aaron smiled. "You always say that, even when I look like shit."

She grinned. "Because I love you."

"Much appreciated," Aaron said. "I love you, too, and I'm going to the police department this morning to apply for a job."

"Good for you! Want some breakfast before you go?"

"I think I'll skip it this morning, Mom. This shouldn't take too long. Do you have a grocery list or anything you want done before I come home?"

"It's on the counter," Shirley said.

Aaron gave her a kiss on the cheek and tore the list off the pad. "If you think of anything else, give me a call."

"Okay," she said, then watched the sway of his shoulders as he walked away, and whispered a quick prayer. "Lord, please let this work for him. He's lost a career and a wife because of his father. It's time something good came his way."

Desk Sergeant Walter Winter was nursing his first cup of coffee of the day when the door opened and a tall dark-haired man entered the lobby.

At first glance, Walter thought it was Cameron

Pope, and then he looked again and realized he was too young. The man walked with a long, steady stride as he approached the desk.

"Morning, sir. I was wondering how I go about applying for a job on the force?" he said.

Walter waved toward a row of chairs against the wall. "Take a seat. I'll be right back," Walter said.

"Yes, sir. Thank you, sir," Aaron said, and made a neat little pivot and sat down in a chair against the wall.

Walter hurried down the hall to the chief's office. The door was open.

Sonny Warren looked up just as Walter walked in.

"Chief, I have a Pope look-alike up front, wanting a job application. Do you have any packets, or do I need to dig in the supply room?"

Sonny grinned. "What do you mean, a Pope look-alike?"

Walter shrugged. "For a second, I thought it was Cameron when he came in. That's what I mean."

"So, what kind of a job is this man wanting?" Sonny asked.

"A job on the force," Walter said.

Sonny's interest was piqued. "Really? Send him to my office."

"Yes, sir," Walter said, and hurried back up the hall and into the lobby. The man looked up. "Sorry, I didn't get your name," Walter said.

"Aaron Pope."

Walter stifled a smile of satisfaction. "Mr. Pope, the

chief would like to speak with you personally if you have the time."

Aaron's heart skipped. "Yes, sir. I have time," and followed Walter down the hall, then into the police chief's office.

"Chief Warren, this is Aaron Pope," Walter said, and then headed back up front to his desk duties.

Sonny stood and shook Aaron's hand.

"Pleased to meet you, Aaron. Take a seat."

Aaron sat, his elbows resting on the arms of the chair, his hands loosely clasped, and looked the chief square in the face.

Sonny smiled. "I thought I knew all the Popes in Jubilee."

"We haven't been here long," Aaron said. "My grand-mother was Helen Pope, who recently passed."

Sonny leaned forward. "Shirley is your mother! I haven't seen her in years. My deepest sympathies for your family's loss. So, are you living on the home place now?"

"Yes. We all moved back to be here with Mom."

"All, as in how many are you?" Sonny asked.

"Four sons. No daughters," Aaron said.

"So, you're all single?" Sonny said.

Aaron took a deep breath. "I'm divorced. The others have never married."

Sonny nodded. "Totally understood. Being in law enforcement is hard on marriages."

"It's not that," Aaron said and then sighed. "Look.

I'm going to be up front with you right now and save us both a lot of time."

Sonny frowned. "I'm listening."

"I'm divorced and unemployed because the police department in Conway, Arkansas, fired me. They fired me because a man named Clyde Wallace beat up his wife and nearly killed her, then killed two people later the same morning in cold blood. The trial was ugly. He got life. Clyde Wallace was our father. Seven solid years with commendations in the department wasn't enough for them. My name alone got me ousted. Our family spent an entire year being hated for something we had no part in. Besides losing my job and my wife, the friends we had quit us. Mom divorced him, but it didn't matter to anyone. We were pariahs by association. Then Grandma died, left the family home to Mom, and it saved us all."

"Wallace? But you're going by Pope?" Sonny asked.

"Not going by. We went to court and legally changed our names. It was Mom's idea. It was the last link we had to that man, and we cut it. Taking her maiden name was a gift. So, if you don't want someone like me on the force, I won't say I'll like it, but I'll understand."

Sonny got up, walked to a file cabinet, and pulled out a job packet.

"You know how this goes. Security clearance. Background checks. Fingerprinting. A physical checkup, etc. I'm always in need of good officers and our budget is generous enough for more. We'll check your service records like we do everyone here. As soon as you turn in the packet, we'll fingerprint you here, and then start the process."

Aaron took the application. "I appreciate the opportunity," he said.

"Of course," Sonny said, and then stood. "Follow me. I'll walk you out."

Aaron wouldn't let himself get excited. Not just yet. But for the first time in ages, he felt hope.

━━━━━━━━

The ensuing weeks after Aaron's interview were tense and nerve-wracking. Aaron couldn't let go of the fear that he'd be rejected again. Only he'd been wrong.

He got a call, and in the middle of April, Sonny Warren pinned a badge on Aaron and issued his service weapon. He had a locker and uniforms on the premises, and the day he began his first shift, he was back where he belonged.

━━━━━━━━

March 1—Monroe, Louisiana

It was half-past 11:00 p.m. and raining again. The streetlight in front of Dani Owens's house was still out, although she'd reported it over a month ago, and night was not her friend. It afforded Tony Bing, her one-time boyfriend turned stalker, too much cover to continue harassing her.

It had been a year now since her nightmare began.

They'd dated for six weeks before it became apparent how controlling Tony was becoming. Seeing nothing but a bad end coming, Dani ended the relationship.

Tony tried cajoling her, sending her bouquets of blue flowers to match her eyes. Making constant calls apologizing for coming across too strong, with promises he'd never do it again. But she knew better and stood her ground. At that point, Tony and his twin brother, Alex, arrived on her doorstep. Tony had a box of chocolates, and Alex was holding a bottle of champagne, supposedly along to speak on his brother's behalf.

It was a Thursday evening, and Dani had taken papers home to grade so she could hand them back to her students the next morning. She was just about to take a break and make herself something to eat when her doorbell rang.

She wasn't expecting anyone, and rarely had friends drop in without calling first, but then she remembered they'd been working in the apartment building when she came home from work, and it might be the manager just checking on tenants, making sure the water pressure was back to normal.

She peered through the peephole, saw a man's

shoulder, and then opened the door, but kept the chain on the lock. When she saw who it was, her heart sank.

"Dani! Darling! Wait, please wait!" Tony said. "Just hear me out."

And then she saw Alex was with him.

"I don't know what game you two are playing coming here like this, but I don't appreciate it," Dani said.

Alex put a hand on his brother's shoulder and moved into view.

"Don't be like this, Dani. Tony's just a passionate man. He overdoes it sometimes, but he's harmless, believe me," he said and flashed a big smile.

"He's not harmless, and neither are you," Dani snapped. "If either of you had a sense of decency, you'd know how to take no for an answer." Then she shut the door in their faces and turned all the locks.

Almost immediately, two hard thuds sounded against her door, like they'd both kicked it. Then she heard one of them say, "You're a bitch, and you're going to be sorry."

"I'm already sorry," Dani shouted. "Leave me alone or I'm calling the police."

She heard muffled cursing, and then the sound of their footsteps as they walked away, and thought that was the end of it. But she was wrong. It was just the last time Tony spoke of reconciliation. His cajoling had moved to anger, and the stalking began.

The first were obscene phone calls in the middle of the night, promising all kinds of torturous things that were going to happen to her. Threatening notes left on the windshield of her car. And even though she lived on the second floor in her apartment building, more than once she'd awakened to a shadowy figure standing out on the balcony beyond her bedroom, trying to peer through the shades she'd drawn.

That's when she contacted a lawyer and filed a protection order against Tony Bing. To her dismay, it only upped his game. Dani made so many frantic phone calls to the police about what continued to happen, that the police began to think she was making it up. He was never there when they arrived, and the shadowy figure caught on security cameras was too indefinite to make an ID.

She was twenty-nine years old and had never felt so helpless, or so alone.

———————

It was late and Dani was tired. She'd run her fingers through her short dark curls so many times this evening that they were standing on end. But there was one more load of laundry in the dryer, and one last set of math papers to grade before she could go to bed. Tomorrow was Friday. The last day of school in Monroe before spring break, and it couldn't come any too soon.

She heard the buzzer go off on the dryer and laid her papers aside to get out the load. Most of it was clothes she wore to work, and leaving them in the dryer wasn't an option. She carried them to the bed and began folding up T-shirts and putting the rest on hangers and hanging the garments in the closet.

She'd just put up the last stack of clean T-shirts into her dresser when the doorbell rang. She glanced at the clock and frowned. It was after 9:00 p.m. Whoever it was could just go away.

But they kept ringing and ringing, and then the banging and shouting began, and she recognized Tony's voice.

"Oh my God," Dani muttered, and made a run for the door. "What's wrong with you? No means no! Go away! Leave me alone! I'm going to call the police."

"Nothing is wrong with me! What's wrong with you?" he shouted. "Why wouldn't you answer the door? You've got another man in there, don't you? You've been cheating on me, you bitch!"

And before she could answer, he kicked the door in, breaking the chain and sending her flying against the wall in the foyer. Before she could get up, Tony grabbed her by the hair and began dragging her through the apartment.

"Where is he? I'll kill him; I'll kill both of you!" Tony shouted.

Dani was screaming. "There's no one here but me! You're hurting me! Let me go!"

He let go of her hair and yanked her to her feet, his hands digging into the flesh of her shoulders. She was staring into the face of a man she didn't recognize. His eyes were wild, his pupils dilated, and his words were no longer making sense, and in that moment, she knew she was going to die.

He drew back his fist, hitting her square on the jaw. She heard it pop, and then she was on the floor and he was on top of her, pounding her with his fists until everything went black.

———————

She woke up in an ambulance, so wracked with pain she thought the siren was her still screaming. With both eyes swollen shut and the scream engulfing her, the EMTs hands upon her body became Tony Bing, still beating her. And then she heard a voice.

"Dani, you're in an ambulance on the way to the hospital. The police caught your attacker. You're safe. You're safe."

The relief was overwhelming, but it didn't last.

———————

She went home from the hospital three days later with broken ribs, a broken jaw, massive contusions and abrasions, and barely able to see.

Tony Bing bonded out of jail before she got out of the hospital. She knew he was still out there, somewhere. He and Alex.

Her heart sank.

There was no justice in this world.

But she was home, and she needed to heal.

———————

Weeks later, after she'd finally been released from doctor's care, she woke up in the middle of the night, certain someone had been standing at the foot of her bed. After a frantic search of the apartment without finding any sign of an intruder, she tried to convince herself she could have been dreaming, even though every instinct she had knew she'd seen Tony Bing. And in that moment, she made a desperate decision.

She bought a gun.

She'd hunted with her father all her life. She knew how to use one.

And the day she picked up the gun, she came home with a plan. She began rearranging everything inside her walk-in closet, then made a bed on the floor inside with a pile of quilts.

Then she stuffed pillows beneath the covers of her actual bed to make it look as if she was in bed asleep. That night when it was time for bed, she went into her closet with her phone and gun, and slept on the floor. Tony Bing liked to play games, and Dani had just changed the rules in her favor.

———————

Five nights came and went without issue, and then on the sixth night, it started to rain. Thunder crashed, followed by the occasional spike of lightning snaking across the sky, unloading a downpour drowning out the sounds of the city. That night when it was time to go to bed, the hair was standing up on the back of Dani's neck. Call it intuition. Call it a sense of self-preservation. But she felt evil coming.

Just like every night, she crawled into her closet with her gun and her cell phone and closed the doors, but this night she didn't lie down, and she had no intention of going to sleep. Instead, she sat within the silence, watching through the slats in the closet door, seeing the intermittent lightning flashes through the blinds on the windows, and the body shape she'd made of her pillows beneath the covers.

She sat in silence, heart pounding. Waiting. Knowing the devil was on his way, but not how or when he would appear.

———————

It was just past 1:00 a.m. when Dani heard a muffled thump somewhere within her apartment. Her first thought was *He's here!* Her second was *How the hell is he getting into my apartment?*

When she began hearing footsteps, and then that one squeaky board in the hall, she grabbed her phone and called 911.

"Nine-one-one. What is your emergency?"

"Someone is in my apartment," Dani whispered.

The dispatcher quickly confirmed her address and apartment number and dispatched police. "Are you in a safe place?" the dispatcher asked.

"I'm in my bedroom, in my closet. He's at the door now! I can hear him. I can't talk anymore," Dani whispered.

"The police are on the way. You don't have to talk, but I'm still here, understand?"

"Yes," Dani whispered, and then gasped, when she heard another squeak. Every time she opened the door to her bedroom, one of the hinges squeaked, and that was what she heard. "Oh God, oh God, oh God. He's here," she whispered into the phone, and went silent.

Even though she'd been expecting it, that squeak nearly stopped her heart. The gun was in her hand now, and she was on her knees, leaning forward, peering through the slats.

When the dark figure appeared beside her bed, her worst fears were realized. *Tony! Oh my God, he has a gun*!

Before she could think, he began firing. POP. POP. POP. And didn't stop until he'd emptied the clip.

———————

Tony felt an adrenaline kick when he began pulling the trigger. It was almost as good as coming inside her. Once he'd emptied the clip, he turned to run.

And then the closet doors flew open, and he watched Dani emerge. In the dark, she was little more than a shadow, and for a heartbeat he thought he was seeing her ghost.

He saw the gun in her hand too late. Her first shot went into his right knee. Even before he felt the pain, she had a bullet in his other knee. He dropped into a spreading pool of his own blood, screaming and writhing in a pain unlike anything he'd ever known.

"Help me! Help me! I need an ambulance!" he shrieked.

Dani leaned over, pushed the barrel of her gun between his eyes, and in a voice devoid of emotion said, "You are a worthless piece of shit! Shut up now, or I'll put the next one between your eyes."

He passed out, saving his own life.

———————

There was no misunderstanding about what had happened.

Dani's neighbors had heard the succession of gunshots when Tony emptied his weapon into her bed.

A 911 dispatcher had heard every shot.

And more than a dozen calls were made to 911 by Dani's neighbors on her behalf.

And there was no mistaking the sound of two other gunshots that came seconds later, or that Dani Owens had defended herself. She had stopped her stalker when the police could not, but her way of life had come to a grinding halt.

During their investigation, the police discovered Tony had rented the empty apartment next door to her and was using the return air duct to get up into the ceiling and crawl to her room, letting himself into her apartment through the grate in the ceiling.

What they didn't know was that Alex had been with him every time, holding the stepladder in the empty apartment while Tony crawled into the vent, and then crawling in behind him and giving him the lift back up from Dani's apartment to help him escape unseen.

The police also found hidden cameras in Dani's apartment, and camera equipment in the empty apartment where Tony had sat watching her. They suspected his brother, Alex, had been helping him, but the only fingerprints belonged to Tony. They couldn't prove it, and Tony denied Alex was ever involved.

At his lawyer's suggestion, Tony Bing opted out of a jury trial and threw himself on the mercy of the court. There was no lawyer on earth who could argue a good reason why Tony Bing shouldn't go to prison for attempted murder.

His parents were horrified at what he'd done and disowned him, and then in indignation for their decision, Alex disappeared.

Tony Bing's cold-blooded attempt at murder, his prior history of violent abuse, and the protection order he'd violated time and again didn't go well with the judge who handed down his sentence. He got the full fifty years for an attempt at first-degree murder, with no possibility of parole. Soon afterward, Tony Bing and his wheelchair were transported to prison.

And after a year of living in hell, when the school year ended, Dani Owens resigned and began looking for a new teaching job, with the caveat that it had to be anywhere but the state of Louisiana.

Chapter 3

June—Washington, DC

NYLES FAIRCHILD WAS A TALL, THIN MAN WHO'D turned forty-five on his last birthday—a confirmed bachelor who wore his long graying hair tied back in a ponytail at the nape of his neck. He had a master's degree in English literature, a PhD in American history, and worked as a cataloger at the Library of Congress in Washington, DC. He lived a quiet life in a tiny one-bedroom apartment on the ground floor of an old apartment building in Alexandria, Virginia. His last pet, a cat named Willie Nelson, died a year ago last Easter. He wasn't lonely, but there were days when he wished he had an alter ego beyond being a mild-mannered cataloger of books.

Still, he fully accepted his life—until he found the journal.

———

Nyles's workday began one morning with orders to oversee the renovation of an old wing on the lower level of the library. It wasn't about moving walls or changing the format. Just overseeing the installation of tiers of new shelving. He didn't like dealing with the public or other employees beneath him, and was mentally cursing the ineptitude of the workers when he saw a packet fall onto the floor from behind an old set of shelves. He quickly retrieved it, opened the soft leather wrapping tied around it, and after a quick glance, realized it was out of place. It didn't even belong in this area of the library.

Then one of the workers knocked over a set of shelving, and he laid it aside in the top drawer of a desk to deal with later and went to see what damage had been done. Hours later, the new shelving was finally in place, and everyone had stopped for lunch.

Nyles always brought his lunch from home and ate at his desk, knowing everyone else would be out and he could enjoy the brief privacy. It wasn't until he was getting ready to leave the basement area that he remembered the packet, and took it back to his office and set it aside as he sat down to eat.

It occurred to him that he probably shouldn't even be messing with it. He needed to check the provenance, and see when it had been entered into the system and where it was supposed to be. He checked the numbers and the coding, and then found the reference section to which it belonged.

NINETEENTH CENTURY JOURNAL DONATED
IN 1942 BY JOHN DAVID POPE.

Personal Journal of Brendan Pope
circa 1833. Ref. State of Kentucky.

"How the hell did you get down here?" Nyles muttered, but now he was curious. It was almost as if someone had gone to great pains to hide it. And in that moment, he ignored his first instinct to just return it to the proper area and decided to give it a once-over.

The journal was wrapped in unprocessed rawhide and bound with a long thin strip of the same material. He took a bite of his sandwich, and then as he was chewing, carefully unfolded the rawhide, revealing the book within. The tiny label at the base of the spine indicated it had been processed into the library at some point, but it was certainly in the wrong place.

His pulse kicked a bit when he saw the age and the style of it, then took another bite of his sandwich and opened it.

The pages were yellow with age, but they appeared to have been made from a thick, heavy paper of good quality. The front and back covers were dark leather that had cracked along the spine and at one corner, but he could see stitches in the paper through a crack on the spine, proving it had been hand-bound.

Gently, he opened the front cover and saw writing on the flyleaf. The script was old-fashioned, and the ink so faded it was difficult to read. He moved it closer to the light and leaned over.

Brendan Pope—In the year of Our Lord—1833
Cumberland Mountains—Kentucky.

Nyles was intrigued, but before he could read further, the door opened, and a co-worker entered. His lunchtime and privacy were over, and without thinking, he dropped it in his briefcase, telling himself he'd look at it later when he had more time.

But then that evening as Nyles was walking through the tunnel beneath the building out to where his car was parked, he thought of the journal in his briefcase. He had no intention of stealing anything, but his curiosity was piqued. He wanted to read it.

What had Brendan Pope been writing about? Why had this particular item been hidden behind a shelf? Was it simply an oversight? Or was there a more mysterious reason why it had not been shelved where it belonged?

As soon as he got home, he ordered in some dinner and, while he was waiting for the delivery, removed the journal and sat down at his kitchen island with it, utilizing the bright lights overhead.

By the time Nyles's food arrived, he knew that Brendan Pope, a twenty-year old man and a native of Scotland, had immigrated to the continent of North America, and after two years of hunting for subsistence and trying to find his place in this land, he set up a trading post on a well-traveled trail in the Cumberland Mountains of Kentucky. The trail went through a valley and then up the mountain beside it, making it convenient for trappers and random settlers to get supplies.

When Nyles's dinner was delivered, he paused long enough to wolf it down before returning to the journal, reading up into the early morning hours. By daylight he was exhausted, but he couldn't let go of the tale and called in sick. He showered, then set his alarm and slept for three hours before waking up and going back for more reading. Brendan Pope was something of a storyteller, and the journal posts, while intermittent, were, for Nyles, like stepping back in time.

He was halfway through the journal when a woman suddenly appeared on the pages. Brendan Pope had taken a wife. A Chickasaw woman named Cries A Lot, and according to the journal, the woman started off as part of a trade.

Cries A Lot had been traveling with a mountain man, who rode off and left her at the trading post with Brendan because, after she saw the big Scotsman, she wanted nothing more to do with the trapper. Brendan Pope's size fascinated her. He was the tallest man she'd ever seen. She told him she would stay with him because she liked the sound of his laugh, but only if he didn't beat her. And it was obvious through the ensuing posts, that she became a huge part of Brendan Pope's world.

He loved her, and he called her Meg.

As Nyles continued to read, the years passed. Brendan's posts were less frequent. He was busy with his work and his family. He and Meg had six sons and one daughter. There was one single line in the journal that mentioned the little girl dying from a snakebite when she was only six.

But as he read through the continuing years that passed, the six sons grew up and claimed their own land up on the mountain. They had their mother's black hair and their father's great size. Four of the boys married daughters of nearby settlers. Another son married a Chickasaw woman, and another married a Cherokee, and they all lived on their homesteads up on the mountain, and that was their life.

But then the journal posts began reflecting the changing times.

Brendan's trading post shifted into a dry goods store, and a blacksmith by the name of Liam Cauley set up shop nearby, and another man named Alfred Glass opened a saloon, and they named their outpost, Jubilee, and their sons and daughters grew up and married and built cabins like the Popes, until the mountain above Jubilee had a larger population than the little settlement below, and when a traveling preacher came through, they built him a church on the mountain. He named it the Church in the Wildwood, and so he stayed.

Nyles was mesmerized. He could see Brendan and Meg's tragedies noted by two or three words. The births, the deaths. Battling weather and thieves, and it was obvious by omission that no one on that mountain was aware there was a civil war brewing in the states beyond, and if they were, they took no claim in it.

Nyles paused long enough to make some coffee,

snagged a sweet roll from the pantry, and was back to reading a post from 1864, when he saw the words *Confederate soldiers* and something about a troop coming through the settlement pulling a wagon rumored to be carrying Confederate gold.

But Brendan only mentioned it in passing, because his main post on that day was that his Meg had gone to the nearby creek to pick berries and never came home. Thinking about those soldiers and worried about her safety, he'd locked up the store, gathered up their sons and some friends, and headed for the creek. They found signs of her berry picking and followed her trail up the mountain, all the way to a place known as the "Big Falls."

They found her berry basket upturned, the highbush blackberries she'd been picking were scattered about, and a large amount of blood was on the ground, as well as the prints of her little moccasins in the crushed berries.

And all over the ground around them were at least a dozen different sets of boot prints. Panicked, Brendan and the searchers began following them. They soon realized there were two sets of prints. One coming to the falls, and a second set going out the same way. They followed them all the way back to the trail.

There, they found the Confederate wagon with a shattered wheel and empty of any cargo. There were signs that the soldiers had gone into the woods, only to come back out later and ride away. But there was no sign of Meg. No more little moccasin footprints. No sign of more blood. No sign of her anywhere. It was as if she'd vanished into thin air.

By now, Nyles was in tears. The little Chickasaw woman was gone, and he felt Brendan Pope's heartbreak and rage as the story continued. Brendan and his sons followed the soldiers' trail over the pass, only to come upon their bodies. Some had been shot. Some had died in hand-to-hand combat. But there was no sign of who they'd fought with, or why. It was almost as if they'd gotten into an argument and killed each other. Whatever they might have known had died with them.

Brendan was miles and miles from home, and with no other trail to follow, he was forced to give up the search. He rode back to Jubilee, grieving the loss of a wife who'd disappeared from his life as unexpectedly as she'd first appeared. The posts ended with Meg's disappearance, and later, in someone else's handwriting, mention of Brendan's death in 1870 and being buried at the cemetery behind the church.

———

But this was where Nyles's focus shifted. It had gone from Brendan and Meg's world to that shipment of Confederate gold. The broken wagon wheel meant they could no longer transport it. And the trail of boot prints leading from the wagon and into the woods was most likely the soldiers taking the gold into the woods to hide, intending to come back for it later. They must have stumbled upon Meg and her berries, and since she would have been a witness to their cargo, they couldn't afford to let her live, right?

Maybe they hid the gold and her body in the same place? If they saw Meg at Big Falls, then the hiding place must have been nearby. He knew Kentucky was rife with caves. What if he could find that cave? And what if that gold was still there? At that point, Nyles wrapped up the journal, went to bed, and dreamed of treasure hunting for gold.

He was already making plans as he got ready for work the next morning. He gave himself a long look in the mirror, trying to decide how he was going to make this work, and then decided he needed a disguise. He already had long hair he could dye, but he needed a beard to hide his face, and there was no time like the present to start growing it.

Once he got to work, he used his lunchtime to research the geography of that area of the Cumberland Mountains and was curious to see if Jubilee had ever made it onto a map. His shock came in finding out that not only was Jubilee still there, but it had become a huge tourist attraction all on its own. And further research gave him yet more startling results.

The mountain was populated by the descendants of the Pope, Cauley, and Glass families. He didn't yet know how, but he knew he was going there, just not as Nyles Fairchild.

A few days later, after setting up leave from work, he

went to his bank to add a fictitious cousin named Dirk Conrad to access his checking account.

The bank employee was helpful and agreeable, and added the name.

"You will need to have your cousin come into the bank in person to sign the authorization slip," the employee said.

"Yes, I'll tell him. He should be arriving within the week," Nyles said, and exited the bank.

Once he took off work, he bought a bottle of temporary color rinse and turned himself into a blond and began coloring his white whiskers along with his hair. Then he bought a hiker-style backpack, a camping shovel for digging, and a metal detector that could be broken down for packing. At that point, he was really into the game.

He knew a guy who knew a guy and, for a small amount of money, wound up with a fake driver's license for his new look. Nyles was pumped. Creating a new identity was like being reborn.

He went into the bank in full disguise, signed the authorization slip, got a personalized debit card in Dirk Conrad's name, and then, at the last moment, realized the license tag on his car was still registered to Fairchild. Dirk Conrad couldn't be seen in Nyles Fairchild's car, so he solved the problem by renting a car under his alias at a rental company in a suburb of Alexandria, bought car insurance through the rental company, and went home to pack.

Two days later, Dirk Conrad was in Jubilee, checking into Hotel Devon. The next day he went into search mode, driving up the road on Pope Mountain only to discover NO TRESPASSING signs all over it.

Shit. No hiking allowed?

The woods hid those who dwelled upon the mountain, but he could tell by the number of mailboxes and dirt roads winding up into the trees, the population did not bode well for sneaking or trespassing.

The next day he explored the tourist side of Jubilee, looking for an answer to his problem. But it wasn't until he drove past the music venues and saw the creek in the distance that he had an idea. After checking his map, he realized he could get to Big Falls by following the creek. He parked and got out, then walked the short distance down the slope to the water flowing past.

Again, there were signs stating PRIVATE PROPERTY on both sides of the creek and warning away backpackers. He could go downstream without issue, but he would be breaking the law if he backpacked up the mountain.

But Nyles hadn't come this far only to be deterred by NO TRESPASSING and PRIVATE PROPERTY signs. The only way to get to where he wanted to go was to follow the creek up the mountain and try not to get caught.

On the morning of his third day in Jubilee, Nyles watched the sunrise from his hotel balcony. He was intimidated by the sheer size of the mountain and the foreboding he felt, but he reminded himself treasure hunts weren't supposed to be easy. With an early breakfast in his belly, he left his hotel room and drove across town, parking in the overflow lot at the edge of the rise and within easy sight of the creek.

The shops were beginning to open, and foot traffic was picking up downtown as tourists began looking for places to have breakfast. But Nyles wasn't interested in fudge making or the blacksmith shop. He had no desire for the woodcarver's goods or the quilt boutique with handmade quilts for sale. He was on a treasure hunt.

Adrenaline was rushing as he pulled his backpack from the trunk of the car and secured the shovel and metal detector to it, making sure his handgun was inside in case of snakes or wild animals. He locked his car, shouldered his pack, and began walking down the slope toward the creek. Once he reached the water's edge, he glanced over his shoulder, then turned left and started uphill on a narrow footpath between the trees and the brushy creek bank.

The woods were thick and, for a man born and raised in cities, a bit mysterious, but the sound of water racing downhill over deadfall and rocks was as hypnotic in its way as listening to waves crashing along an ocean shore. If he hadn't had the creek to follow, it would be easy to get lost. There was a slight breeze, but not strong enough to penetrate the heavy growth of vegetation.

Nyles was out of his element, but his heart was pounding with excitement as he moved ever upward, certain in his heart that he was going to be rich.

———————

It was midafternoon on Pope Mountain when Ray Raines and his thirteen-year-old son, Charlie, finally finished fixing a stretch of downed fence. Now they could turn their livestock back into the pasture to graze. Ray was gathering up their tools, and Charlie had just finished rolling up the old fence wire they'd replaced, and tossed it in the back of his daddy's truck.

"Daddy, are we done now?" Charlie asked.

Ray looked up and, in that moment, saw his son as the man he would one day become, and felt a moment of sadness at how swiftly time was passing. Charlie was already as tall as Ray, and he'd just begun that teenage growth spurt. Charlie took after his mama's side of the family, for sure. The Popes were big people.

"Yes, we're done," Ray said. "I think your mom has some strawberry ice cream waiting on us back home."

Charlie grinned. "My favorite, but could I go to Big Falls to cool off first? I'm already wet with sweat, but that cold spring water sure would feel good."

Ray frowned. "I'm sorry, son. Maybe another day? I need to make a run into Jubilee to make a payment at the bank before it closes."

"Oh, I can walk home, Daddy. It's just barely a mile," Charlie said.

Ray shrugged. "Well, if you want to do that, then sure. Be careful, and don't be late getting home. Your mother will worry."

Charlie beamed. "Thanks, Dad! I'll be careful, and tell Mom I'm only gonna take a quick dip. I'll be along shortly."

Ray nodded. "Will do, and thanks again for all the help. You're growing up to be a real fine man."

Charlie's heart skipped. His dad had just called him a man.

"Will I grow as big as Cameron?" Charlie asked.

Ray laughed. "Who knows. Your mother's people run big. Now go on and cool off, then get yourself on home."

"I will," Charlie said, and took off at a lope across the small meadow, made his way across the cattle guard, and disappeared into the trees.

Ray loaded up the rest of the tools, then drove away.

———————————

Ray's wife, Betty, was sitting in the shade of the back porch when he drove up from the barn. He'd just let their small herd back into the pasture to graze. He could see Betty had been working in the garden, because her sun hat was on the swing beside her, and there was a hoe leaning against the porch railing.

He got out and waved. "Hey, honey."

She waved back, then stood up. "Where's Charlie?"

"He went to Big Falls to cool off. He'll be along soon," Ray said.

He unloaded his tools, then went inside to clean up before heading into town.

———————

Nyles had been on the mountain for hours. He was sweltering, exhausted, and nervous. He'd already passed a couple of small waterfalls before he finally came to one that had about a forty-foot drop. This coincided with the descriptions in the journal. This had to be Big Falls.

At that point, he left the creek bank, took off his pack, and put his metal detector together, grabbed his camp shovel, and shoved the handgun beneath his belt. It was resting against the small of his back as he began sweeping the area with the metal detector, while keeping an eye out for critters.

Twice he'd gotten hits that had been hopeful, but upon digging, the only things he'd found were shell casings from a twenty-two rifle and an old belt buckle. He'd found two small shallow caves that yielded nothing but creepy vibes, and sidestepped a rattlesnake. He'd been spooked by a deer and challenged by a boar raccoon and seen a variety of animal tracks he'd identified with an app on his phone. The only ones that worried him were the tracks made by bears.

Noon had come and gone, and he was back at the falls, sunburned, exhausted, frustrated, and calling himself twelve kinds of stupid for even being here, when he heard something thrashing in the brush, and from the sound, it was running straight toward him! He dropped everything and pulled his gun.

Sweat was running out of his hair and into his eyes. His heart was pounding, and he had an overwhelming urge to pee when he caught movement and fired.

———————

Charlie Raines came out of the trees running, thinking of nothing but jumping into the water, when he saw the man and then the gun. Startled, he stumbled, and in that moment, the man pulled the trigger. He heard the shot, felt the burn, then everything went black.

Fairchild was shaking with horror. He'd been so afraid it was a bear that he'd fired without caution. And now there was a boy lying on the ground with his lifeblood spilling out beneath him.

"Oh my God! Oh my God! What have I done?" Nyles wailed, and rushed toward the boy, kneeling to check for a pulse. But his hands were shaking so hard he couldn't hold them still, he couldn't feel a pulse, and the spreading blood beneath the body made him sick.

He reached for his phone, intent on calling an ambulance, then realized what was at stake. The boy was dead, and Nyles was not only trespassing, but he'd come into this area under a false name! He'd spend the rest of his life in prison.

"Sorry, kid. Wrong place. Wrong time," Nyles said, then ran back to gather his things, frantically throwing it all into his backpack.

He disassembled the metal detector and folded up the shovel, jamming them both down into a side pocket, then took off down the creek, crashing through brush and trees as he went, with his heart pounding and tears rolling down his face.

———————

Betty Raines was worried. Charlie hadn't come home as he'd promised and wasn't answering his phone. Every motherly instinct she had was telling her something was wrong, so she got on their four-wheeler and headed across their pasture and then into the woods. The trail was just wide enough for her to get through the trees on the ATV, and as she rode, she kept calling out Charlie's name.

When her phone began to ring, she stopped to answer, hoping it was Charlie. But it wasn't. It was Ray. He'd come home to an empty house and no note.

"Baby? Where are you?" he asked.

Betty's voice was shaking. "Charlie never came home. I'm in the woods on the four-wheeler and heading for Big Falls to check on him."

Ray frowned. "I'm getting in the truck now. I'll head that way and stay in touch with you by phone."

She started crying. "I'm scared, Ray. This isn't like Charlie. I've got to go."

Ray heard her accelerate and then the call ended. He ran for his truck with his stomach in knots. Charlie promised he wouldn't be long, and his son never broke his word.

Betty drove the four-wheeler across the cattle guard and into the woods, going as far as she could go, and then killed it and got off running, still shouting, still calling Charlie's name.

The earth was spinning, and Charlie didn't know why. He felt weightless, and kept trying to dig his fingers deep enough into the ground beneath him to get a grip, but he couldn't focus enough to tell which way was up and which way was down. He knew he hurt, and he knew he was crying, because he felt the tears on his face, but he couldn't remember what happened. He just kept floating in and out of consciousness, and every time he fell back into the darkness, he thought that he was dying.

Betty kept shouting as she ran.

"Charlie! Charlie! Where are you?"

With every step she took, Betty knew her son was in trouble. She could hear the falls now, and the water tumbling from it down into the creek below. She was looking toward the creek as she ran out of the brush, and then caught a glimpse of something from the corner of her eye and stopped.

It was Charlie. Motionless on the ground.

"Charlie! Charlie," she screamed as she ran to him. She saw the blood, and what appeared to be a gunshot wound in his shoulder, and frantically felt for a pulse. "Please God, please God, don't take my son."

The pulse was weak, but it was there, and for now that was enough.

She grabbed the phone and called Ray, screaming into the phone as he answered.

"Charlie is at Big Falls. He's been shot. He's got a pulse but it's weak. Call an ambulance. Get help. Get the police!"

Then she dropped the phone, tore off the old shirt she was wearing over her T-shirt, and ripped it in two, folding each piece as tight as she could into two pads. Then she rolled Charlie over enough to get one pad beneath the exit wound, eased him back down, and placed the other pad on the entrance wound, pressing as hard as she dared to slow the bleeding, then began to pray.

Ray was in shock. He immediately called 911, relayed the message to the dispatcher, giving them directions, and then parked at the edge of his pasture and took off in a dead run into the trees.

Nyles's trip down the mountain was far quicker than it had been going up, and when he finally got back to his car, every muscle in his body felt like it was melting. He couldn't walk a straight line as he headed for the car park, and was staggering and sobbing. Just as he reached his car, he stumbled and fell. As he did, his backpack slid over his head, jamming his forehead into the concrete and scraping the back of his neck as it went.

He cried out from the pain, then rolled over to slip out of the backpack before dragging himself up. Half-blinded by the sweat in his eyes, and fearing he was going to die of a heart attack where he stood, his only thought was getting away. After fumbling for his keys, he popped the trunk and began grabbing at what he'd dropped. The gun had fallen out, as had the shovel and the pieces of his metal detector.

He slung everything inside, slammed it shut, and staggered to the driver's side of the car. Moments later, the engine started. He backed up and spun out as he sped away, unaware someone had seen everything— from his haggard appearance and the fall, to all that had fallen out of his pack.

———————————

Dani Owens had a new job! Come August, she would be teaching first grade at the elementary campus in Jubilee, Kentucky. She'd been in town for two days now, looking for a place to rent. There were apartments just outside of the city, as well as a couple of small housing additions with some houses for rent, and a few more for sale. She was hot, tired, and a little frustrated from filling out rental applications. As far as she was concerned, the first one that accepted her was the one she was taking. She liked all of the ones she'd seen, and any of them would suit. She just wanted this over with so she could get moved and settled in for a couple of months before she had to go to work.

Now that Dani had covered all the available living options, she decided to drive down to the music venue where Reagan Bullard was headlining. She wanted to get a ticket for one of his matinee performances, and after winding through a maze of parking lots, she found a place to park and went inside, only to learn his matinee shows were sold out for the next week.

But her disappointment was short lived. Since she'd be living here now, she opted not to get that far ahead of herself and exited the building, pausing momentarily to see where she'd parked. As she did, she caught movement from the corner of her eye and, as she turned to look, saw a tall, thin man come lurching up over the small rise between the parking lot and the creek below.

From the distance, he appeared to be crying as he staggered against the load of his backpack. She couldn't tell if he was exhausted or drunk, and when he finally reached his car, he stumbled and fell. The backpack slid over his head as he went down, grinding his head into the concrete and spilling out some of the contents from inside.

She was about to run to his aid when he finally got

to his feet. Blood was running down his forehead as he opened the trunk, then yanked a handkerchief from his pocket and began swiping angrily at the blood running down his face. Cursing loudly, he began picking up what had fallen and throwing it all in the trunk. She thought nothing of the shovel, or water bottles, or what looked like a metal detector that he'd gathered up, but when she saw him pick up a gun, she stepped back into the shadows. He slammed the trunk shut, got in the car, and flew past her without knowing he'd had a witness to his fall.

As she emerged, she looked back at where he'd been and saw something lying on the concrete. She guessed it was something from the backpack and that it likely slid under his car when he fell. It might not be anything important, but on the off chance that it was, she walked across the parking lot to get it.

It was something wrapped in an old piece of rawhide, and she could tell the moment she picked it up that it was likely a book. But when she unfolded the leather for a closer look, she realized it was a very old personal journal, belonging to someone named Brendan Pope.

The name was written in an old-fashioned script and dated 1833, and the first thing she thought was that anything this old had to be something of value. The only thing she could think to do was turn it in at the police station, so she wrapped the journal back up in the rawhide and headed for her car.

After a quick Google check, she found directions to the police station and drove there. As she was getting out of her car, the sharp scream of a siren pierced the air. She flinched, expecting police cars to start speeding away, but when no police cars left the area, she decided it must have been an ambulance and went inside.

The first thing she saw was the backside of a very tall man in uniform, with a loud and rowdy teenager in tow. Unwilling to get in the middle of that, she sat down in one of the empty chairs with the journal clutched against her breasts, and waited.

———————

Aaron Pope was standing at the front desk beside a teenage boy he'd just arrested for shoplifting. Ordinarily he would have taken the boy through the back entrance into the jail area to get fingerprinted and booked, but he'd gotten a call on his way in that an exterminator was on the premises delousing the cells. Someone had booked a transient into jail two days ago, and when he was released this morning, the jailer realized he'd left head lice behind. Just the thought had everyone in the station itching, and business as usual was rerouted through the front door until the area had been fumigated.

The shop owner had caught the teen red-handed, and security footage from inside the store backed up the owner's claim as Aaron arrived to pick him up. But Jason Reece, the teen who'd gotten caught, was loud, demanding, and belligerent. Even after Aaron got him to the station, he was still arguing.

"My father has more money than you jerks will see in a lifetime. He will make you sorry you ever saw my face," he shouted.

"Empty your pockets," Aaron said.

"I don't have to—"

Aaron's voice shifted from an authoritative order to threatening whisper. "Empty your pockets, Mr. Reece, or I'll do it for you."

The teen took one look at Aaron, paled, and began pulling everything out of his pockets and laid it on the counter. The desk sergeant bagged it all in an envelope and called an officer up from booking, who took the kid into an interrogation room, locked him up, and left him sitting until the jail area was cleared for use.

Aaron held up an evidence bag with a black fanny pack in it. "This needs to be logged into evidence. Over two thousand dollars' worth of jewelry lifted from the Cherokee Trading Post, and Mr. Reece just turned nineteen. No more Get-Out-of-Jail-Free cards for him."

"Did you call his parents?" Walter asked.

Aaron shook his head. "No. He's not a kid. He can use his one phone call to let them know."

Walter nodded, then looked past Aaron's shoulder and saw a young woman waiting to approach.

"I'll be right with you," he said, and left to take the stolen property to the evidence room.

Aaron hadn't realized there was anyone behind him until Walter spoke. He turned, eyeing the young dark-haired woman, and then the book she was clutching against her chest.

"I'm Officer Pope. Can I help you?"

Shock rolled through Dani so fast goose bumps rose on her arms. "Oh my God," she mumbled. "What are the odds?"

Aaron frowned. "I'm sorry?"

Then she realized how rude that must have sounded. "No, I'm sorry. It's just that your last name...it took me by surprise." Then she held up the package. "This is probably nothing, but I was coming out of the ticket office down by the music venues when I saw a man come running up from the creek. He was acting strange, like maybe drunk or sick, and then just as he got to his car, he fell and his big backpack slid over his head. A bunch of stuff fell out, including a handgun and what looked like pieces of a metal detector. He threw it all in his trunk and drove away. Afterward, I saw something lying beneath where he'd parked. I think it slid under his car when he fell. I unwrapped the rawhide to see what was in it, and then after I saw what it was and how old it is, I thought it might be valuable. This is the only place I could think to bring it."

"What is it?" Aaron asked.

"A personal journal. It's dated 1833, and it belonged to a man named Brendan Pope."

The skin crawled on the back of Aaron's neck.

"Would you please put it on the counter for me?" he asked.

Dani frowned. "Yes, certainly," she said, and put it

down, then watched him put on a pair of nitrile exam gloves before removing the rawhide.

The first thing Aaron noticed was a small label on the spine. At some point, it had been processed into a library. And when he saw the name and the date, and the condition of the journal, he guessed it was authentic. He had no idea how this had gone from belonging to Brendan Pope to being donated to a library, but the odds of this coming full circle were beyond calculation.

Then he thought about the man who'd dropped it. People carrying handguns didn't sound like someone they needed running loose in a tourist destination like Jubilee. He went behind the desk, dug around in the drawers until he found some evidence bags, and slipped the piece of rawhide and the journal inside one.

"I'm going to need you to tell the chief what you just told me. What's your name?"

"Dani Owens," she said, and took a seat in a chair against the wall as Aaron reached for the desk phone and called Sonny Warren's office.

A couple of minutes later, Sonny entered the lobby. He'd just gotten word from county about Charlie Raines being shot, and now there was a woman in the waiting area talking about seeing a man with a gun.

"Miss Owens?"

Dani nodded.

"I'm Chief Warren. Will you please follow me to my office? Aaron, I'll ask you to come, too."

"Yes, sir," Aaron said.

Dani's heart skipped a beat. Calling attention to herself was the last thing she needed.

"I just wanted to turn in a lost book," she said.

"This one," Aaron said, holding up the bag.

"Yes, ma'am. If you'll please follow me, I'll explain," Sonny said.

Dani was already regretting getting involved, but she did as she was told.

"Please, have a seat," Sonny said as he closed the door behind them.

Aaron laid the journal he'd taken into evidence on the chief's desk, then stood at attention beside the door as Dani sat down.

"Now, I need your name and phone number, and where you're staying, then please tell me exactly what you saw and when," Sonny said.

Dani nodded. "Daniella Owens, but I go by Dani," then gave him her phone number and the Serenity Inn, the hotel where she was staying, before repeating everything she'd just told Aaron.

"I did unwrap it, and I did open the book to look for a name, but the name and date written in the flyleaf was obviously very old, which made me think it might be valuable, so I brought it here."

Sonny eyed the evidence bag. "If this is legit, then Officer Pope is a direct descendant of the man to whom this belonged."

Dani glanced at him again. "I guessed it was something like that when he introduced himself."

"Can you please describe the man you saw?" Sonny asked.

She thought a moment. "He was probably in his late forties, maybe early fifties. He was tall and thin, with a long blond ponytail and beard. He looked like he'd been running for miles. His clothing was soaked with sweat, and he was staggering and crying as he came up from the creek. Then just as he reached his car in the parking lot, he stumbled and fell."

Sonny nodded. "And you said he had a gun. Was it a rifle or a handgun?"

"A handgun," Dani said. "What's going on?"

"Someone shot a young boy named Charlie Raines up on Pope Mountain this afternoon. They think he was shot with a handgun. His family just found him. He's still alive, but barely, and they have no clue as to what could have happened. And then here you come with this story, and this book that appears to be a journal belonging to the very man for whom Pope Mountain was named. The man who founded Jubilee. And the man you saw was in possession of a gun."

Aaron grunted like he'd been punched.

"Charlie was shot?"

Sonny frowned. "Oh man, sorry, Aaron. I blurted that out without thinking. He's related to you, isn't he?"

"It's okay, sir. I'll check on him later," Aaron said.

Sonny returned to questioning Dani. "Did the man see you?"

"No, at least I don't think so. Once I saw him pick up the gun and throw it in the trunk, I ducked back into an alley and watched from there."

"Okay. Say nothing more about this to anyone else. We need to try and identify him ASAP. It may mean nothing. And it could mean everything. Are you here as a tourist?" Sonny asked.

"No, sir," Dani said. "I've been hired to teach first grade here this coming August. I've been here a couple of days looking for a place to rent."

"There are a couple of large apartment complexes just as you head east out toward the campgrounds, and the rental property is almost all outside of the tourist part of Jubilee," Sonny said.

"Yes, sir. I've already filled out several rental applications. I'm just waiting to hear back."

"Right," Sonny said.

"Is that all? Is it okay if I leave now?" Dani asked.

"We'll need to fingerprint you to eliminate them from what's on the book, but I may need to talk to you again later. Officer Pope will walk you down to the lab. When you've finished there, I need to ask you to lead my officer and a team from the crime lab back to where you found the book. If he bled as much as you indicated, we might be able to collect some DNA. You won't have to stay, just show them where it happened, and then you'll be free to go."

"Yes, sir. I'm happy to help," Dani said.

"Excellent," Sonny said, and handed the journal to Aaron. "The exterminator is gone. Log this into evidence, then leave it at the lab for fingerprinting. When Miss Owens is finished, escort her out of the building."

"Yes, sir," Aaron said, then glanced at Dani. "This way, please."

Chapter 4

DANI WAS VERY AWARE OF THE MAN KEEPING PACE beside her. She appreciated his consideration in making small talk, trying to ease her nerves, when he'd just received bad news of his own.

"Don't be worried," he said. "Digital fingerprinting is painless."

Dani glanced up. "It's okay. I've been fingerprinted before. Any time a teacher applies for a job in a new district or a new state, we go through a thorough background check, which includes fingerprinting."

"Oh, right. You did say you'd come here to teach first grade." He flashed back on his own first-grade teacher. She looked nothing like Dani Owens. "That's wonderful," he added. "You get to be in on the beginning of so many lives."

Dani had never heard it put quite that way before, but that's how she always felt with a new class, and his insight touched her. Without thinking, she glanced down at his left hand, looking for a wedding ring, but it wasn't there. It didn't mean he wasn't married, and then she reminded herself his marital situation didn't have anything to do with her.

Then he abruptly stopped.

"We're here," he said, and opened the glass-front door to their right.

It broke the fantasy of the good-looking cop and revived her anxiety, knowing she only had herself to blame. She'd put herself in this mess because she'd picked up that book.

Aaron called out across the room. "Hey, Terry. This is Dani Owens. Chief needs you to fingerprint her strictly for elimination purposes. I've got to log in some evidence. I'll be back to escort her out in a few minutes. Be nice. She's had a rough day."

"I'm always nice," the officer said, and smiled at Dani. "This won't take long, and if Pope gets lost, I'll be happy to show you out."

Aaron's eyes narrowed. "I don't get lost. I'll be back in a few, Miss Owens. Trust me."

Dani hid a smile. She'd seen little boys on the playground with the exact same mindsets as these two. It wasn't a squabble. It was just two male egos pecking at each other without trading blows.

And true to his word, after logging in the evidence, Aaron returned to the lab with the journal in the evidence bag. "Chief wants this dusted for prints."

"Will do," Terry said, and went to work as Aaron escorted Dani out of the building, then gave her his card.

"Just in case you remember anything else later. Go ahead and get in your car, then give me a couple of minutes to gather up the crew. You'll lead us to the place where you found the journal, and then you'll be free to go, okay?"

"Yes," Dani said as she palmed the card, then glanced up. "I'm very sorry about the boy who was shot."

"Thanks. He's a really good kid," Aaron said, and then went back inside.

Dani was a little bit in shock as she headed for her car, thinking how randomly she'd become involved in something this sinister.

Aaron hurried through the station and out to his cruiser. The team from the crime lab was already waiting in the van. He waved as he got into his cruiser, and then left the parking lot with the van behind him.

When Dani saw them coming around the corner, she backed away from the curb and led the way back through town, past the music venues and to the farthest parking lot before she stopped to roll down her window.

She watched from her side mirror as Pope emerged from the cruiser, unfolding his long legs as he stood, and wondered how he was able to fit inside that car. He was strikingly handsome, which would have been obvious to anyone, but she would have had to be blind to ignore that sexy walk.

Then he was at her window and leaning down to speak to her.

"This is the place?"

"Yes. See that faded yellow strip? He was parked beside it."

"Got it. Thank you again for helping, and remember, if you think of anything else, you have my number."

"Yes, I will. Am I free to go now?" she asked.

"Yes, you are. Have a good evening."

Dani rolled up the window and drove away, thinking this was the end of her good deed.

Aaron watched until she was completely out of sight before he remembered he was there to set up a perimeter, so he strung up yellow crime scene tape before calling his mother about Charlie getting shot.

———————

Shirley was outside in the porch swing with a glass of iced tea melting in her hands when her phone rang. Seeing Aaron's name come up on caller ID, she set her tea aside to answer.

"Hi, honey. How's your day going?"

"Not so good, but that's why I'm calling. The news is probably already spreading on the mountain, but I wanted you to hear it first from me. There was an incident at Big Falls this afternoon. Someone shot Charlie Raines and left him for dead. County is working the case, but we're assisting. I don't know anything other than he was still alive when they got him to the hospital, and he's in surgery now."

"No! Oh my God, no!" Shirley cried. "He's just a boy! This makes me sick. Poor baby! Poor Betty and Ray."

"I know, Mom. Listen, I may be late coming home, so if I am, don't worry. This will be the reason why."

"Okay. You be careful. I love you," Shirley said.

"Love you, too, Mom," Aaron said, and then pocketed his phone and went to check on the techs' progress.

They'd already found evidence, taken pictures of the scene, gathered blood and skin samples from where the man had fallen, and were packing up their gear.

"Are you done?" Aaron asked.

"Yes, and heading back to the lab."

Aaron nodded. "I'll follow you in," he said, and jogged back to his cruiser.

———————

Dani wasn't in the mood for sightseeing and was on her way back to her hotel when she noted the time. It was almost five o'clock, and she hadn't eaten since breakfast. There were dozens of wonderful places to eat in Jubilee. She'd tried a couple at lunchtime, but had always gone back to the hotel before dark. Being overcautious now was a holdover from the Tony Bing episode, and she knew it. She was slowly getting past being afraid of everyone and everything, but it was a process.

As she was driving, she remembered seeing a café called Cajun Katie's, and she'd grown up in Louisiana. Maybe a little food from home would settle her nerves, so she drove back downtown until she found the restaurant again, and went inside. The aroma of Cajun spices, fried fish, and gumbo met her at the door, along with a hostess who quickly seated her.

Hunger pangs hit as Dani began scanning the menu. Dinner was about to be served.

Nyles Fairchild was in a panic. His head was throbbing and still seeping blood from the cut on his forehead. When he got back to his hotel, he quickly shed his clothes and showered, then bandaged the cut and put on clean clothes. In a panic to get out of town, he was shaking profusely as he began throwing his things into his suitcase.

Once he was certain he'd left nothing behind, he headed for the elevator to go down to the lobby to check out but, once there, kept looking over his shoulder for fear he'd see cops coming in the door.

And then the desk clerk asked him a question that stopped him cold.

"Sir, do you want to leave your bill on this credit card or...?"

"No!" Nyles said, and then lowered his voice and made himself smile. "Sorry. That was a bit abrupt. I once had my identity stolen, so I don't like to leave that kind of info behind me anymore. I'll pay cash and ask you to erase that card number from your system, please."

"Certainly, sir," the desk clerk said, and handed him a printed copy of the bill.

Nyles dug through his backpack for the backup cash he'd brought with him, and counted out several one-hundred-dollar bills. The clerk gave him his change, and he walked out of the lobby without looking back.

He drove away from Hotel Devon and out of Jubilee with only one thought in mind. To get home. He had a gun in his car that had killed a boy. It had once belonged to his grandfather, and to his knowledge, it had never been registered. Maybe he'd bury it somewhere along the way or throw it in a river. No one would ever know he'd had his hands on it.

Nobody had seen him. And Dirk Conrad didn't exist. He was just one among thousands of tourists. He'd seen the sights, and now he was going home. With a little bit of luck, he might get away with this.

He didn't breathe easy until he'd put a hundred miles between himself and Jubilee, and the farther he drove, the easier he felt.

Charlie Raines was in surgery, still hanging on to life by blood infusions and a surgeon's skill. When the news began to spread on the mountain about what had happened and how dire Charlie's chances of survival really were, every relative Charlie had headed to the hospital to donate blood.

Ray and Betty were in utter shock, and despite Sheriff Woodley's questioning as to whether they or Charlie had enemies, they were adamant that it could not have been anyone they knew.

The first pieces of evidence the sheriff's forensic team found at the scene was a cartridge casing from an old-style revolver and dozens of boot prints. Then they found a trail along the creek indicating someone had followed it up to the falls, and then more recent tracks showing the same footprints going back down. They found evidence of recent digging in several places, and the ground cover was trampled all around the area and far up into the brush. They found even more of the same prints inside a small nearby cave, took castings of the tracks, and bagged a wrapper from a protein bar.

Sheriff Woodley sent two of his officers to the creek to follow the footprints, which led them all the way into Jubilee, but from there, the trail went cold.

They couldn't tell if the person took to the shallow water there and kept following the creek, or if he had a vehicle parked somewhere nearby. After checking all of the security cameras in that area, they discovered that none of them had been aimed toward the creek or the overflow parking lot. The only other security cameras were inside buildings, which didn't help. Tracking was a bust.

Sheriff Woodley was still at the crime scene with his forensic team when he received the call from his men that the trail had come to a dead end. Frustrated, he'd just hung up when his phone rang again.

"Sheriff Woodley."

"Rance, this is Sonny Warren. I'm assuming you are still at the crime scene."

"Yes, but there's not much to go on. My men followed tracks all the way back to Jubilee and then lost him."

"I may have a lead for you," Sonny said, and told him about the woman who'd come into the PD, and what she'd witnessed.

Woodley's pulse kicked.

"This is either a freakish coincidence, or we've just gotten our first break in this case. Is she a local or a tourist? Do you have her contact information?" he asked.

"She's in the process of moving here, but she's staying at the Serenity Inn for the time being. I'll text you her phone number. You can go from there."

"What about that book? Did it have the owner's name in it? We'll need it fingerprinted," Rance said.

"Already on that for you," Sonny said. "We also got some trace evidence at the scene. Blood drops and tissue samples from where his head hit the pavement. We sent it all to the lab here, with orders to send you copies of the results. But get this. The original owner of the journal was Brendan Pope. There's a date on the flyleaf of 1833. This is the man who founded Jubilee."

There was a moment of silence, then shock in the sheriff's voice.

"Holy shit…but wait. It's just a book someone wrote about the man, right?"

"No. It's a personal journal, and old…very old. If we're lucky, the man who dropped this will be in the system. If it's okay with you, and since it was turned in here at the station, I'm going to visit with some of the Popes about it. They may have more information regarding the journal and who might have had possession of it."

"Yes, sure. I appreciate the help. That way when the lab reports come back, I can focus on the shooter," Woodley said. "I don't suppose your witness took any pictures?"

"No. All I have right now is the description she gave. Is there any word on Charlie Raines?" Sonny asked.

"He was alive when they left here with him. That's all I know," Rance said.

"Then we'll hold on to that and pray for recovery," Sonny said. "Charlie is a really good kid. I'm just sick about this happening to him."

———

John Cauley heard all the sirens coming up the mountain and knew in his heart that something terrible had happened. The sounds were all below his place, but he was guessing they had either gone to the home of Marcus Glass, or Ray and Betty Raines. Either way, he needed to know. He stopped what he was doing and ran for his truck, then headed down the mountain.

He was coming up on the road leading into the Raines property when he saw an ambulance come flying out of their driveway onto the blacktop and take off down the mountain with lights flashing and sirens screaming.

"Oh lord, oh lord," John muttered, and took the turn. He was just pulling up to the house when Betty rode up on their four-wheeler with Ray in his truck right behind her.

John got out, running.

"Ray! What's happened?" John cried.

"Somebody shot Charlie down by Big Falls and left him for dead. The sheriff is already on the scene. Say a prayer for Charlie, Uncle John. He's gonna need it."

Then Betty came running, jumped into the truck and they drove away.

John was in shock. His hands were shaking by the time he got back into his truck and called his wife.

It had been a busy day at Granny Annie's Bakery, and Annie had given over the front counter to her daughter, Laurel, and retreated to the kitchen to organize end-of-day cleanup. There were still a few deliveries to make, and she was directing her new delivery driver, B.J. Pope, as to the orders yet to be delivered.

B.J. was carrying them out to the van when Annie's phone rang. She smiled to herself when she saw it was John.

"Hello, honey. How's your day going?" she asked.

"We've had big trouble up here. Someone shot Charlie and left him for dead down by Big Falls. The ambulance just left their place with him, and Ray and Betty aren't far behind."

"What? John, no! Shot him? Do they know who did it?" Annie cried.

"I doubt it. The sheriff is on the scene. You go check on Ray and Betty before you come home. I've got some calls to make."

"Yes, yes, I will. Oh my God, John. What is this world coming to? Are you at home?"

"No, I'm still at their place, but I'm going back home now."

"Drive carefully. I'll call you before I start home."

"Okay, sweetheart. Love you," John said.

Annie sighed. "I love you, too," and disconnected.

After telling Laurel and B.J. what had happened, Annie left Laurel in charge and headed for the hospital.

━━━━━━━━━

Aaron's phone call about the shooting had shaken Shirley to the core, but she wasn't sure what to do. She'd been to Ray and Betty's house a few times in the months since their arrival, and when the evening began to grow short, she knew there would be chickens to put up for the night and barn cats to feed, and decided to call her aunt for advice. She didn't want to overstep her bounds, but she needed to do something for them, and this was all she could think of that might help.

Annie was just leaving the bakery for the hospital when her phone rang. Shirley's number came up on caller ID, so she stopped to answer.

"Hello?"

"Aunt Annie, this is Shirley. Aaron called us about Charlie. Are you going to the hospital?"

"Yes, I'm on my way there now."

"Okay. Would you please give Ray and Betty a message from me? Let them know we're praying for Charlie. Also, I know there will be dozens of family members there, so I thought it best we don't add to the confusion. Just tell them Sean and I will see to feeding and putting their chickens up for the night, and feeding the barn cats."

"That's so thoughtful, Shirley. Yes, I'll tell them."

"If you get news, please let us know. We're just sick about this. Charlie was just here last week fishing in our pond. I can't believe this could happen."

"That's pretty much what we're all thinking," Annie said. "Nothing like this has ever happened up here in my lifetime. I'll talk to you later."

Rusty Pope heard the news from her sister-in-law, Rachel, and made a frantic call to Cameron.

Cameron had taken Ghost for a walk in the woods

an hour earlier and was on his way back home when his cell phone rang. When he saw Rusty's name come up on caller ID, he smiled.

"Hey, darlin'. Were you worried? We're almost home."

"No, no, it's not that," Rusty said. "Rachel just called. Someone shot Charlie Raines. Betty found him unconscious at Big Falls. He's in surgery now. Rachel said it's touch and go."

The words sent a chill up Cameron's spine. "Shot him? He's just a kid! What the hell is going on up here now?"

"This is one of those times when I'm sorry I'm no longer in law enforcement. I don't know where we can help most," Rusty muttered.

"We'll figure it out. I'll be home in about ten minutes. See you soon," he said.

━━━━━━━━━

Ray Raines was pale and tight-lipped, trying not to cry. Betty was doing enough for them both. Family kept coming into the waiting room in silence, giving them a hug or a pat on the shoulder, then sitting down to wait, and the families continued to gather in the waiting room until they'd run out of chairs and people were sitting on the floor. But it was the silence of that many people in one small space that was most telling. There was nothing to say that could make this nightmare better, but they wouldn't let Ray and Betty bear this nightmare alone.

And then two hours later, Charlie's surgeon walked into the waiting room, did a double-take at the number of people present, then gazed around at the faces.

"Is anyone here for Charlie Raines?"

Ray stood, keeping his hand on Betty's shoulder.

"Ray and Betty Raines. We're his parents. Everyone else is family. Say what you have to say to all of us."

The surgeon nodded. "He's in recovery. The bullet hit his clavicle and ricocheted down, breaking two ribs. It just missed his heart. He's lost a lot of blood and will be in critical care for at least the next twenty-four to forty-eight hours so we can monitor him closely."

"When can we see him?" Betty asked.

"Critical care is on the fourth floor. There is a waiting room there as well. The visiting hours are posted but, for now, parents only. You can check in at the nursing station to let them know you're there. I will follow up on him off and on throughout the night, but his family doctor will be the doctor of record throughout the rest of his time here in the hospital." The surgeon paused. "Do you have any questions?"

Ray shook his head. "No questions. Just our undying gratitude for saving Charlie's life."

The surgeon nodded, shook their hands, and then left the room.

As the family began to leave, Annie went straight to Ray and Betty.

"Shirley sends her love and prayers. She also said to tell you that she and Sean will get your chickens fed and put up for the night, and feed the barn cats. And they'll tend to them tomorrow morning, too, so you don't need to fret about your livestock."

"Oh my God. I hadn't even thought about all that," Ray said. "Give her our thanks."

"I will. You two try and get a little rest when you can. I'll bring breakfast for you early in the morning when I come to open the bakery."

Betty was crying with relief, just knowing Charlie made it through surgery.

"Thank you, Auntie. Thank you for always being there," she said.

Annie hugged them both, and left with tears in her eyes, praying all the way home that Charlie would heal.

It was late by the time Aaron got back to the station. The chief had gone home. The night shift was on duty. The kid he'd arrested for shoplifting was no longer in lockup. He wondered how much money it had taken the man's father to pay off the Cherokee Trading Post to get them to drop the charges. It was the only way the kid would have been released that fast. But Aaron had bigger issues to worry about besides a spoiled rich kid burning bridges at such a young life. He clocked out, swung by a drive-through to get some food and drinks for Ray and Betty, then went straight to the hospital to check on Charlie.

———

Ray and Betty had the ringers turned off on their phones and were letting messages go to voicemail. There was nothing new to tell, and they couldn't even look at each other without bursting into tears.

It was getting dark. Betty felt like she should be home cooking supper, not sitting here like this, waiting to see if her son lived through the night.

Ray's mind was in free fall He kept trying to think of who he'd pissed off, or if Charlie had a run-in with a friend and they hadn't known about it. Was it someone they knew? Or was it a stranger?

And then Aaron Pope walked into the room carrying two to-go sacks and a drink carrier, and set it down on the table beside them.

"Burgers and fries. Two sweet teas. Don't tell me you don't want it. Charlie's gonna need two healthy parents when he goes home."

Betty burst into tears.

Ray stood and hugged him, then opened the sacks and began passing out food to Betty.

"Here, sugar. Aaron's right."

Aaron sat with them as they began to eat. "Have you heard any news from Sheriff Woodley?" he asked.

Ray shook his head as he was chewing his first bite.

"That's par for the course," Aaron said. "Don't lose heart. Cops don't talk about leads, or lack thereof. But rest assured, the local police and the county are both on this. Have you been allowed to see Charlie yet?"

Betty took a sip of her drink before she could talk, and even then, her voice was trembling.

"Yes," she said, and explained the extent of Charlie's injuries. "And I have to say, seeing him in that hospital bed hooked up to God knows how many machines is far less frightening than finding him in the woods all covered in blood. I have never been so scared in my life. I thought he was dead."

"Charlie's come this far. I have to think there's a reason he's still with us," Aaron said. "Anyway...I just wanted you to know we're here for you. If you need anything. Anything at all...just call."

"Your mother and Sean have already stepped up to help. They're tending to our animals until we can get home," Ray said. "We are so grateful, and thank you for the food."

"Absolutely," Aaron said. "I'm going to leave you to eat in peace. Try to sleep when you can. I'll be back on duty tomorrow. I'll try to stop by to see you before I leave town."

And then he was gone.

Ray watched him walking away and then glanced at Betty.

"He looks like a younger version of Cameron, doesn't he?"

She nodded. "Yes, and Charlie has that same build and look. All that black hair and he's growing so tall." Then she took a bite of her burger and leaned back to chew. "I didn't think I could eat, but this does taste good. I wonder how he knew?"

Ray shrugged. "Shirley and her boys have been through their own seven levels of hell. I think they've learned the hard way what really matters in life."

Unaware he was the topic of conversation, Aaron was already leaving Jubilee and headed up the mountain. The road was dark and winding, but he was getting used to the dips and curves. He now knew to watch out for random deer leaping out of the woods and freezing in the headlights, and to slow down for the occasional raccoon waddling across the road.

He was a little surprised at how easily they'd slipped into the footsteps of their people, and how quickly his grandmother's house had become their home. Without the constant reminders of his father's crimes, the memories from Conway were beginning to fade.

He was pulling up to the house when he thought of Dani Owens, and the shocked look on her face when she heard his name. But it wasn't the look of hate or disgust that had come with their connection to Clyde Wallace. It had been a look of disbelief that he was connected to the man from the journal she'd found.

She was pretty, but there was something fragile about her. She appeared to be a little leery of the mess she'd unintentionally become involved in, but that was fair. And since she was moving to Jubilee, odds were that he would see her again.

He heard a hound baying somewhere on the mountain as he got out of the car, and paused, letting the sound roll through him. The hound was hunting, likely chasing, and whatever it was chasing was running for its life. Being alive in the world was hard when there was always something or someone who could bring you to an end.

Then he shrugged off the melancholy and went inside to the welcome sound of laughter, and the voices of the people he loved.

Dani was in her hotel room, fresh from a shower and curled up on the bed in her pajamas, watching TV. She kept thinking about her day and how convoluted her life had become just because of what she'd witnessed. She thought of the boy who'd been shot, and how frightened his parents must be.

If the man she'd seen was truly the shooter, she was glad she'd seen him and found the journal. Hopefully they would catch him and put him away for good.

It had been hours since her early supper, and she was thinking about raiding the mini-fridge for a snack when her cell phone rang. She muted the TV, then rolled over and grabbed her cell phone.

"Hello, this is Dani."

"Miss Owens. This is Amber Collins from Jubilee Realty. Your application has been approved, and if you're still interested in the little two-bedroom, bath-and-a-half cottage on Glass Avenue, it's yours."

Dani stifled a squeal. "Wonderful!" she said. "Yes, I am. I want it."

"Great," Amber said. "If you'll come by the office anytime tomorrow, we'll do the paperwork, and you can pick up your keys."

"Thank you! I'll be there," Dani said.

The moment the call ended, Dani leaped out of bed and did a happy dance. This called for that cold drink and one of the cookies in her mini-fridge. She ate while she was going through the numbers on her phone and making notes to herself about what she needed to do tomorrow.

She had already packed everything she owned before leaving for Jubilee and had a moving company on standby. Now all she had to do was call the apartment manager tomorrow, make sure he was still willing to meet the movers to let them in, and then call the utility companies and have her services discontinued.

The little cottage she was getting was adorable, and her furnishings would fit perfectly. She was especially pleased to have the cottage rather than an apartment. That little bit of extra privacy would be welcome. The past year of living in fear and always looking over her shoulder had been hell. Dani needed to feel safe again.

Chapter 5

NYLES FAIRCHILD HAD A HEADACHE OF IMMENSE proportions, and a crick in his neck from being hit in the back of his head with the damn hiking pack. It made driving miserable, but that misery would go away. Nothing was going to change the fact that he'd killed a kid. He still couldn't believe what he'd done.

Last week he'd been living a quiet single life, and now he was on the run for murder. He wished to God he'd never seen that journal. He'd gotten wrapped up in the fantasy of finding gold and lost his fucking mind. He just wanted to get home, regroup, and decide what his next best bet would be.

Could he just go back to work and pretend none of this ever happened? Or did he need to disappear?

About two hours from Jubilee, as he was passing through a small town, he stopped long enough to get food from a fast-food drive-through before getting back on the road. He ate as he drove, with the sun setting behind him, and kept moving late into the night before he finally gave out. He had to sleep.

He found a motel in Charleston, West Virginia, and

once inside the room, stripped by the bed, stepped into the shower, and began washing the blond rinse from his hair. The water was cold before it got hot, but he didn't care. He didn't think he would ever feel clean again. He shaved off his beard after he got out, and then hacked off his ponytail with his hunting knife. His hair was in shambles, but the man who'd killed a boy was no longer looking back at him from the mirror. Still, he knew divesting himself of his alter ego was only a whitewash. He couldn't wash away the damage he'd done.

When he finally went to bed, he couldn't sleep. Every time he closed his eyes, he relived the sight of that boy running out of the woods, the sudden fear on his face, the echo of the gunshot, then the blood pooling beneath his body and seeping into the ground.

The few times he drifted off to sleep, he'd wake abruptly with his heart pounding. He kept breaking out in cold sweats, and the weight of guilt made it hard to breathe. Panic grew to the point of thinking he was having a heart attack, then deciding he didn't care. Death would end this horror.

But he didn't die. He just kept falling asleep, killing the boy again, and waking up crying. Finally, he got out of bed, got dressed, and was back on the road at sunrise.

He drove east through the Monongahela National Forest of West Virginia without being conscious of its beauty. The roads were steep and winding, taking all of his attention. When he finally reached Highway 81, he turned north and followed it all the way to the junction of 81 and 66, and took Highway 66 eastbound.

His first glimpse of the Potomac River brought tears to his eyes, but it wasn't until later, when he saw his apartment building looming on his street, that his panic finally settled. He was home. Nobody from here knew where he'd been, and he looked nothing like the man he'd been in Jubilee. He pulled into the apartment complex and into an empty parking space, then killed the engine. The silence should have been reassuring. But there was a huge black hole before him, waiting to swallow him whole. He closed his eyes, leaned forward until his forehead was resting on the steering wheel, and prayed.

"Please God, I'll give up everything that makes me happy if you'll just make this go away."

Then he leaned back and looked up.

Although his journey was over, his hands were still on the steering wheel. He'd gone as far away as he could from what had happened and had a feeling it would never be far enough.

One glance into the rearview mirror reassured him it was the same brick sidewalks lined with trees he'd known before. The little coffee shop down on the corner. The laundry across the street that did his clothing.

This was it.

Lift off.

Either he got out now, or backed up and kept on driving. But the familiar won. He took the keys from the ignition and got out, bagged up all of his trash, and tossed it in a dumpster in the alley, then went inside the building and down the hall into his apartment.

It was the quiet, the picture of his parents hanging in the hall, and the sight of all his things that finally broke him.

He began to shake, and then dropped to his knees and burst into tears. He was home. But by his actions, he'd forever destroyed what it meant and what he thought he knew about himself.

He didn't know how to be.

What to do.

His first mistake had been curiosity—finding that journal and taking it home to read. The old saying "Curiosity killed the cat" kept going through his head. But his curiosity didn't kill a cat. It killed a boy. And for the first time in his life, the thought of suicide was real.

He went from tears to nausea as he staggered to his bathroom. He threw up until his throat was raw, then dragged himself to the sink to wash his face. His eyes were swollen. His cheeks red and splotchy. He couldn't remember the last time he'd cried. Maybe when he buried his mother. Then he frowned. That haircut he'd given himself was a mess.

Shit. I didn't know crying made me look this ugly.

He dried his face and hands, then went back outside and began emptying his car, carrying in his luggage, stuffing everything back into his backpack that he'd tossed in after he fell, then took the metal detector and the shovel into his apartment. It took two trips to get it all back inside and he still had to return the rental car.

He stared at the mess for a few moments, then began pulling out all of his dirty clothes, including the clothes he'd been wearing at the falls, stuffed them into a laundry bag, dropped it off at the laundry across the street, then went back to his apartment. He stared at the hiking shoes, then put them in the bathtub and ran the tub full of water. He didn't care if he ruined them. He just wanted every miniscule bit of Jubilee washed down the drain. Removing the DNA of a place from his things was of paramount importance.

There was also the matter of the gun. He didn't know what to do with it, but it needed to be gone. Then he thought of the Potomac. As soon as it got dark, he'd drive down to the shore and throw it in the river. The gun was unregistered. Even if somebody found it one day, it could never be traced back to him.

Satisfied so far with his decisions, he unpacked his toiletries, then continued to empty the backpack. It wasn't until he was staring down at the empty pack that he realized the journal was missing.

"What the fuck?" he mumbled, and grabbed the backpack again, tearing through all of the separate compartments, certain that he'd just overlooked it.

"Oh God, oh God, oh God! Where the hell could it be?" Then he dropped onto the side of his bed and closed his eyes, trying to remember when he'd seen it last. "Yesterday morning! I put it in my backpack before leaving the hotel. I had it with me on the mountain, but I never took it out."

And then it hit him! The parking lot! When he fell. Shit came flying out of that backpack like confetti at a wedding. It must have fallen out then and he didn't see it!

He broke out in a cold sweat, and once again, his heart began to pound. It took a few moments of sheer panic before it dawned on him. Finding that book still didn't pin him to it. Nobody would know who lost it. And there were Popes everywhere. They'd just claim it and go on about their lives without knowing how it got there.

"Fine. I'm glad it's gone," Nyles muttered. "Nobody knows me. Nobody saw anything. Now there's nothing linking me to that place. I was just one of thousands passing through Jubilee. It's going to be all right. Thank you, God. It's going to be all right."

He breathed a shaky sigh of relief and went to the kitchen to get something cold to drink. But the contents of his refrigerator left a lot to be desired, so he began dumping out all of the spoiled food and the milk that had gone sour, then made out a grocery list and left.

He drove straight to the bank to remove his "cousin's" name from his account, apologizing for the inconvenience, and giving them the excuse that his cousin had decided against moving to DC after all. Once that was done, he drove into Virginia to return the rental car; then he called an Uber to take him home. Once he returned, he got into his own car with the grocery list in his pocket. He needed a haircut and fresh food, in that order.

That night he drove to the Potomac and tossed the handgun into flowing water as far as he could throw, then went home, took a sleeping pill, and slept without dreaming. He woke up the next morning with a drug hangover and took himself to work.

Walking back through the tunnel from the parking lot, and then into the auspicious Library of Congress, he was convinced he'd just gotten away with murder.

The sad part? Not a single soul had even noticed he'd been gone. No one remarked upon his new look. Or welcomed him back.

He was fucking invisible, and he hoped it stayed that way.

———————

Charlie Raines was still unconscious when his doctor made rounds the next morning, but his vital signs were stronger. The news gave Ray and Betty fresh hope they would not have to bury their only child after all.

Annie Cauley arrived at the hospital the next morning with a half dozen fresh biscuits from home already split and buttered, with pieces of fried ham between them, and a thermos of hot coffee, along with napkins and disposable cups.

Betty was stretched out on a small couch, and Ray

had bunked by shoving some chairs together to make a cot. Nurses had furnished each of them with a pillow and a blanket. They were just waking up when Annie walked in. Betty sat up and began combing her fingers through her hair as Ray shoved chairs back in place and began folding up their blankets.

"I brought breakfast as promised," Annie said, and set it down on a table as she greeted them with hugs. "Also, I asked Shirley to get fresh clothes for the both of you when she and Sean went to your house to do chores. They're in this bag. Call if you need anything. There are a dozen people just waiting to help. Now, tell me how Charlie is doing."

"His doctor already made rounds. Charlie's still unconscious, but his vital signs are stronger," Betty said as she grabbed a couple of cups and poured them full of hot coffee, then took a quick sip and sighed. "You're just what the doctor ordered."

Annie smiled.

Ray picked up his own coffee and took a quick sip before he spoke.

"We got to see him a couple of times in the night. I have a feeling he knows we're there. We just keep telling him he's safe and to rest so he can heal."

Annie sighed. "I don't suppose you've heard anything from the police?"

"Not since Aaron stopped by last night. He said both local and county officers were working the case, but they couldn't be talking about it to anyone," Ray said.

"It's good to know we have family in on the hunt," Annie said.

"Yes, it is," Betty said. "Thank you for breakfast, Aunt Annie."

"You're so welcome, sugar," Annie said. "I'll leave you to it. I need to get to the bakery. Call if you need me."

And then she was gone.

Betty went to wash up, and when she came back, she and Ray ate what they could, saved the rest for later, then took turns changing clothes. A shower would have been welcome, but the simple act of fresh clothing was a comfort.

———

People were also stirring up on the mountain.

Aaron left for work while Shirley and Sean were at the Raines' house tending livestock and chickens.

Wiley and B.J. were only minutes behind Aaron. The day was just beginning.

———

Dani was up early, excited about signing the lease for the little cottage, and thinking about the new job and new life ahead of her. She was about to go down to breakfast when her phone rang. She sat down to take the call.

"Hello?"

"Hello. This is Sheriff Woodley calling for Dani Owens."

"This is Dani," she said.

"Miss Owens, Chief Warren has informed us of what you witnessed yesterday evening, and of the journal you found. We have a copy of your statement, but there are a few things we'd like to talk to you about, as well. To make it easier for you, we'd be happy to speak to you at the police department in Jubilee, rather than ask you to come here. Are you free this morning?"

"I am going by the Realtor's office this morning to sign a lease on a rental property and pick up the keys. I guess I could go back to the police station after that."

"Good. Good. Will around 11:00 a.m. work for you?" Woodley asked.

"Yes, sir. I'll be there," Dani said.

"See you then," Woodley said, and disconnected.

"Shoot," Dani muttered, then dropped her phone and room key into her purse and went to breakfast. She should have known it wouldn't be over this easily.

While she was eating, she made the calls to her landlord and then the movers, and got a date for the van's arrival in Jubilee. She was going to have to wait four more days, but it was what it was.

A couple of hours later, Dani walked into the Jubilee PD with her new house keys jingling in her purse, dreading this meeting. The deeper she got into this mess, the more it felt like she was putting herself in danger. But there was a boy fighting for his life. If she could help find the man who shot him, then she was willing to take the risk.

What she wasn't expecting was the same good-looking policeman waiting for her in the lobby.

"Thank you for coming, Miss Owens. I'm your escort to the conference room we have set up," Aaron said.

Dani paused. "How is Charlie?"

"He's holding his own and getting stronger. Not awake yet, but progressing. Thank you for asking."

"Of course," Dani said, and then glanced around the lobby, checking out the people waiting.

Aaron frowned. "Miss Owens? Is everything okay?" he asked.

"Yes. Sorry. Please call me Dani," she said.

"This way, then," he said, and walked her down to one of their conference rooms.

Aaron saw her frown as they entered the room, then saw her relax. He didn't know what was going on with her, but she was obviously unsettled.

Chief Warren pulled out a chair for her, then began introductions.

"Miss Owens, this is Sheriff Woodley. He's handling the Charlie Raines case because the crime happened in his jurisdiction. However, since you turned in evidence in this jurisdiction regarding his case, the Jubilee PD is officially assisting Sheriff Woodley at his request."

Dani nodded at the sheriff and shifted anxiously in her seat as Chief Warren continued introductions. "And this gentleman is Keith Taggert. He does composite drawings for police departments all over the state. The rest of us, you've already met. Now I'm going to turn this over to Sheriff Woodley."

Rance Woodley could tell the young woman was nervous and hoped to put her at ease.

"Thank you for agreeing to meet me here. I'm recording this interview for my case file, so would you please state your full name, address, and occupation?"

Dani took a deep breath. "Daniella Maria Owens. I just rented a property at 211 Glass Avenue. I was hired as the new first-grade teacher at Jubilee Elementary School this coming August."

"Thank you. Now would you please describe the incident you witnessed yesterday regarding the man you saw coming up from the creek north of the music venues?" Woodley asked.

And once again, Dani repeated the story, from the moment she saw him until the moment he drove out of sight.

"Do you think you could recognize him again if you saw him?"

"Yes, sir," Dani said.

"How long have you been in Jubilee?" he asked.

"Going on four days. I'm still at the Serenity Inn, but now that I have leased a home, I'll be moving in. Unfortunately, I'll be waiting four more days for the moving company to get here with my belongings."

"Have you, at any time, seen the man previous to

seeing him in the parking lot? Maybe in a café or sight-seeing?" Rance asked.

"No, sir, but during the time I've been here, I haven't done much sightseeing. I came to find a place to live and have spent most of my time viewing apartments and houses."

"Right," Woodley said. "Now I'm going to trade places with Keith. Can we get you some water? Or a soda?"

"Water would be fine," Dani said.

"I'll get it," Aaron said, and left the conference room while seating arrangements were being shifted so the composite artist could get to work.

Aaron came back with a cold bottle of water and a folded paper towel for a coaster. He broke the seal on the lid so it would be easier for Dani to open and then set it down near her elbow.

"Thank you," she said, then unscrewed the lid and took a quick sip.

"Welcome," Aaron said, then watched her tilt her head to take a drink. Afterward, he noticed a tiny drop of water lingering on the edge of her lip. It felt like for-ever, but it was only seconds before he made himself look away.

As they were getting set up, Sonny Warren got a call and excused himself, leaving Aaron in charge, so Aaron took a chair from the table and moved it to a point that would give him a clear view of Dani's face.

It was a beautiful sight upon which to gaze, but he

wished he knew what was bugging her. Every time foot-steps passed the door to the room they were in, she glanced toward it, as if she was afraid of who might be coming through it.

It took an hour of the artist's questions and Dani's answers, as she had Keith move the eyes farther apart, then at another viewing, add sharper bone structure to the face, then a longer neck, and finally a slight hook to his nose.

With that last touch added, Keith turned the image toward Dani once more.

"How does this look?" he asked.

Her eyes widened, and then she shuddered. "Like he's looking straight at me and knows I saw him."

Keith glanced up at the sheriff.

"I think we're done, sir."

Woodley took the sketch. "Thank you, Keith. Good job. We'll get copies of this distributed to precincts in the area and go from there. Thank you again, Miss Owens."

"Happy to help," Dani said, and then glanced around the room. "I have a question. My identity won't be mentioned in any public reports, will it?"

Aaron's eyes narrowed. *I was right. She is hiding something, or she's in hiding. And for her sake, we need to know what or why.*

"Absolutely not," Rance Woodley said. "Your name will be kept completely out of this."

Dani nodded. "Thank you."

"I'll walk you out," Aaron said and, once again,

escorted her through the building and back out into the lobby. But this time, instead of holding the door open for her, he walked outside with her, out of earshot of everyone else.

"I have a question," he said.

Dani paused. "About what?"

"What are you afraid of?" he asked.

The startled expression on her face told him all he needed to know. She *was* afraid of something.

Dani's heart skipped. "I don't know what you mean," she said.

Aaron shook his head. "I'm not prying for the hell of it. But I'm a cop, and I'm good at my job. You scan the faces of everyone around you. You jump at unfamiliar sounds, and making sure your name isn't made public is just another signal to me that you are hiding something or hiding from someone. Which is it?"

She glanced up, then looked away.

Aaron sighed. "I'm sorry. I'm not prying, it's just…"

Her expression blanked. The tone of her voice became sharper, and there was a muscle jerking at the side of her eye.

"I had a stalker. It was someone I dated. He got possessive and then controlling, and it scared me. I broke it off with him, and he didn't take it well. Months of unwanted flowers turned into obscene phone calls with a disguised voice, to threatening notes left on my windshield. The protection order I took out on him didn't work. And the cops began to doubt me when I called.

Then one night he broke into my apartment because he thought I was with another man. I was alone, but he was already set on 'teaching me a lesson.' He beat me senseless, broke my jaw, and two ribs. They put him in jail for assault. He was out on bail before I was released from the hospital. The rest of the year was a living hell. The cops got so fed up with my calls for help that they would show up late or not at all. One night I woke up and saw him standing at the foot of my bed. He ran as I was calling the cops. So I bought a gun and began sleeping in my closet and stuffed pillows in my bed to make it look like I was there. I was so scared and so sleep-deprived that I was barely getting through my days at school. And then one night during a thunderstorm, I heard a thud in the living room, and then footsteps in the hall. I called 911 and watched from my closet as he emptied a handgun into the pillows. Then I walked out of the closet and shot him in both knees. He got fifty years with no chance of parole for attempted murder." Then she looked up, straight into Aaron's face, her hands curled into fists. "I should have killed him," she snapped, and walked away.

Aaron was too stunned to stop her. It was his mother's life all over again, only she'd been married to the brute. He saw the angry set to her shoulders, the long steady stride of a woman with someplace else to be, and realized the sacrifice she'd made by coming forward to help find Charlie's shooter. An abused woman does not seek the spotlight. She was on her own again, and without backup.

Horrified that she'd just spilled her guts to a stranger, it was all Dani could do not to run. Then just before she got in her car, she looked back and caught him watching her.

The intensity of her gaze was like a fist to the gut. Aaron flinched, but stood his ground. Then she got in her car and drove away.

In that moment, Aaron's world shifted.

She did have someone who knew her story.

She did have someone who could protect her.

She had him.

Aaron couldn't stop thinking about the rage in her eyes and the sight of her walking away.

Monroe, Louisiana

Alex Bing still had a key to the apartment next to Dani's. The apartment had been rented once since his brother's incarceration, but was empty again. He'd made it his business to know. In his eyes, she was the ultimate bitch, and she'd crippled his brother for life. Being separated from his twin was daily torture, and it was only getting worse. Now that the next-door apartment was empty again, he was going to finish what Tony started. Dani had destroyed his brother. He was going to destroy her. Only quieter. And neater, and make it look like she'd killed herself.

He had it all planned out, right down to the overdose. He knew where the security cameras were, and when it got dark, he snuck into the building, disabled the cameras on that floor, then let himself back into the empty apartment. He crawled back through the ducts and dropped down into her apartment, only to see boxes everywhere. The beds had been stripped. The kitchen packed up. She was gone!

"Son of a bitch!" Alex muttered.

He left the building in despair. He'd missed his chance.

And then it hit him!

If her things were still there, she would be moving them somewhere else. All he had to do was stake out the building, then watch for a moving van. He knew what her furniture looked like. He'd know if it was her things they were loading. After that, all he had to do was follow the van straight to her.

He went home to gather up food and blankets and his binoculars, and then was up before daylight and back at the apartment building. She'd destroyed his family and he wasn't going to let her get away with it.

After five days on stakeout, Alex's persistence paid off. A moving van arrived. He moved his car to a better position in the parking lot, and when the movers began bringing out the furniture, he knew what they were carrying belonged to her. At that moment, he would have given a year of his life for a bath, but personal comfort had to wait. Wherever that van was going, he was going, too.

―――――

The same night back in Jubilee, when the family sat down to supper, Shirley could tell something was bothering Aaron. He was unusually quiet. Her other sons kept the conversation going with stories of their day, so his lack of input wasn't noticed. If he wanted to talk about it, he would. Otherwise, she wasn't going to pry. She knew both local and county officers were working on trying to find the person who shot Charlie, and if that was what was bothering him, he couldn't talk about it anyway.

But when it came time to serve dessert, Shirley put an extra spoonful of cobbler in Aaron's bowl. He noticed, and glanced up at her with a smile. She winked, and the moment passed.

Later, after everything was cleaned up and put away, Shirley went out onto the back porch and settled into the porch swing to watch the sun falling below the treetops. Up here on the mountain, that was as much of a sunset as anyone could see. After that, it was just a matter of watching the sky turning into a painter's palette before the stars were allowed to shine.

She was still watching and savoring the sounds of nightlife on the mountain when she heard the squeak of the screen door behind her, and then Aaron sat down beside her on the swing and put his arm around her shoulder.

"You're glad you came home, aren't you, Mom?"

Shirley nodded. "Yes, very much. Are you sorry you came?"

"Never," Aaron said. "Moving here is the best thing that's ever happened to us. Your life was hell before, and we were helpless to stop it. Clyde is pure evil."

Shirley sighed and leaned her head against his shoulder.

"I wish I had picked a better man, but I know in my heart that I would do it all over again just to have the four sons I have now. Getting to be your mother made up for everything else."

Aaron put his arm around her. Together, they watched as the evening sky erupted in a wash of final brilliance. Dusk came quickly, blurring their vision of the land around them.

"Time to go inside," Shirley said. "I feel a bubble bath calling my name."

"I'll lock up," Aaron said, and followed her inside, then began going through the house, locking everything up for the night.

He was still thinking of Dani later, wanting to find a way to help her, when a notion struck. She would soon be moving into her new house. She'd packed alone. She'd come all this way alone to find a new job and a new place to live. The moving van would soon be here with her things. They could at least help her get settled in, like his family did for them when they arrived.

———————

Dani couldn't sleep. Revealing the ugliness of her past today had just resurrected the horror. Every time she dozed off, she fell back into the dream, hearing the gunshots, then emerging from the closet and shooting Tony. Watching him regain consciousness as the police arrived. Hearing his screaming and cursing as the EMTs carried him out of the room. Watching techs from the crime lab digging bullets from the bed and bagging them and the gun. Seeing the shock on the officers' faces when they realized where she'd been sleeping. Unable to face her, knowing they'd belittled her previous fears. Reliving the trial and the angry shouts from Alex when Tony's sentence was handed down. The look Alex gave her on the courthouse steps, saying over and over, "I'll make you pay," before his parents dragged him away.

She woke up crying and bathed in sweat, then repeated the process until just after 4:00 a.m. Finally, she abandoned the idea of sleep and took a shower instead, sobbing beneath the spray until her eyes were so swollen it hurt to blink. Afterwards, she got a cold drink from the mini-fridge and crawled back into bed to watch TV while keeping a wary eye on the clock, count-ing down the hours until the town of Jubilee awoke. She was going to Granny Annie's Bakery for cinnamon rolls and coffee or know the reason why. She needed some-thing sweet to take away the bad taste of her life.

———————

Charlie Raines was waking up to sounds he couldn't identify and scents that had nothing to do with home. He knew he was lying down, but there was pain.

Why do I hurt?

Someone was talking to him. *Mama? Is that you?*

Betty glanced at Ray.

"Look! His eyelashes are fluttering! I think he's trying to wake up," she said. "Talk to him, Ray. He needs to hear our voices. He needs something to hold on to, to find his way back."

Ray moved closer and put his hand on Charlie's leg.

"Charlie, it's time to wake up now. You're my buddy. I can't do anything without my buddy," Ray said, and then his voice broke and he shook his head, unable to talk anymore without crying.

Charlie was confused. Something had happened. What was wrong? He had a few seconds of confusion, and then an image popped into his memory. *There was a man at the falls. He shot me!*

He felt his mother squeeze his hand.

He squeezed back.

"Ray! He just squeezed my hand!" Betty cried.

Ray wiped away his tears and leaned over to whisper in Charlie's ear.

"Good boy, Charlie! You're safe now. Come on back, son. All you need to do now is open your eyes."

So he did, just enough to get a blurry glimpse of his parents' faces.

"He shot me," he whispered.

"Who shot you?" Ray asked.

Charlie sighed, then closed his eyes.

Ray leaned closer. "Did you know him?" he asked.

They thought Charlie had gone back to sleep.

"No," he said, and then slid back into the shadows.

"Then it *was* a stranger," Ray said.

"Go tell them Charlie's waking up!" Betty said, and then she kissed Charlie's cheek. "You're safe now. Rest. Heal. We're close by. We love you so much, and you aren't alone."

It didn't take long for the mountain grapevine to spread the good word.

Charlie Raines was waking up. He spoke. He knew his mother.

God was good!

Chief Warren notified Sheriff Woodley of the news.

Charlie had seen the man who shot him, but didn't know who he was. He was still in no condition to be questioned, but he was waking up, and that was all that mattered.

Chapter 6

LATER THAT SAME DAY, AARON DROVE BY THE HOUSE Dani had rented just to see where it was. When he saw her car in the driveway, he pulled in behind it and then called her.

Dani was in her bedroom measuring windows. There were rods and blinds already in place, but she liked curtains, and as soon as she got measurements, she was going to order some online. She was writing down the measurements when her phone rang. Once she saw Aaron Pope's name come up, she frowned, wondering what he wanted now as she answered.

"Hello?"

"Hello, Dani, this is Aaron Pope. I have something to ask you, but I didn't want to scare you by just ringing your doorbell. I'm sitting out in your drive. Can we talk?"

"Yes, of course, but the front door is locked. Give me a sec," and disconnected as she went.

By the time she opened it, he was on the porch with his hat in hand and a sheepish smile on his face.

She smiled, then stepped aside.

"Come in. I'd offer you a chair and something cold to drink, but as you can see…"

"Maybe a rain check?" Aaron asked. "If it will make you more comfortable, we can sit outside."

"There's a porch swing out back. It's in the shade and it's a place to sit," she said.

"Works for me," Aaron said, and followed her through the house and then out to the swing. He glanced at her then, thinking her eyes were as blue as the sky above them, then blurted out the first thing that came to mind. "This is a great little cottage. Benny and Lisa Abrams are your neighbors to the south. Benny works at the PD and Lisa works in Granny Annie's Bakery. My Aunt Annie owns it."

Dani's face lit up. "Really? I love that bakery! The cinnamon rolls there are to die for!" She ducked her head a moment and then glanced back at him. "How's Charlie?"

"Funny you should ask," Aaron said. "Good news is he woke up this morning. It was brief, but he spoke, and he knew his parents. He did see the man who shot him, but didn't recognize him, so that's where we are, but his prognosis is way better than it was. We're all really happy about that."

Dani beamed. "That's wonderful! I can only imagine how his parents must feel."

Aaron hadn't been prepared for how that smile changed everything about her. Her eyes were sparkling. Her cheeks had a slight flush, and Lord have mercy, she had dimples. It took him a few seconds to regain his equilibrium and to remember why he was here.

"So when do your movers arrive with your belongings?" he asked.

"In three days. My old landlord called last night to tell me they'd picked up my stuff, so I know they're on the road."

"Great, and that's actually why I'm here. Being new to Jubilee, I know you're on your own, and that the movers will bring everything into the house for you and set up your bed. That's the routine, right?"

Dani nodded. "Yes. It will be heaven to sleep in my own bed again."

Aaron let that settle a moment before he continued. "We moved here from Arkansas back in March after my grandmother passed. Mom inherited the house and property, and we all needed a fresh start, so there was Mom and my three brothers and me. We didn't know what we were getting into, but we knew what we were leaving behind, and this town and Pope Mountain saved us. When we drove up into the yard, the entire length of the front porch was lined with our people, three generations of relatives. They'd cleaned everything, brought us food, and helped us unpack everything we brought. By the time we were ready for bed that night, it looked like we'd been there forever."

Dani was silent now and reading between the lines of his narrative. So she wasn't the only one who'd been running away, and knowing that also explained the empathy he kept showing her.

Aaron continued. "After what you told me, and knowing how really alone you are in this new place, I'm offering assistance." He grinned wryly, then shrugged. "It's why I'm a cop. But it's also the way Mom raised us. What I'm trying to say is, that if it wouldn't offend you, my family and I would really like to help you in the same way we were welcomed home. Mom is great. My three younger brothers are good men, but don't tell them I said so. I have this 'big brother' image to maintain. If we showed up here after the moving van has come and gone, would you like some help unpacking?"

Dani was stunned. Her eyes welled before she knew it, and then the tears were running down her cheeks, which scared the holy shit out of Aaron.

"No, no, don't cry! I didn't mean... I was just trying to..."

Dani shook her head. "Don't apologize for being nice. These are emotional tears. I can't remember the last time anyone offered to help me do anything. I would appreciate you and your family's help. You'll be my first friends in Jubilee."

Aaron breathed a quick sigh of relief.

"Thank God. I thought I'd just made everything worse."

"Well, you didn't, Officer Pope. You just made everything better."

Aaron frowned. "None of that 'officer' business. Whenever you see me, wherever you see me, in uniform or not, it's just Aaron." And then he held out his hand. "Deal?"

Dani hesitated briefly, then clasped his hand and shook it.

"Deal."

"Great! You have my number in your phone now; will you add it to your contacts list?"

She nodded. "Yes, I will do that."

"So, in three days, just text me when the moving van arrives. By the time I get everyone gathered up and get to your house, the movers should be finished and gone. We can help move boxes to the right rooms and help you sort what needs to be sorted," he said.

"I will, and thank you, so much."

"No thanks needed. We haven't done anything yet," he said, and got up.

"You've done more than you know. Thank you," she said, and stood to see him out. As she did, the breeze tousled her hair and plastered the T-shirt she was wearing against her body.

It would have been all too easy to cast an appreciative eye on her shapely body, but instead he just shifted his gaze. "I look forward to it. Now, follow me out so you can lock the door behind me."

Dani stood in the doorway, watching until he drove out of sight, then went back inside and locked the door. She had butterflies in her stomach and her heart was racing just a little. Just enough to remind her Tony Bing hadn't beaten the life out of her, after all.

———————

To Alex's undying relief, when the movers stopped for the night, he stopped with them. He'd cursed Dani's name every mile that he'd driven, and the farther they went, the angrier he became.

After the movers registered and went to the rooms, he went into the office and got his own room next to theirs. The first thing he did when he entered was lock the door and strip. He showered and washed his hair, and then hand-washed his underwear and his T-shirt and hung them on the shower rod to dry.

He had pizza and a liter of Coca-Cola delivered to his room, and ate his fill before crawling into bed. The last thing he did was set his alarm for 4:00 a.m. He didn't know when the movers would leave, but he couldn't afford to lose track of them. He could sleep all he wanted after she was dead.

———————

After his talk with Dani, Aaron went home that night feeling happier than he had in months. He kept telling himself it had nothing to do with the pretty witness. She was alone. They could help. End of story.

Later that evening when they all sat down to supper,

Aaron listened to everyone's chatter and the stories of what happened at work, laughing when it was appropriate, commiserating with them at the roadblocks in their day.

It wasn't until Shirley took a chocolate pie from the refrigerator that Aaron broached his request.

"Hey everyone, in three days, a new friend is moving into Jubilee and I offered to help in the move. Would you guys be willing to help?"

Wiley waved his fork in the air. "I'll check to see if I can get that day off."

B.J. frowned. "I don't know. Maybe…if I ask Aunt Annie when I get to work tomorrow morning. I'll let you know."

Sean nodded. "There's something to be said for being your own boss. Yes, sure. What's up?" he asked.

"I can help, too," Shirley said. "Who are we going to move in?"

"The new first-grade teacher at Jubilee Elementary. She's rented a cottage in town next door to Benny and Lisa. A moving van is due to arrive tomorrow afternoon. They'll unload all the boxes and set up her bed and dump the furniture, but she's going to need help settling in, and I sort of volunteered us for that. I kept remembering how it felt to drive up to a place I barely remembered and meet family I only knew by name. It took away so much confusion. I just thought we could do that for her."

Shirley gave Aaron's hand a quick squeeze.

"That is so thoughtful of you, honey. I'll bring some food, too. So they'll let you off work to do this?"

Aaron nodded. "Unless some huge emergency arises, I'm sure I can."

He didn't mention why, but he knew how appreciative both police forces were for Dani's help, and getting off work a couple of hours early to help her out shouldn't be an issue.

Sean eyed his brother curiously, but said nothing. They all knew how shattered Aaron had been by his wife's swift exit from his life. This was the first time Aaron had even mentioned another woman, even in passing. Maybe he was finally healing, after all.

"How did you meet her?" Shirley asked.

"Through the PD. She found something a tourist had lost and dropped it off at the station. I just happened to be there and took her call."

"How old is she?" B.J. asked.

Aaron grinned. "Too old for you, bub."

"But not too old for you?" Wiley asked.

"Stuff it," Aaron said.

Shirley gave Wiley a look, and that ended what might have been a brotherly round of teasing. Aaron wasn't at the point of even talking about his divorce, let alone another woman.

They finished their meal, and then Aaron sent Shirley out of the kitchen to relax.

"You cooked. We'll clean up," he said.

"Yes, we've got this," B.J. said.

Sean poked B.J. on the arm. "You just want to eat that last pork chop," he said.

Wiley laughed. "B.J. always eats the last whatever. He's still a growing boy."

"I'm not a kid," B.J. snapped. "I don't know if I ever was…if any of us ever were. We grew up fast so we could take care of Mama, and we're still taking care of her. Besides, one pork chop would just junk up the fridge."

They were still laughing when Shirley walked out the back door and sat down in the porch swing.

There were clouds gathering. It looked like it might rain tonight. If it did, the creek would be running high tomorrow; then she smiled at the thought. It had been years since she'd ever worried about such things. Evidently, the mountain was still strong in her blood. She'd fallen right back into its ways as if she'd never left.

━━━━━━

Roll Call—Jubilee PD

The sky was still overcast from last night's rain when Chief Warren walked into the briefing room the next morning. He gave his officers a quick scan, and then moved to the front of the room.

"Good morning, gentlemen. I need to update you on the current situation regarding the Raines shooting. As you know, the bulk of the investigation is happening at county, but since we received evidence pertaining to the crime here, we are working in conjunction with them on this."

"The fingerprints we hoped would give us a lead weren't in the system, so county has decided to release the composite drawing of the suspect to the public. We have no reason to believe he's still in the area, but we can't be sure, so pick up a copy as you leave. It's a setback, but it's not a dead end," Warren added. "Sheriff Woodley and I have decided that because of the tourist element in Jubilee, the release will go nationwide, which means we'll have to be prepared for an influx of phone calls. We've already set up a phone bank, and our job will be to follow up on every tip within our jurisdiction, no matter how random, understood? Woodley and I will assimilate and deal with the out-of-state calls, and rely on those police departments to check them out. On the local front, tourism is up, and so are the shoplifting complaints. Bullard Campgrounds outside of town is open for business. Our local music star, Reagan Bullard, not only revamped the place, but has hired twenty-four-hour security for the premises, so unless there are big problems, our calls out to that location should lessen. Two cruisers are in for repairs, so we're pulling from the motor pool for backups." He paused while a groan of dismay rolled through the room. "Seriously? I didn't ask you to walk your beat," he said. Laughter ensued, and then he ended with his usual, "Are there any questions?"

The officers were silent.

Sonny nodded. "Good. So that's it for now. Stay safe,

and have a good day. You are dismissed." As the officers were getting up, the chief pointed at Aaron. "Officer Pope, I need a word with you before you leave."

"Yes, sir," Aaron said, and stayed behind.

"Two things," Sonny said. "Info from the lab says the library the journal came from was the Library of Congress, in Washington, DC."

Aaron frowned. "You don't check stuff out from there. Researchers and the like have to request permission to access it, and then use one of their reading rooms. Nothing ever leaves the premises."

"Exactly. So how did that man come by it, and why bring it here? And there's more. Dani Owens needs to be informed about the sketch going public. I feel like she has concerns about her privacy. Do you know what that's all about?"

Aaron nodded. "Actually, sir, I do. Before she came here, she had a stalker who escalated to an attempt to murder her." Aaron told him the whole story. "She's a strong woman on her own in a new place, but the police force let her down back there, and I don't think she knows who to trust."

Sonny shook his head. "Damn. I knew something was off. Listen, I don't want her to see this in the papers or on TV without a warning. Either call her or tell her in person that we're going to release the sketch. Assure her that since Charlie Raines has regained consciousness, the public will assume it was Charlie who gave us the information."

"She is moving out of the hotel into her rental property in a couple of days. My family and I are going to help her settle in after everything is unloaded," Aaron said.

Sonny was surprised Aaron had become this friendly with her. "Okay, that's good to know. Whatever day you need time off to help her move, let me know. She's the key witness to this whole thing, and it's our job to keep her anonymity and identity safe. Reassure her of that."

"Yes, sir, and thank you. I'll let her know about the sketch before anything airs."

The dream was an old one.

The scar upon Dani Owens's psyche that would not heal.

She was back in her old apartment in Monroe with the sound of gunshots still ringing in her ears when she came out of the closet, her weapon aimed straight at Tony.

One shot. That's all it would take to remove him from the face of the earth, and she would be safe. The thought was still in her head when she pulled the trigger and shot his legs out from under him instead. His screams of pain were so real she woke up with a start, her heart hammering. Despite the comfort of her air-conditioned room, she was drenched with sweat.

She threw back the covers and staggered to the bathroom, turned the shower on full blast, and, without waiting for warm water, took off her nightgown and stepped beneath the pounding spray.

An hour later she was just getting ready to go downstairs for breakfast when her cell phone rang. When she saw the name that came up on caller ID, her heart skipped. It was Aaron Pope.

She paused to answer. "Hello?"

"Dani, it's me, Aaron. Have you got a minute?"

"Sure," she said, and sat back down. "What's up?"

"About the fingerprints on the journal. We got results back from the lab, and yours were the only ones we could identify. The man who dropped the journal isn't in the system."

"Oh no," she said. "So how do you proceed?"

"That's why I'm calling. Chief Warren wants you to know ahead of time that we're releasing the composite sketch. There's no need for you to worry about it. The public will assume Charlie provided it. We just didn't want you to feel blindsided by it, okay?"

She shuddered. She couldn't help it. She was losing control again, and it was scary.

Her silence was all the answer Aaron needed about how she was taking the news.

"I'm sorry. I'm sorry this feels threatening to you, but I'm here for you, okay? And on a better note, my family is all hyped up to help you move, so keep me updated on their arrival day and time, okay?"

She smiled at the thought of seeing him again. "Yes, okay."

"Awesome," Aaron said. "Have a good day."

"You, too, and be safe," Dani said, and then dropped her phone back in her bag and left her room.

All the way through breakfast, she kept remembering the last time she'd moved. It had been from her childhood home outside of New Orleans to Monroe. But her parents had been alive then, and she was still trying to process Aaron Pope's offer to bring his family to help her get settled in.

He was tall, dark, and handsome, and a cop, but she was unsettled about trusting another man and, at the same time, rattled by her attraction to him. All she had to do was calm down and remember that he wasn't out to win her over. He was just being kind. It did not, however, stop her from thinking about him.

The very first thing she'd noticed about him was that he smiled first with his eyes and was good at not giving away what he was thinking, likely from his years in law enforcement. On the surface, she liked him. But she didn't know if she trusted him. Or maybe it was herself she no longer trusted. Tony Bing had done a number on her. She'd slept with a man who tried to kill her. She didn't trust her own judgment anymore.

━━━━━━

Charlie Raines was on the move. They'd unhooked him from everything long enough to get him from critical care to a private room. He was still groggy and inclined to go to sleep in the middle of a sentence, but he was cognizant enough that he'd told his parents the extent of what he could remember. Only now he didn't know where they were or if they knew he was being moved.

"Where's Dad? Have you seen Mom? They won't know where to find me," he mumbled.

An orderly at the foot of his bed gave his leg a quick pat. "Don't worry, Charlie. They're already waiting for you in your new room."

Charlie sighed. "Yeah, okay," he said, and then closed his eyes because watching the overhead lights moving past his line of sight made him nauseous.

As they rolled him onto the elevator, he had a moment's sensation of falling and quickly opened his eyes to see what was going on. Once he realized it was just the elevator moving downward, he closed them again.

It was weird, but he'd been in the shadows so long that coming back to reality was unnerving, almost frightening. He knew they hadn't caught the man who shot him, which was horrifying. Charlie hadn't voiced his fears, but they were real. Since he had no idea why he'd been shot, in his mind, he was afraid the man would come back and finish the job.

The elevator jerked once as it stopped, and once again, his eyes flew open. He didn't know any of the people around him and wouldn't feel safe until he saw his parents' faces again. Then they were rolling him off the elevator and down the hall. When he finally saw his mom and dad standing in the hall outside a room, he breathed a sigh of relief.

"Mom," he said, and reached for her hand as they rolled him past.

"We're right here, honey. We'll be right in as soon as they get you settled, okay?"

"Dad, too?" he asked.

"Dad, too," Ray said.

"Okay," Charlie said, but when they pushed him through the doorway, he lost sight of them again.

Transferring him from the bed they'd brought him in on to the one in his room was painful. Moving hurt. It made him dizzy, and there were tears in his eyes by the time they had him settled in bed and hooked back up to all the machines again.

He closed his eyes to make the room stop spinning, and when he opened them again, his mother was on one side of his bed and his dad on the other.

"Don't leave," he whispered.

"We won't, darling," Betty said.

Charlie sighed as his eyelids closed over his eyes once more. "He might come back."

Ray frowned. "Who, Charlie? Who might come back?"

"Man who shot me. I didn't die. He might come back," and then he was asleep.

Betty looked across the bed at Ray in horror.

"Oh, Ray!" she whispered, then started to cry.

Ray wasn't shedding tears, and the rage on his face was real.

"I don't know who the son of a bitch is who did this to our boy, but he better be running far and fast. If I ever get my hands on him, it won't be pretty."

───────────

Aaron Pope was on patrol when he got a call to return to base, so he headed back to the precinct to see what was going on.

As soon as he arrived, Walter, the desk sergeant, pointed toward the hall.

"Chief wants to see you in his office," Walter said.

Aaron nodded and headed that way.

The door was ajar. He knocked.

"Come in," Sonny said, then looked up from his desk as Aaron entered the room. "Thanks for coming. I just got word that Charlie Raines has been moved out of critical care and is in a private room. His doctor says we can talk to him, but not for long, and his parents are there with him, so we're covered on that account." Sonny picked up a copy of the composite sketch, slipped it into a folder, and handed it to Aaron. "I started to go do this myself, and thought better of it. I think it will be easier on the boy if he talks to someone he knows. Someone who's family. Take a recorder when you get his statement. He's in no shape to come in and give one."

"Sure thing," Aaron said.

"Report back to me in person when you've finished. I'll share the info with Woodley at county."

"Yes, sir," Aaron said. He took the folder, picked up a recorder in Supply, and left the building.

Aaron was an old hand at being a cop, but he wasn't a detective, and other than the day they arrested Clyde for murder, he'd never been personally involved with a case until now. He knew what to do, but that wasn't the point.

This was Charlie, the kid who liked to fish more than anyone he'd ever known—the kid who liked his catfish fried and his hush puppies with jalapeños in them, and had a soft spot for the new litter of kittens up in their barn.

Aaron didn't know what this had done to Charlie emotionally, but he didn't want to make it worse. Whatever he had to ask, he had to be careful how he worded it.

Chapter 7

A SHORT WHILE LATER, AARON EXITED THE HOSPITAL elevator and headed down the hall to Charlie's room. He'd called Ray to let them know he was coming, because he didn't want his appearance to be a surprise. When he reached the room, the door was standing open, obviously on his account.

"Hey guys," Aaron said, then walked in with the recorder and folder in hand, closing the door behind him as he went.

"Aaron, good to see you," Ray said.

"And it's good to see all of you, and especially you, Charlie. You're my fishing buddy, and as soon as you're up to it, we've got a date down at the pond. Okay?"

Charlie was a little intimidated by seeing Aaron in uniform and with a gun on his hip, but this was Aaron. He was family and one of the good guys.

"Yeah, sure," Charlie said.

Aaron walked up to the foot of Charlie's bed. "Did they tell you why I'm here?"

Charlie nodded. "You want to ask me questions about what happened."

"I'd rather you just tell me first," Aaron said.

Charlie relaxed. He didn't have to have answers. But he did have a story to tell.

"Yeah, okay," he said.

Aaron moved to the side of the bed and put down the recorder.

"I have to record our talk. It's called giving your statement of what happened. This way you'll only have to tell this once, and we can share it with the sheriff's department. Is that okay with you?"

Charlie nodded.

Aaron turned on the recorder. "This is Officer Aaron Pope, in room 317 of Jubilee Hospital. I'm with shooting victim 13-year-old Charlie Raines, and his parents, Ray and Betty Raines." Then he gave Charlie a quick wink and began.

"Okay, Charlie, let's start with why you were at Big Falls, and then everything you can remember afterward."

Charlie glanced at his dad, then took a breath.

"Dad and I had been fixing fence all afternoon. It was really hot, and when we finished, I asked Dad if we could go to the falls for a quick swim to cool off. But Dad said he had to go to the bank before it closed. I begged him to let me go on my own and promised I'd walk home. Dad said I could, and when he went to the house, I took off for the creek. It's not far from our pasture, maybe a ten-minute walk. As soon as I got in the trees, I started running. I could hear the falls. I imagined how good that water was gonna feel. I didn't hear anything weird. I didn't see anyone in the woods until I came out of the trees running. There was a real tall man standing in the clearing with a gun aimed straight at me. I was so startled that I stumbled. I heard the gunshot and everything went dark. I think I came to once, but everything was spinning, and I passed out again. I sort of remember hearing Mom's voice later, and then nothing until I woke up in critical care."

"That's great, Charlie. Can you tell me what the man looked like, besides being tall, I mean?"

"Yeah. He was tall and skinny. He had long blond hair pulled back in a ponytail, and a beard the same color. He looked scared...or mad. It was hard to tell."

"Did he have any hiking gear with him?" Aaron asked.

Charlie's eyes widened. "Yeah! A backpack! I forgot that! One of those kinds with the big metal frame, like hikers wear when they camp out in the woods."

"Excellent, Charlie. Now, one last thing. I have a sketch to show you. It may or may not be the man you saw, but I'd like you to take a look at it anyway. There is no right or wrong answer. You either recognize the man, or you don't. Understand?"

Charlie nodded, but when Aaron took the sketch from the folder, Charlie immediately looked away.

Betty put her hand on Charlie's shoulder. "Don't be scared, son. This is just a drawing, and you're helping the police by either identifying or eliminating this sketch as the man who shot you, got it?"

Tears were rolling down Charlie's face again.

Ray grimaced and then turned to Aaron.

"Charlie's afraid the man will come back and finish him off. He's scared because he doesn't know why the man tried to kill him."

"Son of a bitch," Aaron whispered, then took a deep breath. "No, that's not going to happen, Charlie. The entire sheriff's department and the police department in Jubilee are looking for the man who shot you. And I'll bet a year's wages he's no longer in Kentucky. Whatever he was trying to do, he failed, and he's on the run."

Charlie raised his head and swiped away tears.

"Show me," he whispered.

Aaron held it up into Charlie's line of vision. When he saw all the color leave the boy's face and his eyes widen in sudden fear, he knew before the words came out of Charlie's mouth what he was going to say.

"It's him! That's the man who shot me. Do you know his name?" Charlie asked.

"Not yet, but we will, and you're helping us catch him. Good job, Charlie."

Charlie nodded, but his knuckles were white from the grip he had on Betty's hand.

"Thanks to all of you," Aaron said, and picked up his phone and ended the recording. "I've got to get this back to the precinct. Take care, Charlie, and don't forget that fishing date."

And then he was gone.

Ray looked at Betty, then frowned. "Now how did they happen to come by that sketch?"

Betty shrugged. "We know the sheriff's men followed a trail of footprints all the way back to Jubilee. Maybe they caught a man on security cameras that led them to believe he could be their suspect. And they just had to make sure their guess was right."

"Maybe," Ray said, but he wasn't satisfied. If that was the case, then they could have just enlarged the footage, made a print from one of the images, and showed them a photo. However, he didn't care how they came by it if they could just find the bastard and put him behind bars for life.

———————

Aaron raced back to the station and straight to Warren's office.

"Hey Chief, I'm back. We have a positive ID."

Sonny looked up. "Awesome," and took the recorder Aaron laid on his desk.

"That's the interview," Aaron said. "I listened to it on the way back. And FYI, Charlie is scared out of his mind. He doesn't know why the man tried to kill him, and is afraid he'll come back to finish him off."

Sonny frowned. "Damn it. That makes it more imperative to find him and get him behind bars."

"Are there any results from the DNA samples taken from the parking lot?" Aaron asked.

"Again, we processed the DNA, but he's not in the system, so we don't know who it belongs to. But the picture will be in the paper tomorrow and there are security cameras all over town. Hopefully, someone will recognize him."

———————

A day later, Dani got a call from her movers. They'd be in Jubilee tomorrow. She was looking forward to getting out of the hotel, and if she was honest with herself, looking forward to seeing Aaron Pope again. And since she'd promised to let him know when she had confirmation from the movers, she sent him a text.

> This is Dani. You asked me to let you know about my movers. They'll be here tomorrow in the early afternoon. I'll text you when they arrive.

A couple of minutes later, she got a text back.

> Awesome news for you! See you then!

She smiled, then chided herself for the spurt of excitement. "He was just returning my message. Not asking me out. Calm the hell down, girl," she muttered, then got dressed and left the hotel. She went straight to the supermarket and began shopping for cleaning supplies and basic groceries. That way she'd be one step ahead when her furniture arrived.

———————

The next day, Aaron reminded his family about the movers' arrival today, and to be watching for his text. They'd all worked out getting time off, and Shirley was already in baking mode when he left the house.

———————

Dani was up early, packing to leave the hotel, when she got a call from the movers telling her they were planning to be in Jubilee around 1:00 p.m. She checked out after breakfast, and by 10:00 a.m., she had everything loaded into her car and was headed across town to her new home.

She pulled into the garage and then carried in her suitcase and the two boxes she'd brought with her, full of her family keepsakes and her mother's good silverware. After carrying them into the house, she set up a folding chair on the front porch and settled in to wait.

A short while later, she got another call from the movers, telling her they were about an hour outside of Jubilee. After verifying the delivery address, they disconnected. As Dani sat watching the activity in the neighborhood, she felt such a sense of peace. The day was clear and the slight breeze kept her cool in the shade.

As she sat, she began hearing a squeaking sound, and then a child's laughing. She looked up the street and saw a toddler in jean shorts and green T-shirt pedaling toward her on a tricycle. The woman she took to be the mother was walking behind her, talking on her phone as she went. The toddler's pink bike helmet was sitting sideways on her head, completely covering one eye, but she just kept pedaling away.

Dani grinned. Kids like this were why she loved teaching. Even when things weren't exactly perfect, they just kept going.

As they approached her house, the mother looked up and waved.

Dani waved back, smiling, and pointed to the little girl's helmet.

The mother jogged ahead to see what was wrong, then burst out laughing. She stopped the little girl long enough to straighten the helmet and tighten the strap, then gave Dani a thumbs-up as they continued down the sidewalk.

Dani glanced at her phone to check the time, then looked up the street all the way to the main road. The van should be appearing any time now.

She thought of Aaron and the family he was bringing to her house. It was such an unexpected and generous gesture that she didn't quite know how to take it other than with the obvious gratitude she felt.

A screech sounded high above her head. She looked up. A huge hawk was circling the skies above her, likely looking for dinner in the fields beyond the housing addition.

"Hide, little babies, hide. There be a dragon," she whispered.

And then she heard a big truck downshifting and looked back up the street. It was the moving van! She walked out into the yard to wave them down and was watching the driver backing the moving van up into the driveway when a gray Ford Bronco drove past the house.

Dani paid no attention to the vehicle, but the driver of the Bronco was paying all kinds of attention to her. It was Alex Bing, and his decision to follow the movers had just paid off.

"Hell yeah!" he muttered.

Now all he needed was to find a place to regroup and figure out what came next.

Dani had no idea her past was coming back to haunt her. She was focused on the movers and watching the truck doors opening and a portable ramp coming down. The crew boss introduced himself; then Dani did a quick walk-through to show them where things went, then sent a text to Aaron.

Movers are here.

Within a couple of minutes, she got a reply.

Gathering up the family.

After that, all she had to do was stand in the hall-way and direct traffic. It took a little over an hour and a half to get everything into the house, set up the bed and mattress, and then do another walk-through to make sure they had not damaged what had been delivered. After that, it was all about the paperwork, payment, and signing off on their delivery.

Dani watched them drive away and then went back inside, plopped down in her favorite easy chair for a moment, reclaiming her things in this space.

She was trying not to make a big deal out of seeing Aaron again and was a little overwhelmed to be meeting his family in such a mess. However, if the mess wasn't here, she wouldn't be meeting them, so there was that. Still, she wasn't going to sit and wait. She wanted to find the boxes with all her sheets and towels, then make her bed and have towels and washcloths for her nighttime shower.

Her television was sitting on the stand in her living room, waiting to be hooked up to the cable access TV, and her desk was in the spare bedroom, which was going to be her office. She had everything she needed for Wi-Fi and Internet, but it needed to be hooked up, too.

She headed for her bedroom, hoping the movers had put the right boxes in the right rooms, but to her dismay, the first one she saw in her bedroom was marked KITCHEN.

"Shoot," she muttered, shoved it aside, and kept digging until she found some marked BEDROOM and began opening them, only to find shoes and purses. She shoved it into the closet and kept looking. Finally, she found the box of bed linens and took out a set of sheets and a couple of pillowcases and laid them on her bed, then began looking for a larger box with her bedspread and pillows.

She found that box in the office and dragged it across the hall. She'd never been so happy to make a bed in her life. She had the fitted sheet on and was about to unfold the top one when her doorbell rang.

They're here!

She glanced at herself in the mirror on her dresser, then rolled her eyes. She was already a mess, but it didn't matter. She headed for the door and opened it wide.

"We're here," Aaron said, and handed her an arrangement of flowers in a clear pink vase. "Happy housewarming from all of us."

"They're beautiful!" Dani said, and held them against her chest and stepped aside. "Come in," then glanced nervously at the slim middle-aged woman with graying hair and a sweet smile, and the towering crew of men behind her wearing different versions of the same face.

"Dani, I'm Shirley Pope. Welcome to Jubilee."

And then the men began walking in behind her.

"Hello, Dani, I'm Sean. Really nice to meet you," he said, then shifted the big box he was carrying. "We brought food."

"Hi Dani, I'm Wiley. It's a pleasure. I brought soft drinks."

"Hi, Dani. I'm Brendan, but everyone calls me B.J." And he was smiling as if he were holding the last piece of a puzzle. "I know you! I mean, I didn't know your name, but I've seen you at Aunt Annie's bakery. I work there. Aunt Annie sent a box of cookies."

Dani smiled. "I'm a big fan of her cinnamon rolls," she said. "The kitchen is that way. Follow me," and then talked all the way. "This is so kind of you. The movers got everything inside quickly, but I swear to God, I don't think a one of them could read. I wasted my time labeling boxes when I was packing because it's all mixed up. Kitchen stuff is in my bedroom. My bedroom stuff is in the office. And the books and lamps that go in the living room are all over the kitchen floor."

Shirley saw all the boxes, then laughed and gave her a quick hug.

"You're right! What a mess, but we do know how to read, and we'll have you sorted out in no time."

Sean and Wiley didn't wait for orders. They just started opening bags and putting food into the refrigerator, and left the box of cookies on the island.

Dani blinked and then stepped aside to keep from getting in the way.

Aaron walked up beside her. "They're a little overwhelming, but they're highly capable, okay?"

Dani sighed. "No need to worry. Your family is darling, and I'm so grateful. Thank you for everything."

Aaron kept watching her expression, seeing everything from delight to utter confusion. He wanted to hug her, to tell her everything was going to be okay, but he didn't. And the moment passed.

"Where to first?" he said.

"Honestly? Just getting the boxes into the right rooms is a priority. After that, we can open them. I'm going to have to call someone to hook up all my electronics. I have the stuff. I just don't know how to do it."

Aaron grinned. "Oh, you're gonna love this. Sean! Tell Dani what you do for a living."

Sean turned. "Uh, I'm an IT specialist. I have an office at home and a growing list of new clients. Why?"

"Because Dani has an office and a television just waiting for hookups."

Sean looked at Dani. "Are the services already on?"

"I've been assured they are. I've already set up accounts and paid the fees," she said.

Sean all but clapped his hands with glee. "Then I'm your man," he said.

"Exactly," Aaron said. "When it comes to technology, Sean is in his element."

"Oh my gosh, that's great!" Dani said.

The impulse to throw her arms around him was huge, but she didn't. He was just the cop being nice.

"Do you want us to start by getting boxes into the right rooms first?" he asked.

"Please," Dani said. "I'm going to finish making my bed while that's happening."

"I'll help," Shirley said. "Two can do it faster," and followed Dani out of the kitchen.

The brothers began grabbing boxes and carrying them to the proper locations, leaving Aaron still locked into the sight of her dimples and what they did to his heart when she smiled. Then he realized all the action was elsewhere, grabbed a big box marked OFFICE, and carried it out of the room.

Dani's initial shyness disappeared the moment Shirley grabbed the top sheet, unfolded it, and gave it a flip. The sheet spread out and then floated down across the top of the bed like a feather.

Dani's eyes widened. "Wow. That's a skill I have yet to master."

Shirley grinned. "A skill that comes with making many beds for four little rough-and-tumble boys. Do you like the ends tucked in at the foot or left hanging?"

"Hanging please. Tucked always makes me feel like I'm being restrained."

Shirley laughed. "Well, there you are! My boys are the same way. They grew tall so fast that they outgrew their beds along with their clothes."

Dani smiled, trying to picture the four big men in her house as little boys.

"I can see how that might happen," she said, and together she and Shirley finished making her bed.

"Love the design on the bedspread," Shirley said.

Dani nodded. "Me, too. I'm a sucker for anything floral, and the softer the pastel colors, the better I like it." She plumped up and added a couple of decorator pillows, and called it done. "I cannot wait to sleep in my own bed tonight."

Shirley sighed. "That's exactly how I felt when we moved home. I was so grateful to be there, and at the same time, after the nightmare we left behind us, it felt like I was coming home with my tail between my legs. Our mountain family changed all that for us."

"I don't know what happened to you, but I can empathize with needing a fresh start," Dani said. "Aaron knows. I told him not long after we first met. Secrets are like poison. If you keep them forever, it just takes them longer to die."

Shirley was silent for a moment, and then her eyes welled. "My husband, my sons' father, was a man I came to fear. It's been well over a year since it all happened, but he got high on something one day and nearly beat me to death. He stormed off, leaving me for dead, then went on a rampage that ended with him killing two innocent people. I finally got the courage to divorce him after he was jailed. He's in prison now, serving a life sentence without possibility of parole. But my sons and I became pariahs through no fault of our own. Then my mother passed, and I inherited my childhood home here. It was a godsend. A way to cut ties completely with that life. And the last thing I did was take back my maiden name, and so did my sons. His name was the last link we had to him, and we cut it and left him behind."

At first, Dani said nothing. Just handed her a tissue.

But it was best telling her truth now when it mattered before she got too close to people who would judge her again.

"I had an ex-boyfriend who turned into a stalker. I, too, was beaten. My neighbors heard the screams.

He bonded out of jail before I got out of the hospital, and spent the ensuing year trying to get me back; then it turned into stalking. Scary stuff. I got a protective order that didn't work. The police got tired of me calling only to have him disappear by the time they arrived. I woke up once and saw him standing by my bed. I don't know how he got in, but I had become his enemy, and I knew it was only a matter of time before he killed me."

Shirley pulled Dani down onto the side of the bed they'd just made and held her hand.

"Dear lord, child. What did you do?"

Dani looked up. "I changed the game he was playing." Then she told her about stuffing pillows in her bed and sleeping in the closet, and then finally hearing him in her apartment again. She was shaking by the time she got to the part where she was watching him from the closet when he emptied the gun into the pillows.

"Did he get away again?" Shirley asked.

"No. I'd already called 911 before he got into the room. The dispatcher heard everything as it was happening. When I knew his gun was empty, I came flying out of the closet before he could run, and shot him in both knees. He's in prison. In a wheelchair. He got fifty years for attempted first-degree murder, without a possibility of parole. That's why I'm here. Because I couldn't be there anymore."

Shirley hugged her.

"We belong to a select club of women who have

survived their killers. We hold our heads up. We do not walk in their shame."

Dani looked at her then. "No. We do not walk in their shame. Now, let's go see where we are in unpacking."

They stood up in unison, but when they turned around, the brothers were standing in the doorway.

Before Dani could react, they spilled into the room and surrounded her and their mother, wrapped their arms around both of them, and pulled them close.

"Some men are sons-a-bitches," Wiley muttered.

"They don't deserve to draw breath," Sean said.

"Some men are good men," B.J. whispered.

"Yes, and children are not responsible for their fathers' sins, and neither are their victims," Aaron said.

Shirley looked up from within the circle and saw the look on Dani's face.

"I'm hoping you're just overwhelmed by all the love, and that expression on your face is not claustrophobia, because my boys are huggers. And if you don't toss us away after all this, this won't be your last group hug."

Dani shook her head. "No claustrophobia here. Yes, overwhelmed, but in a really good way."

"Good news," Shirley said, then looked at her sons. "Well? Are the boxes in the right rooms?"

"Yes, ma'am," they echoed.

"Then Miss Dani, what would you have us do next?" Shirley said.

"Yes. Give me a job," B.J. said. "The sooner we get through, the quicker I get to eat."

The ensuing laughter swept the room clean, and happiness returned along with a new sense of belonging to people who were not her kin, something Dani had never felt before.

"Well, B.J., there are two boxes of books in the living room. You can put them all in that bookcase and plug in the lamps," Dani said. "Wiley, if you don't mind, all the boxes marked LINENS, if you can put the contents in the cabinet in the hall, I'll sort them later. And Sean can do his tech magic with my electronics."

"What about me?" Aaron asked.

"You can come lift the heavy stuff in the kitchen for us while Shirley and I get the dishes and pans put away. Lord knows we don't want B.J. to starve."

B.J. grinned. "Yes, ma'am. I like the way you think," he said, and bolted for the living room.

———

Being single meant not having a lot of belongings.

They had everything out of Dani's boxes in only a couple of hours, and then broke down the boxes, tied them in a bundle, and left them at the curb for trash day.

Sean had her computer connected to Wi-Fi and Internet, and her TVs were ready for viewing. One in the living room. One in her bedroom. Her pots and pans were on the shelves beneath the kitchen counter, her glasses and dishes in the cabinets above. They'd moved the living room furniture around enough to accommodate her area rug, and had the table in the kitchen wiped off and loaded with Shirley's fried chicken, potato salad, and deviled eggs, along with paper plates and plastic cutlery. They'd left the soft drinks in the bottles for easier cleanup. There would be no dishwashing tonight. Just eat their fill and carry out the trash.

Dani was exhausted and it showed. She didn't feel like she could eat a thing until she took that first bite of fried chicken, then rolled her eyes.

"So good," she mumbled.

Shirley beamed. "Thank you, sugar."

"Mama is a really good cook," B.J. said.

Shirley accepted the compliment with her usual grace, and the same comment she made at their table every night.

"Thank you, son. Please don't talk with your mouth full."

"Right!" B.J. said, still chewing.

Laughter rolled around the table.

Dani felt like a different person. Today, this family had found the dead weight of grief within her, and buried it with laughter.

She ate what she'd taken out on her plate and was reaching for her soft drink when Sean raised his fork and pointed at Aaron.

"Hey, Aaron, would you pass the potato salad and eggs, please?"

"Sure," Aaron said, picked up the bowl, and quietly put another spoonful of potato salad and another half of a deviled egg on her plate without looking at her or even saying a word, then calmly passed the bowl.

Dani looked at what he'd just done and up at him, and kept staring until she made him look at her.

He sighed. He didn't know if she was insulted or just pissed. He lowered his voice and leaned closer.

"Sorry. Didn't mean to offend. But you didn't take enough food to matter first time around. Sean asked me to pass the potato salad and eggs, so I did. But before I let it go, I gave you a little extra just in case. In this family, if you wait around trying to decide if you want more, then it's too late. You didn't know this. I was just helping. And now you know."

Every fear she'd had that he was going to be another manipulative man controlling her choices just went out the window.

She whispered back, "I had no idea. I was an only child. Thank you for the egg and taters."

Aaron blinked, then saw the twinkle in her eyes, and threw back his head and laughed.

The startled looks his family gave him were because they hadn't heard him laugh like that in years. They looked at each other and grinned, then just kept eating. Whatever she'd said had their blessing.

The Popes left her house just before dark, with the constant words of Dani's thanks still ringing in their ears.

The brothers had loaded B.J.'s Harley into the back of Wiley's pickup truck so he wouldn't be riding it up the mountain in the dark, and then left in a convoy, with Aaron and his mother bringing up the rear.

Dani stood on the front porch watching until the taillights of the last vehicle had disappeared, then she went inside and locked both doors, before going through the house to make sure the shades were pulled. She paused in the middle of the house, listening to the quiet hum of the air conditioner, and felt a sense of peace and a knowing she was where she belonged, then flipped on the night-light in the hall, and went to her room.

She was exhausted, but her hunger had been sated and her house was in order. It was more than enough for today. She ran the bathtub full of water, sprinkled in some aromatic bath salts, and stripped where she stood before slipping into the hot steamy water.

"Heaven. Pure heaven," she said, and leaned back and closed her eyes, focusing only on the heat of the water and the aroma of lavender beneath her nose.

Shirley and Aaron rode in silence until they were almost home before she spoke.

"I like your girl."

Aaron's fingers tightened slightly around the steering wheel.

"She's not my girl," he said.

"She will be," Shirley said.

Aaron glanced at her. "When did you become psychic?"

Shirley shrugged. "I said what I said. I like your girl."

Minutes passed, and Shirley was thinking about a shower and bed when Aaron let out an audible sigh.

"So do I."

She patted him on the knee and then pointed up the road.

"There's our turnoff, and none too soon. I'm getting in the shower before all of you use up the hot water."

Aaron chuckled. "I'll warn the brothers you called dibs on the hot water tonight."

"Thank you, darling. You're my favorite eldest child."

Aaron laughed again, and the sound wrapped around Shirley's heart like a hug.

Alex Bing had driven all over Jubilee before opting for a less noticeable presence and rented one of the little cabins at Bullard Campgrounds. He was aware of the security cameras, but this was a tourist destination. They were everywhere, but nobody knew him. Nobody knew where he was, and he wouldn't be here long enough to be remembered. He just needed to scope out Dani's new situation. Being in a house instead of an apartment building changed the dynamic of his plans. He didn't know what kind of security setup she had, or if there was one. He didn't know her routine and had no idea of what to expect. This would all take time. But Tony was doing time, and Alex had time to spend to do this right.

As soon as he was settled in at the cabin, he went back into Jubilee, got some cash at an ATM, then headed for a supermarket to stock up on some food and drinks. It was going to be tricky scoping out Dani's location in a residential area. Likely nosy neighbors and security cameras were everywhere. He would have to wait until dark to get anywhere near her house. There were alleys behind the houses so he'd try there first and see how close he could get to her house. He needed to see the layout and the access points before he went any further.

Still, just to be on the safe side, he shopped wearing sunglasses and a hoodie pulled over his head, and didn't meet anyone's gaze the whole time he was there. As soon as he got back to his little cabin, he put away his food, then stretched out on the bed, turned on the TV, and promptly fell asleep.

It was after sunrise the next day before he woke, which messed up all of his plans. He decided to lay low all day and wait for sunset before venturing out. Vengeance was a strong incentive for patience, and staying inside the cabin where it was cool seemed the obvious choice. All he had to do was wait until it got dark.

Chapter 8

THE NEWSPAPERS HAD BEEN RUNNING THE COMPOSite sketch of Charlie Raines's shooter for days, with the headline reading DO YOU KNOW THIS MAN?

The story running below it illustrated the highlights of the Charlie Raines ordeal and referred to the sketch as being of a possible suspect who was wanted for questioning.

Dani had seen the initial release and long since relaxed. The police had kept their word. No mention was made of any witness. Just that Charlie Raines had identified the man in the sketch as the one who shot him.

After finishing her errands, she stopped by Granny Annie's Bakery for a loaf of sourdough bread. She had barely entered the store before B.J. spotted her from the kitchen and came up front.

"Hi, Dani!" he said.

"Hi, B.J. Thanks again for helping me out," Dani said.

"No problem," B.J. said, and then introduced her to Annie. "Hey, Auntie, this is Dani Owens. She just moved into Jubilee."

Annie smiled. "So, you're Aaron's friend. Welcome to Jubilee," she said.

"Thank you, thank you for sending those delicious cookies with B.J. last night," she said.

Annie smiled. "It was my pleasure. How can I help you?"

"I'd like a loaf of your sourdough bread, please."

Annie bagged it up, took Dani's money, and handed it over.

"Enjoy!"

"I will," Dani said. "Bye, B.J. Nice to meet you, Annie," and then she left.

"She seems like a nice person," Annie said.

B.J.'s usual buoyant demeanor suddenly shifted.

"She's not just nice, Auntie. She's a warrior," and then he went back into the kitchen in silence.

The word rolled through Annie with a gut punch. That's what Shirley's sons said about their mother, which told Annie that Dani Owens wasn't just another pretty face.

———————————

Michael Devon was in the penthouse suite of the Hotel Devon, getting ready for the day. His fiancée, Liz Caldwell, had just left for work across town at her father's hotel, the Serenity Inn, where she worked as an event planner.

The fact that they were competitors for the tourist

trade often made for awkward situations, but they'd learned to adapt. Love worked like that.

Michael was finishing his cup of coffee and scanning the local paper before going down to his office on the second floor. The sketch was impossible to miss, even though he'd seen it when it first ran. But he kept staring at that face, thinking of what that poor kid must have gone through. He also knew that Liz's cousin Rusty had married into the Pope family, and that she'd once been an agent for the FBI. He couldn't help but wonder if she was involved in this investigation.

He glanced at the time, then folded the paper and took it with him as he rode his private elevator down to the second floor. His secretary had yet to arrive, and he liked walking into the quiet, knowing it would erupt soon enough with the usual drama of managing a hotel.

The first thing he did each morning was check emails and messages. Quite often there would be one from his father, Marshall, who'd left Hotel Devon to him to manage nearly a year ago so Marshall could focus on building a new apartment complex in another state.

He'd barely begun when there was a knock at the door. He looked up from the computer and sighed. So much for quiet.

"Come in," he called.

Ron Daley, the head of their hotel security, came in carrying a copy of the same paper Michael had brought with him.

"Sir. Have you seen the morning paper?" he asked.

"Yes, I have. Why?"

"As you know, I was out of state for my brother's wedding. Today is my first day back at work, and I'm seeing this story has been running for a few days. I thought the sketch looked familiar and had one of our guys check security footage. This man was staying at our hotel! I think we should notify Chief Warren."

The skin crawled on the back of Michael's neck.

"Are you serious?" he asked.

"Yes, sir. We have the footage pulled up in security if you want to see it for yourself."

Michael stood. "I'm right behind you," he said.

They both left the office in haste and hurried to the security area of the hotel. There were dozens and dozens of cameras throughout the hotel, and as Daley promised, they had footage of him checking in, of him going in and out of his room. Having breakfast in the hotel. Of coming in and walking out. And then there was the footage of him coming back with a bloody head wound and the appearance of being in some distress. Then less than an hour later, they had footage of him at the front desk checking out. But the kicker was footage of the back of his car as he left the area, with a clear view of his license tag.

Michael was in shock.

"Do we know his name?"

"He registered as Dirk Conrad. I have billing pulling up the details now," Ron said.

"Make stills of every one of these shots as quickly as

possible. I'm calling the police. They're going to want to see this footage, and they're going to need the still shots for their files. Good job! Good job all of you!" Michael said, hurried back to his office, and made the call.

Sonny Warren was on his way to roll call when his cell phone rang.

"Chief Warren speaking."

"Chief! This is Michael Devon. That man you're looking for. My security chief just informed me that he was here. He registered under the name Dirk Conrad. I'm getting the billing info now. We have footage of him all over the place and a shot of him leaving after he checked out. His car tag is in plain sight."

Sonny was stunned. "He's just now seeing this?"

"Oh. He's been out of town for several days. He just got back this morning and saw the story in the paper."

"Excellent catch, Michael. Give me about thirty minutes to finish what I'm doing, and I'll be right there."

"Take your time, sir," Michael said.

Sonny was smiling when he walked into roll call. His officers were seated. Some were talking to each other. A few more were checking their phones, but they all snapped to attention when he reached the podium.

"Good morning, officers, and it is indeed a good morning. It appears our composite sketch hit pay dirt. Security footage at the Hotel Devon has a man on

camera matching the description we put out. He registered under the name Dirk Conrad. They're pulling the info on him now. What we're not going to do
is make any announcements to the public until this
man is located, because he's already checked out, and
we don't yet know where he's from or where he's gone.
Understood?"

"Yes, sir," they echoed.

"Excellent," Sonny said, and proceeded to issue
updates and BOLOs before dismissing them to their
assignments. "Officer Pope, I'll be needing a ride to
Hotel Devon."

"Yes, sir," Aaron said.

———————

Ron Daley, the hotel security chief, was watching for
their arrival. When Aaron pulled up at the entrance and
parked, Daley walked out to meet them.

"Pope, you're with me," Sonny said.

"Yes, sir," Aaron said, and followed the men into the
hotel. The array of cameras in their security area was
dizzying, and the number of people watching the cameras impressive.

Michael Devon was in the room waiting for them.

"Show me," Sonny said.

As Aaron moved up beside the chief to watch, he
spied the man almost immediately.

"Yes!" Sonny said. "That man definitely matches the

sketch, but we'll show it to Charlie Raines for verification before we move forward. You said you were getting some stills for us from the footage?"

"Yes, sir," Michael said, and handed him a file. "There are stills and the info we received when he checked in. I thought we'd have a credit card to help you run the man down, but I'm told that while he used one when he checked in, when he checked out, he paid everything he owed in cash and requested the card number be removed, which we did."

"Damn it," Sonny muttered. "Did he say why he wanted to do that?"

"Something about having had his identity stolen before."

Aaron was frustrated but said nothing. It sounded far-fetched, but identity theft was a thing.

"Well, we have a license tag, a name, and a city, which is way more than we had before you called," Sonny said. "I'll ask you not to say anything about this. Not to the press. Not to your friends. No one. Until we can verify this is our man, and we know where he lives, we don't want to spook him into running, understand?"

"Absolutely," Michael said. "We pride ourselves on top-notch security here, which also means, at times, keeping our mouths shut," he added, eyeing Ron Daley to make his point.

"You can count on us, sir," Daley said. "I'll make sure my people know."

"I would ask if you'd please send clips of your

security footage to the county sheriff's office. Officially, this is Sheriff Woodley's case. I'll give him a heads-up to be expecting it and to call you to give you contact information."

"Will do," Michael said. "If that's all you need, I'll walk you out." Then he glanced at Aaron. "We haven't met, but I know who you are, and I think it's time we did. My fiancée is Liz Caldwell, Rusty Pope's cousin."

"Ah," Aaron said, and quickly shook Michael's hand. "Nice to meet you, Michael. I've heard Rusty speak of her family here but had yet to meet them."

"They're good people, even if they are our biggest competitor," Michael said, and then grinned.

"Marrying into the family should smooth all that over," Aaron said.

Michael laughed. "You'd think. Liz lives here with me but is still working for her dad at the Serenity Inn. Follow me. I'll escort you through the maze."

As soon as Aaron and Chief Warren got back into the cruiser, Sonny was on the phone to the sheriff's department. He gave Rance Woodley the news and contact information for the security chief, Ron Daley, at the Hotel Devon.

"Also," Sonny said. "I've given all my men orders not to release any of this information or tell anyone about this until we verify the ID with Charlie Raines. Since he's still here in the hospital, I can do that for you if you'd like."

"Yes, that would be helpful," Rance said. "I'm

shorthanded as it is right now, and we're already getting calls in from everywhere about the sketch. I can focus on that, if you'll run the photos by Charlie and let me know his reaction."

"Will do," Sonny said.

"Thanks again," Rance said. "This is good news… really good news."

Sonny ended the call, then glanced at Aaron.

"Take me by the hospital next. We'll show Charlie the stills pulled from the security footage. I haven't been to the hospital to see him, and now's a good chance. Afterward, drop me back at the office, and then you take the stills and show Dani Owens. If we get the go-ahead from both of them, then we can start running a search on this man."

"Yes, sir," Aaron said, and took the next right turn and headed for the hospital while hiding his delight that he'd be seeing Dani this soon again.

———————

Charlie was dozing, already worn out from sitting up to eat breakfast and getting a bath. Afterward, when the two nurses began rolling him from side to side to change the sheets on his bed, he cried out in pain.

"I'm so sorry, Charlie," the nurse said. "We've finished with your bed now, and your pain meds are on the way."

"Where's Mom?" he asked.

The nurse gently patted his arm. "She's out in the hall. We'll let her know we're through here. Maybe you can get some rest now."

As they walked out, Betty Raines walked back in. She saw the tears on his face and hurried to him.

"Oh, sweetheart, I'm sorry this is so hard."

"It's okay, Mom, I just hurt, but they're bringing some pain meds. Did Dad go home?"

"Yes, to check on the house and the animals. Shirley and Sean have been taking care of them while we were here, but now that you're doing better, Daddy and I are going to trade visiting times."

"Tell him to check on the kittens. There are five of them," Charlie said. Betty swept Charlie's hair from his forehead and then cupped the side of his cheek.

"Don't be worrying about all that. Your daddy already knows to look after your kittens."

Charlie sighed. "Yeah, okay."

Betty glanced at the remote. "Do you want to watch TV?"

"You can if you want," he said.

Betty was about to reach for it when there was a knock at the door. She turned around just as Aaron and Sonny Warren entered the room.

"Morning, Betty. Morning, Charlie," Sonny said.

Aaron went straight to Betty and gave her a hug, then winked at Charlie. "How's it going, buddy?"

Charlie rolled his eyes. "They've violated my modesty and rolled me around in this bed like a burrito."

Betty chuckled. "The nurses just gave him a bath and changed the sheets on his bed. It was an ordeal. He's hurting a lot right now and we're waiting for pain meds."

Aaron stifled the urge to laugh. "Hospitals don't have to follow the rules of society when they're busy saving people's lives. Next time just close your eyes. If you can't see them, then they can't see you."

Charlie snorted. "I'm too old to fall for that line."

Sonny let them talk. After learning how frightened Charlie was of the man who'd shot him, putting him at ease was the best way to introduce the photos again.

Aaron glanced at the chief and then took a deep breath.

"Hey, Charlie. Are you okay to look at some photos for us?"

Charlie's eyes widened, and then his gaze shifted from Aaron to the police chief.

"Is it the man?" he asked.

"We don't know," Sonny said. "He looks like the sketch, but we want to know what you think. You'll have the final word."

"Okay," Charlie said.

Sonny pulled out the stills and handed them to Charlie one by one.

Charlie's hand shook when he took the first one, but the more he looked at it, the calmer he became. Sonny didn't know whether that was a good sign or a bad sign until he handed him the last one.

Charlie looked at it, then handed the pile of them to his mother.

"Get a good look at him, Mom. That's the man who shot me."

"Are you certain?" Sonny asked.

"Yes, sir. I'm absolutely certain," Charlie said. "Are you going to arrest him?"

"When we find him, yes, we are. He's already left town, but it's just a matter of time until we track him down. And don't worry," Sonny said. "Our job is to run down the criminals. Your job is to get well, okay?"

"Yes, sir," Charlie said.

Betty wasn't as calm as Charlie. Looking at the face of the man who'd shot her son and left him to die had triggered a visceral response within her.

"You better find him before Ray does, or there won't be enough of him left to arrest," she said, and handed the photos back to the chief.

A chill ran up Sonny's spine. The last thing they needed was a vigilante parent on the loose.

"Betty, you tell Ray to take care of Charlie and leave the hunting to us. And Charlie, rest easy knowing you've done an amazing job in helping us identify your shooter. You're a very brave young man."

A nurse walked into the room as they were leaving.

"Looks like Charlie's pain meds arrived," Sonny said as they headed for the elevator.

"And none too soon," Aaron said. "He was in a lot of pain. I could see it in his eyes."

A few minutes later, Aaron dropped the chief back at the station and then called Dani.

She answered on the second ring.

"Hello?"

"Hey, it's me, Aaron. We've had a hit on the composite sketch and some photos to show you. Are you home?"

"Yes, and fresh coffee made. Come on over," she said.

"Thanks," he said, and headed to the east side of town.

One witness down.

One to go.

———

Dani was waiting for Aaron to arrive when her cell phone rang. She glanced down at caller ID and, for a few seconds, forgot to breathe. Tony Bing's mother? Why the hell would Arlene Bing be calling her? And how did she get this number? She started not to answer it, but then reminded herself that his parents had been horrified by what he'd done, so this couldn't possibly be any kind of harassment.

Curiosity won out, and she finally answered.

"Hello?"

"Dani, this is Arlene Bing. Please don't hang up. There's something I need to tell you. I can only imagine how you feel about our family, but as you know, we were horrified by what happened to you, and there is no way an apology is even a proper response."

"I really don't want to have this conversation. Why are you calling?" Dani asked, then heard Arlene take a deep breath. When she spoke again, it sounded like she was crying.

"Alex has disappeared. He's gone completely off the radar. He isn't answering his phone, but we know where he is, because we put a tracker app on it after Tony went to prison. You know how close they were, being twins and all, and he became completely irrational about what Tony did. In his mind, he has justified every action Tony made and blames you."

A chill ran through Dani so fast she shivered and dropped onto the sofa before her knees gave way.

"I already know this! He pretty much said it in front of a judge, a courtroom full of people at the sentencing, so stop beating around the bush with this. What are you trying to tell me? Where does the app say Alex has gone?"

"He's somewhere in Kentucky. At some big tourist attraction in a place called Jubilee."

Dani moaned. The room was beginning to spin. She put her head between her knees before she passed out where she sat, and realized Arlene was still talking.

"We heard you quit your job here in Monroe, and we certainly can't blame you. I don't know where you went, but if it's anywhere around that area, then beware. I wish I had an answer for why my sons turned out this way, but I don't. We've been afraid of them for years." Then Arlene was crying. "By the time they were teens,

Hank and I were sleeping with our door locked at night. There's something wrong with them. I'm so sorry you became a victim."

The disconnect in Dani's ear was the slap she needed to bring her back to reality.

"God, oh God, why is this happening? How did he find me? Am I going to have to die to ever get peace again?"

She broke into sobs—harsh, choking sobs of utter defeat.

When her doorbell suddenly rang, she jumped, then remembered Aaron was coming and staggered to her feet. She looked out the window to make sure it was a police car in the driveway before she opened the door.

Aaron had the folder with the photos in his hand, expecting to see a smile, and instead, she was in hysterics. He stepped over the threshold, kicked the door shut behind him, and took her by the shoulders.

"What's wrong?"

She couldn't talk; she just fell into his arms, sobbing as he wrapped his arms around her.

"Dani. Please. Tell me what's wrong."

"I just got a call. He's here. He's after me. I just know it. He screamed it at me in the courtroom the day his brother was sentenced."

Aaron was confused.

"Wait. Who's here, and what happened in the courtroom?"

Dani swiped at the tears on her face and took a breath.

"Tony Bing, the man who tried to kill me, has an identical twin brother. His name is Alex. He threatened me in the courtroom and has been alienated from his family for some time. I guess his mother was still keeping tabs on him about town, because she said he's disappeared. He holds a grudge against me for his brother's imprisonment. He's as crazy as Tony."

"Then how do you know he's here?" Aaron asked.

Dani took a slow, shuddering breath. "She just called me. She located him by a tracking app on her phone. She knows he's in Jubilee, Kentucky, but she doesn't know where I am. All she said was, wherever I was, to be careful, and she hung up."

Aaron's thoughts were spinning.

"He thinks he's pulled a fast one finding out where you are, but he doesn't know his cover is blown. There are only so many places he can be staying, and as soon as we find out where he is, we'll put a tail on him."

Dani shook her head and pushed out of his arms. "That won't help. You can't arrest him for just being in Jubilee. Oh my God, I don't want to have to sleep in a closet again. I thought I was finally safe."

Aaron reached for her again, this time with anger in his voice. "You're going to be safe. I'll make sure of that."

"How?" Dani asked. "There aren't laws for people like them."

"No, but there are bodyguards for people like you."

"I can't hire a bodyguard," Dani cried.

"You don't need one. You have me, every night under this roof with you until this nightmare is over."

She went still. Tears were still rolling down her cheeks as she stared at him in disbelief.

Aaron took a handkerchief from his pocket and began wiping away the tears. Then he locked into her gaze and didn't move.

The silence between them grew as they took each other's measure. Finally, it was Dani who broke the silence.

"You would do that?" she asked.

"In a heartbeat," Aaron said.

Her face crumpled. "But why?"

"Because that's what I do, and because knowing you pleases my heart, and I want you to be safe. Is that reason enough?"

Surrendering to the offer, she nodded. "It is enough."

Satisfied that she'd agreed to let him help, he was all business.

"I don't suppose you have a picture of this Alex Bing?"

Dani frowned. "No. But pull up a mug shot of Tony Bing and that's the same face. They're identical. I never could tell them apart."

"Okay then," Aaron said. "Now back to my initial reason for being here. I need to show you these still shots we pulled from security footage. All you have to do is say, 'Yes, it's him.' Or 'Nope, wrong man.' Again, there's no right or wrong answer. We just need your truth."

"Yes, all right," Dani said. The first one she looked at

was all the confirmation she needed, but she looked at the rest before she answered. "Yes, that's definitely him. Is he still in the area?"

"No, he's long gone, but this is a huge lead. I'll let the chief know so he and the sheriff can proceed. After I get off work, I'll go home long enough to pack some clothes. Is there room in your garage for two cars?"

"Yes," she said.

"Okay, then I'll park there." He stood a moment, then asked. "I'm curious as to how he found you. Are you in contact with any of your friends from Monroe? Like teacher friends or the like?"

"No. My parents are deceased. I don't have siblings, and my old friends are all back in New Orleans. I haven't been in contact with them in ages."

"Did Alex ever visit you in Monroe?"

"We didn't hang out or anything like that, but he knew where I lived, if that's what you're asking," she said.

"If he was set on finding you, the first place he would have gone was to where you used to live then, right?"

She nodded.

"And he would have discovered you were gone. Maybe even learned you were moving."

"Possibly," Dani said. "I mean, my landlord is the one who agreed to let the movers in to pick up my things when I was ready to move. Why?"

"If he was determined to find you, he would have been watching your apartment, waiting for you to come back. But then he finds out you're gone. Maybe he talks to the landlord and finds out you're moving. Landlord won't tell him where you're going, but all he has to do is wait for the moving van to show up and follow it. Straight to you," Aaron said.

Dani shuddered. "That's something Tony would do. Stands to reason Alex would, too."

"It's just a supposition," Aaron said. "But it also gives me a good idea of how serious he is in following through on his threats."

"I feel like a sitting duck," Dani muttered.

"Don't. Just do what you need to do throughout the day. You can't hide from him. Likely he already knows where you live, and he's not going to bust in on you when you're awake, anyway."

"Why not?" Dani asked.

"Because you shot the legs out from under his brother in the dark. He won't give you that edge in broad daylight," Aaron said.

Dani blinked. "Oh. Right." She sighed. "I don't have an extra bed, but…"

"Do not worry about that. I have a very comfortable sleeping bag, and I'll be camped out in the hallway. If anyone breaks into this house in the dark, they'll have to come through me first, and I will not be aiming for his knees."

Dani shuddered. "Thank you, Aaron. We hardly know each other, but this is above and beyond the bond of friendship."

"Well, before this is over, we're going to know even

more about each other. I'm not scared of your past, if you aren't scared of mine." Then he held out his hand. "Deal?"

Dani didn't hesitate. "Deal," she said as they shook on it.

"I'll see you later, and if you get scared, you know who to call," he said.

"Ghostbusters?"

Aaron grinned.

"I've been called a lot of things on this job, but that's a first. Lock the door behind me."

"Oh. Wait," Dani said, and ran into the other room, then came back carrying a key and a small remote, and handed them to him. "To the garage and the front door."

Aaron's fingers closed around them. "Right," he said, then grabbed the file of photos and left.

Dani turned the lock, then went through the house making sure everything was locked. Afterward, she wrote an email to her new principal, letting her know that she was officially in residence in Jubilee, that she was looking forward to the new school year, and hit Send, then laid her head down on the desk and started to cry all over again. If only she could stay alive long enough to start the new year.

Chapter 9

AARON RETURNED TO THE PRECINCT AND WENT straight to the chief's office and knocked.

"Come in," Sonny said.

Aaron shut the door behind him as he entered, and laid the file back on Sonny's desk.

"Ah, you're back. What's the verdict?" Sonny asked.

"Positive ID. This is the man she saw."

"Excellent," Sonny said. "I'll let the sheriff know. He'll take over the case from here. I'll be calling in your Pope family to talk to them about this journal."

"Our lead witness has a problem," Aaron said.

Sonny glanced up. "What kind of problem?"

"It's regarding Tony Bing, the man who's in prison for trying to kill her," Aaron said.

Sonny frowned. "If he's in prison, then how can he be a problem?"

"Because his twin brother is not. Dani got a phone call from Bing's mother this morning, warning Dani that Alex Bing, the twin, is in Jubilee, Kentucky. Apparently, Alex Bing threatened her life in the courtroom when his brother was sentenced. Dani was in hysterics when I got to her house. I know this isn't police business...yet. He hasn't threatened her here or approached her in any way. But his previous behavior toward her precludes the assumption that he's just here as a tourist."

Sonny frowned. "You're right about that. We have no reason to approach him at all, assuming we even knew where he was or what he looked like."

"According to Dani, he and Tony are identical twins. All I have to do is pull up Tony Bing's mugshot and go from there," Aaron said.

Sonny frowned. "You can't go vigilante on a citizen without a reason."

"Not planning on it," Aaron said. "But I will find out where he's staying, and I am going to be the backup she needs when he comes calling."

"How do you plan to do that?" Sonny asked.

"I'll be spending nights in her house until this issue is resolved," Aaron said.

"Don't you think you've gotten too involved too fast with this woman?" Sonny asked.

"I'm not involved. I'm empathetic. She's just a younger version of my mother, only she has no one for backup. Mom had us. She should have left the man she married years ago, but she didn't. She thought four boys needed a father. And we did, but not him. Not Clyde Wallace. Dani Owens did fight back. And she did leave her entire life behind to start over, and I'm her backup...sir."

Sonny gave Aaron a long, steady look and then nodded.

"Understood. And since she's a key witness in the Raines case, the Jubilee police force will be your backup if the need arises."

"Thank you, sir. I'm going to need a mug shot of Tony Bing. Maybe I'll spot him when I'm on patrol."

"Stay focused. Don't lose your cool," Sonny said.

"Always," Aaron said. "Is it okay to ask one of the detectives to pull up that mug shot for me?"

"Yes," Sonny said. "Tell them I sent you."

"Thank you, sir," Aaron said, and left the office.

A short while later, he was back in his cruiser and patrolling his sector of Jubilee. When lunchtime arrived, instead of eating, he went by both hotels, showed them the mug shot, asked if a man named Alex Bing had checked in, and struck out both times.

That left Reagan Bullard's campgrounds, so he drove out to the office and went inside. Within a couple of minutes, he learned a man named Alex Bing was registered there. He showed the mug shot to verify the ID and got a description of the man's car and tag number.

"Is he wanted for anything?" the clerk asked.

"No. It's for something else entirely," Aaron said. "However, you're being asked to say nothing about my inquiry to him or anyone else. Understood?"

"Sure, sure," the clerk said. "As long as he's no danger to the other guests, we're fine, too."

Aaron eyed the cabin in the distance as he walked back to the patrol car, verified that a gray Ford Bronco was parked at one of the small cabins, and drove away.

Now he knew what he looked like, what he drove, and where he was holed up.

He called home on the way back into town.

Shirley saw Aaron's name come up on her phone as she answered.

"Hi, honey. On your lunch break?" she asked.

"Sort of," Aaron said. "Listen, I'm going to be spending a few nights at Dani's house until we get a problem ironed out for her. I guess you could say the past has come back to haunt her," Aaron said.

"Oh no," Shirley said. "Is there anything I can do?"

"You already did, Mom. We'll talk more when I get home. I need to pack some stuff to take with me to her house, and dig out my sleeping bag."

"I'm so sorry this is happening," Shirley said.

"So am I, Mom. So am I."

———————

Dani went back to the supermarket to get more groceries. If Aaron Pope was going to camp out in her house, she would need to feed him. She was just coming out of the supermarket when she saw a man drive up in a truck and park.

At first, she thought it was Aaron and waved; then he got out, and she realized he was older and taller than Aaron, and she'd just embarrassed herself with a stranger. Then she saw an immense white animal in the back seat, and when she realized it was a dog, she stopped and stared. She'd never seen a dog that size in her life and wondered how much it must cost to feed it.

The man was coming toward her as she walked. When he saw her, he nodded cordially.

Dani paused. "I waved at you because I thought you were my friend Aaron. Then I saw you get out of your truck and realized you're taller and a little older. My apologies."

"No problem. Are you talking about Aaron Pope?" he asked.

"Yes."

"Then your mistake is understandable. I'm Cameron Pope, his cousin."

"I'm Dani Owens. I've just moved here to teach first grade this fall."

Cameron's smiled widened. "Welcome to Jubilee," he said.

"Thank you," Dani said. "I saw your dog, and I have to ask. What breed is it? I have never seen a dog that size in my life."

"Oh, that's Ghost. He's just an overgrown German shepherd."

Dani laughed. "*Overgrown* is an understatement. I didn't know white was a color of that breed, either. I've learned two new things today."

"And you've met another member of the Pope family," Cameron said. "Nice to meet you, Dani."

"Nice to meet you, too," Dani said, and moved on.

She put her purchases in the car and headed home,

keeping an eye on the cars behind her and the cars who were coming toward her, looking at the faces as she went. Alex Bing was here somewhere, and she needed to see him before he saw her.

Now that Rance Woodley had received the info regarding the identification of their suspected shooter, the sheriff's department was in a constant state of turmoil. It was like walking into a den of red ants. Every visible employee was in motion, fielding phone calls, running searches, following up on leads.

Having the tag number of the car was a huge lead, and their expectations were high until the information came back. The car had been rented in a suburb of Alexandria, Virginia, by a man named Dirk Conrad, but it had already been returned, and the street and number the rental car company gave them was for an address that did not exist.

Rance groaned. They had fingerprints and DNA for a man who was not in the system, and now they learned he'd pulled the whole thing off under an assumed name.

If they hadn't had the security footage, it could have been claimed that the man did not exist, so they ran another story, adding clips from the security footage when it aired anew, hoping someone, somewhere, would recognize him.

Sonny Warren was as disappointed as Rance Woodley about the recent twist to the investigation. Woodley had requested security footage from the car rental agency, only to learn their security system was out of order, and had been for the better part of a week.

"I'm running the story again, but this time adding footage we got from the hotel security cameras, rather than the composite sketch. Hopefully, someone will recognize him," Rance said.

"I have the journal back now," Sonny said. "If it's okay with you, I'm going to call in the Pope families and see if anyone has knowledge about this journal and who might have had it."

"Yes, good idea," Rance said. "Just update me afterward."

"Absolutely. I'll make some calls to find out when I can get them in here for an interview. I'll be in touch."

As soon as they disconnected, Sonny called Cameron. So far, the only member of the Pope family who knew anything about the journal's existence was Aaron. It was time to find out how much, if anything, they knew.

Cameron and Rusty were outside, with Ghost running between the flower bed Rusty was weeding and the fence Cameron was building around the backyard. She'd never gotten over the wounded bear coming into the yard before they were married and Cameron having to put it down.

Then last week, Rusty took a pregnancy test, and it was positive. The utter joy Cameron felt turned into instant protective mode. He remembered her fears of raising children with a forest full of wild animals able to walk into their backyard at free will, and ordered fencing.

It was delivered yesterday, and except for a quick trip to town this morning, Cameron had been in the backyard digging holes to set posts. He was measuring the distance needed to dig the next posthole when his phone rang. He saw Jubilee PD come up on caller ID and put down the posthole digger to answer.

"Hello?"

"Cameron, it's Sonny. Got a minute?"

"Sure. What's up?" Cameron asked.

"I need a favor," Sonny said, and began to explain, then wound up with a question. "Did you have any knowledge of the existence of such a journal?"

Cameron was stunned. "No, never."

"Do you think some of the elders might?" Sonny asked.

"Possibly, but I can't say for certain," Cameron said.

"Here's where the favor I need comes in because this pertains to the Charlie Raines investigation. I need you to contact all of the elders of the Pope family and bring them down to the station. The journal is here. It's still evidence in the case, but you can look at it and read some of the passages. It is, after all, your family's history. We're hoping someone knew about it, or knows what happened to it, to lead us to who the man was who dropped it in the parking lot."

"How the hell did you link that journal to the shooting?" Cameron asked.

"I can't comment on that," Sonny said.

The skin crawled on the back of Cameron's neck. "You had a witness."

"Again, I can't comment on the case," Sonny said. "Will you help?"

"Absolutely," Cameron said. "I'll start making calls. When do you want us to come in?"

"You tell me when you can get them here. I'll make the time," Sonny said.

"Right. I'll get back to you by this evening," Cameron said.

"Thanks, and I'll ask you not to mention this outside the family just yet."

"Of course," Cameron said.

The call ended. He picked up the posthole digger and headed for the house.

"Hey, honey, I have some calls I need to make," Cameron said.

Rusty rocked back on her heels and petted the big dog lying beside her.

"Okay. Bring me something to drink when you come back, okay?"

"I'll bring you something to drink first, and then I'll make calls," he said, and disappeared inside, coming back moments later with a cold bottle of water. "I opened it for you."

She grinned. "Thank you, Daddy."

The look that washed over his face stopped her heart.

"I will never take that gift for granted," he said, and leaned over and kissed her. "Don't stay out too long. It's getting hot."

Rusty took a quick drink and then glanced down at Ghost as the screen door banged behind Cameron.

"You better enjoy your peace and quiet while you have it, big boy. It's going to get really noisy around here in a few months. Are you up for it?"

Ghost whined and licked her fingers.

She stroked the top of his head. "You are such a good boy. Just don't say I didn't warn you."

―――――――

Two hours later, Cameron called Sonny back.

"Sonny, it's Cameron. I've called all of the elders. We'll be in tomorrow around 10:00 a.m."

"Awesome," Sonny said. "How many are coming?"

"All of them. You'll need about twenty chairs."

"Thanks for the heads-up. See you then," Sonny said.

―――――――

Aaron found out about the meeting when he went home to pack. Shirley was full of questions about the journal, none of which he could answer.

"Mom, you know I can't talk about ongoing cases," he said.

Sean walked in on the conversation.

"Whoa! Where are you going?" he asked.

"Stakeout," Aaron said.

Shirley frowned. "Dani is being threatened by someone from her past. Aaron is going to stay with her at night until the mess is resolved."

"Oh hell," Sean said. "Does it have to do with the guy who tried to kill her?"

"Twin brother, out for revenge," Aaron said. "Keep it in the family. He doesn't know we're on to him."

"That sounds dangerous," Sean said.

Aaron looked at his brother, then shook his head.

"What do you think I do all day? Hand out parking tickets?"

Sean flushed. "No, of course not, but I just—"

"I know," Aaron said, and clapped him on the shoulder. "I'll be fine. Mom, do you know where we put the camping gear? I need my sleeping bag and an extra pillow."

"I know. I'll get it and the pillow off your bed," Sean said, and left the room.

"He's just worried about you," Shirley said. "We all are every day when you pin that badge on your uniform and go out the door. And now Wiley's going down the same route. But I also know what a good cop you are, so give Dani my love, and if it gets bad down there, bring her home with you."

"No, Mom. There will never be anything bad brought to our home again. We moved past that. I'll take care of her down there, and it will be fine."

Then he gave her a hug, carried his suitcase to the trunk of his car, and, when Sean came out with the sleeping gear, put it in the back seat.

"Take care of Mom," Aaron said.

"I will," Sean said. "Be careful."

"I always am," Aaron said, and then he was gone. As soon as he reached the blacktop, he called Dani.

She picked up on the first ring.

"Hello?"

"It's me. I'm on the way. Be there in about half an hour. Do you need anything? I can pick it up when I get into town."

"No, I'm good," she said.

"See you soon," he said, and hung up.

A half hour later he was pulling up into Dani's drive-way. He opened the garage door with the remote and drove inside, got his things out of the car, and then hit the remote again. The garage door was going down as he went inside.

Dani was standing in the kitchen, her hands clutched against her stomach. Aaron could tell she was anxious.

"I hope that look of panic on your face has nothing to do with me sleeping under your roof," he said.

Dani sighed. "No, of course not. I've wavered between being embarrassed I have allowed you to become involved in my mess, and so damn grateful you're here."

"No more of that," Aaron said. "I offered. Is it okay to use the hall closet to hang up the clothes I brought?"

"Use the closet in the office. It has more space," she said, and followed him down the hall, talking as they went. "I've made space for you on the bathroom counter as well and laid out extra towels." Her hands were shaking. Her world was out of her control again, and she was so afraid of what could happen. "I put out some quilts for you to use for padding for your sleeping bag. They're on the office floor. I used them when I slept in my closet."

Aaron dropped his suitcase and sleeping bag on the office floor beside the quilts and then turned. Dani's eyes were wide and shimmering with unshed tears.

He wanted to hold her. Instead, he held out his hands palms up.

"Dani, take my hands."

She didn't hesitate and immediately felt calluses on his palms, and warmth, and strength.

"This is me, swearing that I won't let him hurt you. I will protect you with my life."

The tears rolled. "I don't want that kind of sacrifice," she whispered.

"But that's what I swear to do every day when I go to work. I have sworn to uphold the law and protect the innocent. I'm doing this because I want to."

She let go of his hands, lifted her chin in quiet defiance, and swiped at the tears on her cheeks.

"Have you eaten?" she asked.

"No."

"Good. Neither have I. We have choices. Follow me."

In that moment, Aaron saw the resilience of her spirit. She wasn't just a pretty face. He'd known that all along. But she'd just given him a glimpse of so much more. His jaw set as he fell into step behind her. He was already attracted to her and knew it would be so easy to fall head over heels in love with her. But the timing sucked. The last thing she needed was another man wanting something from her she wasn't willing to give.

After eating food from the supermarket deli and cleaning up the kitchen in mutual silence, Dani dried her hands and turned to face him.

"What now?"

He shrugged. "I'm up for anything, or I can leave you alone. It's your call."

"TV for a while," she said.

He nodded. "I'm going to turn on porch lights, front and back. There's a door from the garage that leads out into the backyard. Do you ever use it?"

"No."

"Good. Then I'm going to pull my car all the way up against the door. I'll cover the inside of the house and keep a lookout outside. Tomorrow, I'm going to get Sean to install some security cameras."

"Is there a place to buy them here?" Dani asked.

"Yes. I'll deal with that," he said.

"Just keep the receipts so I can reimburse you," she said.

"I'll be right back," he said, took his car keys to the garage, and pulled his car all the way up to the exit door, then went inside and found her on the sofa. "Now then, what are we watching? What's your fancy?"

"What do you like to watch?" she asked.

"You pick first," he said.

"What if you don't like it?"

"It won't matter. This is your house, Dani girl. You're in charge."

She picked up the remote, turned on the TV, and began flipping channels until she found the Food Network.

"I like to watch cooking competitions," she said.

"And I like to eat. Match made in heaven," he said, and sat down at the other end of the sofa.

"Do you think he'll come tonight?" Dani asked.

"He'll scope the place out for sure. But not until later when all the lights are out. Now, back to the contest. Let's see what they're doing and get a look at their skills, and then we'll pick who we think is going to win."

Dani grinned.

Aaron sighed. The dimples just made an appearance.

"So, what does the winner get?" Dani asked.

He couldn't say what he really wanted, and said the first thing he thought of.

"Dibs on the shower before bedtime."

"Deal," Dani said. "And I warn you. I'm really good at this."

"And I'm really good at spotting liars, so we'll see which chef is all talk and which one has the chops."

Dani laughed. "Chef. Chops. You're really punny."

He groaned. "You made me before it even began. I see a cold shower in my future."

Dani smirked.

Aaron sighed. He could see a lot of cold showers in his future before this stakeout was over.

―――――――――

Hours later, they were getting ready for bed.

Dani won the bet and bounced down the hall to shower first, while Aaron began making his bed. The quilts she'd left out for him to spread under his sleeping bag were going to make for easy sleeping. Once he finished, he went through the house, turning out lights and checking the locks.

He was sitting cross-legged on the sleeping bag, reading messages on his phone, when Dani emerged. He glanced up.

"I saved you some hot water," she said.

He was still trying to wrap his head around the thrust of her breasts beneath the oversized T-shirt she was wearing, and how toned and long her bare legs were, when she went into her bedroom and shut the door.

"Jesus," he whispered, then went to shower.

He was wearing gym shorts when he came out, and noticed the door to her bedroom was wide open.

Dani was in bed. The lamp was on. And when she heard him come out of the bathroom, she looked up from the book she was reading.

Okay, he looks as good out of uniform as he does in it.

"Do you want me to close your door now?" he asked.

"No."

"Are you afraid?" he asked.

"Yes, but not of you," she said.

"That's fair. I might snore."

"That's fine. As long as you are asleep, then I can assume all is well," she said.

"Do you mind if I come in to check your window locks?" he asked.

"Not at all," Dani said, and watched him cross the room to the windows.

"All good," he said after checking the locks.

She laid her book aside and started to reach for the lamp.

"You get settled. I'll turn out the light," Aaron said, and watched her slip down beneath the covers and shift the pillow beneath her head. "All comfy?" he asked.

"Yes, thank you."

He pulled a corner of the covers up a little farther over her, then leaned over.

For a fraction of a second, Dani thought he was going to tuck her in and kiss her good night, but he didn't. He just turned off the lamp, touched her shoulder beneath the covers.

"Sleep well, Dani. I've got your back."

The room was in shadows, but there were still street-lights and night-lights, and she could see him clearly as he walked out of her room. She heard him moving around down the hall and knew he was getting into his sleeping bag. As she closed her eyes, she heard the air-conditioning kick on and a dog barking somewhere outside.

There was a man in her home.

She hadn't known Aaron Pope a full two weeks, and yet she'd let him into her world. Alex Bing had pre-cipitated something that might never have happened, except for her fear of the Bing twins and the way Aaron Pope made her feel.

She turned over onto her side facing the open door and listened, but the house was quiet. She called out.

"Aaron, are you still there?"

She heard what sounded like a soft chuckle.

"Yes, I'm here."

"Good night."

"Good night, honey. Go to sleep."

She sighed and closed her eyes.

Later, Aaron was up and moving through the house to look out both front and back, then looked in on her before he laid back down.

His eyes narrowed as he saw her in the bed, curled

up, knees doubled up, her hands tucked beneath her chin, making herself as small a target as possible. The brutality of what had been done to her hurt his heart. Those brothers had made her this afraid, and for no other reason than because they could.

He went back to his bed, put his gun beneath his pillow, and then laid down again, wishing she was lying in his arms.

It was a little after 1:00 a.m. when Alex left the campgrounds and headed into Jubilee, but the amount of traffic this time of night was startling. How could he reconnoiter with all this going on? He couldn't figure out what was happening, until he remembered the music venues had matinee and evening performances. At this time of night, this had to be those employees going home. And as luck would have it, a large portion of the vehicles were all going to the apartments and residential area, right where he was headed.

"Son of a bitch," he muttered.

So, he miscalculated his chance. So what? Next time he'd just come later. He drove by her house, getting a high from being so close, and then left the area and headed back to his cabin, remembering as he drove how this began and where it went wrong.

There had been a time when he and Tony had really enjoyed her company. They always shared their girl-friends. The girls never knew. They thought it was the greatest game.

Tony met her first, but Alex was the first one to date her.

Tony was the first to score sex.

Alex slipped in on the next date and took her to bed, and then the brothers compared notes, laughing all the time because she never knew.

After the breakup, Alex was the first one to get into her apartment, but it was Tony's idea of how to do it. Alex had been standing at the foot of her bed just watching her sleep and wondering what it would feel like to watch her take her last breath.

But as he was watching her, she began to wake up, and he bolted. By the time she got up to look around, Tony had already pulled him back up into the crawl space. They watched her through the grating, and when she finally went back to bed, they crawled back into the empty apartment, high-fived each other, and snuck away.

Neither of them had seen the danger signs. They'd been too high on revenge. They called the shots in their relationships. Nobody quit them, and they were bent on making her pay.

They'd planned the whole thing so carefully, and the thunderstorm that came on that night was like an omen. All the wind and rain and thunder added to the chaos of murder.

Alex lowered Tony down into her living room, then waited to give him a lift up. The sound of gunshots made him envious.

They'd tossed a coin to see who had the pleasure of taking her out, and Alex lost. The moment the last shot sounded, he crawled to the opening on his belly to wait for Tony to come running.

Instead, he heard two more shots and then Tony screaming and screaming, and heard her tell him to shut up, or she'd put the next one between his eyes. Then there were sirens and people pounding on the door to her apartment and people shouting.

In a panic, he replaced the ceiling grate and began backing up as fast as he could go. In the midst of all the chaos, he slipped out of the empty apartment and lost himself among the people in the hallway and disappeared.

The guilt of leaving his twin behind had eaten at him to such a degree he couldn't sleep. He couldn't visit his brother in the hospital. He couldn't visit him after he was jailed. He couldn't look him in the eye and see the blame. He should have saved him. Somehow. Instead, he ran. And in his mind, the only way to absolve himself was to finish what Tony set out to do.

Frustrated with himself, Alex stormed into the cabin, slamming the door behind him. He got a beer from the refrigerator and downed it in gulps, then popped the top on a second and sat down on the side of the bed wishing Tony was sitting there beside him.

Even though Tony was alive, life was over for the both of them. They had always functioned as one, and they'd been split in two. He'd never spend another day with his brother for as long as he lived.

He emptied the second can, then kept going back for more until he finished the six-pack. He was sitting on the side of the bed when he dropped the last empty can in the trash, then rolled over and stretched out.

Within minutes, he was snoring.

Chapter 10

DANI WOKE UP TO THE SOUND OF WATER RUNNING, remembered Aaron was here. She glanced at the time. It was just after 6:00 a.m. He was probably shaving to get ready for work.

She dragged herself out of bed and used the powder room in the hall to wash up before getting dressed. The hall was empty. Aaron had already folded up the quilts and rolled up his sleeping bag. The man was neat, fine to look at, and, right now, her knight in shining armor. But just because he'd stepped up to help her like this, didn't have to mean anything other than he'd done it from the goodness of his heart. All she had to do was keep reminding herself of that.

As soon as she was dressed, she headed for the kitchen to make coffee, then began frying strips of bacon and beat up some eggs to scramble. Bread was in the toaster, ready to pop down, the bacon was cooked, and Dani was just about to pour the beaten eggs into a skillet when Aaron walked in. She glanced at him then quickly looked away, trying to seem disinterested, when she was anything but.

"Morning," Dani said. "Coffee's ready. I'm scrambling eggs. Do you like them soft or well done?"

"You don't have to feed me," Aaron said.

Dani shrugged. "I know that. Maybe I want to."

"Then make them how you like them. I like most everything," he said.

She grinned. "Then you're getting them well done. Coffee cups are in the cabinet above the coffee maker."

Aaron poured himself a cup of coffee and took a quick sip.

"Is there anything I can do to help?" he asked.

"Bread's ready to toast," she said.

He pushed the lever down on the toaster, and then got a plate from the cabinet and stood aside, waiting for the toast to pop up.

"Did you get any sleep?" he asked.

"Enough," she said. "What about you? I'm really sorry I don't have a guest bedroom. I can't imagine the floor was all that comfortable."

"On the contrary," Aaron said. "Those quilts made an awesome pad for the sleeping bag. Just so you know, I already spoke to Sean. He's going to set up the security here at your house today. I gave him your number, so he'll call to make sure it's convenient before he comes."

Dani glanced up. "Thank you, Aaron. Thank you, so much."

"You're welcome," he said, then watched as she turned the fire out from beneath the skillet and began dishing up the eggs.

She was carrying them to the table when the toaster popped its four slices of hot toast. He transferred them to the little plate and followed her to the table. Dani went back for the bacon, then got butter and jelly from the refrigerator.

"Do you need cream or sugar for your coffee?" she asked.

"No, thanks. I drink it black." Then he stood beside her chair, waiting until she was ready to sit down, and seated her before he sat down.

"Can't remember the last time that happened," she said.

He shrugged. "It's second nature. Even if our dad was an ass, Mom taught us how men were supposed to be."

Dani thought about her own family when she was growing up as she reached for a piece of toast.

"My parents were good people, and good to each other," she said, and began buttering her toast.

Aaron frowned. "Were?"

"They died right after I began teaching in Monroe. Car wreck," she said.

"I'm sorry," Aaron said.

"Me, too," Dani said. "My only other relatives live in Oregon. They're from Dad's side of the family and I don't really know them."

Aaron saw the sadness in her eyes and changed the subject.

"You're a good cook. You put something in the eggs besides salt and pepper, and I like it."

Dani smiled. "I'm from Louisiana, remember?"

"Hot sauce!" Aaron guessed.

She nodded. "I like everything hot and spicy."

"So do I," he said, gave her another long look, and then finished his food. "I'll be on duty until five unless something comes up, and then it could be later. There are no certainties in my job. But you can call me anytime. If something doesn't seem right, pick up the phone, okay?"

"Yes, okay," she said, and started to get up when he stopped her with a touch.

"Take your time. Finish your food. I'll let myself out," then he carried his dishes to the sink. "See you this evening, Dani. Have a good day."

She stood. "Be safe," she said as he came back to the table to pick up his keys.

He palmed the keys, then lightly stroked the side of her cheek with the back of his hand.

Dani shivered at the touch.

"Thank you for the blessing," he said softly, and then he was gone.

She was standing by the table when she heard the garage door go up and then down after he backed his car out and drove away. She could still feel his touch as she began her day.

———

Aaron got to the station, headed for the locker room to get into uniform, then appeared for roll call, only to get orders to return to the station at 10:00 a.m. to sit in on the meeting with the Pope family. They were coming in to see the journal, and he had a knot in his gut just thinking about it. They were all going to want to know how it turned up, and what the police knew about the man who shot Charlie, and why he didn't share any of this with them before. This was the hard part about being a cop. Knowing things that you couldn't talk about to people you knew and loved.

As ordered, Aaron was back at the station a few minutes before 10:00.

The chief was waiting for him.

"Aaron, I need you in the lobby to meet the Popes. As soon as they've all arrived, bring them back to the conference room. Sheriff Woodley and I will be waiting."

"Yes, sir," Aaron said, and headed up front, then didn't have long to wait.

They came in a caravan of cars and pickup trucks, and began parking anywhere they could near the station. Sonny had requested the elders, but some had long since given up driving, and it was the younger generations who'd brought them.

They filed into the station and kept piling in until the front lobby was packed.

"Is this everybody?" Aaron asked after the door finally shut behind the last one.

"No. Cameron and Rusty went after Miss Ella. She's the oldest Pope left on the mountain. Never married. Never learned to drive a car, and they had to do some fast talking to even get her to come off the mountain," Annie Cauley said.

"I've never met her, but I've heard Mom talk about her," Aaron said.

"She's ninety-one. Sharp as a tack and still walks the hills. But she has her ways," Annie said.

"Some say she's got the sight, but she never talks about it," Betty Raines said. "And I wish someone would please explain to me why we're even here."

"All in good time, Betty," Aaron said.

"Do you know?" Marcus Glass asked, then got sidetracked when he saw Cameron and Rusty coming up the street with her. "Here they come," he said, and went to open the door.

Cameron and Rusty entered with a tall, thin woman walking between them. She wore her age without excuse or regret, considering every wrinkle in her face as a battle scar to the past. Her shoulders stooped only slightly, and her white hair was wound up in a bun at the back of her neck. She was wearing a gray shirtwaist dress with long sleeves and a hem that fell way below her knees. Her shoes were shiny black leather flats. But in spite of her appearance, her eyes were dark and flashing with an inner light and an intelligence impossible to mistake.

"Sorry to keep you waiting. Miss Ella lives a far distance," Cameron said, then winked at her.

The old woman smiled, revealing a set of perfectly white false teeth.

"He means I live in the boonies, for which I make no apologies," she said.

Aaron liked her on sight. "We're all good here," he said. "If you'll please follow me, Chief Warren will explain everything," he said, and then led the way through the building and down into a conference room. Aaron immediately pointed to a table set up against the wall with cold drinks and coffee. "Feel free to get your drink and take it to the table. Miss Ella, could I get a drink for you?"

"You're one of Helen's grandsons, aren't you?" Ella asked.

"Yes, ma'am. I'm Aaron. The oldest."

"I take my coffee sweet. Two sugars," she said, and then let Cameron and Rusty help her into a chair.

Aaron set the coffee cup on a napkin in front of her, and then because Betty was there on her own, seated her. "Can I get you anything to drink?"

Betty shook her head. "I'm fine, but thank you for asking."

It didn't take long for people to get their drinks and find a seat. As the last ones were sitting down, Sonny Warren walked in carrying the evidence bag with the journal inside, and Sheriff Woodley was right behind him.

"Thank you all for coming," Sonny said. "I know you're all wondering what this is about. We have in our possession a vital piece of evidence in the shooting of Charlie Raines, and Sheriff Woodley will be sitting in on the meeting."

A low murmur moved around the table, and then they were silent.

He held up the evidence bag. "There is an old journal inside this leather wrap that pertains to Charlie Raines's shooting. We know the man who shot Charlie had this in his possession, but we don't know how he came by it, or how it pertains to his presence here. There are fingerprints on it, but the prints are not in the system. We have security footage of him in Jubilee, but we've also learned the man registered under a false name, drove a rental car that's since been turned in. Gave false information to the rental agency and has since disappeared."

"But if you don't know him, then how did you get the journal, and why ask us?" John Cauley asked.

"I can't speak to the details, but suffice it to say, the man lost it here in Jubilee, and we know that for a fact."

"What's so special about the journal?" Betty asked.

"The man who it originally belonged to is your ancestor, Brendan Pope."

A gasp of shock rolled around the table.

"Are you serious?" Annie asked.

"Yes, ma'am," Sonny said. "And I want to know if any of you knew of its existence, and if you did, do you know who had possession of it?"

To his dismay, they all shook their heads, except for Ella.

"Oh my, oh my," Ella said. "Is there an inscription that says, *In the year of our Lord, 1833,* inside?"

Sonny frowned. "I'm not sure if I remember—"

Aaron flinched. "Yes, there is. I saw it when it was turned in."

Ella's eyes welled. "It's the storybook! Granny's storybook. She used to read it to us when we were little. I thought they were fairy tales. I didn't know it was real accounts of Brendan's life."

"What do you know about it?" Sonny asked.

Ella dug a tissue from a hidden pocket in her dress and dabbed her eyes.

"There are stories about fur traders, and Native Americans. And stories about their daily lives. They had a lot of boys, but there was something in there about his only daughter, a little girl who died from a snakebite. That stuck with me because I was a little girl when I heard it." Then she frowned. "Granny wouldn't read the last part to us. We'd beg, but she said it was too sad. I don't know what she meant. Oh! I remember one part we thought was exciting. When the wagon full of Confederate gold rolled through Jubilee."

There was a communal gasp.

Sonny glanced at Rance.

"Did anyone see real gold?" Rance asked.

"I can't rightly remember," Ella said. "Granny would quit reading after that."

"Do you know what happened to the journal?" Sonny asked.

Ella frowned. "Well, not really. I hadn't thought about it in many a year. I do remember Granny's house catching fire, and they got some of their belongings out but had to rebuild the house. Neighbors were pulling out all manner of things until the roof caught. Then they had to leave the rest to burn. I guess I thought the journal burned. I know it was wrapped in deerskin, like that one right there, because when Granny got it out to read, she unfolded it in her lap and left the deerskin draped across her legs as she read."

"Is there anything else you can tell us?" Sonny asked.

Ella shrugged. "Maybe. If I could touch it."

He frowned. "Touch it? Why would—?"

"Because Miss Ella's got the sight," Annie said.

"Everybody on the mountain knows it," Betty added.

Sonny was getting antsy. Solving crimes with psychics was a joke among most cops.

"I can't really let you touch it. We have to preserve the fingerprints that are already on it, and not add to the mix."

"Leave it in the bag. I just need to lay my hand on it," Ella said.

"Can't hurt anything," Rance said. "Let her have a go at it."

"Aaron, would you please pass this to Miss Ella?" Sonny said, and handed him the evidence bag.

"Yes, sir," Aaron said, then carried it around to the other side of the table and laid it before her.

Ella nodded, then laid her hand on top of the book,

closed her eyes, and took a deep breath, remaining silent long enough Sonny was convinced this was a joke. But when she began talking, she fell back into the old-time speech pattern of the mountains.

"He weren't kin," Ella said. "The man who lost it weren't none of us."

"Then how did he come by it?" Sonny asked.

"Found it, he did," Ella said.

"Found it? Found it where?"

Ella shook her head. "They don't say. I'm a seein' shelves full of books, rooms full of books, in so many stories of one building."

Woodley's heart skipped. They already knew this had been taken from the Library of Congress in DC.

"Like a library?" he asked.

Ella frowned. "A grand building. In another place," she said.

Sonny was shocked. She'd done a pretty fair job of describing the Library of Congress.

"Why did the man have the journal? Why did he shoot Charlie?" he asked.

"Treasure hunter," she said, then she started to cry. "The book is us. But something's missing. No…someone is missing." She opened her eyes and shoved the book away. "The sad is there, like Granny said." She looked straight at Cameron. "Read it for us, son. Something terrible happened to our family that's been left undone."

"I'm sorry, Miss Ella, but I can't let the journal leave the premises," Sonny said.

"Would you let me come here to read it?" Cameron asked. "You could put me in an interview room. I'd glove up. It wouldn't leave prints. Not even on the pages. It might help," he said.

"I don't have an issue with that," Woodley said. "As long as it stays on site here, and he does what he says, it can't hurt. We need every break we can get."

"Then, yes, you have my permission," Sonny said.

"When can I begin?" Cameron asked.

"As soon as you wish," Sonny said.

"Then I'll be back after we get Miss Ella home. I know after we go through that journal that what we read will verify what Miss Ella told us."

Ella shrugged. "I just see what I see. Don't anybody have to apologize for me or believe a word of it if it bothers 'em."

"We aren't bothered, Miss Ella," John Cauley said.

"You know what you know," Betty said. "Everybody on the mountain knows that. The valley people will figure it out soon enough."

Sonny grinned. "Is that what you call us? Valley people?"

Betty shrugged. "Where is it you live, again?"

Sonny laughed. "In the valley between these mountains."

"Well then," she said, and grinned.

"Hey, Sonny, is it okay if I bring Rusty with me? She's fluent in three languages and has a lot of experience with deciphering old documents. She might make sense of the old script quicker than I can."

"Yes, I'll help," Rusty said.

"Yeah, that's fine," Sonny said.

"And Ghost? We don't leave him alone for very long."

Sonny's eyes widened. "Jesus, Cameron."

"He's just big, not dangerous," Cameron said.

"Well, hell. Yeah, sure, why not?" Sonny said. "If we have a pickpocket try to make a run for it, you can just set him on the runner like you set him on Danny Biggers when he kidnapped your niece Lili."

"Deal," Cameron said.

"Okay then," Sonny said. "Thank you for coming. I'm sorry I don't have more news for you."

"We're sorry we weren't more help," Cameron said. "If our grandparents had still been alive, this might have turned out better. I don't know how Brendan's journal got lost from the family, but it's come full circle for a reason. We just need to find out why."

After everyone left, Aaron went back on patrol and made a quick pass by Dani's house. Sean's car was in the driveway. For the time being, all was well.

But Aaron wasn't the only one checking up on Dani.

Alex Bing was on the move.

He'd gone into Jubilee to check the timetables at the music venues. He didn't want another surprise like he'd had last night. Then he swung by the crafts area and strolled through a section where the shops all sold handmade crafts. He bought a handmade hunting knife, and a woodcarving of a hawk with wings outspread and a rabbit caught between its talons. It was a stunning piece of work, but a brutal depiction of the circle of life. All he could think was how much Tony would have loved it.

He joined a crowd watching a blacksmith work, and then wandered into a shop selling homemade candy and came out with a quarter pound of chocolate fudge and a bag of peanut brittle.

The scents of hot sugar and melting chocolate made him hungry. He'd skipped breakfast and the day was getting hot. It was time to settle on a restaurant and go inside to eat where it was cool.

The menu at The Back Porch was varied enough to suit him, and in he went. As he was waiting to be seated, he made sure to scan the room first. It wouldn't do to run into Dani Owens until he was ready to be seen. But everyone in the dining area was a stranger, so he felt safe.

When the hostess seated him at a small table, he chose to sit with his back to the wall so he could see who was coming and going. After ordering fried catfish, coleslaw, and jalapeño hush puppies, he settled in to wait. The sweet tea he ordered was icy cold and slid down the back of his throat like silk.

As soon as he ate, he was going to swing past Dani's house on his way back to the cabin, get a good look at it in daylight, and see if there was any access in the alley between the rows of houses.

She thought she'd gotten away. She thought she was safe. But the bitch was wrong, and seeing the fear on her face would be the first step in the revenge he'd come for. Watching her die would be the ultimate high.

He was staring out the window when the waitress arrived with his order. He dug into the food without hesitation, dipping the crunchy catfish strips in home-made tartar sauce and chasing the bite with the jalapeño hush puppies.

He ate until his food was gone and then leaned back in satisfaction, waiting for the waitress to come back with the tab so he could pay and leave.

As he was waiting, he saw a police car drive up, and then two officers got out and walked into the restaurant in single file. They paused in the doorway, staring across the crowded dining area.

Alex's heartbeat kicked. His body tensed.

One of them saw him staring.

Shit. Now they're going to wonder why I was staring, Alex thought, and ever so slowly looked away, as if they were of no importance.

Moments later, a waitress came hurrying up from the kitchen carrying a to-go bag. The officers' focus immediately shifted to getting their food, then paying and leaving. Alex knew the officer was staring at him again, but he was purposefully focused on paying the waitress for his meal, and as soon as they were gone, he bolted out of the café and headed for the housing addition where Dani lived.

He frowned when he saw a car in the driveway. His

frown deepened when he saw the Arkansas tag. That wasn't her car. He circled a block to check the alley access, only to realize there were no access points into backyards from there. He passed her house again as he was leaving the housing addition, and as he did, saw a tall, dark-haired man come out of the house, and slowed down long enough to get a look at his face.

He was tall, good-looking, and the right age for a new boyfriend.

"Son of a bitch," Alex muttered. "She didn't waste any time."

He was still watching the man from his rearview mirror as he drove away and saw Dani come out of the house, take the box he handed her, and then watched him get a box from his car before they both went back inside. If he was moving in, this was going to mess up everything.

Both curious and furious, Alex hung around Jubilee. He needed to know if she had a roommate, because if she did, then his whole plan of attack had to change. And that was fine. She couldn't stay in that house forever. All he had to do was wait and watch for a different opportunity.

A couple of hours later, he swung back through her neighborhood just as Dani and the same man were both exiting the house. They were both carrying boxes out. He pulled over and parked at the curb down the street to watch, thinking to himself that if they left, he'd have a chance to get in and scope the layout of the house. They put the boxes back into the trunk, then shook hands. Dani went back inside, and the man got in and drove away.

Alex breathed a sigh of relief.

"Okay, Tony...I jumped the gun, didn't I? What is it you always say about assuming?" And then he laughed as if his brother was right there beside him, following the conversation he'd just had with himself.

Satisfied he'd just witnessed a man making some kind of service call, he turned at the next block and went back to the cabin.

———————

Cameron, Rusty, and Ghost were at the police station, situated in an interview room with Brendan Pope's journal. Cameron was reading it aloud and Rusty was recording it. When he'd get stuck on a word, she would come to the rescue.

It was coming up on 2:00 p.m. when a 911 call came into the PD about a lost child. A six-year-old boy had become separated from his parents at an outdoor event, and after a few minutes of looking for him on their own without success, they called the police.

Aaron and another officer named Bob Yancy were on patrol together and responded to the call. As they rolled up on the scene at the town square, the parents came running, both talking at once and in an obvious panic.

"Help us! Please, help us! Mickey just disappeared!"

"Yes, sir. I'm Officer Pope. This is my partner, Officer Yancy. Could I have your names, please?"

The man blurted it all out in one breath. "Randy

and Tina Cotton. Our son's name is Mickey. He's only six. One minute he was holding my hand. I turned him loose to pay for the snow cone he wanted, and when I looked back, he was gone," Randy said.

"Is this where you lost sight of him?" Yancy asked.

"No, we were in the craft area at the snow cone stand. There was a big crowd beginning to disperse when we lost him," Randy said. "We looked and looked but couldn't see him anywhere."

"No one in the crowd heard you calling for him? No one stopped to help you?" Aaron asked.

Tina burst into tears. "He's deaf. We didn't call out for him because he can't hear."

Aaron's heart sank. This was going to make searching for a lost child even more difficult. And then it hit him. Cameron was already in town, and he'd brought Ghost to the PD, and Aaron knew all about Cameron's run up the mountain with Ghost when his niece was kidnapped.

"Yancy! Radio the station. Ask if Cameron and Ghost are still there. If they are, get them here, ASAP."

Yancy's eyes widened. "Yes! Good thinking, Pope," Yancy said, and moved a few feet away to radio in, while Aaron kept questioning the parents.

"Do you have something with you that belongs to Mickey?" Aaron asked.

Randy gave Tina a frantic look. "I don't know, do we?"

"I don't think..." and then she stopped and began digging in the tote bag over her shoulder and pulled out a little baseball cap. "He was wearing it earlier. Would this work?" she asked.

Aaron took it. "Yes, ma'am. Do you have a recent photo of your son?"

"Yes, several we took just today," she said, and pulled up the photos on her phone. "It's a clear shot of his face and what he's wearing," she said and then started crying again, remembering the yellow shirt and red shorts she'd put on him this morning thinking he'd be easy to see in the crowd if they should get separated.

Aaron took her phone, sent a copy of the photo to his own phone, and then handed it back.

At that moment, Yancy returned.

"They're on the way. The chief is coming with them," he said.

"What's happening?" Tina asked. "When are you going to start looking for Mickey? What if someone took him? He will be terrified."

"Since your son is unable to hear us calling his name, we have a tracker on the way who doesn't need to hear Mickey. He'll find him with his nose," Aaron said. They all turned at the sound of an approaching police siren. "And they're already here."

Cameron leaped out of the patrol car and opened the back door as the chief approached.

"Who are we looking for?" Sonny asked.

"Chief, this is Randy and Tina Cotton. They've lost their son, Mickey. He's six, and he's deaf. I thought we'd have a far better chance finding him with Ghost than a search team looking for a child who can't hear."

"Good call," Sonny said.

"Is that them?" Randy asked as he saw a tall man approaching with a huge dog on a leash. He looked at Aaron, and then he looked back at the man.

"Is he your brother?" Randy asked.

"A cousin," and then Cameron and Ghost arrived. "Cameron, this is Randy and Tina Cotton. They lost their son, Mickey, in the crowd down in the crafters' area by the snow cone stand. He's six, and he's deaf. This is Mickey's cap. This is what he looks like," Aaron said, and showed him the photo.

"Send the photo to my phone. You and Yancy run interference for me and Ghost. If Ghost suddenly takes off running, it's likely to freak a bunch of tourists into thinking he's going to attack them," Cameron said.

"Will do," they echoed.

Cameron took a firm grip on the leash, looped it around his wrist, and took off at a lope toward the crafters' area.

Sonny had the parents copy the boy's photo to his cell phone, then got back into the squad car and sent a group text with the photo attached to every officer out on patrol and radioed into dispatch for all officers on duty to be on the lookout for that child.

Aaron and Yancy took off in their patrol car, heading toward the crafts area of town, while keeping Cameron and Ghost in sight. Once they reached the area, they got out and followed him on foot.

When Cameron reached the snow cone stand, the line of customers was long, and they looked askance at the size of the dog he had with him.

"We're searching for a missing child. This is his picture. Have you seen him?"

The people gathered around, all looking then shaking their heads. At that point, Cameron pointed to Ghost.

"This dog is a tracker. Just give us some room," Cameron said, and put the little boy's cap under Ghost's nose. "Seek, Ghost! Find!"

Ghost's ears came up as his nose went to the ground. He began moving in an erratic pattern, back and forth behind the stand, then circling back and moving farther out into an ever-widening circle.

All of a sudden, he whined and took off running with Cameron right behind him holding a death grip on the leash. They ran past the woodcarver's shop, beyond the blacksmith shop, behind the homemade candy shop, and then back onto the main artery of the plaza.

Aaron and Yancy were running parallel to them, waving people out of their path as they went.

Then Ghost made a quick swerve to the left and began running north through the park area, past the first music venue, through a parking lot, past the second music venue and that parking lot, heading straight toward the creek at the far end of town.

"Oh shit," Cameron muttered. "The water. Please God, not the water."

Chapter 11

WILEY POPE WAS ON HIS WAY BACK TO REAGAN Bullard's music venue after a late lunch break. The matinee performance would begin at 4:00 p.m., and they'd open the doors for early arrivals at three. Being a security guard was his first step to becoming a police officer. He loved the job. Enjoyed the people he worked for, and took pride in his work. As far as he was concerned, moving to Jubilee had been a godsend for them all. And while he'd never grown up with a fatherly bond, Aaron had always been his touchstone to how a man should be.

He was just pulling into the employee parking area when he saw Cameron and Ghost coming from uptown. They were running like their lives depended on it. And then he saw Aaron and Yancy running in flanking positions with them. When he realized they were headed for the creek, he jumped out of his car and followed.

Aaron was to the far right of Cameron and Ghost when they topped the rise above the creek. Bushes grew in clumps all along the bank, forming a natural boundary, but as he looked down toward the water, he saw a flash of yellow and remembered the yellow T-shirt the little boy was wearing in the picture. He bolted down the creek bank, shouting, "To your right! To your right!" unbuckling his gun and holster as he ran. He dropped it and his phone in mid-step, kicked off his boots, and jumped into the waist-high water a few feet downstream from where he'd seen the flash of yellow.

The water exploded upward and outward as he went in, and within seconds of landing, he saw the child beneath the overhanging bushes, clinging to a lower branch with both hands.

The moment the little boy saw Aaron, the terror in his eyes was replaced with an overwhelming look of relief. But the distraction made the little boy lose focus. He lost his grip and, within a heartbeat, was in the water.

Aaron lunged forward, making a frantic grab for the child, and felt a sharp, burning pain across his forehead from a low-hanging branch. But he caught him before he could go under. Seconds later, the little boy was in Aaron's arms and so cold to the touch that he couldn't quit shaking.

"Did you get him?" Cameron shouted.

"Yes! Call an ambulance!" Aaron shouted.

Yancy was running toward them, but still a distance away.

Then Aaron heard a splash and turned to look. His brother Wiley was in the water beside him.

"Give him to me. You crawl out and I'll hand him up," Wiley said.

Aaron didn't hesitate. They both waded a bit downstream to find an opening through the bushes along the bank.

Aaron cupped the little boy's face for reassurance, then gave him to Wiley.

"He's deaf. Just hold him tight so he'll feel safe," Aaron said, and climbed back up on the bank, then leaned down. The little boy's arms went up and wrapped around Aaron's neck as he lifted him out of Wiley's arms. By then, Yancy was on scene and helped Wiley out of the creek.

They hurried back to where they'd shed their gear and began gathering it up.

"Aaron, I've got your stuff," Wiley said as Aaron started up the rise in his sock feet, moving toward the parking lot with the little boy trembling in his arms.

"Ambulance is on the way," Cameron said, and they could hear the sirens in the distance.

"Yancy, call the family," Aaron said. "Let them know he's been found."

"Will do," Yancy said, and made the call.

Randy Cotton answered on the first ring.

"Hello?"

"Mr. Cotton, this is Officer Yancy. We found your boy. We think he's okay, but he's suffering from shock and hypothermia. He'd fallen into the creek and was hanging on to some bushes to keep from being swept downstream."

"Oh my God! Thank you! Thank you!" he said. "Where do we go to pick him up?"

"He'll be taken to ER," Yancy said.

"We'll go straight there. God bless you all," he said, and hung up.

Yancy took off jogging to catch up, and then saw the bleeding cut on Aaron's forehead.

"Hey, buddy. You're bleeding. Do you want me to carry him?"

Aaron shook his head. "I'm okay. It's just a scratch. Besides, he's got a death grip on my neck."

Then Yancy glanced at Wiley. "I'm guessing this very wet dude beside you is one of your brothers?"

"Yes, my brother Wiley," Aaron said. "He's a security guard at the Bullard music venue. Wiley, this is my partner, Bob Yancy."

"Nice to meet you," Wiley said.

"How on earth did you wind up in the creek with your brother?" Yancy asked.

Wiley shrugged. "I saw Cameron and Ghost running first, and then I saw Aaron. I didn't know what was happening, but I know my brother. He doesn't run away from trouble. He runs toward it, so I followed. When I saw him drop his phone and weapon, and start taking off his boots, I knew he was going in the water. I just didn't know why. Then I saw the kid and went in to help."

"There comes the ambulance," Aaron said, and lengthened his stride as the ambulance came to an abrupt stop at the end of the parking lot.

EMTs Fagan Jennings and Billy Jackson spilled out of the bus.

"His name is Mickey Cotton. He's six years old and he's deaf. Be gentle. He's scared spitless," Aaron said, and started to hand him over.

But Mickey gave Aaron a frantic look and clung tighter. Aaron kept patting him and nodding to reassure him it was okay.

Cameron came running up and gave Mickey the baseball cap Tina Cotton had given them. When Mickey reached for it, Aaron handed him over to Billy.

They quickly wrapped him in blankets, and then Billy climbed up into the back of the ambulance with him.

"He'll ride in my lap all the way," Billy said, and sat down on the gurney with him as the doors swung shut.

Seconds later, they were speeding off toward the hospital with lights flashing and the siren screaming.

At that point, Aaron's focus shifted.

"Cameron, we can't thank you enough for this assist. We would never have found that little boy in time to save him. You and Ghost make quite a team, and if I wasn't so damn wet, I would hug you both."

"No thanks necessary," Cameron said. "Bringing Ghost into town with me proved to be a good decision, and it appears that it was meant to be. If he hadn't already been here, it *would* have been too late."

"I'd heard about the famous Ghost dog, but it was a pleasure to see him in action," Yancy said. "Ah...and here comes Chief Warren. You and Ghost are going to get a ride back to the station."

Wiley dropped Aaron's boots and handed him his phone and gun.

"I'm already late for work. Good thing I keep an extra uniform in my locker," he said. "Take care, brother."

"Always," Aaron said. "Tell Mom I said hi and that I miss her biscuits."

Wiley grinned. "Don't worry. They're not going to waste. Just more for B.J. And I'll take that wet hug if it's okay with you. You made my heart skip a little when I saw you leap into that water without knowing what was happening."

Aaron wrapped his arms around his younger brother.

"You're a good man, little brother. Go put on some dry pants."

Wiley grinned and took off at a lope toward the venue.

"I better get back to Rusty. We're recording the journal," Cameron said, and headed for the squad car.

Aaron's socks were a mess, but he couldn't wear his boots without them, so he sat down on a bench and put his boots back on before they headed to their patrol car, then drove back to the station. As soon as they pulled up at the back of the precinct, Aaron got out. "Tell the chief I'll be back shortly."

Yancy nodded. "Let me know when you get back to the station and I'll swing by and pick you up."

"Will do," Aaron said, grabbed his hat from the back

seat where he'd tossed it, and ran into the station to get a clean uniform, then back out to his car. He could have showered on site, but he also needed to clean the cut on his forehead, so he grabbed a handful of tissues and began wiping the blood off his face before driving back to Dani's.

━━━━━━━━━━

Dani was feeling good about the day.

Sean had installed a Ring doorbell on the front door, a security camera inside the hall aimed at the front door, and another one outside the back door beneath the porch. He'd set up the Ring app on her phone, showed her how to access and use it, and then showed her how to view the cameras via her laptop. He'd also left a small package for Aaron, along with a note. She felt safe again.

But she'd also heard a lot of sirens today, and Aaron's safety was also on her mind. There was some weird connection between them that she hadn't identified, but she liked him a little too much for her own well-being. Everything had gone quiet after the last siren blasted through town, which made her anxious again. That could be a good sign or a bad one. She just wanted him to be safe.

In an effort to focus on something more positive, she began poking through the refrigerator and freezer for ideas for supper when she heard a key in the door. It was too early for Aaron to be off work, and she wondered what was wrong. She stopped and went into the hall just as Aaron walked in.

———

Aaron was thinking he should have given Dani a call to let her know he was coming as he shut the door behind him. He hung his uniform on a hanger, and then he saw her, eyes wide with a thousand unspoken questions and a slight look of panic on her face as she approached. She slid her hand up the side of his face all the way to the cut. Her hand was soft and warm, and he remembered how it had felt to hold her when she was crying.

"You're bleeding…and you're wet. Are you alright?" Dani asked.

"It's just a scratch," Aaron said. "A six-year-old child got separated from his parents. He was deaf, which made the search a little complicated. Thanks to Cameron and Ghost, we found him. He'd fallen into the creek but had managed to grab hold of some low-hanging bushes. I went in after him. I need to shower and change clothes so I can get back to the station. My shift isn't over for a couple more hours."

"When you come out, I'll clean the cut before you leave," she said.

"You don't have to do that," Aaron said.

She gave him another look. "I'm not doing it because I have to."

He grinned. "You sound like Mom."

"Except I'm not your mom, and you won't be the first little boy I bandaged up on the playground," she said, and smiled.

His gaze moved from the dimples to the shape of her mouth. "I'm not a little boy, and I'm happier than I should be that you and I are not at all related."

Shock rolled through her as she watched him grab his uniform and walk away. Her heart was pounding, and there was a knot in her stomach.

Okay. I didn't see that coming. Then she sighed. *Or maybe I did and was just afraid to look.*

She stood for a few moments, trying to remember where she'd put the first aid kit when she unpacked, and then remembered leaving it on a shelf in the utility room and went to get it.

Once she was satisfied that everything was in it, she laid it on the kitchen table and sat down to wait for Aaron to come back. She could still hear the water running, thought about it sluicing down that long, beautiful body, and sighed.

"God, Dani. Get a grip."

She looked down at her fingernails, rolled her eyes, and bit off a hangnail on her thumb, then got up and began emptying the dishwasher. Banging doors dulled the sound of the shower, which was good. If she couldn't hear it, then she didn't have to think about him wet and naked.

The dishwasher was empty and pork chops were thawing in a pan on the counter when he came back into the kitchen, holding a handful of tissues against his forehead.

"The hot water made it bleed again," he said. "I don't want this uniform bloody, too."

"Sit here," Dani said.

Aaron pulled out a chair from the table and sat as she opened the first aid kit.

"Let me see," she said, and gently removed the tissues to get a better look at the cut. "Yikes, Aaron. That's more than a scratch." She got cotton balls and some antiseptic. "This is going to sting," she added, then began to clean out the cut.

"And you were right," he said, wincing slightly.

"I'm so sorry."

Without thinking, she moved between his knees for better access, unaware Aaron was fighting the urge to grip her waist and pull her onto his lap.

He closed his eyes and tried to concentrate on anything but how close she was.

"So, I guess Sean got all of your security installed," he said.

"Yes. Oh! He also left something for you. It's in that packet on the kitchen counter. He said to remind you to take your personal laptop when you leave."

"What is all this?" he asked.

"Don't know. He just said you'd know what to do with it."

"Yeah, okay," Aaron said, then let the conversation lapse because she smelled good, and the sound of her breathing so close to his ear was somewhat erotic, a thing he needed not to act upon.

Once she was satisfied that she'd applied enough antiseptic, she began using butterfly strips to pull the gash back together. "Okay, that part's done," she said, and leaned back to look. "Are you required to wear a hat?"

"Pretty much," he said.

She reached back into the first aid kit for a small gauze bandage and taped it across the cut. "That should protect the cut from the pressure of the hat. I think you're good to go," she said and took a step backward.

"How do I look?" he asked.

She frowned. "Are you fishing for a compliment?"

He grinned. "Maybe."

"You look just dangerous enough to be interesting," she said, and began gathering up the mess.

Aaron reached for her hand.

"I'll take the interesting part, but don't be afraid of me."

Dani shivered. "I'm not. Not like that."

"Okay then," he said, and stood. "What's thawing in that pan?"

Changing the subject was a good move. Dani's panic quickly subsided.

"Pork chops."

Aaron groaned. "My favorite food ever."

"Would you rather have them fried or smothered in gravy?"

"Yes," Aaron said, and then winked, picked up the laptop and the packet Sean left for him, and walked out laughing.

The sound of his laughter made Dani smile, and she was still smiling as she heard him drive away. As soon as she finished cleaning up the first aid mess, she went to the bathroom to see what needed to be cleaned, and found everything hung up and tucked away.

She sighed.

"Lord. He's gorgeous. Funny. Kind to a fault. Picks up after himself. And today a hero. I can't believe some damn fool woman gave him up." Then she caught a glimpse of the look in her eyes. She was fooling herself and she knew it. "Or…maybe I should just thank her for the opportunity."

———

As soon as Aaron got back to the precinct, he parked, called Yancy to come pick him up, then while he was waiting, opened the packet from Sean.

A small tracking device fell out in his hand, accompanied by a note.

If you know what the stalker dude is driving, plant it. I've already loaded the tracking app onto your home laptop. That way you can keep track of the bastard coming and going. And I put a tracking device on Dani's car. If he starts following her, you'll know it.

You can tell which car is which by the color of the
blip. Dani's blip is white. His is black.

"Way to go, bro," Aaron muttered, and dropped the
tracking device into his pocket. He already knew the tag
number and color of the vehicle. All he had to do was
get lucky and see it parked somewhere in Jubilee long
enough to plant the bug.

Nyles Fairchild was back in his old routine. What had
happened felt like a bad dream. Sometimes he almost
convinced himself it hadn't really happened. But then
night would come. The moment he closed his eyes, he
lived the incident all over again. His conscience and
guilt were killing him. What he hoped to put behind
him had become the monster in the closet.

Every day that he went to work, he thought about
applying for early retirement and moving out of the
country. But he didn't know where to go. He needed to
find out what countries did not allow extradition to the
United States. And some days, he just wished he'd get
caught and then the decision would be made for him.

This morning when he'd arrived at work, there was a
message on his desk to report to the archives. He worked
diligently throughout the day, as if doing excellent work
on the job would make up for screwing up his life, and
was satisfied with himself by the time he went home.

He stopped on the way home to pick up some Thai food. The aroma of his to-go order was making him hungry, and by the time he got back to his apartment, he was ready to kick back and eat dinner in front of the TV.

He changed from work clothes to leisure wear and then washed up before heading to the kitchen. He plated up the food he'd brought and carried it to the living room, along with a cold bottle of beer, then settled in his recliner to watch the evening news as he ate.

He was absently listening to world news, wincing over an invasion and continuing news of an earthquake in one part of the world and a volcanic eruption in another, when the newscaster shifted to a story that had taken on a national slant, and all because it had happened in a well-known tourist location in Jubilee, Kentucky.

His heart kicked. He set his food aside and upped the volume, then leaned forward.

"And, we have an update on the random shooting of a young local boy in Jubilee, Kentucky, that we first told you about some days ago. Apparently, the boy who was shot has finally regained consciousness. With the help of a sketch artist, they developed a composite sketch of the shooter, who was immediately identified as a recent guest at one of the local hotels. However, the identity he registered with has proven to be a false one, so the authorities have released video footage of the man coming and going from the hotel in the hope that someone will recognize him and call in. If you

*think you recognize this man, there is a number to
call at the bottom of the screen."*

Nyles went from utter joy hearing the boy was alive,
to a complete meltdown that his Dirk Conrad persona
had been captured on camera. And when he saw the
footage, he groaned. There he was, big as Dallas, caught
on camera for all the world to see. His saving grace was
the beard, the fake ID, and the rental car, also rented
under the fake name. There was nothing to tie Nyles
Fairchild to that man. He'd left nothing behind.

*Except that damn journal. With my fingerprints
all over it.*

But he kept reminding himself that there was no way
to tie that journal to the shooting. It had been in the
backpack when he'd seen the kid. And he'd lost it after
he got back to town. Whoever found it would never
think to tie it to what happened on the mountain. He
had to believe that.

Then he slapped the arms of the recliner in glee.

"The kid's alive! Thank you, Lord, he's alive!"

Aaron finished patrol with Yancy and then went back
to the station to write up the report on Mickey Cotton.

Sonny Warren saw him at the desk finishing up the
paperwork and then saw the bandage on his forehead.

"Hey, what happened to your head?" he asked.

"Collateral damage from getting the missing kid out of the water. That creek bank is lined with brush."

"Oh, right," Sonny said. "Well, it was a good job all around, and quick thinking on your part to call in Cameron and the dog. You and Yancy work well together."

"Yes, sir. Thank you, sir," Aaron said.

"So, get some rest this evening," Sonny added.

"I'm almost finished with the report, and then I'll be headed home," he said.

"Are you still at Dani Owens's house?" Sonny asked.

"Yes, for as long as Alex Bing is in Jubilee. He's bad news," Aaron said. "Sean installed some security in her house today. We'll see how tonight goes."

Sonny frowned. "Just be careful."

"I'm always careful," Aaron said.

"Yes, well…as you were," Sonny said, and walked away.

Aaron finished the report and filed it, then clocked out. He was planning to go straight to Dani's, and then as he was leaving the station in his personal car, he tossed his hat in the back seat and decided to make a quick sweep through the supermarket parking lot, and then drive by some of the restaurant parking lots on the off chance of seeing Alex's Bronco and planting the tracker. He wasn't going to rest easy until he'd "belled the cat."

Sheriff Woodley was frustrated with the Charlie Raines case.

They had fingerprints, DNA, positive IDs from the victim and a witness, security footage of the man they wanted for the crime, and every damn bit of it was untraceable. What he didn't have was a real motive.

Dirk Conrad was a ghost—a man who had assumed a false identity and disappeared on the same day he shot a boy, leaving the boy for dead.

He had hoped the Pope family would have some idea of whose hands the journal had fallen into, but that meeting had come up with no new leads.

Woodley had just gotten off the phone with Chief Warren. Cameron Pope was reading the journal in hopes that something on those pages would ring a bell and give them a reason for the man's presence.

Right now, their only hope was the continuing stories of the incident the media kept running, and the added security footage. Surely to God, someone would see it. Someone had to know him. A man couldn't live unnoticed forever. Could he?

———

By the time Cameron got back to the station, Rusty was waiting.

"How did it go?" Cameron asked as he was escorting her to the car.

She got in, gave Ghost a quick hug, and then buckled up.

"I quit recording because I realized you're the one who needs to read it. It's your family history. If there's any significance in the entries, I wouldn't know it."

"You're right," Cameron said. "I'll come back tomorrow on my own and read some more. How far did you get?"

"Up to the point when Meg shows up in Brendan's life. Did you know her name was Cries A Lot?"

Cameron's eyes widened. "No way! All I ever heard was Meg."

"I think that's what Brendan called her, but her Chickasaw name was Cries A Lot."

"She was Choctaw," Cameron said.

"Not according to Brendan. She was Chickasaw."

"Are you serious? How on earth did the Pope family get that mixed up?"

"Generation gaps?" Rusty said.

"I guess," Cameron said. "Anyway, this will be news for a whole lot of people," and then he started the car. "You must be exhausted, honey. Let's get food to go. No cooking for you tonight, and I'll clean up the kitchen afterward."

She leaned back in the seat. "I won't argue. I'm barely pregnant and all I want to do is sleep."

Cameron reached across the console and squeezed her hand.

"Then sleep all you can. Maybe you can save some

of it up for all the years ahead in which we never sleep soundly again."

They were still laughing when he backed away from the curb and headed uptown.

———————

Aaron had been all over Jubilee looking for Alex Bing's car and was about to call it quits when he saw one just like it in the supermarket parking lot. He wheeled into the lot to check the tag number and got a hit.

"Bingo," he muttered, and pulled up into the empty parking space beside it, grabbed the tracker, and got out. After a quick glance around, he dropped his keys as an excuse to bend over, slapped the tracker onto the underside of the car behind the bumper, picked up his keys, and then strolled into the store.

He bought a six-pack of Cokes, went through self-checkout, and as he was walking out of the store, saw Bing in the distance, getting into the Bronco and driving away.

Aaron ran to his car and headed straight to Dani's. His head was hurting where he'd cut it, and he didn't know what kind of reception he was going to get when he got there. He'd said more than he should have about his personal feelings toward her and hoped it hadn't freaked her out to the point of being afraid for him to stay.

He opened the garage door with the remote as he was coming up the street, and pulled inside. Like before, he rolled all the way up to the exit door and parked against it, hit the remote to close the garage door behind him, and got out.

As he entered the house through the utility room, he paused, feeling the vibes of what it would be like to come home to country music playing and the aromas of something wonderful happening in the kitchen.

As he walked in, he caught her dancing at the island as she was chopping up a salad, and was suddenly starving for more than supper.

Then she looked up, caught him watching, and stopped.

"Smothered pork chops, mashed potatoes with gravy, candied carrots, and a salad. Make yourself comfortable. It should be ready in about fifteen minutes or so."

"Yes, ma'am," he said, and went to wash up.

As he left the room, he heard her up the volume on the music and smiled. A woman to treasure was one who never stopped dancing while music was playing.

He went straight to the office and booted up his laptop to check the tracker app. As soon as he activated it, he smiled. Bing was still in Jubilee. The app was working. He left it open to keep eyes on the predator, then went to change and wash up.

———

Dani was staring down at the chopping board, thinking she should have sliced the radishes for the salad a little thinner, then frowned. What if he didn't like radishes? Then she shrugged. He was a grown man. He could choose whatever he wanted.

He could even choose me. But do I want that to happen? Or am I just clutching at anyone safe to save me from the devil on my heels? Then she frowned at the thought. *Stop making excuses for the fact that you're attracted to a man you barely know. It's not against the freaking law to appreciate what's in front of you.*

Then she did a little two-step along the kitchen island to get a salad bowl from the cabinet and said a prayer for them both. He was giving up his own free time and risking his life for her. The least she could do was appreciate it without rules and conditions.

When he came back a short while later, he was wearing old jeans and a T-shirt, and had changed from work boots to running shoes. He'd taken the bandage off his forehead, leaving the cut and the tiny butterfly strips visible.

"Does your head hurt?" Dani asked.

"A little, but I just took something for it. What can I do to help?" he asked.

"Everything is ready except what you would like to drink."

"I'll have whatever you're having," he said.

Dani poured sweet tea into two glasses of ice and carried them to the table, but Aaron was still standing beside her chair.

"Thank you," she said as he seated her, then himself. "You're spoiling me."

He glanced up. "Want me to stop?"

The look on his face said it all. There was more than the obvious in that question, and he'd just handed all of the control to her.

"No. I don't want you to stop anything. I'm in free fall Aaron, and you're all that's keeping me tethered. I don't want to be afraid. I don't want to be cornered again. And I don't want to die. I appreciate everything about you, including your presence in this house."

He nodded. "Okay then. While I hesitate to quote my baby brother on anything, 'Let's eat.'"

She smiled. "Deal."

As they began their meal, Aaron wisely shifted the conversation to her new job. By the time they'd finished eating, he'd seen a whole other side of her.

He now knew how much she hated mice.

How much she loved the art projects with her students.

How excited she was watching someone who'd been struggling suddenly "get it," and that she considered teaching as being a key that unlocks children's futures.

And that once she'd taught a child to read, she'd given them their own key to the rest of their life.

"I have so much respect for teachers," Aaron said. "You don't just have students to deal with, you have their families or lack thereof, you have your immediate superiors and the administration in your business all day, every day, and they all expect you to work miracles."

"I know," Dani said. "And, yes, the miracles are few and far between, but we live for the days when they happen. Like when the children who are struggling at the beginning of the year have learned to believe in themselves by the time it's over."

"Did you always want to teach?" Aaron asked.

Dani laughed. "I think so. I used to line up all my dolls and stuffed toys, then read to them."

Aaron smiled. "What would you read?"

"Oh…all the books my mother read to me. I didn't know how to read, but I knew the stories by heart and could tell what came next by the pictures on the page. I just told the same stories again…and again….and again, which is helpful now, because some days I think I'm repeating myself the same way to the few kids who struggle. All you can do is keep repeating the words and the rules and the alphabet, and how letters make words, and words make sentences, and sentences tell stories, until they get it."

Aaron was entranced. When she talked about her job, she lit up from within. But when light caught the side of her face just right, he could see tiny scars from the brutal beating she'd suffered, and knew what a warrior she was. What he didn't know was if she'd ever trust a man again. And that mattered because he was falling in love.

Chapter 12

It was a good evening for Randy, Tina, and Mickey Cotton, as well.

After the horrible fright of losing their son, and then learning what had happened to him before he was rescued, they were celebrating in their cabin out at Bullard Campgrounds.

They'd brought pizza back from Jubilee and stored ice cream from the supermarket in their refrigerator. After they ate, they went outside on the front porch to wait for the Saturday night fireworks. It's part of why they'd decided on staying at the campgrounds rather than in town. Mickey couldn't hear them, but he could certainly enjoy pyrotechnic bursts of beauty against the night sky.

They were going home tomorrow, and thanks to the Jubilee police and the man and his big dog, with a happy ending to their vacation.

———

Alex Bing was back in his cabin, lying flat on his back, his belly full of the meal he'd eaten in town. The television was on, but he wasn't watching movies. He was watching the clock. It was already dark outside, but far too early to make a move on Dani Owens.

After learning she was living in a house, he'd had to change his plans. He was planning to access the house through the back door, using the privacy fence in the backyard as cover.

After that, it would be a simple matter to sneak into her bedroom and jab her with the syringe before she knew what was happening, and take pleasure in watching her die.

What he hadn't expected were the fireworks. When the first big boom sounded, he thought it was an explosion and ran outside in panic, looking for the sight of flames.

Instead, he saw the residents all sitting out in the yards in front of their tiny cabins, looking up at the sky. He heard a shrill, high-pitched whistle and then saw a burst of color and sound above him as a shower of blue and silver exploded across the sky.

"Son of a bitch. Fireworks. Who knew?" he muttered, and stomped back inside. He couldn't afford to make friends. He didn't want anyone to remember his face. So, he sat inside with his television on full blast, trying to drown out the noise.

———

Dani was in her bedroom getting ready for bed. She could hear Aaron dragging the quilts and his sleeping bag back out into the hall. She would never take for granted the sacrifices he was making to keep her safe.

Unaware he was on Dani's radar, Aaron made his bed, then began going through the house, double-checking locks and making a perimeter check. He was in the living room when a loud boom could be heard in the distance, followed by a barrage of pops and bangs.

Even though they were a distance away from Bullard Campgrounds, the sound of fireworks was easily audible in the valley between the surrounding mountains. Usually, he was already home by the time all this started, but he'd worked late often enough to have experienced it before.

But for Dani, this was not the case. When she heard the boom, followed by what sounded like a continuous round of gunfire, she flashed back on the night Tony had emptied his gun into the pillows on her bed and panicked.

She was running out of her bedroom screaming Aaron's name when he appeared at the end of the hall. She flew into his arms, wide-eyed and trembling in every muscle.

"What's happening? Is it him?" she cried.

"No, Dani, no! You're okay. It's fireworks from the campgrounds. I'm here. You're safe. You're safe," he kept saying.

"Oh my God," Dani said, and buried her face against his chest.

Aaron wrapped his arms around her and held her without talking until she quit shaking.

"I'm sorry…I didn't… I can't go back in…"

"Come here," Aaron said, and pulled her down onto the pallet in the hall with him. "Just sit here with me for a bit. You don't have to talk. If you fall asleep, then that's okay, too."

It was the tears rolling down her cheeks that did him in. He put his arm around her and pulled her close, tucking her head beneath his chin.

"Don't cry, honey. I've got this."

"I hate this! I hate being afraid. I hate feeling helpless!"

"The fireworks were a trigger. You have PTSD from all you've been through, and in time, it will pass. Hang on a minute. I'm going to turn out the lights."

Without his arms around her, Dani felt vulnerable again—naked to the world. She watched, wide-eyed and shaking, as he walked away. Then, one room at a time, the house began to go dark.

She could hear his footsteps as he moved from place to place, checking windows, checking doors, turning out lamps, until the house was in total darkness, save for a night-light in the hall.

Having Aaron Pope in her space was like having a wall to hide behind. As she waited, she kept thinking of how random their meeting had been. She didn't know what angel was responsible for it, but she would be forever grateful it had happened.

She saw a tall shadow appear against the wall as he came around the corner. He was back! Finally, she could relax.

"It's all good," he said as he sat back down beside her,

then pulled his gun out from beneath the pallet and put it beside him.

The last round of fireworks was over.

The house was quiet.

Dani's heartbeat was a roar within her ears.

She reached out, just to reassure herself he was there.

"I'm here and you're okay," he said.

"Yes, I am now," she said, and closed her eyes.

Aaron took her hand and held it. Was there enough love left in the world to heal women like Dani? Time would tell.

Minutes passed as he felt her grip loosening. When her breathing softened, he knew she'd fallen asleep. Instead of moving her back to her bedroom, he eased her down onto the pallet, stretched out beside her, and pulled the covers up over both of them, waiting and listening for sounds that didn't belong.

Alex Bing was antsy. This was taking longer than he'd planned, and he was wishing he'd done her the same night he hit Jubilee, instead of getting a place to stay. He could have been in and out and already gone.

It was all her fault. Switching up from an apartment to a house. And then there were the damn late-night workers filing into her neighborhood on their way home.

He'd been hoping and praying to hear from Tony, but he didn't know how all of that worked now. Sometimes he had a chance to call, but the days and times were random. He was worried that something might be wrong. What if the inmates were hurting him? He was in a fucking wheelchair, for God's sake. No cripple should be forced to be in prison. Even the monsters of the world deserved a little consideration.

When he finally left the campgrounds, it was after 1:00 a.m. He drove straight into the housing addition where Dani was living, relieved that most of the houses were dark, save for the streetlights.

———

When the neighborhood finally went quiet, Aaron relaxed. It was easier to discern what he was hearing when it wasn't drowned out by voices and traffic.

It was well after 1:00 a.m. when he heard the sound of a car moving through the neighborhood. He thought nothing of it other than noting the distinct sound of a slight knock in the engine and that the owner needed to get that car to a mechanic. But when he heard the same car pass by the house again a few minutes later, he bolted for the office, grabbed his laptop, and checked the app.

It was Bing!

Aaron stood in the dark, watching the blip on the screen as the car made yet another turn around the block.

Aaron bolted across the hall, glanced down at Dani, and then grabbed his gun. It might be nothing, but he was going to check it out. But as he moved through the house, he heard the same engine sound coming from behind the house.

Shit. The alley!

He hurried to the kitchen and parted the shades long enough to look out. The backyard was empty. Nothing was moving. And then he heard a faint squeak and focused directly on the gate. When he saw the silhouette of a man in a dark hoodie standing in the opening, he bolted for the hall, knelt down on the pallet and touched Dani's arm.

"Dani. Wake up," he whispered.

She sat up with a jerk. "What…?"

He put his finger over his lips, handed her his phone, then pointed to her office.

"In there. Close the door, get flat on the floor, and call 911. Tell them someone is breaking into your house," he whispered. "Hurry."

"Oh my God," she whispered, then threw back the covers, crawled across the hall straight into the other room and shut the door. Her fingers were trembling as she made the call, then went belly down, buried her face in her arms and went still.

Listening.

Waiting.

Praying.

———————

Alex had made enough passes through the neighborhood that he was satisfied with the silence. When he came back down her street again, he was driving with his lights off. He circled the block and pulled into the alley behind her house, then killed the engine, patted the pocket of his hoodie to make sure he had his lockpicks and the poison-filled syringe.

Seconds later he was out of the car and moving to the access gate. He opened it without caution, then winced at the unexpected squeak in the hinges, holding his breath as he watched the house for lights to come on or a door to open. But nothing happened. Satisfied he was still undetected, he breathed a sigh of relief and slipped through the gate, leaving it slightly ajar for a quick escape as he headed for the house.

Adrenaline was surging.

His heart was pounding.

This was for Tony.

Unaware of the carefully concealed security camera aimed straight at his approach, he reached the back door and took out his lockpick.

With Dani out of harm's way, Aaron watched Bing moving toward the house, but the moment he heard a footstep on the porch, he darted back into the shadows, still listening.

Bing was trying to pick the lock!

Aaron tensed. Tony Bing had brought a gun to the party. Would his brother do the same? The moment he heard a distinct click, he knew Bing had unlocked the back door. He held his breath, watching as the door swung inward. The deadly silence and the stealth with which the man had entered the house warned of his intent.

Aaron saw Bing slip his hand into his pocket and pull something out, but in the darkness, he couldn't tell what it was. Then he heard another sound, a slight *tick*. Either he'd taken a gun off safety, or something had dropped to the floor.

Aaron flipped on the light.

"Don't move!" Aaron shouted.

The stunned look on Bing's face was as unmistakable as the gun Aaron had aimed at his chest.

Alex was still holding the uncapped syringe. He'd never had a plan B, and the shock of being caught out this fast had taken him off guard.

Who the fuck is he? Where did he come from? Am I in the wrong house?

"On your knees! Hands behind your back!"

And then self-preservation kicked in. Alex spun and ran.

He was almost at the door when he was hit from behind in a flying tackle. The sheer size and weight of the man drove Alex's chin to the floor and crumpled his right arm beneath him, and in the fall, he stabbed himself with the needle as he fell on the plunger.

Fire. Pain. Nausea. Everything all at once. The concoction he'd brought to end Dani Owens's life was now inside of him.

This wasn't… Oh God. Mistake. Not me. Not me.

"Don't move!" the man kept shouting, but Alex was no longer in control of his body.

The room was spinning. Alex felt the man grabbing his arms and yanking them behind his back. He felt the handcuffs, but he couldn't focus for the fire burning through him. He couldn't swallow. He couldn't breathe. He had a faint sensation of being rolled over onto his back. In his mind, he was screaming. But in reality, there was no breath left to implement the act.

━━━━━━━━

The moment Aaron rolled him over, he saw the empty hypodermic needle projecting from Alex Bing's neck like a dart embedded on a pub wall.

That must have been what he'd pulled out of his pocket!

He put a finger on Bing's neck trying to find a pulse, but it was faint, and Bing had begun convulsing and foaming at the mouth. Then his eyes rolled back in his head, and his heartbeat ended.

Aaron was hearing sirens as he ran down the hall, opened the door, and turned on the light. Dani was on her belly against the far wall, and the look on her face marked the horror within her.

"He's down. You're safe," he said. "I hear sirens. Sit tight. It'll be a long night."

"What happened?" she asked.

"He fell on a needle full of whatever he'd brought for you. Stay where you are. You don't need to see that."

Dani stood.

"No. I need to see him for myself. I need to know the monster in the closet is dead."

"Okay. But no farther than the doorway. The kitchen is now a crime scene, and you can't touch anything. Look, then wait in the living room, okay?"

She nodded, but when he held out his hand, she took it.

Later, she would have no memory of their walk down the hall. Only the sight of Alex Bing lying at the back door with a syringe protruding from his neck. His face was contorted, his tongue swollen and protruding.

Dani was going into shock and Aaron saw it. He grabbed a blanket from his bed on the floor, led her into the living room, and, despite the heat outside, wrapped her in it.

"Sit here, baby," he said gently, and eased her down onto the sofa.

The horror of what had happened was beginning to sink in. Dani was beginning to shake. She was cold. So cold. When she looked up at Aaron, he saw the tears in her eyes.

The look on her face broke his heart. Without thinking, he leaned down, tucked the covers a little closer around her, and then kissed her cheek.

"You're in shock, but it's over. Trust me."

"I already gave you my trust when I let you in my front door," she said, and Aaron was torn between wanting to console her and needing to deal with the chaos. Police were at the door, and an ambulance was pulling up into the drive. Aaron let them in, and after that, everything became a blur.

———————

Thanks to the security cameras Sean had put up inside and outside the house, everything from Aaron and Dani's statements was corroborated by the captured footage, even Aaron's flying tackle as he took Bing down.

Alex Bing was dead by his own hand. Whatever he'd planned to use on Dani would show up in a tox screen when they performed the autopsy.

And then the chief turned up at the scene.

He saw Aaron's bed in the hall, and then Dani curled up on the sofa.

"Is she okay?" Sonny asked.

Aaron glanced at her. "She will be."

"Does she need to go to the hospital?"

"No, sir. Bing never touched her, or me, for that matter. When he saw me and my gun, he turned and ran. I tackled *him* at the door. I didn't even see the syringe until after I had him cuffed. It was only after I turned him over that I saw it. Seconds later, he was dead. It'll be interesting to find out what comes back on the tox screens."

"How did you know he was in the area?" Sonny asked.

"I put a tracker on his car. Sometime after midnight I began hearing the same car driving back and forth past the house, so I got up and checked the tracking app on my laptop. It was Bing. Then I saw the car had stopped in the alley behind the house. When I saw him sneaking in through the back gate, I hid Dani, told her to call 911, and waited. He picked the lock on the back door and came in. I turned on the light with my gun aimed, ordering him to get on his knees. He turned and ran. I took him down at the door."

"Does the investigating team know about his vehicle?" Sonny asked.

"I told them where it was. It will be towed to the lab."

Sonny nodded. "There's no need to put you on administrative leave because you never fired your weapon, but I'm taking you off duty for today. You and Dani will need to come into the station to sign your statements later."

"Yes, sir," Aaron said.

"Good enough," Sonny said. "We can't move the body until the medical examiner arrives. He's driving in from Bowling Green and is about fifteen minutes out. And we'll have to search Bing's hotel room."

"He was staying in one of the tiny cabins out at Reagan Bullard's campgrounds," Aaron said.

"Do you know if he has any next of kin other than the twin who's in prison?"

"I think his parents are still living. Dani will know. The mother is the one who called Dani to warn her, remember?"

"Right!" Sonny said. "We'll get that info from you later."

"If there's nothing else, I'm going to check on Dani," Aaron said, and headed to the living room.

Dani was curled up on the sofa, the blanket pulled up beneath her chin and her gaze fixed on the wall. She couldn't get the sight of Alex's face out of her mind and couldn't quit shaking. If it hadn't been for Alex's mother, she wouldn't have known he was in the area, and if it hadn't been for Aaron, she would be dead. It was a fact.

She'd blocked out the sounds of all the people who'd invaded her space. She'd so loved this little cottage, but this had tarnished it. What happened had sucked all the air from within these walls. It was hard to breathe without screaming.

Then she heard footsteps, and all of a sudden, Aaron was picking her up from where she was lying, blanket and all. Before she knew his intent, he turned around and sat down with her in his lap, tucked the blanket tighter around her, then pulled her close.

"We're waiting on the medical examiner. Chief said it'll be about fifteen minutes more before he arrives."

"I can't imagine what the neighbors are thinking," Dani muttered.

"I've already talked to Benny. He lives next door and works at the PD, remember? He knows there was an intruder. He and Lisa were worried about you. I told them you were upset but unhurt. Is that okay with you?"

"Yes."

He heard the tremble in her voice and saw the tears on her face.

"I'm so sorry this happened, but it's over. Concentrate on that. The only person who still holds a grudge against you is in a wheelchair and he will likely die in prison. You are well and truly safe now. Take a deep breath and close your eyes. I've got you."

Her heard her inhale, then felt the exhale of her breath against his arm. Minute by minute, he felt the tension in her body easing. And because he could do it unobserved now, watched her fall the rest of the way asleep, and thought what it might be like to fall asleep with her in his arms and wake up to her beautiful face every morning.

The ME finally arrived, did the initial inspection of the body, got the pictures he wanted, and then they removed the body and took it back to Bowling Green for an autopsy.

Aaron's partner, Yancy, was on scene, and as everyone began filing out of the house, he and another officer stayed behind to do a quick cleanup, then locked up the back of the house and paused in the hall to let Aaron know.

"We tried to put the room back together," he said. "The back is locked up, and we'll lock the front on our way out. Sorry this happened to your girl."

"She's not my—"

Aaron stopped. He couldn't say the words. Instead, he nodded and watched as they turned the lock, then pulled the front door shut behind them.

After the chaos from before, silence made the house

feel empty. He didn't want to let her go, but she wasn't his to hold. Instead, he brushed a kiss across the top of her head, then pulled her a little closer and stood with her still in his arms.

She stirred.

"It's okay," he said softly, and carried her through the house and back into her bedroom. She roused as he was laying her down.

"What's happening?"

"Everyone's gone. It's over, honey." Then he pulled the covers up over her and brushed the hair from her forehead.

She rolled over onto her side.

He straightened the covers and was about to turn out the lamp when he saw fresh tears on her face.

"Leave the light."

"Okay," he said, and gave her shoulder a gentle squeeze.

"If you need anything, I'll be right outside your door."

She sighed.

He walked out of the room and went straight to the kitchen, found a mop bucket and a mop, filled the bucket with water, poured a cup of pine-scented cleaner into the water, and mopped the entire kitchen from one corner to the other, then mopped the pathway from the front door where the police had come through, wiped down every surface in the kitchen, and turned out the lights.

He paused, then inhaled. Everything felt clean again.

He took his gun back to the office and put it up,

then laid down in his sleeping bag and closed his eyes. Within seconds, he heard her voice.

"Aaron, are you there?"

He sighed, then got up and walked into her room.

"I'm here," he said, and stretched out on top of the covers beside her. "I'm here."

As he was falling asleep, the last conscious thought he had was that he no longer had an excuse to be under the same roof with her. She didn't need a bodyguard anymore, but he needed her.

Charlie Raines was going home, and his parents were overjoyed.

The long frightening hours of uncertainty were over for Ray and Betty, and no one was happier than Charlie.

He didn't feel safe. Would never feel safe again until he knew the man who'd shot him was behind bars. An orderly was taking him to the elevator in a wheelchair. His mother was walking beside him, and they'd told him his dad was waiting in the breezeway with the car.

Nurses on the floor were all telling him goodbye, and he was carrying a giant teddy bear his classmates had sent him. It was all positive and good, but he felt like he was escaping.

And then they were outside, and his dad was coming toward him when the heat of the sun on his face suddenly registered, and tears rolled.

Betty grabbed his hand. "Charlie, honey, what's wrong?"

"Last time I remember the sun on my face was right before he shot me."

"You're safe, son," Ray said, and helped Charlie stand, then eased him into the front seat of their car, while Betty climbed into the back seat. Ray leaned over Charlie to fasten his seat belt, and then paused and looked his son straight in the eyes. "You're going home. You're alive, and you're safe. God saved you. Remember that."

Charlie shuddered. "Yes, sir."

Ray closed the door and circled the car to get in.

"Did you eat breakfast good?" he asked.

Charlie rolled his eyes. "Hospital food is not my mama's cooking."

"You're in for a treat when we get home. Your mama has been cooking for two days."

"Then let's blow this joint," Charlie said.

They were laughing as they drove away.

———

Aaron had awakened before sunrise to the sound of someone breathing beside him, and remembered.

He opened his eyes and saw her then, lips slightly parted. Eyelashes fluttering from wherever her dreams had taken her. Beautifully arched brows as dark as her hair. The faint indentations on her cheeks were where the dimples hid. He didn't see them nearly often enough, but he knew they were there.

There was an ethereal look to her face that belied the true strength within her. The brutality of her recent past had taken its toll. She was a shade too thin, but so beautiful in his eyes. He lay watching her sleep until sunlight began to filter through the curtains. She was waking up, and he didn't want her to know that he'd been watching, so he turned his head and closed his eyes, giving her total control of his presence.

―――――――

Dani woke just after sunrise. Her heart skipped when she saw Aaron stretched out asleep on the bed beside her. She vaguely remembered calling out to him, and then feeling the mattress give from his weight. After that, nothing.

Her first thought at the sight of him sleeping was how handsome he was. Long lashes as black as his hair. High cheekbones. Straight nose with a tiny hint of a bump. Shoulders so wide he didn't quite fit where he was lying. So tall his feet were hanging over the foot of the bed. And with a heart as big as he was. He'd taken off the bandage she'd put on his forehead, and the butterfly strips looked like a tiny zipper holding him together.

She had feelings for him that she didn't know what to do with. Was she attracted to him because he made her feel safe? Because he was the knight in shining armor she'd always dreamed of? Was it lust, or was it the beginning of real love? She didn't know. She wasn't sure of anything but the certainty that she didn't want him to just disappear from her life just because the danger was gone. She didn't want these last few moments with him to end, but today was going to be a day of more chaos.

"Aaron?" she said softly.

He reached toward her, his hand on her arm before he opened his eyes.

"I'm here," he said.

"What happens today?" Dani asked.

"We have to go to the police station and give official statements, and the chief needs a contact number to notify Bing's parents. You said his mother called you. Do you still have that number?"

"Yes, it'll be on my phone. I can't imagine how she's going to feel, finding out her alert saved me, but got him killed."

Aaron frowned. "There's no guilt for either of you, damn it. He killed himself," then rolled over and cupped the side of her face. "You're a survivor, Dani. You're already okay."

"Thanks to you," she said.

Their gazes locked. A long moment of silence passed between them. Aaron had two choices, and the first one was not a good idea. Not here. Not now.

"I'll go make coffee. You get first dibs on the shower," he said, then got out of bed and left the room.

Dani didn't know whether to be relieved or bothered

that he hadn't tried something. Either way, the day was ahead of them, and so was his exit from her house. He'd go home, and she'd be here. Maybe he'd call, and maybe he wouldn't. She didn't like the options, but it was out of her control, so she threw back the covers. It was time to begin the day, but after last night, she was dreading walking back into the kitchen.

She showered, then came out of the bathroom in her bathrobe and shouted down the hall.

"I'm out of the shower!"

"I'm next!" Aaron answered.

Dani heard the water running as she got dressed. He was still in the bathroom when she left her room. Her stomach knotted as she moved down the hall, dreading her first sight of the kitchen. Last night there had been a dead man by the door.

But her fears were unfounded as she turned the corner. Sunlight was pouring into the kitchen from every window. The floor was shining. The room smelled of her pine-scented cleaner and fresh coffee. Not a trace of last night's chaos was visible.

"Oh, Aaron. If I wasn't already falling for you, I would be now," she whispered, then poured herself a cup of coffee and took it outside to drink.

The porch swing squeaked as she sat down and pushed off with her toe, letting it swing as she took her first sip. In her mind, she could almost hear her mother's voice.

"*Today is the day that the Lord has made. Rejoice and be glad in it.*"

Chapter 13

IT WAS THE SQUEAK OF THE CHAIN THAT LED AARON to the back porch. He paused in the doorway as she turned.

"Being alive this morning means more than usual to me. Everything is so beautiful," she said.

"Yes, it is," he said, but he was looking at her.

She eyed his forehead. "The cut on your head. Did it bleed in the shower again?"

"A little. It's fine."

She frowned. "No. It's not *fine*. It's not *fine* until it stops bleeding."

"Yes, ma'am. I'm ready to go when you are."

She rolled her eyes and walked past him, setting her empty coffee cup in the sink.

"I need to go get my purse," she said, and walked out of the room.

Aaron was right where she'd left him when she came back, and when they exited through the utility room into the garage, his hand was in the middle of her back, gently guiding the way.

Cameron entered the front door of the police station as Aaron and Dani came into the lobby from the back.

The moment Dani walked in, she recognized Cameron, and he recognized her.

"You're Dani, the girl from the parking lot!" he said.

"I am, and seeing you and Aaron together, it's no wonder I first thought he was you."

"What?" Aaron asked.

Dani began to explain. "I saw Cameron in the supermarket parking lot the other day. He was a distance away, and at first, I thought he was you. By the time I realized it wasn't, he'd caught me staring. When I apologized for mistaking him, he cleared up the confusion."

"We can't deny the Pope in all of us, and I better get in gear," Cameron said. "I'm off to spend a little time with an ancestor."

"Still reading the journal?" Aaron asked.

Cameron nodded. "Yes, and I left Rusty and Ghost at home today. She's not feeling good this morning, and Ghost is babysitting…literally. We're expecting," he added.

Aaron grinned. "Congratulations! When is she due?"

"It's early days. She's not quite three months along."

"What do you think about the journal? Found anything else interesting besides learning Meg was Chickasaw and not Choctaw?"

"Not yet. But if Aunt Ella says there's a secret in it, I should know something by the end of the day."

Dani waited until he was gone to ask. "Nobody knows it was me who found it, right?"

"Only a few of us at the PD. You're still incognito. Now let's get the statements made and signed. We need to stop by the chief's office first and give him Mrs. Bing's phone number," Aaron said, and walked her down the hall and knocked on Sonny Warren's door.

"Come in!" Sonny called, then stood as they entered his office.

"Good morning. Have a seat," Sonny said. "Were you able to get any rest last night?"

"A little. You asked about contact info for Mrs. Bing?" Aaron said.

"Yes, do you have a number?" Sonny asked.

Dani pulled up the number from Arlene Bing's phone call, then handed him her phone.

"Yes, I do. Her name is Arlene Bing."

Sonny wrote it down. "And she called you to warn you?" Sonny asked.

"Yes," Dani said, and quickly explained about the tracking app his mother had put on his phone before he disappeared. "Right before she disconnected, she was crying," Dani said. "She said something was wrong with her sons. She and her husband didn't understand it or know why, but they'd been afraid of them for years."

"Psychopaths come in all shapes and sizes," Sonny said. "I appreciate the info. Glad you're both okay. I think there's a detective waiting for you in interview room three."

"Yes, sir. Thank you," Aaron said, and escorted Dani out of the chief's office.

While they went to give their official statements, Sonny Warren made the call.

Arlene Bing was at the breakfast table working the daily crossword in her local paper. Her coffee was getting cold, and she'd been unable to finish her food. The knot in her stomach was too hard and too tight to accommodate sustenance.

Her graying hair was long overdue for a coloring. She hadn't put on makeup in weeks. And she and her husband no longer addressed the issue of the elephant in the room. They couldn't even look at each other when they spoke.

She knew Alex was still in Jubilee. But she doubted he was there for the fun. When she'd called Dani Owens, she'd had a horrible feeling that Alex had tracked her there, and felt obligated to warn her. Afterward, she was both heartsick and relieved. Relieved that she'd alerted Dani, and heartsick that she'd had to betray her son to keep someone else safe.

She took a sip of the lukewarm coffee as she read the next crossword clue.

22 Down—*waiting for news*

She counted the spaces. A twelve-letter word for…
"*Anticipating*?" Arlene mumbled, and it fit!

But before she could write it down, her phone rang, and when she saw the caller ID, she froze.

Jubilee Police Department? As in Jubilee, Kentucky? Her hands were trembling when she picked up the call.

"Hello."

"This is Chief Warren of the Jubilee Police Department calling for Mrs. Arlene Bing."

She started crying. "I'm Arlene. Is he dead? Is my son dead?"

Sonny blinked. "Yes, ma'am. I am sorry for your loss."

"What happened? What did he do?"

Sonny quickly explained.

Arlene was too shocked to cry.

"Is Dani okay? Did he hurt her?"

"She's okay. Your warning saved her life."

There was a moment of silence, and then Sonny heard her crying. He began to explain about where her son's body was, and that she would be notified when it was released.

"Again, I'm sorry to have to give you this news," he said.

"My sons…they never fit in this world. Maybe now we can all find some peace."

The line went dead in Sonny's ear. He hung up, then sat for a few moments in silence, staring at the wall and remembering a line from *Macbeth*, a play he'd seen once in college.

Something wicked this way comes.

How horrifying it must have been for this mother to know she'd given birth to such madness.

———————————

Aaron and Dani were silent all the way back to her house. They both knew his departure was imminent, but neither knew how the other felt about it. When he reached the house, he pulled up into the drive, but didn't open the garage door. Instead, he took the remote from the visor and handed it to her.

They both exited the car at the same time, then Aaron unlocked the door and stepped aside for her to enter. As soon as they were inside, he laid the extra key on the table by the door.

"It won't take me long to get my stuff out of your way," he said.

"You were never in the way," Dani said.

Aaron started to say something, then shook off the thought and went to gather up his stuff.

Dani took herself to the living room and sat down, listening to him moving back and forth across the hall, gathering up his toiletries from the shared bathroom and putting the quilts he'd used beneath his sleeping bag back in the linen closet, then carrying his suitcase and sleeping bag out to his car.

When he came back inside, Dani was standing in the hall, trying not to cry.

"I think I have everything, but if you run across a stray item I've left behind, just let me know," he said.

Dani took a deep breath. The speech she'd prepared was stuck in her throat, and all that came out was her truth.

"I will never be able to thank you enough for your generosity and sacrifice. You didn't have to do any of this, and still you chose to, out of the goodness of your heart. I owe you my life, and I am forever in your debt," she said.

"You owe me nothing. I did it because it was the right thing to do, and because you matter to me. Probably more than you care to know. You've been through hell, and I'm afraid to touch you for fear you'd get the wrong idea. I don't want this to be the last time we see each other. I don't want to lose this connection, but I won't ask you for more than you're willing to give," Aaron said.

"I've already given you my trust. If you want more than that, then don't quit me. You know where I live."

Seconds later, she was in his arms.

He moaned as she melted against him, and then her feet came off the floor. Now the wall was at her back and Aaron was holding her, suspended in an embrace that lasted all the way through one long, mind-numbing kiss. When he finally put her down, she was shaking.

There was a long moment of silence as they stood, foreheads touching, feeling the warmth of each other's breath, waiting for their rocketing heartbeats to settle.

Finally, Aaron slipped a finger beneath her chin and tilted her head until their gazes were locked.

"That's what I want," he said softly. "You. In my life."

"I'm already here," Dani said. "Don't forget to take your key before you leave."

His dark eyes flashed, and then he kissed her again, slower, softer, before he stopped.

"Leaving you behind isn't going to be easy, but you're worth the wait."

"I'm going to miss you so much," she said.

"I'm only a phone call away," he said. "Try and get some rest today. Maybe tomorrow after work, I can take you out to eat?"

"I would love that," Dani said, then watched from the doorway as he drove away before she went back inside.

The house felt empty and too quiet, but it felt safe, and she was tired. So tired. From the day she'd found that journal to this moment, her life had been in upheaval.

But now, thanks to Aaron, there was nothing left to hurt her. No one left to fear. There were a dozen different things she could have done to spend this day, but she was crashing. Every step felt like she was walking through mud. Her eyes felt heavy. It was all she could do to get back to her room, and once she did, the bed beckoned.

She kicked off her shoes and stripped out of her clothes, before crawling into bed naked. Soft pillows cushioned her head. As she closed her eyes, the weight of the covers enveloped her. The last thing she heard was the air-conditioning kick on, and then sleep claimed her.

Aaron's drive back up the mountain gave him time to think. He'd been so worried about keeping Dani alive that their time together had felt more like hiding. Knowing she wanted to pursue a relationship was the best feeling he'd had in a very long time.

His mother was outside watering the flowers when he pulled up and parked. She waved, then turned off the water and went to meet him.

"Hey honey! Good to see you! Is everything okay?" Shirley asked.

"Yes. It is now. Let me get my stuff inside and I'll tell you all about it."

"Betty and Ray brought Charlie home today," she said.

"That's great news! It's a good day all around," Aaron said, and then looked up as the door opened and Sean emerged.

"Hey bro! Is this a visit or what?" he asked.

"I'm home. Help me carry stuff in, will you?"

Sean frowned. "Is it over? Is Dani okay?"

Aaron nodded. "Help me get this stuff inside and I'll fill you in on what happened," and then he did, beginning with the end.

"I'll tell you now that the man who was stalking Dani is dead, by his own hand. And Sean, the security you installed was invaluable. There's footage of every time he drove past her house last night, of him coming into Dani's backyard and breaking into her house, thanks to all of the cameras you installed. Everything was recorded. Both of our statements have been backed up by the footage. There are no misconceptions. No concerns of any kind that this was anything other than another attempt on Dani's life."

Sean shook his head. "You're the one who camped out to stand guard. You're the one who put his life on the line, and you're the one who saved her."

"I know she's alive, but emotionally…how is she?" Shirley asked.

"Before, she was triggered by every little sound and noise. It was traumatizing all over again, but this time, it's over. I think there's a sense of relief just knowing there's no one left with a grudge against her. It was the stalker's own mother who called and warned her that he was in Jubilee, or this could have had a far different ending."

"I can't imagine being a mother and knowing your children are capable of such evil," Shirley said.

Aaron shrugged. "Psychopaths are born broken, and she had two of them. It's a tragedy all the way around, but she's safe and that's all that matters to me."

"So, you moved into her life and moved out three days later. How do you feel about that?" Sean asked.

"Lonesome," Aaron said, and then grinned. "Does that satisfy your curiosity enough?"

"Sean, don't start," Shirley said. "Aaron's girl. Aaron's business. Go find one of your own."

Sean laughed. "Maybe I'll join one of those online dating sites. Meet myself a crazy girl scamming for a sugar daddy."

"You don't have the income to be a sugar daddy," Aaron said.

Both brothers burst into laughter.

Shirley rolled her eyes and left them sitting.

———————

Later that night, and after everyone had retired to their rooms for the night, Aaron was still up, missing the sound of Dani's voice and unsettled within himself. Tired of television, and too antsy to focus on reading anything, he grabbed a beer from the refrigerator and went out onto the back porch and sat down in the swing.

The day had been hot and sultry, but up here on the mountain, it was degrees cooler and with an intermittent breeze. The sky above had turned midnight blue, revealing stars a billion light-years away.

He took a sip of the beer and then set it aside. He'd thought he wanted it, but he was wrong. What he wanted was her.

———————

Dani had done everything she could to put off going to bed. She was no longer afraid of who might come into the house, but when she closed her eyes, there was no door she could shut to keep out the dreams.

For all the nights Aaron had been here, all she'd had to do was call out to know he was there. But tonight, there was no one within reach of the sound of her voice to answer if she called.

Finally, she made a final sweep through the house just to reassure herself she was safely locked in, and headed for bed, turning out lights as she went.

The lamp was on by her bed, lighting her way across the room. At the last moment, she turned around and went back, and shut and locked her bedroom door, and then sat down on the bed, trying to psyche herself up to get in it and turn out the last light.

Her cell phone was on the charger as she started to turn off the lamp, and then she picked up her phone instead and called Aaron.

It rang twice, and then he answered.

"Dani?"

She sighed. "I just needed to hear your voice."

"I'm here. Are you afraid?"

"Just a little jumpy, I guess."

"Don't be. I'll always be here for you, and I'll see you tomorrow."

"Yes, tomorrow, and sorry I called so late," Dani said.

"I wasn't asleep. Couldn't sleep. But now that I've heard your voice, maybe I can, too."

The call ended.

Dani turned off the lamp and then crawled into bed.

Aaron finished his beer, then said good night to the mountain and went inside.

The next day, Tony Bing had visitors.

His parents had arrived.

They hadn't once visited the prison since his incarceration, and to learn they were both waiting to talk to him felt off. When the guard pushed his wheelchair into the visiting area and he saw their faces, completely devoid of expression, he knew he'd been right.

As soon as the guard parked Tony's wheelchair at the table where his parents were sitting, then backed off, Tony went on the defense.

"Well, I haven't seen you two since they hauled my ass out of the courtroom. What's up? Did you come to tell me you won the lottery or something?"

Tony thought his father would respond, but it was his mother who spoke up, and there was so much rage in her voice, he actually recoiled.

"No. We came to tell you Alex is dead. He was trying to finish the hell you two set in motion with Dani Owens, and killed himself by his own stupidity. He fell on a syringe full of the poison he'd intended for her."

Shock rolled through Tony in waves. Then he began to weep.

"Oh my God! No, no, no! How will I go on?" he wailed.

Arlene was so angry she was shaking. She leaned forward, her voice barely above a whisper.

"How will you go on? What the hell kind of question is that? Even now you don't see your own truth. What you did put you here. And what Alex did ended his life.

I don't know what is wrong with you two, but neither of you got like you are from lack of love. As far as I'm concerned, the children I raised died a long time ago."

Tony was in shock. His parents had always been in the background of their adult lives, but still an anchor. And they'd just cut him adrift alone.

"You don't mean that!" he cried.

At that point, his father unloaded. "Shut up, Anthony. Your tears are selfish tears. I have watched your mother grieve in ways you will never understand. You and Alexander reaped your own bitter harvest. We're through here."

Tony laid his head down on the table, weeping copiously as they left him sitting. The guard rolled him back to his cell, and when the lock clicked behind him, it was an audible endnote to life as he'd known it.

The same morning that Tony Bing got the news about his brother's death, Cameron Pope reached the end of the journal, and as he was reading the last posts, what happened to Charlie Raines began to make sense. He jumped up from his chair and headed for Sonny Warren's office.

The door was open. Cameron walked in talking.

"The man who shot Charlie! He was looking for gold!"

Sonny looked up. "What? What the hell would—?"

"It's in the last part of the journal. Two things

happened on the same day. Brendan Pope's wife, Meg, went up the mountain to pick berries on the same day that a troop of Confederate soldiers came through Jubilee with a wagon reported to be carrying rebel gold to fund their war. When Meg didn't come back, they organized a search party and followed her trail up the mountain, following the creek. They found dozens of boot prints, a lot of blood, and an overturned basket of berries at Big Falls. Brendan thought of the soldiers and followed their trail back out to the road."

"Holy shit, Cameron! Did they take her?" Sonny asked.

"They never saw any of her footprints after they began tracking the soldiers, but they found the wagon abandoned on the side of the trail with a broken wheel. Their theory was that after the wagon broke down, the soldiers carried the gold into the woods, got as far as the falls to hide it, and walked up on Meg. Now she was a witness to where they were going to hide the gold. They followed the soldiers' trail up the mountain for miles until they came upon what was left of the troop. There'd been some kind of gunfight. They were all dead, and no sign of Meg. Brendan and the searchers went back to Jubilee, believing the soldiers had likely killed Meg and hid her body wherever they hid the gold. I think the man who shot Charlie came upon this journal somewhere and came looking for gold, and Charlie surprised him."

"That could very well be," Sonny said. He couldn't tell Cameron they already had an eyewitness who'd seen their man with a gun, a metal detector, and a shovel, but knowing this, it fit what they already knew about the shooter.

"Good work! I'll let Sheriff Woodley know. On another note, did they ever find Meg's body?"

"No, and my family is going to be devastated when they hear this. This has to be what Aunt Ella was referring to. Why her mother would never read her the end of the journal. Because Brendan's wife went up the mountain to pick berries and never came home."

"That's a tragedy you don't get over," Sonny said. "I can't imagine how Brendan Pope felt."

"I know how I'd feel if I lost Rusty," Cameron said. "Oh...I left the journal in the interview room. Should I bring it to you?"

"No need. I'll get it and return it to the evidence room," Sonny said.

"Thank you for giving me access. I want permission to scan the entire journal. I'm going to make copies and have them bound for our families. I suppose it will go back to the Library of Congress when this is over. It's probably safer there than risking another house fire like Aunt Ella mentioned. I can't imagine how it wound up being donated, but I'm happy to know it still exists," Cameron said.

"Absolutely," Sonny said. "Give Rusty my best, and I hear congratulations are in order with a baby on the way."

"Thanks. We're pretty excited," Cameron said. "If we can be of further help, all you have to do is ask."

Cameron left the station, conflicted by what he'd

learned. Nearly two hundred years had passed since Brendan Pope came to Kentucky, and then some thirty years afterward, his wife goes missing on Pope Mountain. The chances were, she was still up there somewhere, waiting to be found. This was something they all needed to know.

———————

The next morning, the chief caught Aaron in the hall after roll call and told him about what Cameron had discovered in the journal.

Aaron was in shock, first about the reason for Charlie being shot, and then learning about their missing ancestor.

"He was hunting for treasure?" Aaron said.

Sonny nodded. "From what Cameron read, the soldiers who were hiding the gold got Meg killed, and it nearly got Charlie killed when someone went looking for it."

Aaron thought back to Dani's first statement. "Dani did mention a metal detector and a shovel in her initial witness statement, which fits in with what we've just learned, and explains why the man was willing to risk trespassing."

"Speaking of Miss Owens, how's she doing this morning?" Sonny asked.

"Don't know. I went home yesterday, but I'm seeing her later."

"So, it's not all just business between you two anymore?"

Aaron didn't answer.

Sonny grinned.

"As you were, Officer Pope. Go find some lawbreakers."

"Doing my best," Aaron said, and left the precinct.

———————

Dani was both excited and anxious.

She had a date, and she had expectations but didn't know if she and Aaron were on the same page. Growing up, she'd always loved surprises, but after all she'd been through, uncertainty meant *unsafe*, and she'd dumped a lot of trouble into Aaron Pope's lap without really knowing the man.

However, after the last three days, she knew enough. She knew he hadn't taken advantage of her. She knew he'd kept his word. And she knew yesterday when he'd kissed her goodbye that she didn't want to see him go. The fact that he wanted to see her again was a small miracle. Even after all he knew about her, after all the danger her trouble had put him in, he wanted to see her again. It felt like high school all over again, waiting for her date for the prom, only better.

Aaron wasn't sixteen, didn't have acne, and wasn't driving his mother's green Pinto. And when he kissed her, their teeth didn't bump, and he knew where to put his hands. Not all over her, like her prom date. But gently, and in the right spots. She knew they were going out to eat. After that was anybody's guess.

Chapter 14

Aaron changed clothes at the police station before leaving to gas up his SUV, then he swung by the ATM where he banked, made a quick stop at a flower shop for a mixed bouquet of flowers, then headed to her house.

After her phone call last night, he'd thought about her all day and what kissing her had felt like.

Like coming home.

And that was scary.

He'd fallen too hard, too fast, and was so damn scared of losing her he couldn't think straight. Tonight had to be about setting boundaries, and she had to be the one to call the shots. What he wanted was obvious. He wanted her. But it was what she wanted that had to matter first.

His pulse kicked with anticipation as he took the turn into the housing addition, pulled into her drive, and got out with the flowers. He had a key, but he wasn't taking anything for granted and rang the doorbell instead.

The simple act of dressing for a date had Dani anticipating the evening. She was wearing her favorite summer dress made of a cotton-blend fabric with a floral design in shades of blue and green on a white background, and green ballerina flats for easy walking, and had let her hair dry into curls.

The finishing touches were small gold hoops in her ears and the necklace her parents gave her when she graduated college—a single pearl on a gold chain resting just above the crevice between her breasts.

She sat down to wait, but not for long. Minutes later, her doorbell rang.

He's here!

She made herself walk, not run, but when she opened the door, the first thought in her mind bordered on lust. Black hair, dark eyes, that olive cast to his skin, and in his dark jeans and white shirt, he was looking too hot to handle and he came bearing flowers.

"For you," he said.

She smiled. "They're beautiful. Come in."

"Not as beautiful as you," he said, and shut the door behind him.

"You talk as pretty as you look," she said. "Have a seat. I need to put these in water before we go."

She left the room, but Aaron didn't sit. And when she came back, he was still standing in the same place, waiting to see if she looked as gorgeous coming toward him as she had walking away.

He sighed. She'd scored a ten without trying.

"Are you ready?"

She didn't hesitate. "I've been ready for this moment all day," and took the hand he offered as they walked out of the house together.

Moments later they were backing out of the drive and headed into town. It was so normal and so wonderful to be going on a date with Aaron Pope that it almost felt like a dream. Dani kept glancing at his profile and then looking away, and knew he was aware of it. So, she blurted out the first thing she could think of to explain herself. Even if it was a lie.

"Looks like the cut on your head is healing. Does it still hurt?" she asked.

"Not a bit. You're a good doctor," he said. "I have a reservation at The Back Porch. Have you eaten there yet?"

"No, but I love to try new places," she said.

"It will be crowded, but so is every place in Jubilee at mealtimes. It's good, and that's what matters. Afterward, if you're not too tired, I thought we might drop by Trapper's Bar and Grill. I've seen you dancing around the kitchen, and they have a live band and a good-size dance floor."

"I would love that!" she said.

Aaron grinned. "I had a feeling you might."

A few minutes later, they'd reached their destination. After finding a place to park, they went inside and were soon seated in a small booth against a wall of windows. The windows overlooked the wraparound porch and

286 SHARON SALA

the myriad assortment of hanging baskets overflowing with flowers and ferns.

Bluegrass music was playing faintly in the background beneath the rumble of diners' voices. Every so often laughter would break out at a nearby table or from across the room. The aromas coming from the kitchen were enticing, and the ambiance of the whole place was like being at a family reunion without knowing all the relatives.

"I love this place," Dani said as she opened her menu. "Thank you for bringing me."

Aaron reached across the table and grasped her hand. "It's pure selfishness on my part. I like being with you. And forgive me for changing the subject, but you have the bluest eyes I've ever seen. They're beautiful."

She smiled.

"And the dimples are icing."

"I cannot take credit for either of those assets," Dani said. "I have my father's eyes and my mother's smile, dimples and all."

"Then God bless the both of them for sharing," Aaron said.

She laughed.

The conversation shifted to ordering food and then trading work stories while they ate. Two hours later, they were back in his car and headed to Trapper's Bar and Grill.

They'd spent two hours on a meal that could have easily counted as foreplay, and once he got her out on the dance floor, he would have her right where he wanted her—in his arms. Where it went from there was anybody's guess. Music was rocking out into the night as they pulled into the parking lot.

"Sounds like the party's already started," Aaron said, and held out his hand as they headed toward the entrance.

Dani grasped it and held on for all she was worth as they walked into Trapper's.

One song had just ended as they found a table. The band struck a chord, then went into a slow Willie Nelson classic, "Always on My Mind."

"I think they're playing our song," Aaron said as he slipped his arm around her waist, settled the flat of his hand against her lower back, and swung her out into the crowd of dancers.

Cheek to cheek.

Heart to heart.

Their bodies moving in perfect synchrony.

Waltzing her around the floor.

The next song segued into another old song by the Kentucky Headhunters called "Dumas Walker," which called for a lively two-step. Half the people in the bar were singing along with the band, and the other half were dancing.

Three dances later, the band took a fifteen-minute break, so they returned to their table and ordered drinks. While they were waiting for their order, Aaron's patrol partner, Bob Yancy, saw them and came up to say hello.

"Hey, buddy, introduce me to your pretty lady."

Aaron grinned. "Dani, this is my partner, Bob Yancy. Bob, this is Dani Owens. She's recently moved here and will be teaching at the elementary school this fall."

"Pleasure to meet you, Dani. Welcome to Jubilee. My wife Jilly and I have kids in that school. One starting kindergarten, and one going into second grade."

"I'm teaching first grade," Dani said. "Maybe I'll have your little one in my class next year."

"Speaking of Jilly, where is she?" Aaron asked.

Bob pointed at the bar. "See those three women with their heads together at the end of the bar. Jilly's the blond, and they're plotting a baby shower for one of their girlfriends. When conversations go all girlie and every other phrase is 'That's so cute,' I find something else to do."

Dani laughed.

"Saw you two dancing earlier. Nice moves," Bob said. "Enjoy your evening."

The waitress brought their drinks as he moved back into the crowd.

"He seems nice," Dani said.

Aaron nodded. "He's a good partner," and then he picked up his drink. "A toast," he said. "To strong women with gentle hearts."

"And to heroes everywhere," Dani said, her eyes welling as their glasses clinked, and then they both took a drink.

Dani looked away as she put down her glass, but Aaron had seen the sudden shimmer in her eyes and knew she was battling back tears.

Aaron held out his hand, palm up.

Dani looked up at him and then slipped her hand in his, shivering slightly as his grasp tightened.

"It's all good," Aaron said. "No pressure. No demands. If all you need is a friend, then I'm up for the job. Just me enjoying your beautiful self and your fine company, okay?"

She looked up at him and sighed. "Yes, it *is* all good, thanks to you. As for whatever you're offering, you already drew a Get-Out-of-Jail-Free card, passed Go, and are well on your way to winning the game."

Aaron shook his head, then leaned forward so that only she could hear.

"I don't play games, sweetheart, and the only thing I want to win is your trust…and maybe one day, your heart."

The words were still ringing in Dani's ears when the band returned. The first song they played was a ballad. Moments later, she was in Aaron's arms, moving around the floor. And the longer he held her, the more certain she was that it was where she belonged.

When she finally laid her head on Aaron's shoulder, it was like levitating. She was as happy at that moment as she'd ever been.

It was after 1:00 a.m. when Aaron pulled up into Dani's drive. They got out, walking hand in hand to the door, then inside.

"I'm going to do a walk-through to make sure you're secure," Aaron said.

"You don't have to—"

"Shh," he said softly, and stopped her words with a brief kiss. "Yes, I do," he said and left her standing in the hall.

Dani's heart was pounding. All she had to do was say the word and they'd be in bed. That much she knew. But it still felt like too soon, so she waited, listening to his footsteps moving from room to room, and then back again to where she was standing.

"You're good to go, darlin', and from that sleepy look in your eyes, I think you're just about done for the night…or should I say, morning."

"It was the most wonderful night ever," she said. "It feels like I've known you forever, when it hasn't even been a month."

"When you face danger together with someone, it kind of cuts through the bullshit of life and gets down to what matters. That's what happened to us. You keep saying I saved your life, but what you don't realize is that you saved me, as well. I came here feeling bitter and rejected. You changed that. Knowing everything there was to know about me, you still accepted me. You accepted my whole family. I treasure your presence in my life. We have weeks behind us now, and a lot of tomorrows to look forward to. How do you feel about having dinner with us one day soon?" Aaron asked.

"At your home?" Dani asked.

He nodded. "Yes, if it sounds okay."

"Yes, very okay. I would love it," she said, and knew from the look in his eyes that he was going to kiss her.

And he did.

———————

Long after he was gone and she was lying in bed, she could still feel his arms around her, and the pressure of his lips, and the thunder of her heart, and wished she hadn't been a coward. She wanted him. In her bed. Inside her. And it would have to wait.

———————

Aaron was in bed, staring up at the ceiling, listening to Sean snoring in the room across the hall, and hearing the old clock downstairs striking 3:00 a.m. He sighed, aching for her. But there was no deadline on how long he was willing to wait. Things that matter are forever.

———————

Up on the mountain, the revelation of Brendan Pope's missing wife was spreading through the families, while down in Bowling Green, the county sheriff's office was deep into the Charlie Raines case, still running down every lead and following up on tips from the last bulletin they'd released.

After airing the story one more time with the added security footage of the shooter, it had given viewers more to look at than just a composite sketch. They could see mannerisms, like the tilt of one shoulder as he walked and the lanky build of his body. Hundreds of leads had come in from all over the country, but so far none had panned out.

Sheriff Woodley was frustrated. Despite the evidence they had, they still had no motive for the shooting, until he got a call from Sonny Warren.

———

Woodley was in his office when his desk phone rang in the middle of him writing a report.

"Hello. This is Woodley."

"Rance, it's me," Sonny said.

"Oh, hi, Sonny. What's up?"

"Cameron Pope just handed us a possible motive for the Raines shooting."

"What? How?" Rance asked.

"He's been reading the journal. At the very end, there's a reference to a troop of rebel soldiers going through Jubilee pulling a wagon reported to be carrying gold." And then Sonny laid out the whole scenario. "One could theorize that if this journal fell into the hands of a man willing to go looking for treasure, it might explain why he was at Big Falls. Why he had a metal detector and a shovel, and why there were signs of digging near where Charlie was shot."

"Well, I'll be damned," Rance muttered. "Finally. Something is beginning to make sense. The only thing I don't have, is a freaking clue as to where to find him."

"This is progress," Sonny said. "It's more than we knew this morning when we got out of bed. I have faith that someone, somewhere, is going to see that footage and know exactly who he is."

"I hope you're right," Rance said. "Thanks for the info."

"Welcome. Let me know if you need assistance down here in any way."

"Will do," Rance said, and hung up.

———

Then two days later, Rance Woodley had the piece aired again, and a woman named Connie Sanders just happened to be home that day with a sick baby. She was rocking him to sleep when the news anchor led his broadcast with the story and the film clip.

She upped the volume enough to hear what was being said, and then when she saw the video, the hair stood up on the back of her neck.

"It couldn't be," Connie muttered, then hit Pause, then Replay, and watched it over and over, and the more she watched, the more convinced she was that she knew that man, even though he was sporting a beard in the footage and the man she was thinking of was clean shaven.

She made note of the hotline phone number, and as soon as she got her baby to sleep, she made the call.

"Police hotline. This is Paul. Who am I speaking to?"

"My name is Connie Sanders. I live in Alexandria, Virginia. I'm calling about the man you're looking for, the one who shot the kid in Jubilee, Kentucky. I think I know who he is."

"You're certain?" Paul asked.

"Yes, sir. I believe I am."

"Local authorities will be contacting you about an interview to verify your information. May I have your address?"

"I'm not normally home during the day, but my baby is sick, and I stayed home with her today and happened to see the story and the film footage. I'll give you my home address and my place of work. All they have to do is call my number, and I'll make time to talk to them," she said, then gave them the rest of the information.

"Thank you for coming forward," Paul said. "Authorities will be in touch."

The line went dead.

Connie put down the phone and then had a moment of worry. What if she was wrong? Then she thought of the boy who'd been shot, and strengthened her resolve. She knew damn good and well she wasn't wrong. She'd been working in the same building with him for the better part of eight years.

━━━━━━━━━━

Rance was walking out the door when his desk phone rang, and went back to his desk to answer.

"This is Woodley."

"Sheriff Woodley, this is Paul with Police Hotline. I just took a call from a woman in Alexandria, Virginia, who vehemently claims she knows the shooter on the Charlie Raines case. I thought you would want to know."

"I can only hope she does and it's not another wild goose chase," Rance said, and sat down as he reached for a pen and paper. "What's her name and number, and where's she located?"

Paul gave him the info.

"Got it. I'll have this followed up immediately," Rance said, and hung up, but his heart was thumping as he opened a desk drawer, took out the case file, and began going back through the notes until he found the info about the rental car and quickly scanned it. After a few moments, he smiled. He'd been right! The car the shooter had been driving was a rental, with an office located in a suburb of Alexandria, Virginia. The caller was from Alexandria. Could this be the break they'd been waiting for?

Rance immediately made a call to the Alexandria Police Department, identified himself, and asked to be transferred to the crime division. He was briefly put on hold, and then a man answered.

"Detective Sosa."

"Detective Sosa, my name is Rance Woodley. I'm the Warren County sheriff in Bowling Green, Kentucky. We've been working a shooting in Jubilee, Kentucky and—"

"About that kid…what was his name… Charlie Raines?"

"Yes," Rance said.

"I know all about it. I've seen the story run a couple of times. What can I do for you?" Sosa asked.

"We have DNA, fingerprints, and security footage of the shooter, but he came into Jubilee under an assumed name. Even the car he was driving was rented under that name. But we just got a call on our hotline from a woman in Alexandria who claims she knows who he is. And the car that was rented under the assumed name came from a rental agency in a suburb of Alexandria. She's agreed to speak to local authorities and I'm calling to see if you…"

"Consider it done," Sosa said. "I have a thirteen-year-old son. I can't imagine what the boy and his parents have gone through. Is the kid okay?"

"He's healing, and that's a miracle in itself. The shooter left him to die on a mountain," Woodley said.

"Give me the info," Sosa said, and began writing down everything Woodley gave him.

"If it turns out to be our man, put him in a holding

cell long enough for me to get the DNA and finger-prints to you," Woodley said.

"Will do," Sosa said. "We'll be in touch."

Woodley felt a surge of excitement the moment the call ended. This felt right.

———————

The next morning when Connie Sanders got to work, she made a point of going to see if the man was at work. She knew he'd been on vacation, and knew when he came back that his long ponytail was gone, which made sense with what she'd just learned. Once your face is plastered all over the national news, it stood to reason you'd do whatever it took to change your appearance.

She went into the office across the hall and went to work, but every time her phone vibrated on an incoming call, she checked caller ID. Unless it was the babysitter or the local police, she wasn't answering the phone.

———————

It was just after 1:00 p.m., and Connie was back from lunch when her phone rang. When she saw caller ID, her heart skipped a beat.

"Hello, this is Connie," she said.

"Connie, this is Detective Sosa from the Alexandria PD. We understand you have information to share about the suspect in the Charlie Raines shooting."

"Yes, yes, I do," she said.

"Would you be available to speak to us today?"

"Yes."

"Could you come down to the station?" Sosa asked.

"I really think you should come here. The man in question works in the same place I do. At the Library of Congress. You can see him for yourself."

Sosa was stunned.

"Really?"

"Yes, he works right across the hall from me. I made sure he was at work. He was on his vacation just a week or so back, and when he returned, he'd cut off his long ponytail. In the eight years I've worked here, he's never cut his hair. Until now. A poor attempt to change his appearance, I'd say."

Sosa's interest was piqued. He hadn't expected much when he'd agreed to follow up on a lead, but this was suddenly becoming an interesting interview.

"Yes, we'll come to you."

"Call me when you get to the front lobby. I'll walk you back to where we work."

"Thank you," Sosa said. "We'll be there within the hour."

Connie's heart was racing as she ended the call. Who would have thought she'd ever be able to help with an attempted murder case?

She went back to work entering data, with her phone on vibrate and lying face up near her elbow so she wouldn't miss the call.

Nyles had a stack of first-edition classics on his desk and was working on entering them into the system. They'd been bequeathed to the library after the collector's death, and the simple fact that he was holding books ranging in age from three hundred to five hundred years old was a blood-rush.

He was so focused on the task at hand that he never saw the two strangers entering the room, or was alerted to the multiple footsteps coming his way. He only looked up when he realized two men were standing in front of his desk. Then when they flashed their badges, it was all he could do to keep his seat.

"Nyles Fairchild?"

"Yes?" he answered.

"I'm Detective Sosa, and this is my partner, Detective King. We'd like to ask you some questions."

"About what?" Nyles asked.

"Is there somewhere we can talk in private?" Sosa asked.

Nyles frowned. "I'm sorry, but unless you tell me what this is all about, I'm not going anywhere."

Sosa frowned. "It's just a formality. You've been pointed out as a person of interest in a shooting in Kentucky, and we just need to eliminate you as a suspect."

There was a moment when Nyles realized he should never have come home, but it was too late to redo the decision. There were lots of tall, skinny men with ponytails and beards in the world. All he had to do was deny everything.

"How odd," Nyles said, and then stood. "There's a small meeting room nearby. Would that suit?"

"Yes, thank you," Sosa said. "Lead the way."

Nyles led the cops out of the room, unaware they'd seen the security footage that had been aired, and were taking notes on the way he was dragging one heel as he walked, and that he held one shoulder lower than the other. They walked all the way down a narrow hall and then into the room, Nyles turning on lights as he entered. There was a long table in the middle of it, with a dozen chairs around it, shelves of books lining the walls, and a framed photo of the current president hanging on the wall.

"Have a seat," he said, and then purposely sat down at the head of the table. To his chagrin, both cops took seats flanking him and suddenly he felt pinned in, rather than as if he were leading the interview. Still, he chose to speak first. "Now, how can I help you?"

"The first things we'll need are a DNA sample and fingerprints as part of the elimination process, and then we'll need you to answer a few questions."

Nyles blinked. It was the only sign he made of the shock he was feeling.

What the hell? DNA? Fingerprints? He didn't leave any of that behind. He'd felt for a pulse on the kid's neck. And he'd checked out of his hotel room long before the kid woke up. The hotel would have long since cleaned the room and rented it again and again before the kid woke up to give them a description.

He watched in quiet horror as Detective King opened the briefcase he was carrying. The first thing King did was take a swab from the inside of Nyles's mouth to collect DNA. Then he pulled out their digital finger-print scanner, connected it to their laptop, and slowly and carefully took prints of every finger and thumb on both hands, then sent the results into the system, and then sent an email with the scanned prints directly to Sheriff Woodley.

Detective Sosa saw the nervous look on Fairchild's face but said nothing. Instead, he pulled still shots of the security footage Woodley sent him via email, and laid them in front of Nyles, one by one.

"I'd like you to take a look at these," Sosa said.

Nyles leaned forward, looked at each one, then sat back and looked up.

"Is this you?" Sosa asked.

Nyles pretended surprise. "Of course not. I don't look like that!"

"We've seen your DMV photo. We've seen your government ID. And we have witnesses here in this building that claim that, up until recently, this is exactly how you wore your hair. In fact, they state you still looked like this before you went on vacation, and when you came back, you'd cut it all off."

Nyles shrugged. "I just wanted a change. I live alone.

I don't have a social life to speak of and I get lost in my work here. The days off gave me a new perspective on my personal grooming, that's all."

"Where did you go on your days off?" Sosa asked.

"Oh, nowhere really. I just wanted some time off. I took walks to the Potomac. Slept in. Watched movies. Ate out. Things I never take the time to do."

Sosa began making notes. "Where all did you eat?"

Nyles shrugged. "Different places around the city."

Sosa made more notes. "I'm sure that can be verified if we check your credit card receipts."

Nyles folded his hands in his lap to keep them from shaking. "I like to pay cash when I can. Too many thieves stealing credit card numbers these days."

Sosa made more notes. "So, when we check your credit card purchases, will we find purchases for a metal detector or any camping gear?"

Nyles's heart skipped, but he was still in full-on lie mode and answered without a hitch. "Oh. Yes, you would. I did do a bit of metal detecting down by the river on my days off. Didn't find anything, but it was something I'd always wanted to try. I might do it again one day soon."

"And how do you explain the camping gear?" Sosa asked.

"I thought about a camping trip, but it kept raining and I'm not much of a woodsman, so I ruled that out. Also, something to do for another day."

Sosa was still making notes.

"Have you ever been to Kentucky?" Sosa asked.

Nyles frowned thoughtfully. "No, I don't believe I have. I've been to Georgia and West Virginia, though. Specifically, the Appalachia area with some archaeologists when I was in college."

They kept throwing questions at him, and Nyles seemed to have an answer for everything, until they got a return email from Sheriff Woodley.

The prints match!

Detective King elbowed his partner, then pointed to the laptop screen.

Sosa read the message, then looked back at Nyles.

"We're going to need you to come with us," he said.

Nyles felt the blood draining from his face. Wearing the shock he was feeling was a hard thing to hide.

"This is ridiculous! Why?" he cried.

"Because your description fits the man in the security footage, and your fingerprints match the prints the police have on file of the man who shot a boy and left him for dead on a mountain."

"Fingerprints? What fingerprints?" Nyles shouted.

"The ones all over an old journal found in a parking lot there."

Nyles laughed. It sounded a little maniacal and he knew it, but he couldn't let them see the panic he was feeling.

"What's so funny?" Sosa asked.

Nyles waved his hands. "Look around you! Think where you are! I'd bet my entire retirement fund that my fingerprints could be found on a thousand books here, maybe tens of thousands. I've worked here for over twenty-five years. If a book came through here, I probably touched it. That's what I do. I'm a cataloger for the Library of Congress, for God's sake."

Sosa's voice softened as he leaned forward.

"I never said the journal came from this place. Is this where you found it? We'll be checking to verify that it is, indeed, part of the library's collection. What's in that journal that led you to bring it with you to Jubilee, Kentucky? What the hell were you doing up on that mountain that made it worth killing for?"

It was all getting away from Nyles and he knew it! It was time to go on the defensive.

"You're obviously trying to pin a crime on me that I didn't commit, and I'm not saying anything more until I get a lawyer."

"Fine with me. In the meantime, we're taking you in for further questioning. Stand up," Sosa said, and cuffed him.

Nyles's humiliation was at an all-time high as they walked him out of the building in handcuffs, but it was nothing to the tightening knot in his gut. He was in big trouble.

As soon as Nyles was put into a holding cell, Sosa made a call to Sheriff Woodley's private cell phone.

"Hello. This is Woodley," Rance said.

"Sheriff Woodley, this is Detective Sosa. We picked up a man named Nyles Fairchild and brought him in for further questioning."

"What do you think?" Woodley asked.

"He's changed the color of his hair and cut off the beard and ponytail, but his DMV photo and his old ID card looks like the man in the footage. He has all of the same mannerisms of the man, including dragging one foot as he walks and a slight tilt down to one shoulder. And his story is full of holes. He has all kinds of answers for what I asked, but we're about to dig into the background of his finances. We took his prints and DNA. The prints matched. We'll have to wait on DNA results. But when I asked about a recent purchase of a metal detector, he admitted it and said he was using it locally down around the Potomac River. When I asked him about purchasing camping equipment, he said he'd planned to camp, but plans fell through."

"So, his prints did match! That should confirm identity. What does he do? Where does he work?" Woodley asked.

"He's a cataloger at the Library of Congress here in DC. His job is to log in and label all of the new acquisitions to the library, which as you know is immense."

Woodley gasped. "The journal we found with the fingerprints came from the Library of Congress."

"Yes, I know…but we didn't tell him that, and yet when I mentioned his prints were on the journal, he immediately said that because of his job, his prints are likely on thousands of books here. He gave himself away before we barely began."

"Shit," Woodley said. "Listen, I'm going to send you the file of everything we have on the case. You need to be as informed as possible before you question him further."

"Yes. Are you emailing it, too?" Sosa asked.

"Yes," Woodley said. "But keep in mind, he can't lie his way out of a DNA match. What we collected is in the system, and when you get your test results back, see if they match. That will be the nail in his coffin. And if he starts to argue that, tell him we have eyewitnesses."

"I was given to understand that the kid who was shot provided the composite, but you just said witnesses," Sosa said.

"Yes. We have another one who came forward long before the kid ever regained consciousness. But that's need-to-know only. We promised the witness anonymity."

"Understood," Sosa said. "I can hold him for up to ninety-six hours since it's an attempted murder case. I've ordered a rush on the DNA. Hopefully, we'll know something one way or the other before I have to turn him loose."

"Keep me posted," Woodley said. "I'm at the point where I don't care who gets credit for the collar as long as I get Charlie Raines's shooter behind bars."

"Will do," Sosa said, and went back to his desk,

letting Fairchild stew in the holding cell while they waited for a public defender to show up.

While he was waiting for Woodley's file to come through, his partner, Detective King, began going through Fairchild's financial records, trying to make connections to Nyles Fairchild and Jubilee, Kentucky.

Nyles was in a panic. His worst fears about this fuck-up were coming true. He should have disappeared after it happened instead of coming back.

But he hadn't, and here he was. He had an explanation for the prints. He had excused the purchases he made. What else did they know? Or more to the point, if they kept digging, what else would they find out?

Chapter 15

THE FILE FROM WOODLEY FINALLY CAME THROUGH, and when it did, Detective Sosa printed all of it out and began to read through it, while his partner was still searching Fairchild's financials.

Two hours later, King was at his desk on a call, and Sosa was going through the files Sheriff Woodley had sent. They were both still waiting for Fairchild's public defender to show when King hung up the phone.

"Hey, Sosa."

Sosa looked up. "Yeah?"

"I think we've finally got something to connect Fairchild to Jubilee, Kentucky," King said.

"Like what?" Sosa asked.

"Over a week before the shooting, Fairchild added another person's name to his personal checking account, giving him access to withdraw funds, and ordered a debit card for him as well."

"Yeah, so what was his name?" Sosa asked.

"Dirk Conrad. The name of the man who was identified as the shooter. And the bank has security footage of Conrad coming into the bank to sign an access card and pick up his debit card. They're sending the footage over as we speak. Something else I found out about Fairchild: after he supposedly came back from vacation, he returned to the bank, removed the name from his account with the excuse that the person changed his plans and access was no longer necessary. But the bank has Dirk Conrad's debit card used at check-in at the Hotel Devon in Jubilee, Kentucky. And when Conrad checked out, he paid cash, and the deposit from the card was returned to his account."

Sosa's eyes widened. "That fits in with what I've been reading in Woodley's files. Conrad asked the hotel to wipe the card from their system and paid cash when he checked out, supposedly to protect his number from being stolen."

At that point, Sosa's computer signaled the arrival of a new email. It was from the bank, with an attachment of the security footage.

"It's here," Sosa said.

King moved to Sosa's desk to view it. It only took moments to realize it was the same man from the hotel footage.

"It's Dirk Conrad," King said.

Sosa nodded. "But it's also Nyles Fairchild. See how he drags his foot as he walks and tilts his shoulder down the same way? The only difference is Fairchild didn't wear a beard, but if he intended to hide his identity in other ways besides a fake ID, he'd want to change his appearance, too. Growing a beard would be the easiest and quickest way to do that."

"Looks like we're on overtime tonight," King said.

"Check to see if his lawyer ever showed," Sosa said. "If he's there, tell them we're about to pay Fairchild a visit."

King went back to his desk and made a call. After being on hold for a couple of minutes, he got his answer.

"The lawyer showed up about thirty minutes ago. By the time we get there, they should be ready to talk," he said.

Sosa picked up the file he'd been reading, slipped his notes inside, and stood.

"Let's do this," he said.

Cheryl Vlasek was a lawyer who served as a public defender. She was at the dentist when she got a text to go see a new client named Nyles Fairchild, who was in custody in a holding cell in the Alexandria Police Department.

She signaled her dentist to stop for a moment and texted her response, letting them know it could be as long as a couple of hours before she could get there, hoping they'd send someone else in her stead. But they didn't. She was told to proceed to the address as soon as possible.

She groaned, then eyed the dentist. "How much longer?" she mumbled.

"About thirty minutes," he said.

She leaned back in the chair again, gave him a thumbs-up, and closed her eyes.

About forty-five minutes later, Cheryl was in her car and driving toward the police station. One side of her face was numb, and her mouth didn't quite close all the way. All she could do was hope she could talk well enough to make herself understood, and began practicing as she drove, saying aloud, "Jack be nimble. Jack be quick. Jack jump over the candlestick," over and over.

By the time she reached the police station, the numbness was beginning to wear off and she could feel her lips. The downside was that her mouth hurt like hell.

A few minutes later, she was escorted to an interview room. She asked for a bottle of water and sat down to wait. After they brought the water, she downed a couple of painkillers and was ready to proceed when they brought her client into the room. But she could tell by the look on her client's face that he was not happy.

"I thought it would be a man," he said.

Cheryl stood. "I'm Cheryl Vlasek. Have a seat, Mr. Fairchild."

"I wanted a man," Nyles persisted.

"When you ask for a public defender, you get the luck of the draw. Sit down and start talking. What have you been accused of, and did you do it? What you say in confidence stays with me. But if you don't tell me the truth, then I can't defend you against your own lies."

Nyles blinked. She sounded tougher than she looked, and beggars can't be choosers. He started talking.

By the time the detectives arrived, Cheryl was a little bit in shock. She'd seen the national news reports about the shooting. She even remembered the kid's name, Charlie Raines. She'd been horrified at the time, thinking what the hell kind of man would shoot a kid and leave him to die like that? Now they had this man in for questioning in the case, and after what he'd just told her, she was smack-dab in the middle of it. She knew only what Fairchild had told her, and was absolutely certain he had not told her everything, which meant this was probably going to blow up in both their faces.

Nyles was scared. His lawyer hadn't given him any straws to hold on to.

"There are no arguments for murder," Cheryl told him.

"But I didn't mean to do it," Nyles said.

"You might not have intended to shoot a person, but you purposely left a boy to die. And you meant to do that," Cheryl said.

"You have to do something," he snapped. "You're my lawyer."

"I could argue diminished capacity, but then you blew that out of the water because of the technical aspects of your job, and the fact that you acquired false identification to hide what you went there to do. All you can do is wait and see what they have on you, and we go from there," she said.

Nyles sulked.

"I wanted a man," he muttered.

"So do I," Cheryl snapped. "But the only ones I seem to come in contact with these days are either flat-out mean, or total dumbasses on their way to prison."

Nyles knew what category fit him best and said no more.

And then the detectives came in.

Nyles tried to read their expressions, but they gave nothing away as they introduced themselves to his lawyer, then sat down on the other side of the table. He eyed the files they'd brought with them, wondering how much of his story they could already refute.

Detective Sosa turned on the recorder, gave a date, time, and location, and named all of the people in the room, and then the questioning began.

"Mr. Fairchild, would you please state for the record your name, occupation, and where you're from."

"I'm Nyles Fairchild, from Alexandria, Virginia, and I work at the Library of Congress as a cataloger."

"How long have you held that position?" Sosa asked.

"A little over twenty years," Nyles said.

"Thank you. Now, I'm going to ask you some questions that we've already asked you before. But this time, it's for the record, and if you need to change your answer, keep in mind there are consequences for lying under oath."

Nyles glanced at his lawyer. She'd pretty much said the same thing to him earlier.

"Mr. Fairchild, have you ever been to Jubilee, Kentucky?"

"No," Nyles said.

"Have you recently purchased hiking gear and a metal detector?"

"Yes, but I explained what—"

"*Yes* is sufficient," Sosa said.

"Do you know a man named Dirk Conrad?" Sosa asked.

"No, I do not," Nyles said.

"Then why did you go to your bank and add the name Dirk Conrad to your personal banking account, and request a debit card in his name?"

His face flushed. "Uh, that was a friend who—"

"You told the bank it was your cousin," King interjected. "We have security footage of Dirk Conrad walking into the bank to sign papers authorizing him access to your money. We have record of him receiving his debit card. We have records from your bank of that same card being used when Dirk Conrad checked in at Hotel Devon in Jubilee, Kentucky. How do you explain that?" Sosa asked.

Nyles froze, then looked at Cheryl Vlasek in a panic as if to ask, *What do I say?* She was furious. Just as she'd expected, he hadn't told her the whole truth. She just raised her eyebrows.

Nyles glared at the detectives. "No comment."

Sosa unloaded another barrage of facts in Nyles's lap. "The footage of Dirk Conrad at your bank matches the man in the footage from the Hotel Devon, and that man has been identified by Charlie Raines, the boy who was shot and left for dead, as the shooter. That same man has also been identified by another witness as dropping a leather-wrapped bundle, which turned out to be a missing journal from the place where you work. The same journal with your fingerprints all over it. How do you explain that?"

"No comment," Nyles said.

Sosa shifted the subject. "Mr. Fairchild, I see you have a healing wound on your forehead. How did that happen?"

"I fell," Nyles said.

"And when you fell, did it scrape the skin? Did you bleed?" Sosa asked.

"Obviously. There's a visible scab, or you wouldn't have commented," Nyles snapped.

"Mr. Fairchild, when we first questioned you, did you allow us to take fingerprints and a DNA sample from you?"

A cold chill ran through Nyles so fast he shuddered, then nodded.

"For the record, Mr. Fairchild, please answer aloud," Sosa said.

"Yes, I did," Nyles mumbled.

"So, our witness saw Conrad fall, and when he got up, blood was gushing from the cut, and he was throwing all kinds of things into the trunk of his car, including a camp shovel, a hiker's backpack, and a metal detector. Oh…and a handgun."

"I don't own a handgun!" Nyles shouted.

"So, you deny that," Sosa said. "However, our witness

says otherwise. And the crime lab gathered DNA from the scene of Conrad's fall in Jubilee. When your DNA matches the DNA they have on file belonging to Dirk Conrad, you won't be able to deny that, will you, Mr. Fairchild?"

And in that moment, Nyles knew all was lost. He didn't even look at the lawyer.

"It all began as a lark! I was curious. I just wanted to verify information from the journal for myself. It was an accident! I didn't mean to shoot anybody. I thought it was a bear! And then I panicked and ran. I'm sorry. I'm so sorry. I didn't mean to do anything wrong! It just snowballed and I didn't know how to stop it!" Nyles said, and then began to weep.

"Where did you get the gun?" Sosa asked.

"I inherited it from my grandfather," Nyles said.

"Where is it now?" Sosa asked.

"I threw it in the Potomac," Nyles moaned, and covered his face.

The surge of elation that went through both detectives was huge, and having the shooter confess on record was icing on the cake.

"Detective King, would you please read Mr. Fairchild his rights and put him under arrest for the attempted murder of Charlie Raines, and add fraud and possession of an unregistered weapon to the charges?"

King stood up, and as he was cuffing Fairchild, read him his rights, then led him away.

Cheryl Vlasek's head was throbbing as she began gathering up her things.

"Thank you, Ms. Vlasek," Sosa said as he removed the tape from the recorder.

"Just doing my job," Cheryl said. "I'll see you at the sentencing."

Sosa followed her to the door and waved down an officer.

"Will you please see Ms. Vlasek out?" Sosa asked, and then watched them walk away before he headed back to his desk. He needed to enter the tape into evidence and write up the report, but before he did that, he had a phone call to make.

———————

Rance Woodley was on his way home, driving through a late evening thunderstorm when his cell phone rang. He answered on Bluetooth so he could keep both hands on the wheel.

"Hello, this is Woodley."

"Good evening, Sheriff. This is Detective Sosa."

"Did you get the files I sent okay?" Rance asked.

"Yes, I did, and I have something for you," Sosa said.

"Oh yeah? What's that?" Rance asked.

"We got your man. He broke under pressure and confessed to everything."

Rance let out a whoop. "This is the best news ever. I've got a kid who's been afraid that man would come back and finish him off. I've had a whole mountain full of his family on my ass for days, asking if there was any progress. This is wonderful news! Did he say why he did it?"

"It was an accident. He thought the kid was a bear and shot before he looked. He said he'd gone to Jubilee to verify information he'd found in the journal, but he didn't say what that was."

"We think he was hunting for Confederate gold. A damn treasure hunter," Woodley said. "We found an entry in the journal about some Confederate soldiers coming through Jubilee with a wagon full of gold. Then the soldiers who were guarding it were all found dead and the wagon broken down on the trail. Either they hid the gold to go back for it, or someone stole the gold and killed the soldiers…or some such story, and he shot and left a kid to die for his stupidity."

"Good to know," Sosa said. "Even as he confessed, he was still lying about why he was there. Well, tell Charlie Raines the man who shot him is going to spend the rest of his life in prison. Maybe that will help."

"Will do, and thank you for your assistance. I'd like a copy of your arrest report for my files so I can close the case."

"Certainly, Sheriff Woodley. Been a pleasure working with you," Sosa said, and disconnected.

Rance drove the rest of the way home with a smile on his face, and as soon as he got into his house, sat down and called Sonny Warren.

It was almost 7:00 p.m. in Jubilee, but Sonny Warren was a long way from getting to go home. Between a three-car pileup in town, an attempted robbery at Reagan Bullard's music venue, which Wiley Pope busted and had the perp in cuffs by the time police arrived, and a woman using a stolen credit card in three shops before she got caught, he and his officers were still wading through the arrests and paperwork involved. When his phone rang, his first thought was *Now what?*, even as he answered.

"Chief Warren."

"Sonny, this is Rance. I have good news. We caught the man who shot Charlie Raines. His name is Nyles Fairchild, and he's sitting in a jail cell in Alexandria, Virginia, as we speak."

"Oh man! This is the best news we've had all day! How did you make the connection?"

"A strong tip came in on the hotline. I contacted the Alexandria PD to follow through. They took him in for questioning. One thing led to another, and he ran out of lies and excuses. The reason he even shot at Charlie was because he thought it was a bear coming through the woods. Then he thought he'd killed him and ran. I've asked them for copies of the arrest so I can close my file. I'll get a copy to you as well when it comes through."

"Much appreciated," Sonny said. "Are you going to make the notification to Ray and Betty Raines?"

"As soon as we hang up," Rance said. "And thanks again for everything. Your help was invaluable to the case…as was Dani Owens, our secret witness. Be sure and let her know."

"I will," Sonny said. "Thanks for calling."

Rance disconnected, then looked up Ray Raines's number and called him.

———————

Betty Raines was at the stove frying chicken, and Charlie was already sitting at the table, playing a game on his iPad. Ray had just come in the house from doing chores and was at the sink in the utility room, washing up for supper, when his phone rang. He grabbed a towel to dry his hands and answered.

"Hello."

"Ray, this is Rance Woodley. Got a minute?"

"Yes, sure," Ray said, talking as he entered the kitchen. "Do you have news?"

"Yes, I do!" Rance said. "We got him, Ray! We caught the shooter. He confessed and is in jail in Alexandria, Virginia."

"Oh my God! That's great! That's wonderful news! Who was he? Why did he do it?"

So Rance explained once more, giving him what he knew about the case.

"Charlie doesn't have to be scared anymore. The man who shot him is going to prison, which will likely be his last stop in this lifetime."

"Will Charlie have to testify in court?" Ray asked.

"No. The man confessed. He's not denying anything. It will be up to the judge to sentence him, and the only reason he won't be charged with murder is because Charlie didn't die. He's going down for attempted murder and a whole list of other infractions."

"Thank you, Rance. From the bottom of our hearts," Ray said.

"You're welcome. I don't always get good conclusions from the cases we get, but this is a winner all the way around, and most especially for Charlie."

The call ended.

"That was Sheriff Woodley," Ray said.

Betty shoved the skillet of chicken off the fire as Charlie looked up from his game.

"And?" Betty asked.

Ray started smiling. "They caught him! They caught him, Charlie! The man who shot you is in jail. He confessed to the whole thing. He shot at you because he thought you were a bear, and then when he thought he'd killed you, he ran."

Betty started crying. "Oh my God. What a cold-hearted, callous thing to do," and then fell into Ray's arms.

Charlie was quiet, just listening to his parents rehashing their horror and fears, and their anger at the stranger who'd nearly killed their son, but Charlie wasn't satisfied.

"Daddy?" he said.

Ray turned. "Yes, son?"

"Why was he there to begin with?"

Ray glanced at Betty. They'd heard through the family grapevine about what was in the journal and the theory that the shooter might have been looking for Confederate gold, but they hadn't said anything to Charlie. However, now that the man was no longer at large, it was only fair to let him know.

"They think he was hunting for treasure," Ray said.

Charlie frowned. "What? What treasure?"

"Gold or something that got lost during the Civil War," Ray said. "Your mom and I just learned this today. Cameron thinks it's why the man was there."

"But why would he think that?" Charlie asked.

"It was something that was written in a journal in the 1800s. Your ancestor, the first Brendan Pope, wrote the journal. The shooter found the journal in some library and came looking for buried treasure."

"But why on our place?" Charlie asked.

"Because Big Falls was mentioned in the journal and that's where the man went."

Charlie's expression shattered. His eyes welled, and his voice sank to a whisper.

"I nearly died because some old man wanted to play pirate?"

Ray and Betty wrapped their arms around their son and hugged him. "You're looking at this backward," Ray said. "You lived because of your mother's love. She went looking for you because you matter most in our world. You're okay, you know that, right?"

Charlie could feel the rough scratch of his daddy's day-old whiskers and the softness of his mother's face against his cheek. The scent of home-fried chicken filled the room, and they were holding him close, and all he could think was, *It's over.*

"Yes, Daddy," Charlie said. "I'm okay."

Sonny Warren started to call Dani Owens, and then stopped and went looking for Aaron Pope instead. After all Aaron had done on Dani's behalf, he deserved the privilege of giving her the good news.

———

Aaron was at a desk, finishing up the report on his last call before going home, when he heard footsteps approaching and looked up. It was the chief.

"Hey, Chief. What's up?"

"I have good news, and I need a favor," Sonny said.

"I'm all about good news. What do you need?" Aaron asked.

"I just got a call from Sheriff Woodley. Long story short, the shooter we've been looking for has been arrested in Alexandria, Virginia. The local authorities picked him up for questioning, and he confessed to shooting Charlie by accident. Thought he heard a bear. He thought the kid was dead and ran. And if it hadn't been for Dani Owens, I would venture a guess we'd still be treading water, looking for a suspect."

"This is the best news ever for the Raines family,

for sure. Charlie won't have to be afraid anymore!"
Aaron said.

"Yes," Sonny said. "And good work all around, which
brings me to the favor. You have developed quite a
rapport with our secret witness, and she deserves to
hear this from the source, so would you like to tell her
in person?"

Aaron grinned. "I'd be happy to, sir."

"Thanks," Sonny said. "And let her know there's
every possibility that her name will come out in the
case against him to corroborate seeing him with the
gun and metal detector, and then finding the journal
that links him to the crime."

"I will, and now that she's no longer in danger from
the Bing brothers, I doubt she'll have any concerns,"
Aaron said. "As soon as I finish up here, I'll drop by
her house."

"Thanks," Sonny said. "It's been a long day. See you
tomorrow."

"Yes, sir. Thank you, sir," Aaron said, then finished
the last of his report, saved it in the computer, and
printed and filed a hard copy as well before giving
her a call.

Chapter 16

DANI SPENT THE MORNING RUNNING ERRANDS AND the afternoon cleaning house. By the time she finally finished mopping the floors, she was exhausted. She took a quick shower to cool off, then grabbed a cold drink and went out to the swing on the back porch and plopped down. Her back was aching, and she'd kicked off her shoes earlier when she was mopping. Sitting down with her glass of iced tea was a treat. She had just taken a drink when her phone began to ring, and when she saw it was Aaron, she smiled.

"Hi, you," Dani said.

Aaron smiled. "Hi yourself. Are you home?"

"Yes. Are you coming to see me?" she asked, and heard laughter in his voice as he answered.

"Yes, please."

"Yay! Let yourself in. Grab yourself something to drink on your way through the kitchen. I'm on the back porch."

"That's the best invitation I've had all day. See you soon," he said, and hung up.

All of a sudden, Dani's exhaustion turned to

anticipation. She ran back into the house, plated some of the cookies she'd bought at Granny Annie's Bakery, and took them outside. What was left of the day had taken on a whole new perspective. The sun was already sliding below the treetops. Night was imminent. And her favorite person was coming to see her. She grabbed a cookie from the plate and took a bite, then pushed off in the swing as she chewed.

Granny Annie's snickerdoodles were good, but it was Aaron Pope who rocked her world!

―――――――――――

Aaron dodged a street parade by taking back streets to get out of the tourist part of Jubilee. A few minutes later, he was in Dani's driveway. He had news to share but all he could think about was what she felt like in his arms.

As directed, he let himself in, grabbed a cold long-neck from the refrigerator, and then exited the kitchen onto the back porch, pausing just long enough to take in the sight of her. Long legs beneath short pink shorts, a white T-shirt with an I TEACH LITTLES logo on the front, and bare feet. A half-eaten cookie in one hand. A glass of iced tea in the other. But the smile on her face was all his.

"Come sit!" she said as she set her glass aside and scooted down the length of the swing to make room.

He sat. "Hey, beautiful," then leaned over and kissed her. "Long time, no see," he whispered.

She shivered from the all-too-brief feel of his mouth on her lips and shook her head.

"It was yesterday," she said.

"Is that all?" Aaron said. "Felt like forever."

Dani laughed. "Your words are as pretty as you are, but I won't hold it against you. Help yourself to cookies. Don't worry. I didn't bake them. Your Aunt Annie did."

Aaron grinned as he snagged a cookie and took a quick bite, then washed it down with a long drink of the cold beer.

"Umm, thanks," he said. "I missed lunch. It's been crazy at work. Even Wiley got into the act today. Stopped a robbery in progress at the ticket office and had the perp in cuffs before we got there. He's probably home right now, telling the family all about it."

"Oh my gosh! He wasn't hurt, was he?" Dani asked.

"No. He's got some moves, and he's good at his job."

"Thank goodness," Dani said. "I can't imagine being your mother and having two sons in law enforcement."

Aaron went quiet, then reached for her hand as the swing rocked back and forth.

"Can you imagine living with someone who has that job?"

Dani's heart skipped as his grip tightened slightly. He was afraid of what she was going to say.

"I can imagine it. But imagination only goes so far. I'm more into reality," she said.

Aaron saw the twinkle in her eyes. "So, that's a yes?"

She nodded. "Pretty much."

He grinned. "Just checking. And…I come bearing good news."

Dani laid her cookie by her drink and dusted the cinnamon sugar from her fingers.

"Tell me!"

"They caught the man who shot Charlie Raines."

Dani gasped. "Oh my gosh! Best news ever! How? Who was he? Where did they find him?"

Aaron began laying out the story as he ate, beginning with the tip on the hotline about Nyles Fairchild, to the Alexandria police following up and then getting Fairchild's confession. But it was the reason he shot Charlie that floored her.

"He thought he was shooting at a bear? Oh my God! People like him have no business even owning a gun. And then to leave Charlie just lying there and run away? An idiot and a coward, to boot."

Aaron nodded. "You just summed up the basic makeup of nearly every person who winds up getting arrested. They do something stupid and then won't admit they made a mistake. However, Chief Warren wanted me to advise you that there could be a possibility that your identity may come into play now. Nyles Fairchild confessed, so there's really no point in a jury trial. The sentencing will be up to the judge. But your name and your witness statement will be part of the total package."

"Fair enough," Dani said. "And since there's no one

left from my past wishing me dead, the need for ano-nymity no longer exists. This is such good news. Thank you for letting me know!"

"Any excuse to come see you is a plus," he said.

Dani frowned. "You don't need an excuse."

Aaron put his arm around her shoulders and pulled her close. "Maybe not, but I need you."

Dani put her arms around his neck. "I can easily be on call, day or night as the need arises," she said.

Aaron buried his face against the curve of her neck and pulled her into his lap. "No pressure or anything, but you should know that you are single-handedly heal-ing every broken piece of me."

Dani shivered with longing as she turned in his arms and cupped his face with both hands.

Aaron tunneled his fingers through her hair, feeling the short curls wrapping around his fingers just like she'd already wrapped herself around his heart, then stroked the curve of her chin with his thumb.

"I dream of making love to you, but I don't want it to be hit and run. I want to see you come apart in my arms, then hold you as you sleep. I want to wake up beside you for the rest of my life. I keep reminding myself you barely know me, but that's how I feel."

Dani slid off his lap, then held out her hand.

"Where are we going?" Aaron asked.

"To bed, to make a dream come true."

Sunset had come and gone.

There were two piles of clothing at the foot of the only bed in the house.

And a man and a woman in the bed, in the act of making love.

Again.

Like thirsting for water, they couldn't get enough of each other.

This moment had been a long time coming for both of them, and the timeline of when they'd met no longer mattered.

Aaron felt whole again.

Dani felt safe again.

They were already in love but had yet to say the words, and at the moment, thinking was out of the question.

There was nothing between them but the feeling.

Rocking body to body, chasing that single moment when the blood-rush hits.

Muscles tightening.

Nerves burning.

Bodies humming from the energy they'd built between them.

Riding the high.

Holding on to that high because it hurt so good.

And then the tipping point!

Time stopped.

Breath caught as the climax rolled through them.

For that moment, they were one.

Dani moaned and held him tighter.

Aaron collapsed and buried his face in the curve of her neck.

With sweat dripping from their bodies, they lay entwined, motionless, waiting for their heartbeats to catch up.

Finally, he rose up long enough to look at her.

Her eyelids fluttered as she finally opened her eyes and caught him—watching her.

"Oh my God," she whispered.

Aaron sighed. "Can you walk?"

"I don't think I can even stand," she said.

He rolled out of bed and then scooped her up into his arms.

"Where are you taking me?" Dani asked.

"To shower," he said as he crossed the hall and deposited her in the shower. "I'm turning on the water. Don't fall."

Dani sat down on the side of the tub, and once the water got warm, Aaron stepped into the tub with her, pulled the shower curtain, and took her into his arms to steady her, then stepped into the spray.

She was in his arms, her cheek against his chest, standing entwined as the shower spray sluiced the sweat from their bodies, cooling everything, including ardor, and leaving them sated in every way.

Long after he was gone, and she was back in bed alone, she couldn't sleep. What happened between them made her feel alive again. Whole again.

Impulsively, she reached for her phone and sent him a text.

Did I dream you, or did tonight really happen?

And then she laid the phone beside her pillow and closed her eyes, thinking he would get the message when he woke up the next morning. But moments later, her phone signaled a new message. She quickly opened it and then sighed.

It's real, and it's just the beginning. I want to take you home with me after work tomorrow. I promise good food. Mom's cooking. And there's a great view of the sunset from the back porch. Will you come up the mountain with me?

She sighed. He didn't know it yet, but she'd follow him to the ends of the earth if he asked.

I would be honored. See you then.
Awesome. Probably pick you up a little after six.

Dani disconnected, put the phone back on the charger, and closed her eyes. Within minutes she was asleep.

The headline in the local paper said it all.

SHOOTER CAPTURED

The ensuing story elaborated on the capture with no mention whatsoever of treasure hunting, praising both local and county authorities in their diligent pursuit for justice. Nyles Fairchild was painted as a backpacker who was knowingly trespassing, and the shooting as an accident compounded by the fact that he ran off and left Charlie Raines for dead.

Every citizen of Jubilee was relieved that justice was served, but while the residents on Pope Mountain were overjoyed by the news, they had deeper concerns. Concerns that somehow the reason for Fairchild's presence on the mountain would become known and trigger an invasion of treasure hunters.

Cameron Pope had been thinking about this ever since he read the journal, and once he learned the shooter was in custody, he went into his office with Ghost at his heels and called Brother Farley, the pastor at the Church in the Wildwood.

The old man was having coffee out on the front porch of the parsonage when his phone rang. He set his cup aside and took his phone from his pocket to answer.

"Hello?"

"Morning, Brother Farley. This is Cameron Pope. Do you have a minute?"

"Yes, certainly, son. What can I do for you?" Farley asked.

"We need to have a family meeting, and by we, I'm talking about the residents of Pope Mountain. I was wondering if we could have it at the church? It's the only place I can think of that would be big enough and private enough for what we need."

"Of course," Farley said. "Let me know the day and time, and I'll make sure to have the air-conditioning set properly."

"Thank you so much," Cameron said. "And, if it's not too much trouble, your presence would be welcome."

"I'll make a point to join you, and await your call," he said.

Cameron disconnected, then looked up as Rusty walked into his office.

"Are you going to use the church?" she asked as she sat down on his knee.

Cameron slipped his arm around her waist to secure her, and then gave her a quick kiss.

"He said we could, but now we need to start notifying as many people as we can to let them know."

Rusty nodded. "Okay then, when do you want to do this?"

"As soon as possible. Maybe day after tomorrow? And we should probably do it after hours. Maybe seven o'clock. That will give a lot of people time to get home from work. I have a list of everyone's info on my computer. I guess I'd better start calling."

"Give me half the list. I'll help call," Rusty said. "But what do we say to impress upon them the importance of coming?"

"Just tell them we have a mystery to solve, and it's going to take all of us to make it happen."

———————

The calls went out, and then the family grapevine began speculating. What was wrong now? The man who'd shot Charlie was in custody. Nobody they knew had gone missing. Nothing they knew about had been stolen, but by the time the sun went down on the day, everyone had come to the same conclusion. They were going to the Church in the Wildwood to find out what was going on.

———————

Like everyone else, Shirley got the call about the meeting, but she was busying about the house getting ready for company. Aaron hadn't even pretended interest in a woman since the world came down around them until he met Dani Owens.

Shirley liked Dani the first time she met her, and now all she could do was hope their relationship worked. They both deserved to be happy, and when he came home this evening, she'd grill him about Cameron's phone call. Aaron always knew more about what was going on than he told.

―――――――

It was just after six when Aaron clocked out at work, then showered and changed into street clothes in the locker room before leaving the station. Driving across town was always a process. Because it was so full of tourists and foot traffic, it was slow going until he crossed the main highway and drove into the residential area. He couldn't wait to see her.

He pulled up into the drive and let himself into the house, calling out as he walked in.

"Knock, knock, pretty girl!"

Dani came out of the kitchen laughing and threw her arms around his neck.

"I missed you!" she said.

Aaron wrapped his arms around her and pulled her close. "I missed you, too," he said, and kissed her.

Just a brief brush of lips at first, but it wasn't enough, and they went back for more, until he remembered where they were supposed to be, and stopped.

"God, you smell good," he whispered as he kissed a little freckle below her left ear. "As much as I hate to stop, we are expected elsewhere."

"Yes…elsewhere," Dani said, and grabbed her purse and set the security system before they walked out.

Minutes later, they were on the blacktop going up

Pope Mountain and leaving Jubilee behind. It was like stepping into another world, and Dani couldn't quit staring, marveling at the height of the trees and the impenetrable forest surrounding them. The farther up they went, the denser it became. All there was to see was the road in front of them, the forest surrounding them, and the intermittent mailboxes on the side of the road, marking homesteads somewhere within.

The farther up they went, the more wildlife they began to see. Then when a couple of deer bounded across the road a short distance ahead of them, Dani cried out.

"Look, Aaron! Two of them. How beautiful!"

"Very beautiful," he said, but he was looking at her.

Farther up, she caught sight of a racoon waddling through the underbrush, and then later, a rabbit bounding from the road into a ditch, and farther up, a lone bobcat slipping through the trees.

"This mountain is so mysterious and a little daunting. I can't imagine the centuries of secrets that lie hidden up here."

He glanced at her then, surprised by how perceptive that remark had been, but she didn't notice. She was too busy looking into the undergrowth as they passed by.

"Have you ever seen bears or cougars?" she asked.

He nodded. "From a distance. They shy away from people as readily as we shy away from them, and we're almost home. That mailbox up ahead is ours."

Dani shifted anxiously in her seat. She'd already met them and shared a meal with them, but now, after what had passed between her and Aaron, this felt a whole lot like a formal "meeting the family for the first time."

"Mom's so excited you're coming to eat with us," Aaron said as he turned off the road onto the driveway leading to the house.

"Really?" Dani said.

"Yep. You'll see. And don't blame me if you're hugged to death again. Remember, we're all huggers."

"It's a good feeling…belonging," she said.

"You miss your family, don't you, honey?"

Dani nodded. "Very much, but I'm also really happy that you're sharing yours with me."

"Maybe one day soon, if it suits you, you won't be on the outside looking in," he said, and then pointed at the sprawling house nestled among the trees. "We're here."

Dani was immediately charmed by the house and the porch across the entire front of the house, and then the door opened and his brothers came out to greet them, pushing and shoving to beat each other down the steps.

Aaron rolled his eyes. "You'd think they had yet to reach puberty from the way they're acting. But take heart. It's also a sign they really like you."

Dani laughed, and before they could get out, Sean opened her door and Wiley offered his hand to help her out.

"Welcome to Pope Mountain," he said.

"Welcome to our home," Sean added.

"Mom made pot roast and all kinds of good stuff," B.J. added.

Aaron laughed. "Leave it to the kid to know the menu."

Dani was still smiling as they started escorting her up the steps, and then she looked up, and Shirley was standing in the doorway with her arms wide open.

"Welcome, honey! It's so good to see you again. Come in, come in!"

Aaron saw the joy in Dani's smile and the delight of being welcomed in such a fashion. It made him grateful for the people he called his own.

It was, as Aaron had predicted, a hug fest, and then a continuous stream of chatter and brotherly arguments during supper, with Shirley quieting the outbursts before they got out of hand, while keeping up a conversation with Dani.

But it wasn't until Shirley got up to plate dessert that the focus shifted.

"I'm assuming everyone wants a piece of coconut cream pie?" she asked as she made the first cut into the first of three pies lining the sideboard.

"Yes, please," they all echoed, then Aaron got up and carried the servings to the table as she plated the slices.

As soon as they were all seated again, Shirley cleared her throat.

"I received a phone call from Cameron this morning. He's called a special family meeting up at the church day after tomorrow. It's at seven o'clock, and I expect all four of my sons to be present with me. Is that understood?"

They nodded.

Shirley glanced at Dani. "I don't know what it's about, but we all just found out that the man who shot my nephew has been arrested, so we don't think it has anything to do with that."

"Aaron told me. It's wonderful news," Dani said. "I also heard about Wiley's big day at work. Congratulations on catching the bad guy, sir."

Wiley grinned, pleased by the praise.

"Indeed," Shirley said, and then looked straight at Aaron. "But I have questions about Cameron's call. What do you know that we don't?"

"Bits and pieces," Aaron said, then glanced at Dani.

"It's okay if you tell them," she said.

All of a sudden, everyone was looking at Dani.

"Tell us what?" Sean asked.

Aaron put down his fork and reached for her hand.

"I'm not certain what Cameron's call is about, and I'd prefer that this conversation stays between us until after Cameron's meeting. I don't want to blow his news out of the water, and I'm not sure what he's planning, but what you can know...what the whole family needs to know, is that Dani is the one who found the journal the shooter dropped. She also witnessed him dropping it, along with a metal detector, a shovel, and a gun that fell out of his hiking gear after he came running up from the creek. She's the reason we had a composite sketch before Charlie regained consciousness. She's also the one who identified him from security footage. If it had not been for Dani, we'd still be kicking up rocks and looking for ghosts."

"Oh my God!" Shirley said.

The brothers stared.

"Why did it have to be a secret?" B.J. asked.

Aaron hesitated, and Dani answered for him.

"Remember when you were helping me move in, and you found out I'd had a stalker who tried to kill me?"

They nodded.

"Well, I didn't know it at the time, but his twin brother, Alex, was looking for me to finish what his brother started. I'd purposely left Louisiana to get away from all that, and I didn't want to advertise my new location to anyone from home. Then right after you helped me move in, I found out Alex was in Jubilee looking for me. That's why Aaron came to stay with me. It's why he asked Sean to install all of the security in my house. Your brother turned himself into my bodyguard and ultimately saved my life."

The room was silent. The family kept looking at Aaron, and then Dani, and then over again, stunned by what they'd just learned.

"And all of this was going on in the middle of trying to find Charlie's shooter?" Shirley said.

Aaron nodded. "Yes, ma'am. Dani was indirectly involved in the crime we were trying to solve, and a direct target to a psycho as well. As far as I'm concerned, she's as good as it gets."

"No arguments about that from any of us," Sean said.

"Thank you all, and especially Aaron, for all of the obvious reasons and then some," Dani added.

Aaron grinned. "No problem."

"Okay," Shirley said. "But I'm absolutely certain that's not why Cameron is calling a meeting. So, what's up?"

Aaron sighed. He should have known his mother wasn't going to let this go.

"Cameron finished reading that journal Dani found. He knows the secret Aunt Ella said was in the journal. And I suspect he's going to let the family know as well."

"So, what is it?" Shirley asked.

"Well, we now suspect the man who shot Charlie was looking for a missing shipment of Confederate gold, because there's mention of it in the journal, and that it was supposedly hidden somewhere around Big Falls. But what was important to Brendan on that same day, was that his wife, Meg, went up the mountain to pick berries and never came home. They never found her body. I think Cameron is going to send us all on a treasure hunt, but not for gold. To find Brendan's Meg and bring her home."

The shock on their faces was stark.

"I can't imagine that kind of grief," Shirley said.

Dani glanced at Aaron.

He brushed his finger down the side of her cheek.

"You didn't know how intuitive your remark was on the way up here, did you?"

"What do you mean?" Shirley asked.

Dani sighed. "As we were driving up here, I remarked about how beautiful it was, but because of the density of the forest, also a little overwhelming. I wondered how many centuries of secrets this mountain was hiding."

B.J. had seen Pope Mountain as their saving grace. He loved everything about it, but hearing about this great tragedy had shocked him. He couldn't imagine anything worse than losing someone and never knowing what happened to them or where they were. His eyes were swimming with unshed tears, and because he didn't want to cry in front of God and everybody, he picked up his fork.

"This is too damned sad to talk about. I'm eating pie."

Dani saw his tears, and felt an immediate need to protect him.

"I agree," she said. "It's too damned sad to talk about," and stabbed her fork into the slice of pie before her and took a big bite.

She didn't know it, but in that moment, she sealed her fate with this family in helping hide B.J.'s tears.

Shirley gave Aaron a look.

"Does Cameron know about Dani's part in all this?"

"No, ma'am. I don't think so," Aaron said.

"Well, he should," Shirley said, and left it at that.

After finishing dessert and helping clean up the kitchen, Dani finally had to say goodbye. Aaron still had to take her home and he was on duty tomorrow. Shirley and her sons stood beneath the porch light waving goodbye as Aaron backed up and then went down the driveway to the main road.

"That was the best time I've had in years," Dani said. "Thank you for tonight."

"You're welcome, and it was truly my pleasure," Aaron said, and gave her a quick glance as he braked at the end of the drive. "Mom and my brothers adore you."

"What about you?" Dani asked.

Aaron reached for her hand, lifted it to his lips, and kissed it. "Oh, I'm way past adoration, lady. I love you. Simple fact I can't deny."

Dani saw the truth on his face by the dashboard light.

"My knight in shining armor. Always wanted one. How blessed I am it's you. Take me home, Sir Aaron. I very desperately want to make love with you."

Aaron's pulse kicked. "Oh my God, woman! We're a good four mountain miles away from a bed and you tell me this now!" Then he threw back his head and laughed. "It's gonna take a sec to get there."

Dani leaned back in the seat. "I can wait."

"Lord," Aaron said, and pulled out onto the blacktop and headed down the mountain. "Starting up a conversation after that request is like being the juggling act that had to follow Elvis."

Dani laughed out loud. "Now that put an image in my head I'm going to remember for a while."

Aaron grinned. "You're a hot mess."

"Just don't forget I'm your mess," she said.

"Not a chance," he muttered, and kept driving.

When the bright lights of Jubilee finally came into view, Aaron was cruising, and silently thanked the Lord for all the green lights as he drove toward the residential area on the far side of town. When he finally pulled up into her drive, she was holding the door key.

He killed the engine.

They opened their doors at the same time and exited in unison. Dani beat him up the steps, unlocked the door, and walked in.

Aaron came in behind her, locking the door as he went.

Dani was halfway down the hall when he caught up, swept her into his arms, and carried her the rest of the way to the bed, and they had yet to turn on a light.

Clothes flew in every direction and then Dani was flat on her back.

The long drive down the mountain and the waiting invitation had been all the foreplay they needed.

Aaron was fully erect and sliding into the soft, wet heat of her body when she wrapped her arms around his neck and her legs around his waist.

All they had to do was let go, and so they did—of every inhibition, of every hesitation. Moving in perfect unison without conscious thought of the spark they'd started, their only intent to chase after the fire.

There was nothing on their mind but each other and the building rush of imminent climax. When it finally came, it was in a flash, without warning, in one long wash of ecstasy. They collapsed, still wrapped in each other's arms.

Silence followed.

Neither wanted the inevitable ending, even though it was already happening.

"I hate leaving like this," Aaron whispered.

"No regrets," Dani said. "You have laughed with me, fed me, and made love to me in the most perfectly beautiful way. I love you, Aaron Pope. I have faith you will be back."

He sighed. "You know I'll be back. I'm bound to you, soul to soul. You know the magic words."

"Magic words?"

He nodded. "Three little words are the key to my heart."

Her eyes widened. "I love you?"

"Those are the ones," he said, then kissed her again, long and hard, before getting up and going across the hall to the bathroom.

When he came back, she'd turned the lamp on by the bed and was sitting up in bed cross-legged, wearing one of his old T-shirts that he'd obviously left behind. She had his clothes neatly laid out for him to put on.

"I hope you don't mind, but I found it after you left, and when I sleep in it, I pretend I'm sleeping with you."

A muscle jerked at the side of his jaw. "Jesus, Dani. It already hurts to leave you, and now I gotta be jealous of a damn T-shirt?"

She smiled.

He eyed the dimples as they appeared, then shook his head and dressed before he changed his mind, then tucked her in as he was leaving.

"Sleep good, sweetheart. I'll text you in a bit to let you know I got home. Talk to you tomorrow, okay?"

"Watch out for deer on the road, and drive safe," she said, then watched him walk out of her room, turning out the hall light as he went.

She heard him reset the security system and lock himself out as he left, but she still listened, waiting for the sound of his car until he drove away. Only then did she relax and close her eyes. But her hand was on the phone beside her pillow. She wouldn't sleep until she got the text.

Twenty minutes later, it came. She rolled over on her back to read it.

I'm here...but my heart is still there with you.

Dani smiled, sent him a whole row of heart emojis, and then put the phone on the charger and fell asleep.

Chapter 17

SHIRLEY POPE HADN'T STOPPED THINKING ABOUT the revelation of Dani Owens's part in the Charlie Raines investigation and woke up with a certainty that, while the rest of the world might never find out, their family needed to know.

So, she called Cameron.

———

Rain was predicted for later in the day, so Rusty left early to go into town to pick up groceries and have brunch with her cousin Liz Caldwell at the Serenity Inn, where she worked.

Cameron was in the backyard with Ghost, hanging a gate on the privacy fence he'd just finished. At first, he'd fenced in the yard for Rusty's peace of mind about having a safe place for their baby to play, but the longer the fence was there, the more he liked it. Now, he didn't have to worry about Ghost dashing off into the woods, or anything bigger than squirrels coming into the yard.

He'd just put the last screw into the latch when his

cell phone rang. He saw Shirley's name pop up on caller ID and put down his tools to answer.

"Hello?"

"Cameron, it's me, Shirley. Got a minute?"

"Sure thing," Cameron said, and started walking back to the porch to get in the shade. "What's up?"

"Did Sonny Warren ever tell you how he came by Brendan Pope's journal?"

"No. He was vague about how they acquired it, and said it was part of the ongoing investigation into Charlie being shot. Why?"

"They had a witness. Her name was Dani Owens. And, as Aaron told us last night when he brought her to supper, if it hadn't been for her, the authorities would still be looking for leads."

Cameron was stunned. "I had no idea."

"No one did. At the time, keeping her anonymity was important to her own personal safety. Someday you'll find out what she's been through, but I wanted you to know that she sacrificed her safety to help our family and to help find the man who left Charlie to die."

"Thank you for letting me know. I'll talk to Aaron," Cameron said.

"Give Rusty my love," Shirley added.

"I will," he said, and as soon as they disconnected, he called Aaron.

It didn't take long for Aaron to fill him in on the details, and by the time he'd heard the story, he was shocked.

"Aaron, will you do me a favor?" Cameron asked.

"Yeah, sure," Aaron said. "What do you need?"

"Bring Dani with you to the family meeting tomorrow evening. We all need to pay homage. She brought this family full circle, and she doesn't even know it."

"Sure. I'll let her know, and bring her with us," Aaron said.

"Thanks," Cameron said. "We owe her."

As soon as their call ended, Cameron went back to working on the gate. Aaron was on patrol but took the time to give Dani a call.

Dani was planting flowers in the front flower beds when her phone rang. She quickly wiped her hands on her jeans and then sat down on the front steps as she answered.

"Hello, favorite person ever!"

Aaron smiled. "You stole my line."

"Sorry. What's up?" she said.

"It appears Mom told Cameron about your part in this whole Charlie/journal thing. He was both surprised and very appreciative, and asked me to bring you to the family meeting tomorrow evening."

"Oh, Aaron. I don't want a big deal made about—"

"Too late," Aaron said. "What you did was a big deal to us. And since I'm still holding on to the idea that you'll be part of the clan one day, you might as well see them all at once and get it over with."

Dani laughed. "You make it sound a little like trial by fire."

"It's not a bad thing. But there are a lot of us. That's all."

"Okay, sure. I'm honored."

"Great. I'll pick you up tomorrow as I'm leaving work, and I'll stop by for a hug and a cold beer before I leave town this evening, if that's okay?"

"It's very okay. Love you and be safe," she said.

"Always to both," he said, and hung up.

Dani stood for a moment, hanging on to the sound of his voice in her ear, then sighed and went back to planting flowers.

———

Nyles Fairchild was in jail awaiting a court date.

The horrors of imprisonment were already a reality. He knew jail was just a place to be on the way to somewhere else, but if prison was worse than where he already was, it would be hell.

He'd always thought of himself as a scholar—a highly educated man of refinement who'd turned into something of a loner as he moved toward middle age. But he would have bet his life that he'd be honest. That he would never do anything harmful or illegal. But he'd already lost that bet with himself, and he wished he *was* dead. He no longer had a future. He'd destroyed his life and his good name, and was too big of a coward to kill himself.

And all because of gold fever.

He'd heard of it.

He'd made fun of it before.

Only now, he knew it was real.

Men killed for it.

Lied for it.

Died for it.

And he'd just joined the club.

He was glad his parents were no longer living to see him come to this ignominious end.

Nyles's only saving grace was knowing the boy he shot had lived. He wasn't asking for understanding or forgiveness. At this point, he was grateful they couldn't add murder to his list of crimes.

Dani woke up thinking about the meeting on the mountain. She wavered between being overwhelmed, and anxious to meet so many of Aaron's relatives at once. What if they didn't like her? What if they felt like she didn't belong there? She was at the point of wishing Cameron hadn't invited her, even as she was getting ready to go.

She'd called Shirley earlier, just to ask her what to wear, and the warmth and laughter in Shirley's voice eased some of her nerves.

"Oh, honey, it's not a party. It's just us being present when some announcement is being made that affects us all. It happens here from time to time. It's just the easiest way to get family news without hearing it thirdhand. The church is air-conditioned, but there could be as many as two hundred people there. Dress for comfort. Pants. A dress. Shorts. Whatever suits your fancy."

Dani exhaled a sigh of relief. "Thanks, Shirley. This helps."

"You're welcome, sugar. See you soon," she said.

Dani returned the dress she'd planned to wear to the closet and switched it for navy-colored slacks and a pale blue short-sleeved T-shirt that made her blue eyes shine, and a pair of brown Docksides for walking comfort.

She'd washed her hair earlier and let it dry naturally in a tumble of soft, dark curls. Her only makeup was a slash of lipstick in a color called Antique Rose. After that, she was as ready as she was going to be.

Aaron arrived before six. He'd worked without a lunch break so he could leave an hour early because of the meeting, and he showed up at her house with his black hair still damp from the shower he'd taken at work.

He rang the doorbell, then let himself in, calling out as he crossed the threshold.

"Hey, pretty lady. Your Uber awaits."

Dani came hurrying from the hallway.

"Wow. You look beautiful," Aaron said.

"So do you," she said. "I'm nervous. Talk me down from this panic on the way up the mountain, okay?"

"Aw, honey, don't be scared. Before tonight's over,

you're going to be everybody's heroine." Then he pulled her into his arms and hugged her. "Now let's go. If we're lucky, Mom will have sandwiches or something ready and waiting so we can eat a bite before we leave."

"Shirley's food is a lure to anything. And I think I'm beginning to sound like B.J., but a fact is a fact, so there," she said.

Aaron was laughing as they headed out the door. He flipped on the porch light and set the security system before he closed the door, and then they were off.

This time the trip up the mountain was less intimidating to Dani, and the farther up they went, the more the world behind them disappeared.

"I'm starting to get this mountain vibe," she said.

"How so?" he asked.

"What's behind us doesn't belong up here, does it?"

He smiled. "Is that how it makes you feel?"

She nodded.

"Is that a good thing or a bad thing?" Aaron asked.

"A good thing! Definitely a good thing," Dani said. "The absence of noise is when you hear thoughts the clearest."

He reached for her hand and gave it a quick squeeze.

"Just when I think you couldn't get more perfect, you go and say something like that. You are the blessing that keeps on giving."

Dani's vision blurred. "And I'm just learning that you choose to make love in a myriad of ways. What you just said...that's a high I'm not likely to forget. I keep thinking if we hadn't gone through our own kind of hell before…and if we hadn't had a need to escape…we would never have met."

"It's just the universe setting things straight," Aaron said. "Before, we weren't where we supposed to be, and now we are. Simple as that."

Then he made a quick turn off the road onto their drive and headed up through the trees to the house.

"Home, and in good time," he said as they went up the steps.

"You're here!" Sean said as they walked inside. He gave Dani a big hug and punched Aaron's shoulder. "Mom's getting ready. She left food in the kitchen. Help yourself. I've got one more client to deal with and then I'll join you."

"Where's Wiley?" Aaron asked. "I didn't see his car."

"He's here. Car trouble. He had to ride home with B.J. on the back of his Harley."

Aaron rolled his eyes. "Why didn't he call me?"

"They've been here over an hour. I guess you were still at work," Sean said. "No matter. They're already in the kitchen. Go get something to eat before they clean it out, and don't worry about me. I got mine early and took it to my office."

Dani grinned as Sean disappeared. "Making sure there's something left to eat seems to be the top topic of conversation in this house."

"You have no idea," Aaron said, and then gave her a quick kiss. "Let's go say hi to the brothers and beg for our food."

Dani was laughing as they entered the kitchen.

"Hey, you two," Wiley said. "Grab a plate and help yourselves. I've already knocked B.J. away from the sandwiches twice."

B.J. grinned. "They're really good. Mom made pulled pork for sandwiches, and there's fried ham between biscuits, but I couldn't decide, so I ate some of both."

Aaron handed Dani a paper plate, and as soon as they made what they wanted, they joined Wiley and B.J. at the table.

Aaron took a big bite of his pulled pork sandwich, chewed, and swallowed. "You're right, B.J. It's really good." Then he glanced at Wiley as he took a quick drink. "Next time you need a ride home, call me."

Wiley glanced at B.J., then grinned. "Trust me. I will. He drives like a bat out of hell."

"I do not exceed the speed limit," B.J. muttered.

"The road up Pope Mountain is two-lane and winding, little brother. Sixty-five miles an hour on that road is like one-fifty on the Bonneville Salt Flats in Utah."

And off they went, all three brothers discussing the merits of racing on the Salt Flats as opposed to racing the Le Mans Grand Prix, while Dani calmly ate her biscuit and ham, then went back for a second helping of potato salad, and brought back a biscuit and ham for Aaron. She laid it on his plate, then sat down to finish eating.

But Aaron noticed, and remembered the day he'd put food on her plate without asking, and how taken aback she'd been before he'd explained. Now she got it, and just returned the favor. He leaned over and whispered in her ear.

"Thank you, darlin.'"

She smiled. "You're welcome."

A few minutes later Shirley walked in, followed by Sean carrying his dirty plate and glass from the office.

"Ah...my last two chicks are here," Shirley said when she saw Aaron and Dani, and gave both of them a quick hug.

"The food is delicious," Dani said. "Have you eaten?"

"Oh, a taste of this and that as I was making it," Shirley said. "I'm fine."

"No, ma'am, you're not fine," Aaron said. "Have a seat. I'll make a plate for you," and got up.

"You just want an excuse for thirds," B.J. said as Sean went to refill his drink.

Dani burst out laughing.

Shirley rolled her eyes, but she sat down and let Aaron and Wiley wait on her, because it gave them pleasure to think they were taking care of her.

"Don't put a lot on my plate, boys. We need to leave soon."

"We know, Mom," they said, and kept working.

Dani couldn't help but stare at the four men in the room. It was blatantly obvious they were brothers. Some taller than others, but all taller than six feet. All with varying shapes of the same faces, and all with different styles of the same straight black hair.

"Shirley, you sure made four beautiful sons," she whispered.

Shirley beamed. "Why, thank you, honey. I'm proud of them all."

"As you should be," Dani said.

Aaron turned around to take his mother's food back to the table and saw them with their heads together, chattering away, and smiled. Dani fit him like a glove, and she was fitting into the family like the last piece of a puzzle.

"Eat up, Mom. We'll clean the kitchen and put away the leftovers," he said.

"Thank you, son," Shirley said, and picked up her fork.

By the time Shirley had finished eating, they had everything put away and the countertops gleaming. They put her fork into the dishwasher, then started it as Wiley carried out the garbage.

A short while later, they loaded up into two cars and headed up the mountain to the meeting.

Cameron and Rusty came early because he'd called the meeting and because it was protocol to be sure to be on hand to welcome guests.

Back when they'd first discovered the journal's existence and gotten permission to read it, Cameron had recorded the journal as it was read aloud at the police station. But since then, he'd had the entire journal scanned and was having bound copies made for the families.

He knew the existing Pope, Glass, and Cauley families would be shocked, and he felt certain there would be enough of them willing to help in the search. He also knew it would be a daunting task. Maybe an impossible task after all these years, but he also knew if they didn't solve this mystery of the missing gold, they would spend the rest of their lives dealing with treasure hunters, wanting what Nyles Fairchild wanted. Willing to trespass—to steal something that didn't belong to them. And hurt others in the process, just as Charlie had been hurt.

Brother Farley was in the church office going through notes for his next Sunday sermon and awaiting Cameron's request to join them. He didn't know what was going on, but he'd soon find out. And if it affected his entire congregation, he needed to know what they were facing.

John and Annie Cauley were the first to arrive at the meeting because they lived the closest to the church, and they brought Aunt Ella with them. Cameron's sister Rachel, her husband Louis, and their daughter, Lili, arrived next, with Louis's father, Marcus Glass.

Annie's daughters and grandchildren arrived, and went to work with their assignment manning the church nursery to babysit the little ones during the meeting, with snacks already laid out to help pass the time.

After that, one family after another began arriving, including Ray and Betty Raines with Charlie. Each of them greeted the others and settled into little groups to visit until the meeting began.

And then Shirley and her sons arrived, but with a stranger, and the room went silent. She was a woman few of them knew or recognized, and they all looked at Cameron first to see his reaction.

He walked up the aisle to meet them, then gave the woman a quick hug.

"Dani, I'm so glad you could join us. Aaron, thank you for bringing her."

"My pleasure," Aaron said, and slipped his arm around Dani's waist for moral support.

"Thank you for the invitation," Dani said.

After listening to that interchange, the rest of the family relaxed. Whoever she was, she'd been invited. That was enough for them. Then, as the last stragglers arrived, Cameron stepped up to the pulpit.

Aaron felt Dani tense beside him and reached for her hand.

She glanced at him, taking comfort in his presence, and made herself relax. This wasn't an inquisition. Just a revelation of facts, part of which included her.

Cameron adjusted the sound system, making

sure those sitting in the back could clearly hear him, then he began.

"First thing, I want to thank everyone for coming. I'm sure you're all wondering what this is about. Basically, this mystery began when Charlie Raines was shot. We didn't know why it happened, and took it as the miracle it was that he survived. Now, we all know who the man was and where he was from, and we know that because there was a witness."

A resounding gasp rolled across the room, followed by a buzz of whispers. Then Cameron gave Aaron a nod.

"I'm going to ask Aaron to come up and explain the legal ramifications because he's not just a Pope but is also the officer in the Jubilee Police Department who began part of the investigation, and the first person to interact with the witness."

Aaron gave Dani's hand a quick squeeze, and then stood and moved to the front of the room and took the microphone.

"This began before the police in Jubilee even knew Charlie had been shot. I was in the front lobby of the police station when a woman walked in with the sole intention of just turning in something she'd found. It turned out to be Brendan Pope's journal, and you all already know about that, right?"

There was a rumble of voices and heads nodding.

"As we were taking her statement about how she'd come by the journal, and what she'd seen, we received the news about Charlie's shooting. After that, her statement about seeing a man with a hiker's backpack running up from the creek, staggering and drenched in sweat, became something of interest. She'd already told us she saw a metal detector, a camp shovel, and a handgun fall out of his pack when he fell, and at that point, we realized the implications. After the man drove off, she saw something lying on the ground where he'd been parked. Likely it had fallen out of his pack with everything else but slid beneath the car and he didn't see it. This turned out to be the journal. At that moment, we realized there was a real likelihood that she'd seen the man who shot Charlie, but we couldn't prove it. It became a scramble to get prints from the journal, hoping to ID him, but it turned out his prints weren't on file in the criminal justice system. All we had was her. But to keep her safe from the shooter trying to remove his only witness, we didn't let anyone, including the media, know she existed.. Then Sheriff Woodley was informed, and he brought a police sketch artist to create the composite sketch that was released nationwide. After that, the shooter was identified on security footage at the Hotel Devon, and our witness identified him as the man she'd seen dropping the gun and the journal. At that point, it was vital that no one knew of her existence. For all we knew, the shooter might be desperate enough to kill the only person who could identify him. We not only have her to thank for finding the man who shot Charlie, but we also owe her a huge debt of gratitude for bringing the journal, a family heirloom, full circle. Over the weeks of working on this case, she's become an important person to me and to my family, and Cameron wanted you to meet her." Then Aaron looked straight at Dani and smiled.

"Dani, honey, would you please stand?"

Dani took a deep breath and then stood.

"Everyone, this is Dani Owens, Jubilee's new first-grade teacher, and the secret witness who helped crack the case and find Charlie's shooter."

Dani smiled shyly and waved while the people began clapping and cheering.

She sat down as Aaron returned to join her, and Cameron returned to the podium.

"Thank you, Aaron, and now for the rest of the story. I wanted to read the journal, but since it was still evidence in an open case, it was not allowed to leave the police station. However, they let me come to the station to read it. It took me a couple of days to decipher the old script, but it was an eye-opening and moving depiction of our Scottish ancestor's beginnings here in Kentucky, and how he came by his Chickasaw wife. All my life I'd been told Brendan's wife, Meg, was Choctaw, but it's not so. She was a little Chickasaw woman by the name of Cries A Lot, who Brendan called Meg. Their story is wonderful and sad, and the bond between them was obviously strong and loving. But as I read, I began to realize why the man who shot Charlie came to Jubilee and what he was doing at Big Falls. At the end of the journal, two things happen at once that are direct reasons for what's happening now. Brendan and Meg's children were grown and had families of their own by the time the Civil War began. And sometime thereafter, a troop of Confederate soldiers came through Jubilee. They had a team of mules pulling a wagon, rumored to be carrying Confederate gold. They went through Jubilee on the same day Meg went up the mountain to pick berries. When she didn't come home, they went looking for her. They trailed her footprints all the way to Big Falls where they found her basket of berries spilled on the ground, her little footprints mingled among a dozen or more boot prints, and way too much blood on the ground for someone to have survived. They looked all over for Meg without success, then followed the boot prints back to the main road and found the wagon that had gone through Jubilee earlier, abandoned and with a broken wheel. They followed the trail of the soldiers for miles, until they came upon all of them dead, with no further sign of Meg. Brendan and the searchers decided when the wagon broke down, the soldiers carried the gold into the woods to hide it, came upon Meg picking berries, and killed her so she couldn't tell where they'd hidden their treasure, and hid her body, too."

Again, gasps and murmurs filled the air, and in the midst, Ella Pope suddenly covered her face. "The crying woman," she said and began to weep.

Cameron kept talking. "We think Nyles Fairchild came looking for gold. He told the police who arrested him that shooting Charlie was an accident. He heard something coming through the trees and shot because he thought it was a bear. But he left Charlie to die, right where Brendan's Meg disappeared. And that's why I've asked you all here. I believe Meg is somewhere on this mountain, likely with whatever it was the soldiers hid. I want to organize a search with all of the up-to-date technology available to us and find her. Until this journal reappeared in our lives, none of us knew this story, and I don't believe in coincidences. I think there was a reason Dani Owens found the journal. Brendan Pope began writing it in 1833, and almost two hundred years later, it's come full circle for a reason. We need to find our little Chickasaw grandmother. There's a sign-up sheet on the table in front of me if you want to participate in this search. And if you can't, that's totally understandable, too. But she belongs to us. Her DNA is in every Pope who came from this place. She's been alone for centuries. It's time to bring her home."

There wasn't a dry eye in the room as men began getting out of their seats and moving quietly toward the table to sign up, and as they did, women began gravitating to where Shirley and Dani were sitting to introduce themselves to Dani and thank her. Later, Dani would not remember a single name or what they looked like, because she was too overwhelmed to speak and her eyes were full of tears.

They drove home in mutual silence, each thinking about what had transpired, and the search that lay ahead. When they got back to the house, Aaron parked to let his mom and B.J. out.

"Thank you for supper and the moral support," Dani said. "Next time, I'm cooking for you."

"I'll look forward to it," Shirley said. "Rest well, honey. You did yourself proud tonight."

"What are you gonna cook?" B.J. asked.

They all broke out laughing.

"Damn, B.J., give her a minute to think about it."

B.J. grinned. "Just asking. Whatever it is, I'll like it."

"Good to know," Dani said, and then laughed again as Shirley and B.J. went up the steps and into the house.

Sean and Wiley drove up and waved at them as they went inside.

Light was shining from the windows, marking its place in the dark. It was both solace and safety to the family within. Aaron gave it one last look and then put his car in reverse.

"Time to get my girl home," he said as he backed up and took the driveway back to the main road, then headed back down to Jubilee.

They were silent for a couple of minutes before Aaron spoke.

"Are you okay? I mean…being outed like that? I know you were anxious about it."

"I'm fine. Most of my anxiety was about being the only outsider in such an important family meeting, but it wasn't as worrisome as I thought, and everyone was really nice to me, afterward."

"I'm anxious, too, but for different reasons. It's been such a long time since all of this happened. What if we don't find Meg?" he said.

"I don't know. Maybe the family could have something as simple as a memorial service, and Cameron reading sections from the journal about their lives together. Having said that, I can't help feeling she'll be found. Like Cameron said, there has to be a reason why all of this has come full circle."

"I hope you're right," Aaron said. "I sure hope you're right."

Chapter 18

Now that the news had been shared, Cameron began making plans as how to proceed. Just storming the woods in a giant all-out search party was a waste of time. Meg Pope was dead somewhere. If they found anything, it would only be bones, and that was a long shot, depending on where the soldiers hid the gold, because he fully believed they'd hidden her with it. They would not have wanted her to be found and have an angry mob come after them. If she was just missing, there would be uncertainty as to who to blame. None of them would have any idea that they would all be killed in battle hours later, or realize what a mystery they'd left behind them.

But as Cameron and Rusty were discussing the search, it was Rusty who came up with the plan.

"I think your best bet is to use drone-mounted Lidar, and ground-penetrating radar as well. That technology is amazing. Basically, it's laser light, a scanner, and a GPS receiver. Even in an area as heavily forested as the Cumberlands, and with the endless cave systems in this state, you can still pinpoint almost anything from the air with the drone mounts, or beneath the ground with GPR."

"That's a great idea," Cameron said. "What made you think of that?"

"When I was still with the Feds, we used Lidar to pinpoint places in the jungles and deserts, helping us find structures beneath the green growth or sand. The known caves in Kentucky are already mapped, but if we can find anything in or around Big Falls that looks like an old structure, and if it's not on a map, that might be a good first place to look."

"So, my darling expert, who would you recommend?" he asked.

"I'll make a list," Rusty said. "And...you might want to contact a forensic pathologist to be on standby, too, just in case we get lucky. Because no matter where you find a body or how old you think it is, the authorities will treat it like a crime scene. They'll remove bones, then carbon date to verify it as historical before the remains can be claimed."

"Shit. Never thought of that," Cameron said.

"That's why you have me," Rusty said.

"I love that you're smart and capable and gorgeous, but it's not why I married you," Cameron said, and pulled her down into his lap.

Rusty wrapped her arms around his neck. "Then why did you marry me?" she asked.

He kissed her chin, then the tip of her nose, then the soft curve of her lips.

"Because I couldn't live without you," he said.

It was another whole week before Cameron had the techs in place with their Lidar and GPR, and a forensic pathologist on standby.

Since it was the closest way to getting to Big Falls, the tech crews met at Ray and Betty Raines's house. They arrived loaded for bear, with all of their tech equipment in a Range Rover and a Jeep.

Cameron was sitting in the shade waiting and went to meet them as they approached.

"Thanks for coming. I'm Cameron Pope."

A short, blond-haired man in his early forties smiled as he held out his hand. "Brian Chandler. I'm with the Lidar crew."

A bald, heavyset man of middle age nodded at Cameron. "Eddie Young. My crew mans the GPR. Nice to meet you."

"This is Ray Raines, and it's his property we'll be mapping," Cameron said.

"Thanks for coming," Ray said. "Is everybody ready to go?"

"Just lead the way," Brian said. "We'll be right behind you."

Ray got in his truck with Cameron riding shotgun and led the way through his property, taking them as far as they could drive. At that point, they exited their vehicles, loaded up the gear, and continued to the falls on foot with Ray and Cameron leading the way.

The day was hot. And as the crew approached the area where Charlie had been shot, there were still signs in the area from the shooting and subsequent investigation. A piece of yellow crime scene tape caught in the brush. Limbs broken off bushes where Nyles had poked about, and obvious sites of where he'd been digging.

Ray looked down at one of the shallow holes Nyles had left behind and rolled his eyes. "What the hell did he think he was going to find in that little hole? A whole cache of gold lying inches below the surface? Stupid bastard," he muttered, and shoved his hands in his pockets.

The misty spray from the falls soon had their clothes damp and sticking to their bodies, but it was also cooling from the heat, since the woods blocked whatever breeze was in the air. But everybody had something to do as they set to work assembling their technology and programming in a grid.

Finally, Brian's crew sent up their Lidar-mounted drone, programmed to cover a certain area above the falls. Cameron and Ray watched as it rose up into the sky, then began flying around the area.

Down below, Eddie and his crew began mapping the ground all along the creek bank with the GPR.

Cameron and Ray stayed back, watching from the shade of the forest behind them.

"You know what I've been thinking ever since I heard about Meg disappearing?"

"No, what?" Cameron said.

Ray was still looking up at the drone as he spoke. "Aunt Ella said it in the meeting, and it got me to thinking. One of the old legends from the mountain that I grew up with was the one about the crying woman."

Cameron nodded. "I thought the same thing when she said it. When I was a boy, I remember going hunting with my dad and uncles at night when they were running the hounds, and sitting around the campfire and hearing those stories."

Ray was silent for a few moments, then glanced at Cameron.

"Did you ever hear her?" he asked.

Cameron shrugged. "I've heard all kinds of weird things up here. When a mountain lion screams, it sounds like a woman screaming. Heard that plenty of times. Have you heard the crying woman?"

Ray nodded. "More than once, but never in the daytime. Once I heard it when I was out in the pasture, looking for a cow and calf that didn't come up. It was almost dark when I finally found them. The calf was caught in the fence, and of course the cow wasn't about to leave it. Took me a bit to get the calf loose without getting stomped by the old mama. When the calf got loose, the old cow quit bawling, and the calf went straight to her to suck. So, as I sat waiting for the calf to feed before I headed them back to the house, I began hearing the sound of a woman crying…sobbing. I got my flashlight and climbed over the fence to check it out, but there was nothing there. And the farther I went into the woods, the farther away the crying became. Felt like I was being lured away. Got the chills all over. If I'd kept walking in that direction, I would have wound up where we are right now, and I'm wondering if the crying woman was Meg's ghost, trying to show me where she was at."

Cameron shuddered. "Just because I've never seen something, doesn't mean I don't believe it exists. Ever since I read that last post in Brendan's journal, I've had a feeling of obligation to right this wrong. Maybe part of it is my military training. Never leaving a soldier behind, but I want answers, you know?"

Ray nodded and looked up at the drone in the sky above them.

"Old Brendan would be hard pressed to believe what the world has come to," he said.

"Not always for the better," Cameron said. "But if we're going to find any answers, it's going to take modern technology to lead us to it."

So, they sat, watching the drone overhead and the men running the GPR over the ground. One looking for structures hidden above ground, and the other looking for answers below.

━━━━━━━━━━

The drone was in the air for almost three hours until the power pack began running low. They brought it down long enough to replace the battery, and sent it back up to finish the grid, while the crew running the GPR had moved away from the clearing and were pushing it through a narrow path through the woods that was encircling the cliff around the falls.

Every family on the mountain knew what was happening, and that a physical search would not take place until the area around the falls had been scanned. They needed a starting point and were hoping this technology would give them one.

―――――――――

It was midafternoon when it all came to a halt.

"I think we've gotten all the footage we need," Brian said. "What about you, Eddie?"

Eddie Young nodded. "We're good."

They packed up their gear and headed back through the woods to where they'd parked, loaded up, and then turned to say goodbye.

"How long will it take before you can get back to us with footage?" Cameron asked.

"There's a lot to go through. It will take at least a couple of days to view it and correlate the findings," Brian said. "I'll call you when we're ready, and Eddie and I can come back and meet with you anywhere you say."

Cameron nodded. "Then we'll be in touch."

They all got in their respective vehicles, turned around, and left the same way they'd come in. When Ray and Cameron stopped at the house, the two crews drove past the house to get back to the main road and head back to the Serenity Inn, where they were staying during the trip.

"Thanks for this," Ray said as Cameron got out.

Cameron shook his head. "I don't need thanks for anything. I just want to find her."

Ray's shoulders slumped. "I know it's a long shot, but so was Charlie's survival. He made it, and I have a good feeling about this. Finding Brendan's Meg will mean the world to all of us. Say hi to Rusty and give that giant dog of yours a good ear scratch from me."

Cameron smiled. "I'll do that. Take care and I'll be in touch," then he got in his SUV and headed home.

He felt good about today even though they still knew nothing. But it was a start, and that was something.

———

After what Annie Cauley had learned at the family meeting, she'd thought of little else. She'd heard the stories all her life of the crying woman on the mountain, but never to the point of relating to who it might be. But on the evening of the second day after the meeting, as soon as she got home from the bakery, she went straight to her bedroom and opened up an old trunk that once belonged to her granny.

She hadn't looked in it in years and wasn't certain what all was in it anymore, but she had a vague memory of being shown a piece of Native American jewelry when she was little and hearing her granny say it once belonged to a woman named Meg who'd been her great-great grandmother. But after what she'd learned, she couldn't help but wonder now if the crying woman might be Meg, and, if the jewelry was in Granny's trunk, she was going to take it to Aunt Ella to see what she could see.

Ella Pope was sitting on her front porch, fanning herself with a folded newspaper and sipping from a glass of iced tea when she saw her niece coming up the drive. She set her glass aside and waved as Annie pulled up at the front gate and got out.

"Evening, girl! Good to see you!" Ella said.

"You, too," Annie said. "I brought blueberry muffins."

Ella beamed. "You know they're my favorites. Would you take 'em in the house for me and get yourself a cold pop before you come back?"

"Yes, ma'am," Annie said, and went inside, returning moments later carrying a cold can of Mountain Dew, then sat down in an old cane-back chair beside her and slipped the strap of her purse over the arm of her chair.

Ella leaned back in her old rocking chair, smiling as she watched Annie take a drink.

"What's botherin' you, girl?" Ella asked.

Annie sighed. "You know. You said it yourself at the meeting when we learned Brendan's Meg was lost. I heard you say it under your breath. You said, "The crying woman." Do you think what we've been hearing all these years is Meg's spirit wandering this mountain, wanting to be found?"

Ella's smile faded.

"I can't know a thing for certain. I can only feel things."

Annie reached inside her purse and pulled out a worn and faded blue velvet pouch, and laid it in Ella's lap.

"What's this?" Ella asked.

Annie shrugged. "It was in my Granny's trunk. Will you 'see' it for me?"

"What if it tells me nothing?" Ella asked.

"Then it will keep its secrets just like this mountain," Annie said.

Ella nodded, and then dumped the contents into her lap.

The necklace was obviously Native American and old, very old, made of trading beads and bear claws, strung on a thin strand of rawhide.

"Meg's," Ella said. "I heard the elders talk about it when I was little, but I didn't know this still existed."

Annie sighed. "Granny said it was hers, but I wasn't sure. If you held it, would it talk to you?"

Ella picked it up, then held it loosely in her palms, letting the claws fall between her fingers as she closed her eyes and took a deep breath.

Annie's heart was pounding. Waiting like this was worse than waiting for Christmas when she was a kid, and then Ella started talking.

"Mist on my face. Taste of berries on my lips."

Annie froze. *Oh my God!*

Ella shuddered. "Many men. Afraid. Begging." When Ella made a sudden grab at her own chest and cried out in pain, Annie jumped, afraid Ella was having a heart attack, but then Ella shuddered and relaxed. One minute passed, and then another before she opened her eyes.

"They shot her, just like that man shot Charlie. And like Charlie, she was still alive when they put her in the dark. Wherever she is, she died alone, calling for Brendan."

"Could you see where she was?" Annie asked.

Ella shrugged. "In the dark. They put her where it was dark. That's all I saw."

"Had to be a cave," Annie said.

"But they're everywhere," Ella said.

"It had to somewhere near Big Falls, because the soldiers wouldn't have been there unless they'd gone there to hide the gold. What I don't understand is how soldiers, people who didn't grow up here, even knew where Big Falls was, or that there was a place to hide something like that?"

"But what if one of the soldiers *had* been from the mountain? Lots of people joined up when the war began, even a few from here. And think about this. Why did they even choose to take such a steep and treacherous route up a mountain with that gold unless someone knew it would be less traveled and they were more likely not to be attacked? They didn't plan on breaking a wagon wheel, but once it happened, that same person would have been the one who knew exactly where to put it for safekeeping until they could come back to retrieve it," Ella said.

Annie gasped. "Oh wow. Yes. I never thought of that, but it makes sense."

Ella's eyes narrowed as she stared off into the trees, remembering.

"There were old trapper's huts still around when I was growing up, but I'd reckon they've all fallen down and turned to dust." Then she put the necklace back in the velvet pouch and gave it back to Annie. "I reckon you should return this to your granny's trunk. If they do find Brendan's Meg, it would be fitting to give it back."

Annie nodded as she put the pouch in her purse. "Yes, yes, I'll do that very thing, Aunt Ella. I promise."

"Meg would like that, I think. Brendan made it for her."

Annie sighed. "All of this just breaks my heart."

"I've lived a long time, and if there's one thing I've learned, it's that life can be heartbreaking, but as long as it's given to us, it's precious despite the pain," Ella said.

"Thank you for doing this for me," Annie said.

"You're welcome, girl. But there were no revelations. Only verifications of what we already suspected."

"Except for one thing," Annie said.

Ella frowned. "What's that?"

"We didn't know she was still alive when they hid her. This is why she's crying on the mountain. She's been waiting for Brendan to find her, which in my mind, makes this a rescue a hundred and fifty years in the making."

Annie went home and immediately told John about the visit, then said nothing about it to anyone else until she got to the bakery the next morning. She liked opening up the shop and being the first one in the kitchen long before daylight. It was a quiet time. A time for contemplation as she went through her morning routine. Starting yeasts to proof, measuring flour, turning on the ovens to preheat. Starting coffee to brew in the big coffee maker.

She was taking her second batch of cinnamon rolls from the oven when her crew began to arrive.

Her daughters began working on cookie doughs and pie crusts, while B.J. began mopping the front area and wiping down tables. Once he was finished, he went to the galley area and began cleaning up the baking equipment for reuse. There was little to no talking, just people doing their jobs, when Annie suddenly stopped and turned around.

"I have something to tell you. You're all family, and this has been weighing on my heart all night." Then she began to relate her visit to Aunt Ella and told them everything Ella had said about the crying woman and believing it was Meg. When she stopped, tears were running down her face.

"Mama, what's wrong?" Laurel asked.

"Aunt Ella said Meg was shot, but when they hid her

body, she wasn't dead. Meg died in the dark alone, crying out for Brendan. I can't get that image out of my head."

B.J. was in shock. "Just like Charlie," he said. "Only his mama found him in time."

They all turned to look at him. He was pale and obviously shaken by Annie's story.

"I used to be afraid of the dark," he muttered, then went back to cleaning without looking up.

After that, it was a long day for all of them, trying to stay upbeat for the constant stream of customers as the sadness settled upon them.

That evening when B.J. went home, he was unusually quiet at the supper table and only picked at his food, behavior that alerted every family member into thinking he was sick.

"B.J., honey, are you okay?" Shirley asked.

"Yes, ma'am," he said, and shoved a piece of meat through a pile of ketchup, then put down his fork.

"If you're not sick, then what's wrong?" Aaron asked.

"Is Aunt Ella psychic?" B.J. asked.

That was the last thing they'd expected him to say.

Shirley shrugged. "The family has always claimed she had some kind of knowing. I don't think they ever called her psychic. Why?"

But the moment he told them what Annie said, they had the same reaction he'd had, that of shock and then dismay.

"Mom, is there really a legend about a crying woman?" B.J. asked.

Shirley frowned. "I don't know, but I've known the story all my life. Once, my brother and I thought we heard her, but Mama wouldn't have us talking ourselves into being afraid of the mountain and just told us whatever happened in the past did not have the power to hurt us in the present." Then she sighed. "But that was before that crazy man found the journal and came looking for gold. Gold that got Meg killed and nearly killed Charlie, so I don't think Mama covered all the bases."

"I hope we can find her," Aaron said.

"I want to be on the same search team as my brothers," B.J. said. "I remember being afraid of the dark."

Aaron gave B.J. a quick pat on the shoulder.

"I'll make sure you're with me," he said.

"Thanks," B.J. said, and then carried his plate to the sink and walked out.

Sean sighed. "I think our little brother is becoming quite a man."

"Agreed," Wiley said.

Shirley sat, listening to them talk and wondering what kind of a miracle it was going to take to find Brendan's Meg and the missing gold.

———————

The next morning, Cameron got a call from Brian Chandler, telling him they had finished going through the Lidar scans and were ready to meet.

"I can be there in a couple of hours," Cameron said. "Would ten o'clock work for you?"

"Sure. We can meet in my suite. Room 404 at the Serenity Inn," Brian said.

"I'll be there," Cameron said, disconnected, then went to see if Rusty was awake. Pregnancy was taking its toll, and waking up early was no longer on her agenda. He opened the door to take a peek, then smiled. She was curled up on her side, her long red curls scattered across her pillow and in her face, sound asleep.

The mere sight of her filled him with such joy, and knowing she was carrying their baby was enough to put a lump in his throat. He carefully closed the door, left a note for her telling her he was taking Ghost for a run and would be back in an hour, then grabbed Ghost's leash. Within seconds, Ghost was at his heels.

"You heard the jingle of the clasp, didn't you, boy?"

Ghost looked up with anticipation.

Cameron chuckled, fastened the clasp to Ghost's collar, and out the door they went.

As always, he took to the blacktop and headed up the mountain at a lope with Ghost beside him. It was already getting warm up here, so he could only imagine what it must feel like in the valley below.

He was anxious to find out what the Lidar scans revealed, but he was also a realist. This search was such a long shot. But he couldn't forget those last few posts in the journal. After Meg's disappearance,

Brendan's zest for life ended. There was no mention of anything of note afterward. Losing her had been the end of him.

And that kind of loss, Cameron understood.

———————

Dani was dressed and in the kitchen making coffee when she heard a car pulling up into her drive. Before she could get to the door to see who it was, she heard a key in the lock and smiled.

"It's just me!" Aaron said.

"I'm in the kitchen," Dani shouted.

Moments later, he walked in, put a sack on the kitchen island, then took her in his arms.

"I'm on duty. Calling this a welfare call. I am absolutely certain I cannot get through this day without this hug. I brought you cinnamon rolls from Aunt Annie's bakery. I love you."

Then he swooped in, tunneling his fingers through her hair as he aimed for her lips. The kiss rocked her to her toes and ended as abruptly as it began.

Aaron groaned as he turned her loose. "Never forget how much I love you."

And then he was gone, leaving Dani speechless and breathless, trying to absorb the kiss and run, but all she could remember was the rock-hard surface of his chest, the scent of his aftershave, and the cinnamon rolls as proof that he'd really been here.

Cameron arrived on time at the Serenity Inn and took the elevator to the fourth floor, then went down the hall to Brian's room and knocked. A few moments later, the door swung inward.

"Come in," Brian said. "Eddie's here, too. The rest of the crew left for home this morning. There are cold drinks and coffee on the bar. Help yourself."

"I'm good, but thanks," Cameron said. "I'm just anxious to see if you've got anything for us."

Brian grinned. "We have stuff. Whether it's anything that will aid in your search, I can't say. But it's interesting, to say the least. Have a seat at the table. We'll explain things as we go."

As Cameron sat, Brian took the chair beside him, then opened his laptop.

"First off, I'm going to show you all this in real time, although we've loaded it all onto a flash drive for you and have a whole series of still shots printed off as well. So whichever works best for your search, you'll have it. Now we begin."

Cameron leaned forward, listening as Brian began explaining what was on screen. It was like deciphering a whole other language, and it took a bit for him to realize what he was looking at. The drone-mounted Lidar had given him in-depth images of what lay hidden beneath the dense forest and undergrowth, while the GPR would reveal disturbances to the soil below. The area around Big Falls was where the search was focused, and there were two things that stood out.

"What's this?" Cameron asked, pointing to a specific shot captured near the falls.

Brian frowned. "We're not sure. Lidar doesn't penetrate water very well, but a best guess is some kind of aperture behind the waterfall itself."

Cameron's eyes narrowed. "That's weird. I swam in that pool beneath the falls many times, and I never noticed any kind of opening."

"That's understandable. Like I said, Lidar doesn't refract properly through water, even when it's in the ocean or in a lake. And this water coming off the falls is falling hard and fast, which stirs up a continual mist. It may be nothing, but if there's a crevice or an opening in the wall of the falls, there could be a containment spot of some kind behind it."

Cameron made a mental note to check that out, while Brian kept talking.

"Here's another interesting point. This would be in the woods south of the falls. We think it's some kind of structure. There aren't any walls, of course, but what appears to be remnants of a foundation," Brian said.

Cameron frowned. "There aren't any existing buildings back there and haven't been in my time. I've spent too many hours in the woods around Big Falls not to know that. So this is interesting."

Brian nodded. "Another verification of a possible home or cabin once being there is in this footage." Then he pointed. "In this image, we're looking at treetops. Looks like a big green carpet, doesn't it? Different varieties of trees grow to different heights, of course, but see here, where it looks like a big indentation…like a giant used the trees for a bed and left an impression when he left?"

"Yes. What does that mean?" Cameron asked.

"While we know the variety of trees growing on Pope Mountain haven't changed, in this particular area we're looking at, the growth is considerably shorter than the growth surrounding it. You don't notice this from the ground, but it's obvious from aerial views. This might indicate it had once been a clearing, and the growth there now is considerably newer than the surrounding area. It's near the indication of a hidden foundation. Maybe trees were cut down in the past century or so to build a cabin?"

Cameron kept staring, trying to picture where this was from ground level. "It's amazing how this aerial view can be interpreted with Lidar. I knew the technology existed because I've seen documentaries about new findings on Mayan cities lost to the jungles from centuries past, but to see it used on a place I know is a revelation." He leaned forward again, pointing to a different configuration on the laptop screen. "What's this area here?"

"Those are indicative of cave entrances, like the caves and tunnels that have been present for thousands of years. Not man-made holes, like graves or where something large has been buried, which GPR would pick up."

This was info Cameron would have to compare to the cave maps he had of the state. "Did you find anything on the GPR?" Cameron asked.

At this point, Brian turned it over to Eddie and traded places.

Eddie opened his laptop so Cameron could see what he was talking about.

"As you know, we were limited to scanning, because GPR only works in open areas. We tried getting into the forest, but GPS isn't made for use in small intermittent areas, so it's impossible to get good data from it. What you're seeing here is the creek bank area only, and a little bit around the rock face of the falls. See how the striations stay even through most of it? That means the earth beneath hasn't been disturbed. Nothing dug up or buried. But we do have this odd anomaly near the falls. We did some research, and it seems that when the New Madrid quake happened in 1811, it was devastating in ways these people had never before encountered. Not only was it pivotal in this area, but in a good portion of the central U.S. as well. The quake first hit in December 1811, and intermittent quakes continued through February 1812. People thought the world was coming to an end and abandoned everything in an effort to escape. The earthquakes were of a magnitude of 7.0 or larger, so we can only imagine the continuing horror and devastation in those times. We think this portion of the scan is representative of that because the timeline fits. Those quakes appear to have changed the formation of how Big Falls looks now. But I don't see anything that would relate specifically to your search."

"I don't think I knew about that quake," Cameron

said. "People must have been horrified." But then he began putting two and two together. "It could explain why some of the old trappers' cabins no longer exist. Why I never saw any when I was growing up. If the quake happened in December, then it would be cold on the mountain. Anyone inhabiting those dwellings would be burning wood to keep warm, and if those cabins caught fire during the tremors, people would have fled the area, and there would have been no one left to rebuild."

"Agreed," Eddie said. "Even though our GPR scans didn't turn up much for you, you'll have copies of still shots and scans on the flash drive."

"And here they are," Eddie said as he pushed a large manila envelope across the table, then handed Cameron the flash drive. "If we can be of any further service, just give us a call."

"Do I pay you now?" Cameron asked.

Eddie shook his head. "Naw…you're Rusty's guy, so that's good enough for us. We already invoiced you."

Being considered "Rusty's guy" made Cameron smile. "Thanks again for your prompt response."

"What your family is trying to do is pretty special," Brian said. "Do us a favor. If you do find your lost ancestor, let us know, will you?"

"I'll let you know, one way or the other," Cameron said, and picked up the envelope. "I'll let myself out. Safe travels home."

Minutes later, he was heading to Granny Annie's Bakery. Rusty loved sweets, and he loved Rusty.

Chapter 19

ANNIE CAULEY WAS AT THE FRONT COUNTER OF THE bakery when Cameron walked in. As soon as she rang up her waiting customer, she came around the counter to hug him.

"You're the second good-looking Pope to come in this morning. Good to see you, honey."

"Good to see you, too," Cameron said. "Who else was here?"

"Aaron. It seems Dani loves my cinnamon rolls."

"And Aaron loves Dani," Cameron said, then laughed. "I'm here for Rusty. It appears we're suckers for the women we love."

Annie's smile faded. "Like Brendan loved Meg. I went to see Aunt Ella last night. I had her read a necklace for me that my granny always claimed belonged to Meg."

Cameron was well aware of the family's faith in Aunt Ella's "second sight" and had no reason to dispute it. "Really? What did she say?" he asked.

"Let's sit a minute," Annie said, then called back into the kitchen. "Laurel, will you please come take over for me for a bit?"

Cameron held out a chair for her, then sat down beside her. Annie was already worrying the hem on her apron, twisting it into a wad and then smoothing it out again, a sign she was upset.

"I won't go into details, but Aunt Ella said Meg was shot in the upper chest area, like Charlie. She also said Meg was still alive when they put her somewhere dark and that she died calling Brendan's name. I can't get that image out of my head. It breaks my heart, Cameron. It purely breaks my heart. I hope to God you find our Meg. Ella said she's the crying woman some hear on the mountain. She wants to be found."

Cameron was stunned and, like Annie, horrified by the image of that happening to Meg.

"We're going to begin searching tomorrow. I now have the maps and info I was waiting for. What will be, will be, but we're going to give it our best shot."

Annie wiped her eyes. "I know you will. Now what are we getting for Rusty today?"

"Some kind of pie, I think."

Annie frowned, thinking of what they had on hand. "This weather calls for something cool and refreshing. How about a lemon cream pie?"

"Sounds like a winner. Box it up," Cameron said.

———————

Cameron spent the rest of the afternoon making calls until he had fourteen men on the list, counting himself.

They were to meet at Ray and Betty Raines's home
tomorrow morning at 8:00, with their own backpacks
of food and water, ropes if they had them, hatchets for
clearing brush as they searched, and shovels for digging.
He went to bed that night satisfied by the progress.

———————

Aaron had gotten the call while he was on patrol. For
him, the timing was perfect, because he was off for the
next two days.

B.J. was at work when he got the call, and after
talking to Annie, she'd gladly given B.J. the day off to
help search.

Wiley was pulling a double shift at work and couldn't
go, and Sean had two prior conference calls scheduled
and couldn't change them without losing clients.

Cameron's brother-in-law, Louis Glass, was one of
the searchers, as was his father, Marcus, and the next
morning at 8:00 a.m., the members of the search team
began arriving at Ray and Betty's house. Charlie was sitting on the back porch wishing he was old enough and
strong enough to participate. Instead, he sat watching
as they arrived and began loading up three pickups with
men, gear, and backpacks.

Then once again, Ray led the way through his property all the way to the tree line. From there, the men
piled out of the pickup trucks, gathered up their gear,
and headed for Big Falls.

Cameron, Louis, and Marcus, were riding with Ray. Aaron and B.J. were riding in the bed of a pickup truck belonging to one of Annie's grandsons, along with a half dozen other men, and a third pickup truck with the rest of the men was bringing up the rear.

Once they arrived at Big Falls, Cameron planned to break the men up into two teams. One team would take the area around the falls to see if there was actually a cave behind the falling water, while the other moved to the wooded area to see if they could find any sites that might indicate previous dwellings.

After seeing the Lidar imagining, he knew this wouldn't be a long, drawn-out search because there was only a limited area to consider. The soldiers would not have dragged a heavy trunk of gold all over the forest. They would have had a destination in mind from the start.

"Here we are, boys. Let's do this," Ray said as he drove across the cattle guard, then parked. The other two pickups pulled up beside him, and then everyone piled out, recovered the equipment they'd brought with them, and headed toward the falls with Cameron leading the way.

Aaron knew how invested B.J. was in being a part of this, and he'd already promised his mother to look after him, something B.J. knew nothing about.

"I got a good feeling about this," B.J. said as they followed the rest of the search team.

"Hope you're right, little brother," Aaron said. "It means a lot to the family to make this right."

B.J. nodded. "I know. But we're really new to the mountain. Sometimes I feel like we still don't quite belong, even though everyone is down with us being here."

Aaron frowned. He'd had no idea B.J. felt like this.

"No, no way," he said. "Where you're born isn't who you are. Up here, blood kin is the key to belonging. Mama grew up here, and Grandma Helen before her, and all the way back through the generations to the first Brendan Pope, your namesake. You walk with your head up. You don't have to explain yourself to anyone."

B.J. sighed. "Yeah, okay, you're right. I think sometimes I'll never fully shed the shit from before."

Aaron frowned, shifting his pack as they walked. "Forget before. Today and all of our tomorrows are what matters now."

A few moments later, they reached the falls and joined the rest of the team. Cameron had copies of photos of the areas they were going to search, and handed them out to each man present, then explained his plan.

"These are the two areas of focus. It has been suggested there could be a cave behind the waterfall, so half of us will concentrate on that. Make sure you're a damn good swimmer before you volunteer for that team, because the rocks are bound to be slippery, and if you wind up in the water, at least be able to swim your way out. The rest of us will concentrate on searching the wooded area. The Lidar scan indicated an area that had once been a clearing, and there might be some kind of structural foundation buried beneath a century's worth of decay and undergrowth. You can see the areas from these photos."

That immediately separated the men without argument. All of them could swim, but some of them were leery about dealing with the falls.

Aaron could just see B.J. clamoring over those rocks with the same abandon he showed on his Harley, and volunteered them for the foot search in the woods.

B.J. gave him a look and then grinned. "Mama told you to bring me back in one piece, didn't she?"

"You already know the answer to that," Aaron said, and began looking at the photos in relation to where they were standing. "Okay, whatever we're looking for is on this side of the falls, so let's head back south, and then maybe wind our way west a little and see what we can see."

As they walked away, Marcus Glass followed, as did four other men, and the farther they walked, the more they began to spread out, until some of them were out of sight, while Cameron and the other six searchers began looking for a cave behind the waterfall.

It was slow going, and as the first hour passed, Wade Morgan, one of the searchers at the falls, slipped and fell into the pool beneath, and got hammered by the water pounding down. He came up gasping. By the time he swam to the creek bank, he was out of breath.

"Are you okay?" Cameron asked as he and Louis reached down and pulled Wade up and out.

"Oh, yeah, I'm okay, but the pool is deep, and the

water coming down off the mountain is pretty strong. It pounded the crap out of me before I could swim out."

"Go pour the water out of your shoes and take a rest," Cameron said.

Wade nodded and headed for a stump back in the trees as Cameron and Louis returned to the search.

All of a sudden, they heard someone shout and went running back to the search area. Darren Cauley, one of Annie's grandsons, came hacking his way out of a dense growth of brush, scratched and bleeding.

"Cameron! I found something. I think it might be a cave entrance."

"Did you go in?" Cameron asked.

Darren ducked his head. "I didn't want to go in alone with no one knowing where I was, for fear I'd walk up on a bear."

"No shame in being careful," Cameron said. "Got a flashlight with you?"

"Yes, sir," Darren said.

"So do I. Lead the way. We're right behind you," he said, following Darren through the thick brush until he stopped abruptly.

"It's there," Darren said, pointing to an opening about six feet wide that narrowed upward into a point about eight feet from the ground. Basically, a tepee-shaped opening in the side of the rocks.

Cameron had a handgun in a holster and was suddenly wishing for a hunting rifle as he stared into the black void before them. Then he took a deep breath.

"I'll go in first. You three come in behind me, okay?"

They nodded, watching as Cameron turned on his flashlight and stepped into the opening, pausing slowly to sweep the interior with light.

It *was* a cave, about forty feet deep, and looked like something from another planet. Stalactites hung down from the roof of the cave, while stalagmites rose from the floor. The roar of the waterfall was deafening in here, and as he moved farther inside, he walked into tiny droplets coming down like rain from above.

As he moved forward, the others entered behind him.

"Holy crap," Louis said, and then realized he couldn't hear his own voice above the roar, and went quiet.

Cameron moved forward carefully, looking for any sign of a large chest or box, but saw nothing to indicate skeletal remains or even animal bones, which indicated an unlikely lair for any animal. The roar alone would be enough to put them off, not to mention the water. It would be like sleeping in constant rain.

After a thorough search of the entire area and finding no tunnels branching off in other directions, they retraced their steps out.

"That was creepy as hell," Darren said.

"Agreed. Even the animals seem to be giving that a wide berth," Cameron said.

"Back to the drawing board," Louis said.

Unaware of Wade Morgan's baptism, or that Darren had actually found a cave behind the falls, the men in the woods were still eyes to the ground, looking for signs of anything resembling a crumbling fireplace or pieces of foundation.

It was nearing noon.

Aaron heard men's voices in the distance from time to time, but they were somewhere behind them or to the south, and he and B.J. were still making their way west. He noticed B.J. had paused about seventy-five yards ahead and was digging at something in the ground.

Aaron paused to take a drink of water when he heard B.J. yelp and then call out. He looked up.

B.J. was standing with one arm in the air, waving wildly. "Aaron! Aaron! This way! I think I found something!"

Aaron lifted his arm in response and then watched in horror as B.J. suddenly dropped out of sight, disappearing before his eyes.

Aaron groaned. "Oh hell, no!" he muttered, and leaped forward in an all-out sprint, calling Cameron's phone as he ran.

Cameron answered. "Hello."

"This is Aaron. I need help. B.J. just fell into some kind of hole south and west of the falls. One minute he was waving at me, shouting that he'd found something, and then the ground went out from under him and he disappeared." Then he dropped his phone into his pocket and kept running.

B.J. hit solid ground feet first in a jarring thud. He bit his tongue as he landed, then fell backward onto his backpack. His side was burning, and when he touched it, it felt wet. At best guess, he was at least fourteen feet below ground level, and the daylight shining down into this hole had suddenly become his North Star.

"Jesus," he moaned, spitting out blood and wiping the blood from his hands onto his jeans.

His ears were still ringing from impact as he managed to slip off the backpack before fumbling inside it, trying to find his flashlight. His heart was pounding, and despite the chill below ground, he was sweating.

Damn the dark. Damn the dark. You're not a kid anymore. Get over it.

When his fingers finally curled around the handle of his LED lantern, he breathed a quick sigh of relief and turned it on.

But relief soon turned to shock and then full-on panic at the web of dangling grass roots above his head, as well as the tree roots that had followed the walls down and onto the dirt floor on which he was standing. It was a shocking version of a haunted house at Halloween, and he'd arrived here without having to pay a gate fee to get in.

There were remnants of a decaying staircase on the ground around him, and a large iron box nearby covered in a thick layer of dirt and roots. But it was the little skeleton lying beside it that rendered him speechless.

Meg.

He rolled over onto his hands and knees and began to inch toward it, keeping the light directly on the path in front of him. The last thing he wanted was to get snakebit and die down here, too.

When he finally reached her, he rocked back on his knees and flashed his light, eyeing the way she'd died—on her side, arms curled upward, hands together against her chest in a gesture of prayer.

In this dark ungodly hole, he'd never seen anything more holy. His hands were shaking as he reached toward her, feeling the need to make contact to assure himself and her that they were no longer alone.

"Meg, I'm Brendan, one of your grandsons from this time. We've been looking for you."

Suddenly there was a swirl of air around him and the faint sound of what sounded like laughter. The hair stood up on the back of his neck as he went quiet, then jumped when he heard a voice shouting his name.

He looked up. It was Aaron.

B.J. glanced down at her again. "Be right back," he said, and then painfully crawled to his feet and limped back to the hole and looked up. "I'm down here!" he shouted.

"Crap, kid! Are you okay?" Aaron said.

"I'll live," B.J. said.

"What the hell happened?" Aaron yelled.

"I found Meg."

"Oh my God! Is it a cave? Is the gold down there with her?" Aaron asked.

"It's not a cave. I think it's an old dug cellar. There's a really big iron box beside her, but I don't know what's in it. There used to be a staircase here, but it long since fell apart. I'd appreciate a lift up when you can manage it."

"Lord, have mercy, little brother. Sit tight. I've already called the cavalry. How bad are you hurt? Should I call an ambulance?"

"I'm bleeding some, but I'll live."

Aaron sighed. "Mom's gonna kill me," he muttered, and then heard voices shouting his name.

"Here! We're here!" Aaron shouted back, and kept calling until he saw the others coming toward him on the run.

Cameron was the first to reach him. "Where is he?"

Aaron pointed to the hole behind him. "Down there. He found Meg, and there's a big iron box with her."

"Is he hurt?" Cameron asked.

"He said he's bleeding some, but I think he's okay. He was standing up when I aimed the light down on him."

At that point, the search for Meg turned into a rescue for B.J. The men began assessing the area where B.J. fell, and soon realized it was what was left of the wood floor from an old cabin, and B.J. had fallen through the door in the floor. When the ancient wood shattered, ragged edges of the ancient spikes had ripped through B.J.'s side and across his back on the way down.

"B.J.! Get back!" Cameron shouted. "We need to enlarge the hole where you fell so we can get somebody down to help you up."

"That will be me," Aaron said.

"Anybody up there got something to cover Meg up? I don't want any garbage to fall on her down here!" B.J. shouted.

Cameron took a disposable rain poncho out of his pack. "Dropping down a plastic poncho," Cameron shouted.

B.J. saw it falling and caught it in midair. Then he pulled it out of the pouch, unfolded it, and carefully laid it over the remains.

"Okay! She's covered! Just be careful with what falls in here!" B.J. shouted, and then eased himself down beside her so that he was kneeling between her and any falling debris, and settled in to wait.

He could hear the rumble of men's voices from above as they began to clean up the opening, but he was past caring about what was happening above ground, and doing his best not to panic about where he was or how much blood he could feel soaking into his clothes, and started talking to keep his mind off the pain.

"My mother's name is Shirley. I have three brothers, Aaron, Sean, and Wiley. I'm the youngest. There are hundreds of us up here on Pope Mountain. You and your Brendan left a wonderful legacy for all of us."

The sounds above faded as silence enveloped him. By all rights, he should have been freaked out of his head, but in a strange way he felt safe, and as he continued to speak, his voice kept getting softer, like the whispers in church between him and his brothers when they were small.

"There's something else. We didn't know you'd gone missing. Over the years, Brendan's journal, the one he wrote your story in, went missing, too. Then our family found it again, and that's when we found out that you never came home. Brendan couldn't find you then, so we came looking for you now. You're not lost anymore, Meg. You don't have to cry on the mountain ever again. We found you for him. It's going to take a while, but we'll get you out of here."

And then he took off his belt, removed the ornate buckle with his initials on it, and laid the buckle on top of the cover he'd put over her.

"This is a gift. My promise to you that we'll honor your time in this world and lay you to rest with your Brendan."

As he swept his flashlight across the plastic shroud, it reflected off the silver buckle with the initials BJP. Satisfied, he leaned back, and as he did, a sharp pain doubled him over.

B.J. moaned and then yelled up to the men above.

"Hurry the hell up, you guys, before I bleed out down here!"

Aaron went pale. "Shit. Somebody call that ambulance, give me a first aid kit, and get me down there. Now!"

Within minutes, Cameron had a nylon rope looped around the nearest tree he was using as an anchor and a six-foot lanyard attached to Aaron's harness to absorb the shock of a sudden drop. Then they buckled him in and sent him down.

Aaron was holding on to a first aid kit and his lantern.

"Coming down," he shouted.

B.J. was lying on his back now, in too much pain to stand up. Seeing his brother descending into this hole was like seeing an angel coming to take him out of hell. The moment Aaron's feet hit dirt, he shouted up. "I'm down! Give me some slack."

Moments later, he was out of the harness and rushing to where B.J. was lying. He swept a light beam all around the area, saw the box and the shroud B.J. had placed over the remains. The sight of B.J.'s belt buckle put a lump in his throat. When he aimed the lantern at B.J. and saw all the blood, he had to hide his panic. "Hey, little brother. I need you to sit up so I can get to this wound. Can you do that for me?"

"With a little help," B.J. said.

Aaron lifted B.J. into a sitting position, then pulled B.J.'s arm out of his T-shirt and pushed it aside, revealing three deep gashes and a host of splinters visible both in the wound and under his skin.

"Aw, man, this is so gonna hurt," Aaron muttered as he opened the first aid kit. "I can't do much but disinfect the obvious and patch it up enough to slow the bleeding."

"I can take it. Once you look at Meg, you'll realize that hurts way more than what you're about to do to me. Have at it."

Aaron poured the antiseptic, flushing out as much debris as he could, then tore into a half dozen gauze pads and placed them over the cuts.

"B.J., can you hold them in place for a sec while I tear off some tape?"

"Yeah," B.J. said, wincing slightly as he applied pressure to keep them from slipping until Aaron had them all taped down.

"Okay, shirt back on, kid. After that, you're gonna have to stand up so I can buckle you into this harness. You can lean on me, okay?"

"Do what you gotta do," B.J. said.

Aaron helped B.J. up, hearing his gasps and moans as he buckled him into the harness. At that point, Aaron leaned forward until their foreheads were touching.

"Love you, Brendan."

B.J. grasped his brother's forearm as a wave of pain nearly sent him to his knees. "Love you, too, man. See you up top."

Aaron handed him his backpack, then stepped back and yelled.

"Cameron! He's ready! Pull him up!"

Moments later, B.J.'s feet left the ground. He moaned as the harness began pressing on the wounds, then gave Meg one last glance and lifted his face to the light.

As B.J. went up, Aaron began gathering the refuse

he'd discarded from administering first aid, then pulled out his phone. He began taking pictures of everything in sight, from the web of roots coming down through the old flooring above, the tree roots tunneling down the side of the walls, and then the box covered in dirt and debris, and all the while, the tiny mound of bones beneath the plastic was in his peripheral vision. He'd seen bodies before. He'd seen skeletal remains before, but he'd never had a personal connection to them, and what he was about to do felt like an intrusion. Still, they'd come looking, and he needed to see what they'd found, so he removed B.J.'s buckle and lifted away the shroud.

There was a moment of shock and then a wave of despair as the realization of how her life ended washed through him. He took the necessary photos, and as he was covering her back up, had a vision of Dani cowering in the dark, in a closet, afraid for her life, and gritted his teeth to keep from crying. He put the buckle back where B.J. left it, then stepped back.

"I'm so sorry, little Meg," he said softly, then picked up his lantern and carried it to the iron box.

The lock was huge and rusted, and when Aaron gave it a twist, it came off in his hands. His heart was pounding as he began brushing away the roots and debris, but when he reached to open the lid, it stuck. He wiped his hands on his jeans and tried again and then again, until suddenly it broke free. At that moment, he thought how likely it would be that the hinges were as fragile as the lock had been, and eased the lid up just enough to shine in a light.

At first, he couldn't figure out what he was seeing, and then when he did, forgot to breathe. He just stood there, staring in disbelief until reality took hold. He snapped a couple of pictures before easing the lid back down and turned away, shaking his head.

The silence within this space was haunting, like being buried alive.

Like Meg.

He could tell from the added murmurs of voices above that the paramedics must be on scene. He stood listening as the voices began fading. That meant they were taking B.J. to the ambulance.

He hoped Cameron had called their mom and thought to call Wiley because he was already in town, then gave up worrying about details. Eventually everyone would know, and it would all work out.

They had succeeded in what they came here to do, but Aaron felt sick to his stomach. He just kept thinking, *What a waste. What a waste.*

He wanted Dani. He needed to touch her. To feel her skin beneath his fingertips. To feel her breath upon his face. Have her laughter echoing in his heart. To remember life, and not this death.

He couldn't bring himself to look at the little bones again. But it didn't matter. The image of her last hours and final resting place would be forever etched in his heart.

Then a shout came from above.

"Hey, Aaron! Harness coming down!" Cameron shouted.

Aaron stepped back as they lowered it, then grabbed it and buckled himself in. He looked around to make sure he wasn't leaving anything behind, then picked up his flashlight and the first aid kit.

"Pull me up!"

So they did.

The closer to the light he went, the more he regretted leaving her alone. And as soon as they pulled him up onto solid ground, he handed over the first aid kit and as he began unbuckling himself out of the harness. As he did, he saw his brother's blood all over his hands and his clothes, and shuddered.

"Did they get B.J. out okay?" he asked.

"Yes, some of the men helped the EMTs carry him out. Was the gold down there, too?" Cameron asked.

Aaron stared off into the woods. "The box is there. But there's no gold. It's full of Confederate money. Rotting, crumbling, worthless paper. Meg was murdered for that. Charlie nearly died for that. I'm kinda sick to my stomach."

There was an audible gasp from the men around him, and then they went quiet.

Aaron wiped his hands on his jeans, but the blood had dried, and then he looked back at the hole they'd just pulled him out of.

"We need to cover up the opening and tent it to protect it from the elements until your forensic pathologist gets here." Then his voice began to quaver as he struggled not to weep. "Don't let them take away her bones with some bullshit story about needing to study them. All they need is a tooth or a tiny piece of bone to get her DNA, and there's a mountain full of us with that same DNA to back up who she is, along with entries in the journal. They can keep her in the morgue in Bowling Green until they're satisfied she belongs to us. We have to make sure she never gets lost again."

"I can make that promise," Cameron said. "If I have to, I'll sic Rusty on the powers that be."

Aaron nodded, but he still couldn't look at them without losing it.

The men had all seen B.J.'s emotional state after they pulled him up—tears rolling down his face and mute to what he'd seen, and now Aaron had come out of that hole the same way.

Cameron wanted to console him, but he didn't know how or what had triggered it.

"What happened down there? What did you see?" he asked.

A muscle jerked near Aaron's eye as he pulled out his phone and began sending all the photos he'd taken to Cameron's phone.

Cameron heard the dings as his phone signaled incoming messages. "What are you sending?" he asked.

"Pictures of what's down below. The old cellar became her crypt. I'd say she died praying. I'm gonna head on back to the truck," and then quietly walked away.

Chapter 20

B.J. WAS IN ER, STRIPPED DOWN TO HOW HE'D COME into this world, suffering the indignities of having three different nurses cleaning away the grime and blood before they took him to surgery, but he was at the point of not giving a shit what they saw if someone would just take away the pain.

The doctor had taken one look at the state of B.J.'s injuries and decided on the spot that it would be less painful for the boy if they put him to sleep before they began to remove the debris and repair the damage.

Finally, the nurses finished, and as they were covering him with a sheet, Shirley walked in with Sean and Wiley behind her.

B.J. saw the look on her face and sighed. He'd scared her. Hell, he'd scared himself. And he was on the verge of his own set of tears.

"Hey, Mom."

"Brendan! Sweetheart! What have you done to yourself?" Shirley muttered as she moved past the nurses and went straight to his bed.

"I found Meg," he said, then shuddered.

Sean and Wiley were immediately at his side, touching him and patting him, just like they used to do when he was little.

"You did good," Sean said. "Where's Aaron?"

"He came down to get me and was still in the hole when they took me to the ambulance. He's okay."

"I told him to take care of you," Shirley muttered.

B.J. frowned. "And he did. They lowered him into that god-awful hole. He gave me first aid and hugged me and told me he loved me. Who could have predicted the ground I was standing on would give way? There's no way to prepare for something that bizarre. Don't you dare be mad at him."

Shirley sighed. "Honey, I'm not mad at either of you. But if you'll remember, my hair has been gray since my thirties. You boys and your escapades have made me old before my time."

Then two orderlies appeared. "I'm sorry, but you'll need to go to the waiting room on the surgical wing. That's on the second floor. It will likely take at least a couple of hours."

"Surgery! Oh no!" Shirley said. "Will they have to put him to sleep?"

B.J. groaned. "God, Mom, I hope so. This hurts like hell and feels like I have enough wood splinters in me to build a doghouse. Don't worry. I'm right where I need to be, and Aaron can explain everything when he shows up."

The orderlies took a left as they wheeled him out,

while the family returned to the lobby and took the elevator up to the second floor.

———————

Aaron came home to an empty house and went straight to the bathroom, then wouldn't look in the mirror. He didn't want to see his own expression or his brother's blood. How he felt was bad enough without seeing the physical evidence for himself. He turned on the water to let it get warm, and then thought of Dani and walked out into the hall to call her, but when she answered, the sound of her voice finally broke the wall he'd been hiding behind.

"Hi, sweetheart! How's it going? Are you still on site?"

Aaron took a deep breath as tears rolled. "No. I'm home cleaning up. B.J.'s in ER, but he's gonna be okay. Just getting stitches."

Dani froze. There was an emotion in his voice that she'd never heard. "What's wrong? And don't tell me nothing, because I can hear it in your voice."

"B.J. found Meg. I'm getting in the shower now. I'll tell you details later."

"Aaron…sweetheart…I'm so sorry."

"Don't be. It's what we wanted. It was just harder than either of us imagined. As soon as I get cleaned up, I'm headed to the hospital. Mom and my brothers are likely already there."

"Would it be okay if I went there? I wouldn't want

anyone to think I was insinuating myself into their personal, private space."

"I want you there. You'll never be an intruder. You're already in our hearts. I'll see you soon."

⸻

Thirty minutes later, Dani walked into the waiting room, a little nervous about her reception, then realized by their greeting that she'd worried for nothing.

The moment Shirley saw her walk in, she was on her feet, and Dani started talking. "Aaron called me. I hope you don't mind that I'm here," she said and gave Shirley a hug.

"Of course, we don't mind. I'm glad you're here. Aaron just sent pictures of the place where they found Meg, which just elevates the tragedy of the whole thing. It's strange to be feeling this much emotion for someone we never knew except by name. She's been dead and gone for such a long time, and yet for all of us, because we just learned of her fate and now found her remains, it makes it all so current. And then to have B.J. injured on top of it all…"

Shirley just shook her head and took Dani's hand. "Come sit with us. Do you want something to drink? The boys have already hit the concession area over there."

"No thanks, I'm fine," Dani said. "So tell me what happened to B.J. How did he get hurt?"

"Sean, show Dani the photos Aaron sent you."

Sean pulled them up on his phone and handed it to her, then began pointing at each photo she pulled up.

"They think this used to be a cellar beneath some old cabin. The structure is no longer there, but the flooring and the cellar door were still in place, and covered in a century-plus of grass, decaying leaves, and debris. B.J. was digging on it, unknowingly standing on the old cellar door. It shattered beneath his weight and down he went. Aaron saw him fall. Basically, he disappeared before his eyes, but he was a good distance away. This is what B.J. fell into. The injuries came from the broken wood as he fell through. Dug some pretty deep gashes in his side."

Dani winced at the thought, but the photos were horrifying. "It's like still shots from a horror movie," she muttered, and then she saw the bones, and a chill ran through her. "Oh my God. This is total proof she wasn't dead when they left her down there. They would have abandoned her and made a run for it, not stopped to pose her like that." Dani's eyes welled. "She's so tiny. I never pictured someone like this being the mother of giants."

"Neither did we. But she left her mark on all our babies born with her black hair."

Dani touched her own hair, thinking of making babies with Aaron and growing old in his arms. Then she saw the big metal box.

"Is that the gold?" she asked.

"It's what nearly got Charlie killed, but it's not gold," Sean said. "It's full of worthless Confederate money."

"Not much of a treasure after all," Dani said. "But it's good the mystery of it has been solved. It will be the perfect deterrent for future treasure hunters."

Wiley nodded. "That was part of the reason for the search. Finding whatever had been hidden and making it known, so this would never happen again."

Then they heard the sound of footsteps in the hall—someone wearing boots and walking fast.

"That's Aaron," Shirley said, and moments later, he walked in.

They all stood as he approached.

A look passed between him and Dani, and then for a few moments, he was all business.

"Have you heard anything?" he asked.

Shirley shook her head. "No, but give me a hug. B.J. has given me orders not to make a fuss and informed me you're his hero again, so there's that."

Aaron breathed a quick sigh of relief. They were all past the age of being afraid of their mother's wrath, but at the same time, he never wanted to disappoint or bring her shame.

"Thank goodness for that," he said lightly as he hugged her and kissed her cheek, then glanced at Sean and Wiley who were standing beside him. "Are you two needing a hug, too?" he asked.

"No, thanks," they echoed, laughing as they both punched his shoulders before returning to the concession area.

Aaron turned to Dani. "You're getting one whether

you need it or not, because I do need one…and from you. Today was hell, and I'm needing a reminder of how good it is to be alive, okay?"

"Always okay," Dani said, and wrapped her arms around his waist.

Held fast within the strength of his embrace, her cheek pressed against his chest—the steady thump of his heartbeat in her ear—she knew this man was her "meant to be."

A few moments later, Aaron reluctantly let go. "That'll do for now, but be warned. I'm going back for seconds." Then the moment they sat, he reached for her hand. Today, she was his touchstone to reality.

***

A short while later, a surgeon entered the waiting area. "Are you the Pope family?"

Shirley stood. "Yes. How's my son?"

"He's fine. It was a wise move putting him under. We removed a good deal of debris from those wounds before we stitched them up. Does he live with you?"

"Yes," Shirley said.

"Then he can go home as soon as he's awake enough. He's off work until the stitches are removed, which all depends on how rapidly he heals. Don't remove the bandages. Don't get them wet. Bring him back to his doctor in about four days to check for infections. I've ordered antibiotics and pain pills. You can pick up the prescriptions when you check him out. Let the nurses' station know you're here. They'll let you know when he's awake enough to go home."

"Thank you," Aaron said.

The surgeon left, but Sean was right behind him. "I'll let the nurses know where we are," he said, and hurried from the room.

Shirley was in mother mode again, and began organizing who would go home and get B.J.'s bedroom ready for convalescing, and who would stay behind to bring him home, when Aaron interrupted.

"Mom, you and Sean go home. You'll do a better job of getting things ready than any of us. Wiley can finish his shift, and I'll hang around to take B.J. home, okay?"

Shirley frowned, "I don't like you having to wait here by yourself."

Aaron grinned. "I'm a big boy, and I know the way home."

"I'll wait here with him, Shirley. I promise," Dani said. "I won't leave until they do."

Shirley looked relieved. "That would be wonderful, honey…if you're sure it's not a bother."

"Spending time with Aaron is never a bother. Consider it done."

"Well then. That's that," Shirley said. "Oh, Wiley, go tell Sean to get those prescriptions so we can fill them before we leave town."

"Yes, ma'am," Wiley said, and bolted.

A few minutes later, the others were gone, leaving

Aaron and Dani alone. Without asking, he went to the concession area and got both of them cold drinks and snacks, then carried them back.

"Thanks," Dani said as she opened her little bag of pretzel twists, then took a quick sip of her Pepsi, and all the while felt Aaron's eyes on her...watching everything she did. Finally, she looked up. "Okay, spit it out. What's put that shadow in your eyes?"

"I'm never going to be able to hide anything from you, am I?" he said.

"Nope. Teachers have internal radar on children in their care and the people they love."

He leaned forward, his elbows on his knees, staring at the floor, trying to figure out where to start. In the end, he began with what happened today. He turned sideways in his chair to face her.

"Today, nothing happened like we planned, which amped up the panic when I saw Brendan disappear, so consider this a mind dump. Two things happened that have forever changed me. The first was seeing proof that Meg was still alive when they left her there. I could almost feel her fear and despair in the damn hole, knowing she was dying and might never be found." He stopped, took a deep breath, and then cupped the side of her face. "Then a weird thing happened. Suddenly I wasn't seeing her anymore. I was seeing you, all alone and crouched in your closet in the dark, afraid you were going to die...knowing that if you lived through what was happening, you were going to have to save yourself." He took a slow, shaky breath. "All those years between her and you, and not a damned thing has changed for women. There will always be predators, and there will always be victims. But you changed your story by fighting back, and I honor that in you."

There was a knot in Dani's throat and tears burning her eyes, but she said nothing. She'd asked, and he still had a story to tell.

"The second thing was witnessing how swiftly life can end. Meg's went from picking berries to being killed, just because she witnessed something a troop of soldiers didn't want told. Same damn thing happened to Charlie in the same damn spot, and for the same reason. I want to think that finding her and the so-called treasure has broken that curse. As a cop, I've always known how swiftly life can end, but never on a personal level." Aaron stopped, looked away for a moment, and then started anew. "You know I love you. I say it to you countless times and will say it to you with my last breath. You have become the center of my world. Life is short. Our time here is not certain. I go to bed at night missing you. You're the first thing on my mind when I wake. Every day we're apart feels like a day wasted. There is so much more I want to say, but then I remember your fears. And I understand your hesitation in trusting someone in this short space of time. The last thing I want is to scare you away, but on a scale of one to ten, where are we on the trust factor?"

Dani didn't hesitate. "There is no question. I have zero fear of nothing but losing you."

Aaron held out his hand, palm up. "I'm talking commitment, woman. Now and forever."

She clasped it. "Take B.J. home and come back to me. Bring your toothbrush. I've been waiting for you all my life."

Aaron groaned. "This is where the hero sweeps the woman off her feet and takes her to bed."

Dani's dimples popped as she grinned. "And this is where I say...'Houston, we have a problem.' The second floor waiting room is not ready for that, or us."

"Copy that," he said. "What if I brought a little more than a toothbrush?"

"I'll make room for you...in my house...in my life."

"Deal," he whispered, then sealed it with a kiss.

They were still sitting side by side when a nurse came into the room. "Mr. Pope?"

Aaron stood. "Yes?"

"Your brother is ready to go home. We'll be bringing him down to the lobby in a wheelchair. If you'll pull up your car at the entrance, we can load him in from there."

"Excellent," Aaron said, then grabbed Dani's hand as they headed for the elevator. "It'll take me a bit to help get him settled in at home and pack some stuff before I get back."

"What's Shirley going to say?" Dani asked as they stepped into the elevator.

"Probably something that sounds like 'It's about time. Don't fret. Her heart's desire has been to see all of us married and gone. Not because she doesn't want us, but she's been on the grandchild train for a few years now, and in our world, one comes before the other."

Dani laughed and was still smiling as the elevator landed and the doors opened. They exited the hospital, parted with a kiss, and went in different directions, Aaron to get his SUV and Dani to her car.

But as Aaron was taking B.J. home, Dani was at the supermarket, stocking up for a man in her house.

It never once crossed her mind that she was jumping off a cliff into the unknown, because she knew wherever she landed, Aaron would be there to catch her.

Many things had happened by sunset of discovery day.

Cameron and the searchers had laid a large piece of plywood over the opening into the old cellar and then erected a large camping tent over all of it.

A forensic pathologist and his team were on the way to Jubilee, as were federal authorities to recover the box. Due to the historical content involved, Cameron was covering all the bases.

Once Sheriff Woodley was informed of the discovery of the body, ancient though it may be, he'd sent an officer to stand guard until proper authorities arrived.

Ray and Betty Raines's property had become a thoroughfare, so to make life simpler for everyone, he moved his livestock to another pasture for the time being and left all the gates open at the house for a direct route to the site.

B.J. was home, swaddled in comfort, well fed, and resting. But the incident had changed him. When they'd first come to Pope Mountain, he'd felt like an outsider. Being related to people he hadn't grown up with was like straddling a fence. He had one foot in the past and one in the present, and hadn't known how to get to his own future. He didn't know what he was meant to do. He didn't have a set goal like his brothers. He was nearing twenty years old and delivering cakes and cookies.

Falling into that cellar with Meg had been like falling into his own past. It was the first time he'd ever thought about hell being where you were in life, not some unknown place for dead sinners.

Whether by accident or by God, he'd been the one marked to find her.

Him. Named for the man who'd loved her.

He would never take life for granted again. He was headed to the CIA—the Culinary Institute of America. It would involve moving to New York, but he was willing to do whatever it took to become a first-class chef. And thanks to dividends from PCG, Incorporated, paying for it was no longer an issue.

Down in Jubilee, the tourists oblivious to the drama on the mountain continued their vacations. The music venues sold out every performance. All of the restaurants and cafes were packed, and karaoke night at Trapper's Bar and Grill was a huge draw.

Bullard Campgrounds was a hot spot for families, and its little water park drew its own share of profits from the tourist trade, and all of the people who came to Jubilee to see the sights kept the police department and the hospital busy.

But the residents of Jubilee who lived beyond the hustle and bustle were quietly going about the business of life. Coming home from work. Making meals. Feeding their families. Refereeing fusses. Paying bills. Fighting amongst themselves. And some were in the throes of newly discovered love. It was life with all its messes and successes, in all its tragedies and its glories.

———

The clothes Aaron brought were now hanging in the closet beside Dani's. Their shoes were placed side by side on the floor below. His toothbrush was in the holder next to hers. His shaving kit was lying on the counter beside the hairdryer and her brush.

They'd made a meal together.

Cleaned up the kitchen together.

And now they were curled up in bed together.

Aaron was exhausted from the day, but as at peace as he'd ever been.

Dani had fallen asleep with her arm across his chest and her head cradled against his shoulder. She'd dreamed of the inevitability of this moment, but had never taken it for granted. Like Aaron, she was at peace.

Daybreak was still testing the boundary of dawn when Aaron rolled over, bumped into Dani, and realized where he was and that this wasn't another dream.

He opened his eyes and then smiled. She was not only awake, but had been watching him sleep.

"Good morning, darlin.'"

"Yes, it is, and I know how to make it better," she said, and slipped her arms around his neck.

One thing led to another, and then another, until he was inside her, rocking her world.

Making love was the most glorious, blood-rushing, mind-altering act there was between a man and a woman, but with Aaron, a little insanity was involved. He took her once, then twice to the point of losing her mind before he let himself go.

By the time the sun was up, they'd gone back to sleep. It was Aaron's optimum answer to having the day off.

But they weren't the only ones who had awakened early.

Cameron was up by dawn to take Ghost for his run.

Had breakfast with Rusty, filled her in on the day ahead, then left to meet the forensic team at the Serenity Inn. They were standing outside beside their van when he drove up.

"Welcome to Jubilee. I'm Cameron Pope."

"Good to meet you, sir. I'm Peter Church, forensic pathologist. These are my associates, Ken and Trudy Barnes, husband and wife. I can't tell you how excited we are to see what you've discovered."

"Not a what. She's a who. We already know who we discovered. Her name was Cries A Lot. She was Chickasaw, married to a Scotsman named Brendan Pope, the founder of our family and of the town of Jubilee. She was my five-greats grandmother, and there's a multitude of her descendants living on that mountain behind you. She went missing in 1864, and we have the historical journal of that time to back the story. All we need is to prove to the locals that she's not some recent murder victim, and there are upwards of a good two hundred Pope relatives willing to submit DNA tests to claim her."

"Yes, yes, of course," Church said. "We're ready to proceed. Just lead the way and we'll follow you in our van."

Cameron got back into his SUV and led the way out of town. But he was bothered and beginning to understand Aaron's concerns of yesterday. These people didn't have a personal connection. They'd see bones and artifacts. Something to put on display.

Their excitement was in direct opposition to the sadness the family felt yesterday. They saw the bones as history and nothing more.

————————

After they got to the parking area and unloaded their gear, Cameron led the way through the forest to where the tent had been set up. The officer Woodley had sent to guard the site was still there and moved aside as Cameron began to caution them.

"The tent is strictly to keep out the elements. I cannot guarantee the safety of walking anywhere inside it. Yesterday, none of us knew this was here. My cousin was standing in the spot where the hole is now when the old door to the cellar below gave way. He was severely injured as he fell, so I suggest you move to the opening one at a time to descend. There's no light source. Take your flashlights. And mind your step as you descend. It's a long-ass way down. I'll go first, then steady the ladder for the rest of you, and you can lower your gear with the ropes on site if you wish."

They agreed and stood back watching as Cameron removed the plywood from over the opening, then picked up a large ladder they'd left inside the tent and lowered it into the opening, leaving a good four feet extending above ground once it was down.

Cameron shifted it around until he was satisfied it was set, turned on his LED lantern, and carefully lowered it into the cellar so he could see where he was climbing, then shouldered the small pack he'd brought with him and headed down. Even though he'd seen the pictures, he was unprepared for what he felt. Once he touched down, he untied his lantern from the rope, then swept the bright beam of light past the metal box to the plastic shroud beside it, shuddering at the sight.

Then he set the lantern on the box and moved back to the ladder, took a stance behind it, and grabbed hold with both hands.

"Okay to come down now!" he shouted.

And so they did, lowering their equipment first and then descending one by one, until all three of them were down.

Like Cameron, they took a quick look around the area, but their immediate focus was on what was beneath the plastic shroud.

"Who covered the remains like this?" Church asked.

"My cousin, B.J. Pope, the one who fell. He wanted to make sure no debris fell on her when we began enlarging the opening to get him out."

"Right," Church muttered.

Then Trudy Barnes leaned over, shining her light on the buckle B.J. left behind.

"What's that?" she asked.

"It's B.J.'s belt buckle. I don't know why he left it. Maybe he just wanted her to know she'd been found."

And that was the moment the trio realized how emotional this was to the family. A look passed between them.

"We're going to remove it now so we can get photos of the remains in situ," Church said. "If you want to take the buckle back to your cousin, now would be the time to pack it up so it doesn't get misplaced."

Cameron put it into his pack, then stepped back to watch as they carefully removed the sheet of plastic. With all their lights now aimed at the remains, the position in which she was lying was bitterly poignant.

"Do you think they placed her like this?" Ken Barnes asked, eyeing the folded arms and hands clasped against her chest.

"No. We know she was shot, but she was still alive when they dumped her here. She died alone, and we think she died praying."

"How do you know all this?" Church asked.

Cameron shrugged. "We have people in our family who some would call psychic or mediums. We were told she wasn't dead when she was dumped. We were told this before we ever found her. Then to find her like this is all the proof we need that it was true. The Confederate soldiers who shot her and left her here damn sure weren't worried about how she'd be found. She crawled into this position. She died in this position. And all we need from you is to remove her with dignity. She's not going anywhere to be studied. She'll never be put on display. Your job is to determine how long she's been dead and get a tiny sample of bone to extract DNA. The morgue in Bowling Green has already volunteered their facility as a place to keep her remains until we're allowed to bury her."

The trio was mute. The giant before them had laid down an edict. There was no mistaking how serious the Pope family was. And at that point, all superfluous chatter ended.

"Yes, sir," Church said. "The depth of your allegiance in this matter is commendable. We are honored to be able to help."

At that point, they began carefully wrapping and packing the bones in the containers they'd brought down without uttering a word other than to ask for help or advice from one another on procedures.

Just as they were ready to begin carrying up the containers, they heard a shout from above.

It was Rusty. "Cameron! Are you there?"

"Yes!"

"The feds are here," she shouted.

"Tell them to hang on a bit. We're getting ready to bring up the remains."

"Will do," she shouted, and then the voices from above faded.

Church was surprised. "What are the feds doing here? What's going on?"

"They came to get that box," Cameron said.

Ken swung his light toward the corner where it was sitting. "I saw that. What is it?" he asked.

"It's what got her killed," Cameron said.

Now all three of them were staring at the box.

"What's in it?" Trudy asked.

"Confederate money, which amounts to so much trash now. A boy was shot up here recently because some damn treasure hunter got wind of a treasure and assumed it was gold."

"Oh my God," Church muttered. "No wonder all of this is so personal. One tragedy repeating itself for another. Okay, team, let's get their girl out of this hole and into the light, so they can bring an end to this nightmare."

So up they went, one by one, leaving Cameron to be the one to secure each container into their lifts. Once the last one was out, Cameron climbed out, too.

Rusty was waiting.

"Hey, honey. My guys have been helping them carry the containers to their van. Some guy named Church said to tell you he'd be in touch tonight to let you know she'd been delivered. I assume you know what that means?"

Cameron hugged her. "That I do. Thanks for bringing out the feds, and unless you want to hang around in this heat, feel free to head back to the house. I need to help them get the box out and then send Woodley's officer home."

"What are you going to do about that cellar? It's going to be a liability nightmare for Ray and Betty now that its location is known. I can see kids prowling around down there just for the thrill of being scared."

"Already on that," Cameron said. "I have a construction crew on call. We'll cut up the old flooring, drop it in the cellar, and then fill it in. It was a grave, and now it needs not to exist."

"Agreed, and as soon as the rest of the men get back, I'm going to take your advice and go home."

"There they come," Cameron said, pointing behind her. "Be careful with yourself and baby Pope."

"Always," Rusty said, then turned and walked away.

As Cameron stood watching the red curls bouncing on her head and the sunlight catching fire in their color, he wondered if Brendan Pope had been watching when Meg walked away with her berry basket. Something she'd probably done every berry season for as long as they'd been together.

He would have had no reason to fear for her safety. He couldn't have predicted or prepared for such an atrocity. And yet it had happened.

All of a sudden, he had an urgent need to get that damn box off this property and be done with all of it. The feds were here. They wanted it. They could go down and get it.

And then a couple of federal agents approached him, smiling. "So, you're Cameron, Rusty's husband. We've heard good things about you."

"Not all good, I hope. That would be lies," Cameron said.

They laughed. "Rusty said you were a pistol. But you'd have to be to catch her eye. She's one of a kind."

"Yes, that she is," Cameron said. "What you came for is down in that hole. There are enough ropes here to tie it off and pull it up from above. But you're going to have to go down there first to do that."

One of them shuddered. "Oh hell, I hate caves."

"Not a cave. An old cellar. But it looks like something

out of a horror flick. Be careful. In the past twenty-four hours, I've hauled all the dead and injured people out of there I care to see."

The five of them nodded, grabbed the four lengths of nylon climbing ropes inside the tent, and started down.

"It's pretty big. How do you plan to get it to your car?" Cameron asked.

"Oh…Mr. Raines is en route on a four-wheeler pulling a small flat trailer. He said he can get in here with it and haul it out to our van."

Cameron nodded. "Okay then, down you go. If you need another lantern, take mine." Then he walked over to where Woodley's officer was sitting. "Hey, Kirby. Unless you're just aching to spend another night out here, you can give Rance a call and tell him you've been released from duty and are about to head back to the department."

Kirby Rawls stood, and began gathering up his sleeping bag and backpack. "Best news I've had all day. Thanks, Cameron. I've camped out in the woods all my life, but I've never guarded an open grave before. It was kinda spooky. Don't really want to do this again."

"Understood, but it was appreciated," Cameron said, watching Kirby make tracks as he headed back to his truck.

An hour later, they were all finally up top again. Cameron had pulled up the ladder, and he and the agents were standing on both sides of the opening, holding on to four lengths of rope. They had to pull it straight up, taking up rope as they went. They were covered in dirt, grass roots, and old cobwebs from wrestling the old box to secure it, so they knew it was going to take all of the upper-body strength they had to get it out.

"Are you ready?" Cameron asked.

"Ready," they echoed and began to lift.

———

A couple of hours later, they were gone. Cameron helped Ray and Charlie take down the tent, put plywood back over the hole, and then they shoveled dirt and leaves over it to disguise the location. Hopefully, it would serve the purpose until the construction crew could come out with the dozer to fill it in. They'd have to cut down a few trees to make a path, but it had to be done.

By the time Cameron got home, he was as tired and dirty as if he'd been on active duty. Ghost met him at the door when he walked in, sniffed his clothes, and then dropped to his belly and whined. He'd done it last night, and now he was doing it again.

Cameron's heart broke. No matter how far away he and Ghost had come from war, some memories never leave. He knelt down beside him and began stroking him and hugging him. He knew what was wrong. Two days in a row Ghost had smelled death on him. Didn't matter if it was old bodies or new ones. To a dog, dead was dead.

"It's okay, boy. It's okay," Cameron said. "War's over. Next on the agenda is burying the dead."

Chapter 21

A MOST WONDERFUL SIDE EFFECT OF AARON MOVING in with Dani was being absorbed into his family and his world.

The annual homecoming at the Church in the Wildwood was always held on the Fourth of July, and when Aaron took Dani, it was a first for both of them. She came carrying lasagna and hot garlic bread, and was welcomed profusely, whisked out of Aaron's arms, and taken into the kitchen where all of the women and the smaller children were gathered.

They immediately oohed and aahed over her food, asked for her recipe, and brought her into the world of women. She was enchanted by their openness and willingness to accept her, but it wasn't until the women began witnessing how the children gravitated toward her that they saw her true calling. The teacher in her was shining.

By the time Aaron came to check on her, she was

sitting in a chair in the corner surrounded by littles, telling them a story from her childhood about a little alligator from the swamp with a turtle for a best friend. The basis of the story was about accepting people's differences and not excluding someone just because you didn't understand their ways.

Several women saw Aaron walk in the door and gave him a thumbs-up. He just grinned and kept moving toward her.

Dani looked up and smiled when she saw him.

One of the little girls saw him and held up her hand. "Miss Dani, Miss Dani, is Aaron your boyfriend?"

Dani grinned, because she knew Aaron heard it. "Yes, he is."

The little girl sighed as she leaned against Dani's knee. "I think he's pretty."

Dani nodded. "I think he's pretty, too."

Aaron winked at Dani as he swooped the little girl up in his arms. "I heard that, Lili Glass. I thought Uncle Cameron was your favorite."

Lili giggled. "Mama says I can have lots of favorites."

"Your mama is right," Aaron said, gave her a quick kiss on the cheek, and then put her down, and held out his hand to Dani and pulled her up. "Storytime's over. I want my girl back."

The children giggled, disbanding like a flock of quail—all going in different directions.

A few days afterward, Dani got an invitation to Rusty's baby shower, and a few days after that, she and Aaron went to a family wedding.

From then on, wherever they went, she was introduced first as Aaron's girl and then by name, and she loved it. She'd gone from years of having no family to inheriting a mountain full of people who'd taken her into the fold.

———

It was Saturday, which should have been Aaron's day off, but he'd switched with another officer who needed to attend a family funeral, which meant the day of surprises he'd planned for Dani had to wait.

On Monday, she would be going to school to open her classroom and meet her principal, and he'd be back at work. It would mark the beginning of the hectic reality of their lives—not always being off on the same days and limiting their time together even more. But she was excited, and he was happy she was happy, and so he'd shifted all his special plans to tomorrow.

By the time Aaron left the precinct, clouds were gathering, and he was tired all the way to his bones. He'd spent the entire shift dealing with entitled tourists, shoplifters, underage drinkers, and one elderly man who'd become turned around and lost his way. None of it had been serious, but he'd used up all of his patience and then some. Then the sight of the little house lifted his spirit, and when he pulled into the garage and parked, all the hassle of his day fell away.

He was home.

He walked into the house to the aroma of good things cooking. He was guessing meat loaf in the oven and something chocolate on the counter when Dani came flying into the kitchen, meeting him with a hug and a kiss.

"Welcome home, sweetheart! You look so tired. If you want to shower or rest before supper, the food will wait."

"I showered at work, but I'd take a glass of iced tea if there's any made, and put my feet up for a bit. I want to hear about your day."

"Pick your seat, and I'll get the drinks and join you," Dani said.

He chose the sofa, kicked off his boots, and put his feet up on the hassock, then glanced out the window. The clouds were still gathering.

Dani came in with the glasses and sat down beside him. He lifted one from her hands and took a long drink before he set it aside.

"That hits the spot," he said. "Now tell me about your day. Did your new principal ever get in touch?"

"Yes. Monday is confirmed. I meet her in the office at nine. I'll get the keys to my room, a packet with school info, and meet some of the other elementary teachers for lunch at the Hotel Devon. It seems the hotel treats the teachers to lunch on their first school workday at the start of each new school year."

Aaron loved the animation in her face as she talked, and the dimple action in her cheeks when she smiled. She was talking about clothes and heat and how she hoped the school had good air-conditioning, while his frustration and exhaustion kept fading.

He laughed with her in all the right places and had a fairly good idea of what she'd been saying, but his thoughts had been of what she meant to him and how she'd changed the bitter man he'd been.

There was a whole litany of phrases that fit her.

Most beautiful of women.

Healer of broken hearts.

Peacemaker.

Faithful companion.

Lover.

The person who made him whole.

Daniella Maria Owens.

But she needed a new last name, like Pope.

"Aaron? Aaron?"

He blinked. Dani was giving him that look. "What?"

She poked him on the arm then crawled into his lap. "Where did you go? I was asking if you were ready to eat, but I could tell by the look in your eyes you were elsewhere."

He laughed as he pulled her close. "I was thinking about you and about us," he said. "And yes, I'm hungry and everything smells so good, including you," and nipped the side of her neck.

Dani jumped out of his lap, then grabbed their glasses.

"Follow me, hungry man."

"Always…to the kitchen and beyond."

It began raining after supper as they were cleaning up. And the later it got, the stronger the storm became. By the time they went to bed, the wind was howling, and rain was blasting against the windows.

Dani fell asleep in Aaron's arms, sated and satiated, then hours later, she began to dream.

She was back in the closet, hiding, on the phone with 911, and scared to death they wouldn't get here in time to save her. It was thundering and raining, and she knew Tony was in her apartment, but she didn't know where he was until she heard a board squeak out in the hall. Her fingers clenched around the gun in her hand, praying with every breath, knowing he was just outside her bedroom door. She heard it open, saw him moving toward her bed, then saw the gun. When he took aim and began firing, she began screaming.

Aaron awoke abruptly, turned on the bedside lamp, and took her in his arms. "Dani, sweetheart! Wake up! You're safe. Open your eyes."

It was the sound of Aaron's voice that pulled her out of the nightmare. He wasn't part of that time. He shouldn't be part of the dream. She opened her eyes, saw the bedroom of her little house, the thunder and lightning from the storm outside, and the worried look on Aaron's face.

"I'm sorry. I'm sorry. I was dreaming. Tony was shooting at the bed." She went limp in his arms and began sobbing. "Damn it. Just when I think that's all forgotten, something triggers it. It was the storm. I know it was the storm."

"I know, I know. It's okay. We're okay. It was just a dream," he kept saying and held her until she calmed. "Let's go for a walk," he said, then got up, put on a pair of gym shorts and dropped something in the pocket, then held out his hand.

Dani sat up in bed, looking at him in disbelief. "A walk? Are you crazy? If we don't get fried by lightning, we'll drown standing up."

He was still holding out his hand. "Don't you trust me?"

Dani sighed. "That's not fair. You know I do," she muttered.

She got out of bed, grabbed the nightgown she never put on, and slipped it over her head.

Aaron took her by the hand and led her through the house, then through the kitchen, making their way outside to the back porch.

Rain was blowing sideways, blasting beneath the overhang and across the length of the porch. Dani's nightgown was immediately drenched and plastered to her body. Just before she lost her footing, Aaron was suddenly behind her, his hands clasped beneath her breasts, holding her fast against his chest. He'd become her anchor, standing steady against the wind as he leaned down near her ear and began to talk.

"Every tear you shed hurts my heart. I know horror came to you in a storm. But look at us now. You're standing with me in a storm, just as we stand in life. Together— secure in the world because I'll always keep you safe. But you keep forgetting that, in the beginning, it was you who saved yourself. You're the least helpless woman I've ever known." He hugged her, then planted a kiss on the top of her head. "We're about as wet as we're ever gonna be, but since we're standing out here in the sight of God almighty, then you should consider yourself getting washed clean. Made whole again with the tears from heaven. Your past can't own you anymore. Nobody owns you. But somebody sure does love you, and that somebody's me."

Then he abruptly let go.

The wind hit her, and this time she staggered. Reeling from the blast, she turned around and he was on one knee, holding a black velvet box. The lid was open. Something glittered deep within.

"Marry me, girl. I don't want to do life without you. While the world is new within you, please say yes."

Dani gasped. "Yes, you crazy man. I say, yes!"

Aaron slipped the ring onto her finger and then stood, swept her off her feet and into his arms, and held her close. So close. His heart was near to bursting as he whispered in her ear.

"Love you, Dani. Love you forever," and then he kissed her.

———————

Aaron invited his family out to Sunday dinner at The Back Porch the next day. As soon as they were seated, Aaron reached for Dani's hand.

"We have an announcement," he said. "I asked Dani to marry me, and she said yes!"

Dani was beaming as the family began cheering and exclaiming over her ring. Their little celebration caught the attention of other diners, who quickly caught on to the reason and the ring on Dani's finger. At that point, the diners in the room clapped for them and raised a few glasses on their behalf.

Dani couldn't stop smiling. She'd never known this kind of love. Or this kind of happiness.

The weight of the world was off Aaron's shoulders. He had a partner for life. And what a partner.

Shirley was both teary and ecstatic.

The brothers teased Aaron and cheered Dani, welcoming her to the family. It took forever to calm down, and even longer to order. But the meal progressed, and they parted in total joy.

Shirley wasn't losing a son. She'd just gained a daughter, and this time, one who loved them back. She couldn't have been any happier.

The next day Dani went to meet her principal, wearing a new red and white outfit, and flashing her new engagement ring. The principal walked her down the hall, showing her the way to the gym and the cafeteria, and introducing her to teachers on the way. And then after they turned a corner, they walked into the first room on the left.

"This is your domain. You're free to arrange seating, begin decorating your classroom and the bulletin board outside your door…all the usual beginning-of-school activities. Don't hesitate to ask for help, and if you start moving desks, get on the intercom and ask for Mr. Henry. He's the custodian and all-around handyman here," Mrs. Lowrey said. "We're so glad to have you. Poke around the school all you want, and don't forget to meet up at my office about fifteen minutes to twelve. We'll bunch up in cars to go to the Hotel Devon for lunch. See you then," she said, and handed Dani a key.

Dani added it to her key ring, then set her purse on a windowsill and dug out a tape measure. Within seconds, she was seeing the possibilities of the room, counting the cubbies, and planning the way she'd move the desks to allow for learning centers. By the time they met up at the office, she was in total teacher mode.

Life was about as perfect as it could be.

Two days later, Cameron was on the back porch giving Ghost a bath when his phone rang.

"Rusty! Will you get that, honey? My phone's on the counter. I'm up to my elbows in soap and wet dog."

Rusty went inside and grabbed it. "Hello, this is Rusty. Cameron can't come to the phone right now."

"Is this Mrs. Pope?" a man asked.

"Yes, I am. Can I take a message?"

"Yes. This is Peter Church, the forensic pathologist confirming the remains he found. Will you please let him know that the identity has been confirmed, and the age of the remains confirmed as well? The remains have been released and can be picked up from the morgue in Bowling Green at any time now."

"Yes, I'll tell him. This is great news for the family. Thank you for helping verify her identity."

"You're most welcome," Church said, and disconnected.

Rusty hurried out. "That was Peter Church. They've verified and released Meg's remains. She can be picked up at any time now."

"That's great news," Cameron said. "As soon as I get the whiny baby rinsed off here, I'll call the funeral home in Jubilee and have them pick up the remains."

Rusty eyed Ghost and then Cameron, careful to stay far enough away from the pair of them not to get splashed. "You'd think he would be used to baths by now. I don't know who is wetter, you or Ghost."

Cameron grinned. "Getting wet in this heat is fine with me. But Ghost has worked himself up into a state. As you well know, he'll pout all night."

Rusty laughed at the despondent look on the big dog's face. "Poor baby. It's what you get for rolling in that dead possum on the road."

Cameron laughed.

Ghost just stood there, water dripping, waiting for it to be over.

———————

That night, Cameron began making calls regarding Meg's funeral service. He knew they needed to honor her, and he knew just how to make that happen.

———————

Pope Mountain—One week later

Families came in droves, using up all the parking spaces at the church, then parking on the side of the blacktop road and walking the rest of the way, carrying babies in their arms and toddlers on their hips, approaching the cemetery in reverent silence.

A kilted piper stood just beyond the graveyard, the plaintive wail of the bagpipes filling the air around the mourners' approach, then echoing within the surrounding hilltops and into the valley below.

The pipes were for Brendan, welcoming his beloved home.

When the crowd was finally gathered, the piper ended, letting the last notes of the pipes fade into the air.

In those passing moments, a tall, brown-skinned man dressed in traditional Chickasaw clothing walked into their midst. His hair was white and long, hanging straight behind his back. His shoulders had yielded to the weight of life, his face a reflection of the years he carried with him.

Johnson Strong as Bear, a tribal elder honored and revered for his guidance and wisdom by his people, had already done his part in preparing the bones for reburial in the ways of their people.

Where once Brendan's Meg had laid alone in the dirt and dark, her little bones now rested upon a soft Chickasaw blanket in the colors of red, blue, and gold, spread inside a satin-lined casket. The front of her skull had been painted red, and the treasures representing her past had been placed around her—the bear claw necklace Brendan made for her. The buckle B.J. had placed upon her body when he found her. A bound copy of Brendan's journal that had led them to her. A braid of sweet grass. A bundle of sage. A pouch of tobacco. A red feather from a cardinal. A seashell. And a blue rock.

All things that had come from the mountain were going home with her.

Her grave had been dug beside the rock marking Brendan Pope's final resting place, with the casket lowered into the grave with her head facing west. Off to the side sat a little wooden house, three feet in height and five feet in length, that would be placed over her grave when all was done.

Johnson Strong as Bear looked down into the open grave and at the small wooden casket within, then lifted his arms above his head.

As he did, the mourners began to hear a drumbeat from somewhere back in the woods. A steady, repetitive *thump-thump* that became a dirge.

And then the elder's voice rang out among the stones as he called out to the Old Ones.

"*Aba`binili`.* Look now!"

"It is Cries A Lot, daughter to the Chickasaw."

"Woman of two worlds."

"Woman with two names."

"First mother to Pope Mountain."

"Look now! She is coming."

The drumbeat grew louder as the elder's voice rose.

"Your daughter became lost in the time before us. In the time of the highbush blackberry of 1864."

"And she has been found in the time of the highbush blackberry of 2023. Look now, *Aba`binili`*"

"Send the Old Ones to meet her."

"She is coming home."

The people standing had begun to weep.

The birds went quiet.

Children stood motionless, sensing the momentousness of the occasion without understanding why.

The drums grew louder still as the elder's voice rose again.

"Listen now!"

"Cries A Lot! Daughter of the Chickasaw."

"As you take your final journey, take the words of your people with you."

"Chiholloli!"

"You are loved."

The drumbeat ended abruptly, followed by one sharp, resounding war cry, and then the mountain went silent.

Someone sobbed.

Someone was praying beneath their breath.

Then, one by one, the mourners began to file past the grave, taking a handful of dirt from the pile beside it and tossing it on top of the casket as they passed. When the line finally ended, the people stood back, standing witness as the gravediggers began shoveling the remaining earth back into the ground.

When the burying was over, Cameron, Aaron, Louis, and Marcus stepped out of the crowd, picked up the little wooden house, and settled it on top of the grave before stepping back into the crowd.

When they looked up, Johnson Strong as Bear was gone.

After that, it was all about the leave-taking. As each family separated from the crowd to go home, they picked up their own bound copy of Brendan's journal, safe in the knowledge that the original was back in the Library of Congress, in its place of history where it belonged.

The piper packed and left, leaving the mourners to disperse as they chose, until finally there was no one left but Brother Farley locking up the church before driving away.

Silence filled the area.

The world was holding its breath.

A bird took flight from a nearby tree.

A rabbit hopped out from beneath a bush.

An eagle circled in the sky above.

And the sun continued its downward descent into the western horizon, guiding a lost soul home.

Epilogue

RUSTY POPE WENT INTO LABOR ON THE FIRST DAY OF February, subsequently giving birth to a nine-pound, six-ounce baby boy with a thatch of straight black hair and eyes the color of a hot summer sky. He was screaming bloody murder as his father held him, laughing from the pure joy of having the child in his arms.

Another generation of Popes was in the making.

———

B.J. came home from New York City for Easter weekend to see Aaron and Dani get married. He'd grown his hair long and was sporting a ponytail with his tux. Some things about Shirley Pope's baby boy had changed, and some things had not. He bore the scars from finding Meg like a badge of honor, and he knew within the depths of his soul that no matter where he was in the world, Pope Mountain would always be home.

———

After the old cellar was demolished and filled up, Ray and Charlie planted it with highbush blackberry plants as an homage to Brendan's Meg. Creating something good from something bad seemed the most likely way to remove the stigma of the past.

———————

Aaron and Dani took each day as it came.

Being husband and wife solidified everything good in their lives.

She thrived in the classroom through the days and came home every evening to her real-life hero.

While Aaron, ever the protector, made it his daily mission to never be the one to make her cry.

She was his love everlasting.

It was a Pope thing.

**Read on for more page-turning
romantic suspense with *Heartbeat* from
New York Times bestselling author Sharon Sala**

Chapter 1

THE DAY WAS NEW, AND THE SUN WAS IN AMALIE Lincoln's eyes.

She was driving eastbound on the Tulsa Crosstown Expressway, coming up on a pretzel loop of rebar and concrete, also known as the Interstate 244 and US-169 junction, when her very normal day turned into chaos.

Suddenly, the car a few yards in front of her swerved, over-corrected, spun sideways, then overcorrected again, and broadsided Amalie's car. It sent her into a spin before hitting her again, then slamming her car into a concrete abutment. When everything finally came to a stop, the ensuing pileup had traffic at a standstill.

Amalie was dazed, bleeding, and trying to unbuckle her seatbelt when her car suddenly burst into flames.

"No, no, no!" she cried, then began screaming for help, trying to unbuckle her seatbelt as smoke rolled up around her.

She kept screaming and screaming, trying to open the door even as the first fingers of fire were licking at the legs of her slacks, then the arm of her jacket, when all of a sudden, the door came open! She could hear voices shouting, and the whoosh and hiss of fire extinguishers, and then some man's voice in her ear, telling her, "I got you lady, I got you," and a voice whispering inside her head… *You're going to be okay.*

Then everything went black.

―――――――――

The time afterward was a blur. She went from an emergency room to a burn unit in Hillcrest Medical Center, and ensuing days and nights of living hell. Time was measured by recurring debridement, the administration of pain meds, and wrapping and unwrapping the burns, and complete isolation.

It was a week before Dan Worthy, her across-the-hall neighbor in her apartment building, learned what had happened to her.

He was an accident lawyer. He knew she had no family so he called the burn unit, asked a nurse to deliver a message to her, and that he'd wait for the answer.

The nurse listened, wrote down what Dan Worthy said, and headed for Amalie's room, gowned up, then moved to the side of Amalie's bed.

"Amalie, can you hear me?"

Amalie moaned, opened her eyes, and then nodded.

"Do you know a man named Dan Worthy?"

"Neighbor," Amalie said.

"He says he's an accident lawyer. Is this so?"

Amalie blinked. "Yes."

"He says he just heard about what happened to you, and if you say the word, then he's going to sue the pants off the drunk who hit you."

Amalie chuckled, but tears were rolling.

"Tell him, yes and thank you."

"Consider it done," the nurse said. "Oh, and by the way, your next round of pain meds are on the way."

Tears were still rolling when Amalie closed her eyes.

The nurse went back to the phone. "Mr. Worthy, are you still there?"

"Yes, ma'am. What's the verdict?"

"She says, 'yes, and thank you.'"

"Awesome," Dan said, and disconnected.

After that phone call, Dan went into action. He had the accident report. The man's blood alcohol level was off the charts when he was arrested, and it wasn't his first DUI. He filed a lawsuit on Amalie's behalf, against the man and his insurance company for all they were worth, suing for loss of wages, emotional distress, criminal intent, all medical costs, legal fees, and the list went on. He was fighting for Amalie as she was fighting for her life.

———————————

The first wave of condolences from her colleagues at the CPA firm where she worked came in the midst of her worst days, and then as she began to heal, they dwindled to no contact at all.

In the months she spent healing, her job had been

filled, her so-called friends had moved on, and the ones she happened to see either couldn't stop staring, or looked away. She didn't look like she had before. There was a white streak in her hair that had never been there. From shock, the doctors said. She had pink healing scars and grafts on the left side of her neck, shoulder, arm, hand, and down the left side of her lower leg.

There was a healing scar on her lower jaw from being cut by broken glass. She didn't like to look at herself in the mirror, but she felt selfish for caring because so many people had worked hard to save her life.

———

The upside to it all was when Dan won the case on her behalf, to the tune of millions. A year to the day of her accident, he knocked on her door to tell her was the only good news Amalie had had in months. When she opened the door, Dan was standing on her doorstep with a bouquet of flowers and a box of chocolates.

Amalie smiled. "It's not Christmas. What's up?" she asked, as she let him in, then led him into the living room.

He handed her the flowers and put the candy on the table between them. "We did it, Amalie. The courts awarded you everything I asked for on your behalf."

Amalie gasped. That had to mean millions.

"Everything?"

"Yes, ma'am. Everything."

Amalie leaned back in her chair, holding the bouquet

like a talisman. "You are a rare man, Dan Worthy. We've traded cookies and wine at Christmas for four years, and barely said more than hello in passing. I don't know what prompted you to take all this on for me, but I will be grateful for the rest of my life."

Dan shrugged. "I get paid, too, but I chose this job because I've witnessed the system shafting people who needed help most, and seen the ones with the most money and power get away with murder. The bastard who hit you had already been let off twice for driving drunk with little more than a hand slap, and look what he did to you. They don't change. And the only options left to the victims is to, literally, make them pay. As we discussed, it was deposited directly into your bank account. You are officially, good to go."

"Thank you. The trucker who pulled me out of the burning car saved my life, and now you've just saved my future. I owe both of you more than I can ever repay."

"Just pay it forward and we're even," he said. "Gotta go or I'll be late to court. Take care, Neighbor. I'll let myself out."

———————

November
One year later

Amalie Lincoln had come a long way since her accident two years ago and was tired of being overlooked. No matter how many resumes she submitted after her accident, she'd never gotten past the first interview. The moment they saw the pink scars, their expressions froze in the smile they'd been wearing, and they never looked her in the eyes again.

That's when she decided the only way to get work, was to be her own boss. But she was done with Oklahoma. She needed a fresh start, and since she'd never been farther east than Arkansas and Missouri, she started looking for other options, which was not unusual because Amalie had been looking for answers most of her life.

The day she turned eighteen, she sent off for a DNA test kit from Ancestory.com. By the time it arrived, she was having second thoughts about submitting it. Whoever had abandoned her didn't want her to begin with. Why was she doing this? Then rationale won out. If for no other reason than knowing the medical history of your people was valid, she took the test and sent it.

The results came back weeks later. Like most Americans, she had ancestors in different countries, obviously on the move from one place, looking for something better in another. She saw the irony. That was her to a T.

But she never got a hit from the website, and was never contacted by anyone claiming to be related. Nobody wanted her when she was born and, obviously, nobody wanted her now, so she forgot about it. However, Amalie had dreams and a life yet to be lived. It was time to get out of Tulsa, and out of this rut.

Now the holidays were upon her, and with no office

parties to go to, and no friends left to invite her over for Thanksgiving or Christmas, she decided to spend the time on her own and in a new place. Somewhere she'd never been before.

After a little research, she found a tourist attraction she'd never heard of, in a place called Jubilee, in the state of Kentucky. She scanned the website, admiring the shops, and the little valley in the Cumberland Mountains where it was nestled, and decided this was it! She loved country music, mountains and the draw of stepping into a place that not only held onto their past, but had found a way to share it with tourists. It seemed delightful. She made a reservation at a hotel called The Serenity Inn for two weeks, arriving the week of Thanksgiving.

Once she arrived, she knew she'd made the right choice. The changing color of fall leaves visible from her hotel window covered the mountains like a patchwork quilt. The days were sunny but brisk, and every day she lost herself within the hustle and bustle of tourists and shops, and the friendly faces of the storekeepers.

She ate Thanksgiving dinner in the hotel dining room along with dozens of other diners. Every day she became the tourist going in and out of shops, watching fudge being made, and quilt makers at work. She watched the blacksmith at the forge, wandered into a store with Native American jewelry and bought a handmade ring made of silver with a turquoise setting. She walked the streets eating funnel cake, listening to fiddlers playing blue grass music in the square. She went to a Reagan

Bullard concert at one of the music venues, and caught a matinee performance of a different musician at another.

When she learned the mountain looming above Jubilee was called Pope Mountain, she felt a connection like being introduced to someone new.

Every day afterward as she looked toward the mountain, she felt something she'd never felt before. A connection—a longing—a sense of wanting to stay, and she began thinking about living here. It didn't take long to fall in love with the concept.

At that point, she thought of work, and started scoping out options. The first thing she noticed was the lack of public accountants. There was only one small CPA firm in the whole town. But she wasn't looking for a job there. She was checking out the competition.

A couple of days before she was due to leave, she rented an office space in the business complex next to the bank with a window facing the street. Hired a sign painter to mark her presence in that place, then rented a house in the residential area of the town. On the morning she left Jubilee, it was with the knowing that she was coming back to stay. It took a while to pack up her life in Tulsa and get out of her lease, but she'd done it.

It was just the first week in January when she returned to Jubilee, and when she drove into town, her eyes went straight to the mountain. The colorful leaves were gone, but there was green from the ancient growths of evergreen and pines, and the mystery of it still called to her.

About the Author

New York Times and *USA Today* bestselling author Sharon Sala has more than 135 books in print published in six different genres—romance, young adult, western, general fiction, women's fiction, and nonfiction. First published in 1991, her industry awards include the Janet Dailey Award, five Career Achievement awards, five National Readers' Choice Awards, five Colorado Romance Writers Awards of Excellence, the Heart of Excellence Award, the Booksellers' Best Award, the Nora Roberts Lifetime Achievement Award, and the Centennial Award in recognition of her 100th published novel. She lives in Oklahoma, the state where she was born. Visit her at sharonsalaauthor.com and facebook.com/sharonkaysala.